Praise for

GREETINGS FROM SOMEWHERE ELSE

"A cozy, lighthearted romp, highly recommended."
—The Australian Women's Weekly

"Her best yet . . . a funny and poignant story . . . a novel which fairly cracks along with a mix of humor, a touch of blarney, and insight into the pressures and strains in contemporary relationships." *—Courier-Mail* (Australia)

"Fresh, funny, and engaging . . . This is comfort reading— warm buttered toast with Irish honey spread right to the crusts." *—Adelaide Advertiser*

"There's something about Monica's book that makes you want to escape into its world." *—Sunday Tribune* (Ireland)

"A highly entertaining tale of self-discovery, friendship, and romance." *—Country Living* (Australia)

"A page-turner . . . McInerney has a great insight into human nature and relationships and a good line in humor."
—Sunday World (Ireland)

"A real page-turner to curl up with on the beach this summer."
—Modern Woman (Ireland)

Praise for

THE FARADAY GIRLS

"Crossing the globe, from Australia to Manhattan to Dublin, McInerney's bewitching multigenerational saga lavishly and lovingly explores the resiliency and fragility of family bonds."
—*Booklist*

"It's always an almost-sinful pleasure to delve into anything written by Monica McInerney, whose delightful prose brings her rich characters to sparkling life." —*Irish American Post*

"McInerney is a talented storyteller. . . . A great story and a great read." —*Library Journal*

"This warm, compassionate book shows great insight into sisterly relationships. McInerney is Australia's answer to Maeve Binchy, a modern-day Jane Austen."
—*The Sun-Herald* (Australia)

ALSO BY MONICA McINERNEY

AT HOME
WITH THE
TEMPLETONS

AT HOME
WITH THE
TEMPLETONS

A Novel

Monica McInerney

BALLANTINE BOOKS TRADE PAPERBACKS ⬛ NEW YORK

A Ballantine Books Trade Paperback Original

Copyright © 2011 by Monica McInerney
Random House reading group guide copyright © 2011 by Random House, Inc.

Published in the United States by Ballantine Books,
an imprint of The Random House Publishing Group,
a division of Random House, Inc., New York.

Previously published by Penguin Books Australia Ltd., 2010.

Library of Congress Cataloging-in-Publication Data

McInerney, Monica.
At home with the Templetons : a novel / Monica McInerney.
p. cm.
ISBN 978-0-345-51865-1 (pbk.) — ISBN 978-0-345-51864-4 (ebook)
1. English—Australia—Fiction. 2. Friendship—Fiction. 3. Country life—
Australia—Fiction. 4. Victoria—Fiction. 5. Domestic fiction. I. Title.
PR9619.4.M385A8 2011
823'.92—dc22   2010049227

Printed in the United States of America

www.randomhousereaderscircle.com

2 4 6 8 9 7 5 3 1

Book design by Mary A. Wirth

For my mum, Mary,
with my love and thanks

AT HOME
WITH THE
TEMPLETONS

Prologue

London
October, 2009

From the moment Gracie Templeton knew she was going back to the Hall, she started to see him again.

He walked past her in the Tube station. She saw him studying at a table in the local library, his head bowed, engrossed in a book. Every second customer in the restaurant where she worked part-time sounded like him. An actor on TV had his shy smile. Everywhere she went, there was a man who reminded her of him. The same height, six-foot-three. The same dark curls. The easy, lanky walk. The same clothes—faded jeans, a dark reefer jacket. For eight years she'd been trying to put him out of her mind, to forget him, to rebuild her life. Now it was as if no time had passed at all.

As she watched the departure date grow closer, packed her suitcase, tidied her flat, she could think only of him. Three days before her flight, she gave in. Even as she typed his name into an Internet search engine, she knew it was a mistake. When his name appeared, she clicked on the link and began to read, then turned quickly away, shutting the laptop, breaking the connection. Quickly but not quickly enough. A line from the entry had leapt out at her: "A promising career cut short—"

If she'd dared to read on, would she have seen her name there? *A promising career cut short by Gracie Templeton.*

The phrase haunted her throughout the twenty-two-hour flight.

Until, there she was, stepping out into Melbourne airport for the first time in sixteen years.

The man behind the car-rental desk was the perfect mixture of efficiency and good humor. "That's all great, Gracie Templeton aged twenty-seven of London, thank you." He handed her English driver's license back across the desk. "So, is this your first time here?"

Gracie hesitated, then shook her head. "I used to live here, with my family. For three years."

"But you all left again? Summer got too hot?"

"Something like that," she said.

Minutes later she was in the small rental car, breathing in the too-sweet air-freshener fumes, unfolding the map and plotting her route. It was unsettling to see the place names again. Turning up the radio loudly to drown out her thoughts, she focused her attention on the road ahead.

Just over an hour later, something about the landscape made her slow down. A sign came into view: CASTLEMAINE 25 KM. She wasn't far away now. She hadn't been sure she would find her way so easily. There were no longer any roadside signs pointing to the Hall, after all. But it felt so familiar. The broad paddocks, gentle tree-covered hills, the big sky, the space. So much light and space. She stopped briefly to double-check her map, and the smell when she opened the car door almost overwhelmed her: warm soil, gum leaves, the scents of her childhood.

Five kilometers later, she was at the turn-off. The huge gum tree at the junction of the highway and the dirt driveway had always been their landmark. She indicated left and drove slowly, jolting over potholes and loose stones. As she tried to negotiate her way around the worst of them, she saw broken tree branches, crooked posts, gaps in the fencing. Her father would never have let the approach road look this uncared for. "First impressions are everything, my darlings," she could almost hear him saying.

The closer she came, the more neglect she saw: uneven patches of grass where there had once been smooth green lawn, bare brown earth where she'd once picked flowers, rows of fruit trees now left to grow wild, their branches heavy with unpicked, rotting fruit.

One final bend of the driveway and there it was in front of her. Templeton Hall.

She slowly brought the car to a halt, feeling as though her heart was trying to beat its way out of her chest. She'd expected the building to look smaller, but it seemed bigger. Two stories high, large shuttered windows, an imposing front door reached by a flight of wide steps made from the same golden sandstone as the house itself. It needed painting, several roof tiles were broken, and one of the window shutters was missing a slat, but it was still standing, almost glowing in the bright sunshine, as beautiful as she remembered.

As she walked toward it, the sound of the gravel crunching beneath her shoes mingled with unfamiliar bird calls from the trees all around. She automatically reached for her talisman, the antique silver whistle she always carried in her bag, and held it tight in her hand. He'd given it to her when she was just a child. Back then it had been a good luck charm. Now it was her only reminder of him.

She climbed the first step, the second, the third, wishing, too late, that she hadn't offered to arrive early, hadn't volunteered to be the first to step back inside the Hall again.

The front door opened before she had a chance to put the key in the lock.

In the seconds before her eyes adjusted completely from the bright sunlight, she registered only that a man was standing there. A tall man with dark, curly hair, holding something in his right hand. As she saw his face, she felt a rushing sensation from her head to her feet. She heard herself say his name as if from a long distance away.

"*Tom?*" She tried again. "Tom?"

"Hello, Gracie."

He took a step forward into the light.

"I've been waiting for you," he said.

PART
ONE

Chapter One

Templeton Hall,
Victorian Goldfields, Australia
1993

GRACIE TEMPLETON had just turned eleven when she discovered there were people who didn't like her family as much as she did.

It was Saturday morning, June fifth. She woke at seven, knocked on her two older sisters' bedroom doors, waited for them to shout at her to go away, then knocked again, twice as loudly. Ignoring their second wave of sleepy insults, she went in search of her little brother. He was inclined to sleep in cupboards rather than in his bed, but on this particular Saturday he was, surprisingly, in his bedroom. Under his bed, rather than on it, but easy to find at least. After three failed attempts to wake him, she returned to her own small bedroom at the back of the east wing, the one with blue wallpaper that her father called the Red Room, for reasons he seemed to find funny and she didn't quite understand.

It was the first Saturday of the month and Gracie's turn to be the head of the house. She put on the well-ironed long blue cotton dress she'd hung up in her wardrobe the previous evening, adjusted her petticoats, tied on her apron, brushed her unfortunately flyaway white-blond hair until it was a little less flyaway, checked that her black patent leather shoes were shining and her bonnet neatly fastened.

After a final look in the mirror, she went downstairs and opened up the dining room, the library, and the morning room. She switched on all fifteen of the lamps, from the small table ones with the colored glass shades to the large standard models with the heavy brocade covers. Next, she polished the dining-room table. It was eight feet long and four feet wide and she couldn't quite reach the middle of it, but with the lamps turned low she hoped any dust wouldn't show.

She lit the incense in the small Chinese-themed room. She straightened the rugs in the entrance hall, tweaked the runner on the main staircase (it always seemed to stick on the fifth stair), and turned the bronze statuette of Athena on the side table in the smoking room so it was correctly facing forward rather than staring at the wall. Her brother, Spencer, thought it was funny to move the statue around in unexpected ways and at unexpected times. One Saturday, Gracie was about to open the heavy front door and welcome the first of the day's visitors to Templeton Hall when she noticed Athena was standing on her head, balanced precariously against the wall, her bronze legs akimbo. Gracie only just had time to rescue her before the first visitor appeared.

Returning to the morning room, Gracie used a broomstick to gently nudge the portrait of her great-grandfather above the fireplace back into position (it tended to tilt to the left) and set a record of Beethoven's sonatas playing on the old gramophone in the corner.

Her preparation was almost done. Even though she'd checked the appointments book the night before, she checked it again, trying to memorize where each group was coming from. Her sisters, Charlotte and Audrey, always mocked her diligence.

"Who cares who they are or where they come from?" Audrey would often say. "They're just *tourists*, Gracie. Here to pay our bills for us."

"Not tourists, stickybeaks," Charlotte would correct her. "People with more money than sense."

For years, Gracie had heard that saying as "more money than cents," which didn't make any sense to her at all. Not that she dared ask Charlotte for an explanation. She'd learned from an early age that it was best not to question any of Charlotte's pronouncements. There was less chance of being a victim of her sharp tongue that way. Her "legendary" sharp tongue, as Charlotte herself proudly referred to it.

Gracie loved both her big sisters, but preferred them separately rather than together. Seventeen-year-old Charlotte was quick tempered, but on her own she could also be surprisingly patient. And if sixteen-year-old Audrey wasn't busy gazing at herself in the mirror or complaining that she wasn't receiving enough attention from their parents, she could be quite kind to Gracie.

At least their father approved of his youngest daughter's passionate interest in the Hall. "That's my girl," Henry would say if he came across Gracie sitting on the staircase with the appointments book. "If only the others were as good at this whole malarkey as you."

"I *am* as good at this whole malarkey," Charlotte said once, overhearing. "Better, probably. I just can't be bothered. There's a difference."

Gracie put the book back neatly where she'd found it. This morning was going to be busy. The first group was due in at ten, and three others before lunch, but as all the Templetons knew from experience, casual visitors could also arrive at the Hall anytime. She caught sight of the family motto written in curling Gothic script around a framed portrait of her grandfather, Tobias Templeton. It was in Latin, but her father had translated it for her—loosely, he explained—as "Fail to prepare; prepare to fail."

Gracie would never admit it to her sisters, or to Spencer, but that motto was like a life message to her. She did her best with her schoolwork and her share of the housework and gardening, but she *really* tried to be prepared when it came to the family business. She bit her lip as she stood in the hallway, mentally checking her to-do list. Something was missing. She walked through the rooms again until it hit her. Flowers! There were no flowers. And there *had* to be flowers.

She ran up the two flights of stairs and this time opened Audrey's door without knocking.

"Did you get the flowers?"

"I'm asleep."

"Audrey, did you?"

"I'm sleep talking. Go away."

Gracie's voice got louder. "You promised you'd get them. We made a deal. I'd polish the silver if you got the flowers. You promised."

"I forgot." Audrey's voice was muffled by the pillow.

"That's not fair!" Gracie was shouting now.

"Can you two shut up?" Charlotte's voice sounded clearly from her room across the hallway. "I'm trying to get some sleep here."

Gracie surprised them both, and herself, by giving a loud shriek that lasted nearly ten seconds. It hurt her throat but it worked. Before the last note finished sounding, both Audrey (in a silk nightdress) and Charlotte (in plaid pajamas) were standing in front of her. Their expressions were murderous, but they were at least paying her attention.

"Bloody hell, Gracie. Shut up. You'll wake Mum and Dad and Hope," Charlotte hissed. "You know the rules. No sleep-in on Saturdays, no pocket money for any of us."

Gracie stood her ground. "Audrey was supposed to get the flowers and she didn't."

Charlotte rolled her eyes. "So what? Who cares? If anyone asks, blame it on the maids."

"We don't have maids."

"People don't know that. Tell them we had a maid but she turned out to be light fingered—"

"Flower fingered," Audrey interrupted.

Charlotte laughed. "So we had to dismiss her. Hence, no maid and no flowers."

Gracie wanted to cry. She hated it when her sisters ganged up on her like this. She also hated it when there were no flowers in the rooms. At any other time of the year, she would have gone out into the large gardens surrounding the house and picked what she needed. But there were no flowers at the moment, just lots of dry autumn leaves.

"Stop fretting so much, Gracie," Audrey said, more kindly. "It really doesn't matter."

"It matters to me."

"'It *matters* to *me*.'" Charlotte and Audrey both mimicked her passionate tone, before laughing again.

That did it. She stomped, as noisily as she could, down the hallway.

"Shut *up*, Gracie. You'll wake everyone," Audrey hissed again.

"I don't care. I hope I wake them all, Mum *and* Dad *and* Aunt

Hope. Then I'll be able to tell them about the flowers. About your broken promise."

"I'm going back to bed," Charlotte said, turning away.

Gracie turned back toward her. "You can't. You're supposed to be dressed and ready by now, too. I checked the roster. It's you and me on today. I'm downstairs, you're upstairs."

"Check the roster again. It's you and Spencer on today, not me. I did a deal with him."

Gracie felt a sudden rush of anger again, secretly enjoying the feeling. It gave her the courage to stand up to Charlotte and Audrey. She borrowed one of her aunt Hope's phrases: "You two are absolutely and completely bloody incorrigible." She headed downstairs, muttering to herself but loudly enough so they could hear her, borrowing another one of Hope's favorite sayings. "If this was my house, I'd throw you all out."

She did her best to ignore their laughter as she tramped back down the polished stairs to the entrance hall. Audrey was probably right, none of the visitors would notice the lack of flowers. They were usually so busy noticing everything else about Templeton Hall, as well as whispering to one another about the age of their tour guide and the whole unusual setup. But this kind of fine detail mattered to Gracie. Unlike her two sisters and brother, she longed for her turn as head guide. She didn't do it purely for the pocket money on offer, either. She loved sharing everything she knew about the Hall: its history, its beautiful contents, all it meant to her whole family, stretching back for generations. . . .

"We're just a tourist attraction, Gracie. You have to understand that. People don't care if we're descended from English aristocracy, Australian squattocracy, or a pack of werewolves," Charlotte had said once. "We're just one more stop before they drive on to their hotel or caravan park. Something to fill up the day. A place to take a photo or go to the loo. Don't take it so seriously."

But Gracie did take it seriously. She couldn't help it. She checked the time now on the large grandfather clock ticking beside her in the hallway. Nearly nine a.m. A glint of metal on the side table caught her eye. Charlotte's car keys. They shouldn't have been there, for two reasons. One, all signs of their "modern" life were supposed to be hidden on the weekends when the Hall was open to the public. And two, their parents had asked each of them repeatedly to please hang any keys on the hook behind the pantry door. The house was so big that a few rules and regulations had to be made. The alternative was many wasted hours searching through eighteen rooms.

Gracie did some quick mental arithmetic. Templeton Hall was out in the countryside, a long way from a shop. It would take her twenty minutes to drive into Castlemaine, their nearest big town. Ten minutes, if she was quick, to buy flowers from the grocery store where the family had an account. Twenty minutes back. It was possible. If there were no delays, she'd be back with ten minutes to spare before the Hall opened to the public.

There was the minor matter of it being illegal for her to drive. But she'd been driving Charlotte's car, a little automatic, since she was ten years old, over a year now. So far, only in the paddocks around Templeton Hall, but Charlotte had always expressed amazement at how quickly she'd caught on. Her lack of height was the main problem, but a couple of folded wheat sacks from the stables had always given her the inches she needed. A coat or jumper or two would do the same now, surely?

Five minutes later, she was at the wheel, turning from the Hall's long dirt driveway onto the main road to Castlemaine. Her heart was beating so fast she could almost hear it. She was up a little high in the driver's seat (she'd decided on three coats rather than two, and regretted it slightly now). Her steering was good, her braking impeccable, and the roads were thankfully quiet. As she passed the *Welcome to Castlemaine* sign twenty minutes later and drove into the wide main street, she started to breathe more easily. She could see the greengrocer ahead, setting up his outside display of fruit and vegetables. Yes, he had roses there. And she could see carnations, too, and chrysanthemums.

She was so busy looking at the flowers that she didn't see the car pulling out in front of her. There was, however, no missing the bang that sounded as the front of Charlotte's car hit the back of the other vehicle, or the sound of her car horn as she fell forward against it for ten long seconds, that later would re-sound in her ears as lasting for hours.

Afterward, she wondered where all the people had come from, and so quickly. The street had been quite empty. But within seconds of the collision, people came rushing from shops, from other cars, from side streets. She heard snatches of sentences.

"I didn't see her. She just appeared." "What the hell is a kid doing driving a car?" "Why is she dressed in that weird gear?" "She's one of those mad bloody Templetons, that's why. They think they own the bloody place."

The greengrocer's concerned face was replaced by a fiercer face attached to a body dressed in a policeman's uniform. "What do you think you're doing? You could have killed yourself or someone else."

"I was getting flowers. We're about to open."

The policeman looked away from her, around the crowd, as if hoping they might be able to make sense of Gracie's words. It was clear he couldn't.

A bystander stepped in. "You're new here, aren't you? She's one of the Templetons."

"The mad bloody Templetons," someone added.

"Up to another publicity stunt."

"From Templeton Hall."

"Tembledinall?" the policeman misheard. "What is it, a religious cult?"

More murmurs as locals hurried to offer explanations. Gracie didn't have time to listen, or to worry about her family being called the mad bloody Templetons twice in five minutes. The town hall clock was striking nine-thirty. She had to hurry. She struggled out of the seat belt. One large brown arm pushed her back in her seat.

"You're not going anywhere, kiddo."

MUCH LATER that night, Gracie's father, Henry, announced that he found it very funny. Hilarious, he said. Her mother, Eleanor, was still in a shocked, rather than amused, state and also angry—Gracie's arrival at Templeton Hall in a police car just as a bus filled with tourists pulled up had caused such a fuss that Hope, Eleanor's younger sister who stayed with the family on and off, had taken a "turn," as Eleanor usually put it. "Threw a wobbly," Audrey preferred to describe it. "Went psycho," Spencer would say. "Exhibited pure attention-seeking behavior, more like it," Charlotte would insist.

Charlotte, as the oldest, had plenty of opinions on the relationship between her mother and Hope. "It's Queen Elizabeth and Princess Margaret all over again," she'd announced once. "The youngest is jealous of the older sister's standing and marriage, so she goes wild and hits the bottle, resulting in the older sister having to take care of her for the rest of her days—the ultimate revenge."

"Hope got upset at the sight of the police, nothing more and nothing less. Stop talking about her like that, please," Eleanor had said, in the voice they'd all learned to obey.

"On the bright side, at least Gracie can't lose her driver's license," Henry said, as the family sat around the kitchen table that evening. "Unfortunately it's because she doesn't *have* a license."

Gracie's arrival in the police car had set off a domino effect of arrivals, with cars following buses following caravans and camper vans, all filled with tourists, as well as more than a few people from the nearby area. Usually the locals avoided Templeton Hall, but word had obviously spread quickly about Gracie's accident, and curiosity had overcome their usual aversion to the family.

"On the extra bright side, at least they all got the full 'At Home with the Templetons' experience," Charlotte said cheerfully. "'Welcome to our world, where chaos reigns—'"

"Flowers are missing," Audrey added.

"And where the souvenir biscuits are always stale," Charlotte finished.

"It wasn't the full experience," Gracie said, sulky now that the excitement had passed and she just felt achy and cross. "I was the only one dressed up, even though I *begged* you to go and put your proper clothes on."

Charlotte laughed. "I'd forgotten that bit. You, draped over the policeman's shoulder, shouting at us all to go and get dressed. You should have seen his face. I'm sure he thought you were hallucinating, that we were greeting you in the nude."

"I don't think anyone asked for refunds, Gracie," Audrey added, in a kind voice. "It was all quite festive, actually. Until Spencer let off that stink bomb, at least."

"That was Spencer?" Eleanor wasn't happy to hear it. "I told everyone it was the drains."

Ten-year-old Spencer said nothing, just smiled secretly to himself from his hiding place under the table.

"I think we pulled together beautifully in what were very trying circumstances, actually," Henry said, leaning back in his chair and beaming at his family. "Triumph over adversity, as our ancestors might have said."

"I still think you should all have got dressed up," Gracie said. "It's false advertising otherwise. It wasn't the full colonic experience."

No one pointed out her error. Gracie often confused "colonic" with "colonial." It had been Henry's idea not to put her right. "It makes a funny story, which leads to word of mouth," he'd said. "We'll get more visitors out of that story than any advertising we do."

Now, though, Henry took pity on his youngest daughter. "Poor Gracie," he said, pulling her onto his lap in one easy motion. He was nearly six feet and very fit from all the outdoor work he did on the grounds. "My poor lawbreaking Gracie. How can I make it better?"

Gracie wriggled out of his arms and sat up straight. "Put me in charge again tomorrow," she said.

Chapter Two

THAT NIGHT Gracie could barely sleep from the excitement. It was possibly turning out to be the best weekend of her life. Not only had she been the center of attention for the whole day, not only had she survived a car crash (it was getting more spectacular every time she thought about it), and not only had her father agreed that she could be head guide again on Sunday—"As long as you're okay, Gracie. Any dizziness or headache at all and you'll have to stay in bed"—but best of all, she'd just had a whole hour of her mother to herself. All to herself; no sign of Charlotte or Audrey or Spencer or, especially, Aunt Hope, who seemed to take up more and more of their mother's time these days. Just Gracie, in her bed, the room made cozy by the lamplight, the rose-patterned curtains drawn against the cool night air, and her mother lying beside her, stroking her hair and talking in that low voice she used only when she was especially worried.

"Promise me you'll never do anything like that again, Gracie, please. It was so dangerous. Anything could have happened."

"But the flowers—"

"You're a good girl to be so meticulous—that means concerned with details," Eleanor added without a pause—she was always very good at explaining the meaning of any long words she used, whether they were in the middle of home lessons or not—"But sometimes you have to be a little more relaxed about things. Think of the consequences. Be careful not to put either yourself or others in danger."

"But I wasn't hurt when I hit the other car." Eleanor winced at her words and Gracie immediately felt guilty.

"No, you weren't, but you could have been. And other people might have been hurt as well."

"Sorry, Mummy." Now that she was eleven she tried to call her mother Mum, like Audrey and Charlotte did, but sometimes it felt so comforting to call her Mummy.

Eleanor pulled her in close and kissed the top of her head. They lay there in silence for a few moments. Gracie relived the accident in her mind, in slow motion this time, relishing and exaggerating the sound of the impact, the blare of the horn, the rushing feet as crowds gathered, all the comments. The comments! She sat upright and told her mother all she'd heard people say about the "mad bloody Templetons" and "another publicity stunt." She paused. "What's a publicity stunt?"

"It's a way of getting people to notice you and talk about you."

"People thought I did that crash to make people notice me? I didn't!"

"I know, Gracie. It was just an accident."

"So what other publici— What other stunts did they mean?"

"I can't imagine," Eleanor said, but in the voice Gracie knew her mother used when she was pretending she didn't know something.

"And why would they call us the 'mad bloody Templetons,'" she asked. "Don't people in town like us?"

"Gracie, please don't swear. It's not nice, even if you're just repeating what other people have said. Don't worry about what you heard."

"But that wasn't all. Another man kept saying that we carry on as if we own the whole bloody place. We do own it, don't we? The Hall and the gardens and everything? Or whose is it if we don't own it?" Gracie turned as her mother made a sudden odd noise. "Are you laughing at me? Is what I said funny?"

"Not in the least bit funny, darling. And you're to ignore that as well. Some people just don't like other people and it sounds like unfortunately you met a few of them today."

"Maybe I should have run those people over?"

Eleanor laughed out loud. "You could have, but all around I think it's best you didn't."

"So we're not the mad bloody Templetons?"

"No, Gracie, we're not. We're not mad or bloody. We're just the very ordinary Templetons."

Ordinary? Gracie wasn't sure she liked the sound of that, either.

ACROSS THE HALL, Charlotte lay in bed, disgruntled and not just because of the damage to her car. Usually she liked action-packed dramatic days, but she'd had other plans today involving a leisurely bath and a new paperback, all canceled when it became clear it was going to be one of those all-hands-on-deck Saturdays at Templeton Hall. She'd put up a feeble kind of resistance when her father insisted she do the guiding upstairs instead of Spencer.

"That's not fair! I'd swapped with him. Why do I get stuck with it again?"

"Because you're my daughter, because I'm asking you, because today is an unusual day, and because if you don't, I'm pulling you out of boarding school and you can start going to the local high school again."

That clinched it, really. She'd suffered through one term at the local school before announcing to her parents that if they made her go back there again she would set her bedroom on fire. It was a bad threat to choose. Her aunt Hope had recently tried to do something similar, stopped only by Spencer coming into the bedroom to investigate the smell of kerosene as Hope was trying to get her lighter to work. Charlotte had swiftly apologized for her lack of tact, while just as swiftly insisting that she was serious, that after years of being homeschooled by Eleanor, having her intelligence taken for granted, her brain nurtured and encouraged—she'd laid it on thick, if she did say so herself—it felt like a personal insult to be lumped with the local kids who treated her like she'd arrived from another planet, and taught by teachers who didn't know even half as much as she did.

She was prepared to argue her point for days, if necessary, but to her amazement her parents gave in that night. She'd started researching the best boarding schools herself and quickly decided on one in Melbourne, far enough away from Castlemaine for independence yet not too far to prevent her coming home on the train on weekends. It was only later she discovered that while she'd been complaining about the local school, the local school had been complaining about her. She was "a disruptive influence," according to the letter from the principal she happened to find in the desk in her father's study. "Her arrogance prevents her from easily making friends, and the teachers find her lack of regard for their methods off-putting and unacceptable."

Charlotte took great pleasure in tearing the letter up into pieces and mixing them in with the kitchen scraps. Her father wouldn't miss it, she knew. His filing system was a mess.

At least she'd spared Audrey the horrors of that principal and her half-witted cronies. When the time came for Audrey to move from homeschooling to secondary classes, there was no question of the local school. She was enrolled in the same boarding school as Charlotte, and the two of them had been students there since. Charlotte preferred not to let Audrey forget it, either. "If it wasn't for me . . ." she liked to say, until Audrey turned on her one day.

"If it wasn't for you, I'd be happily living at home with friends from my own area rather than exiled with girls from miles away. But if banging on about it makes you feel less guilty about your own bad behavior, you go right ahead."

Charlotte just laughed. She knew they both liked being away from the family for weeks during the year, far from the Hall, far from being tarred with the "one of the Templetons" brush, and, best of all, far from the tedium of trying to maintain a property as large as theirs without the help of an army of servants or a tribe of gardeners.

Charlotte argued with her father about that, too. "It's ridiculous. Here we are re-creating the authentic colonial experience, giving visitors a glimpse into yesteryear, yet we're doing it without the most basic element of life of that era: maids. How can I act the part of an aristocratic miss if twenty minutes earlier I was cleaning the toilet?"

"We call it a lavatory, Charlotte. And you know why we don't have servants. Because unlike your esteemed ancestors, we don't have a gold fortune to pay them."

That was the most annoying thing of all, really. There she was, not just snatched from her happy life in London and forced to leave all her friends behind, but locked in this strange historical bubble that was Templeton Hall, gaily spouting detail after detail about life in the goldrush days, wearing the clothes, pretending—*pretending*, for God's sake, the humiliation of it—that they were living in that era, and yet it all seemed to be built on such flimsy financial foundations.

Oh, she knew that her father was still dealing in antiques, heading away from the Hall now and again on buying and selling trips. Selling with some success, too, from what she'd occasionally overheard him say to her mother. Not that Charlotte cared much for old glassware or furniture, but she'd always known that her father had a very good eye for spotting valuable pieces and selling them on just as quickly. But was the antique trade as lucrative a business in Australia as it had been back home in England?

One day she'd had a poke around her dad's study in search of some answers. She was the oldest of his four children, after all. Someday, all this would be partly hers. It was only right she should have some knowledge of the family's financial picture beforehand.

Unfortunately the snooping session was interrupted before Charlotte had time to even work out which was the best drawer to start looking through. Aunt Hope came in, silent as ever, giving her a fright, though Charlotte did her best not to show any alarm, not until she could work out what her aunt's mood was that day.

Fiery, it turned out. Aunt Hope was melodramatic at the best of times. At the worst of times, too. Catching her niece in her brother-in-law's out-of-bounds office was a heaven-sent situation. She slammed the door, lifted her chin, and said in her mannered, husky voice, "And what do you think you're doing, young lady?"

Charlotte knew it annoyed Hope to hear the relaxed hybrid English-Australian accent in her nieces and nephew, after the elocution lessons she and Eleanor had suffered back in England. "They just sound so common," Hope liked to say, with a theatrical shudder. But that Australian accent could come in very handy, Charlotte had discovered. She used it now, dragging out her vowels, leaving out letters, enjoying the sight of Hope's disgust.

"Just havin' a look around, Hope." She pronounced "around" as "arind." "I'm doin' a school project on the psychological impact of clutter"—she pronounced it "cludda"—"and Dad's office seemed a perfect place to start."

"He wouldn't be happy to find you here." Hope's vowels were as sharp as diamonds.

"Nor you, I'd wager," Charlotte answered, switching to a well-bred English accent to deliberately annoy Hope further. "What were you doing here? Dad's office is out of bounds to all of us, isn't it?"

Charlotte watched with interest as Hope, flustered by the direct question, changed the subject and started to talk in great detail about the hot weather instead. Quickly bored, Charlotte decided to get out before Henry came in and started interrogating the pair of them.

For as long as she could remember, Charlotte had disliked Hope. She felt plenty of other emotions toward her as well. Anger, mostly, when Hope drank too much and threw the tantrums that upset not just Eleanor, but the whole family and any poor visitors who happened to be in earshot. Hope in full flight could be a terrifying spectacle, with tears and shouts and objects being hurled around the place.

"She can't help it. She's unwell." They'd heard the excuses from their parents for years.

"So send her to a hospital," Charlotte snapped back one night. She'd been angry and hurt on that occasion, just a few months after they arrived in Australia. It was her birthday, the only day in the Templetons' newly established family schedule when the birthday girl, or boy, was truly able to be the center of attention, get out of tour-guiding, cleaning, and gardening, and instead spend the day doing just as they pleased, finishing with a dinner made up of all their favorite dishes.

That day, though—Charlotte's fifteenth birthday—Hope had one of her "episodes." Not a standard plate-throwing or screaming one, but a get-completely-drunk-and-slash-at-herself-with-a-broken-glass one. They were all in the kitchen, about to start serving dinner, the usual teasing and joking flying around, Charlotte the center of attention. One moment Hope was standing at the sink, obviously drunk, yes, but apparently happy, the next she was weeping loudly, a broken wineglass in one hand and a gash down her other arm. Pandemonium followed, Charlotte remembered; attempts to stop the blood with a tea towel, then a bath towel, before a rushed trip to the Castlemaine hospital, Henry driving and Eleanor in the back cradling her sister. There was no time for apologies to Charlotte about her ruined birthday dinner. By the time they'd arrived back, after midnight, her birthday was over in any case.

"I'm so sorry," Eleanor had said, coming into her room. "What did you do, darling? Did you manage to have any fun at all?"

Charlotte took perverse pleasure in telling her the truth. "How did I spend my birthday? As a matter of fact, I spent it cleaning your drunken sister's blood off the kitchen floor."

She'd regretted it afterward, seeing the hurt expression on her mother's face, but anger had eventually won over regret. Her mother needed to know the impact Hope had on the family. Secretly, when they were sure their mother wasn't listening, it amused Charlotte and Audrey to call their aunt Hope-less, to imagine the joys of a life without Hope, to bemoan the fact that Hope springs eternal. But no matter how they joked, before long the same drama would play out, the whole family held hostage to Hope's drinking, her mood swings and temper. The only saving grace was that Templeton Hall was so big they could at least try to avoid Hope as much as possible, except on days like today when there was a fuss about something and she would place herself in the center of it.

Sighing, Charlotte turned her pillow over, thumped it twice, then lay down again. The sooner she finished school, turned eighteen, and could get away from this madhouse, the better. On the bright side, her father owed her now, for having given up her day off. It had to be worth double pocket money. As she lay there waiting unsuccessfully for sleep to come, she took great pleasure in concocting a long shopping list.

IN HER BEDROOM, Audrey couldn't sleep either. She pulled out the sheet of paper from under her pillow and read it one more time. She'd intended to show it to her family today, but changed her mind after the drama with Gracie. She wanted everyone's full attention when she made her announcement. Charlotte already knew, of course, but she'd been sworn to secrecy until Audrey decided the time was right to tell the others. For once, Charlotte had seemed to understand how important it was, and also what a recognition of her talent it was. The drama teacher had said it, too, in front of the whole class, after he announced the cast. "I think we have the makings of a fine production of *Hamlet,* girls, with a very special Ophelia in Audrey Templeton. Here's to a marvelous end-of-year production."

It was like a wonderful dream, except it was actually real, Audrey thought, gazing down happily at the play's rehearsal schedule. There it was, in black and white, a list of cast members, with her name beside one of the *lead* roles!

This wasn't just some ordinary school production, either. Word had it that drama scouts for film production companies, acting schools, and advertising agencies came to all the Galviston Girls' School productions. Whether it was because their daughters attended the school Audrey didn't know, and preferred not to think about. This was her chance, her moment, and, more important, the only way to show her parents she was serious about a career as an actress.

When she'd tentatively raised the subject a year before, armed with brochures from her school career guidance counselor, she hadn't gotten very far. Her parents hadn't even looked at the information on drama studies. They both concentrated on the weighty documents explaining the courses on offer at Melbourne University, the best tertiary institution in the state, in their opinion. A chemistry degree for Audrey, they'd decided.

That day, and many days since, Audrey had cursed her own easy ability with scientific formulations and chemical compounds. So what if she could sort out formulas in her head? She could run fast, too, but that didn't mean she wanted to be an Olympic athlete. But any hints from her about chasing her dream were met with blank stares from her parents.

"Acting's not really a career, darling. It's a hobby."

"We didn't even know you liked acting. You never show much interest in it here."

This isn't acting, she'd wanted to shout. This is some weird family business involving ill-fitting costumes and dull facts, spouting information to motley groups of tired and sweaty people in shorts and T-shirts who think it is somehow funny to follow a costumed teenager around an old building for a family outing. Acting was different. Acting on a stage, in a darkened theater, was a suspension of disbelief, a way of blocking out the real world, of seeing other people's lives and stories brought to life—she had listened attentively through every one of her drama theory classes and had her arguments ready. Except her parents didn't ask for her arguments. Before she'd had a chance to object, Henry had filled out the form requesting she be coached toward a chemistry degree.

"And don't worry, of course you can keep acting," Henry had said. "Melbourne University has a terrific drama society. It'll be a great outlet for you—give that right brain of yours a workout after all the left-brain study."

But this piece of paper in her hand could change everything. Her parents' minds, her future, everything. Once they saw her as Ophelia, they would realize just how talented she was and how serious she was about acting. After the play was staged, she'd ask her drama teacher to write a letter, begging for their understanding, urging them not to make the mistake of denying the world a great dramatic actress.

Audrey climbed out of bed, too excited to sleep now. Silently crossing the room, she took a seat on the elegant antique stool in front of her dressing table, lit two of the candles that formed a waxen guard around her extensive collection of makeup brushes and hair ornaments, and stared at her reflection in the beveled mirror. She'd decided recently that the best way to describe her looks to any possible casting agent was "classic English beauty." Pale skin, high cheekbones (not high enough, in her opinion, but her experiments with various shades of blusher were helping toward her ideal look), and shoulder-length dark-red hair that she liked to wear in, yes, "classic" styles. Her role models, she'd decided, were the silent screen goddesses of the 1920s, with their immaculate grooming and strong femininity. Elegance never went out of fashion.

Not that she'd shared her thoughts with anyone in her family. Her mother had started to grow very impatient with the time Audrey spent sitting in front of the mirror. Audrey suspected it was jealousy. Her class had studied female psychology at school recently and it was apparently a common phenomenon that aging mothers became envious of their daughters' blossoming beauty. Not that that was a problem in Charlotte's case. In Audrey's opinion, Charlotte might look reasonably attractive if she took a bit more care and particularly if she went on a diet, but Charlotte just didn't seem to bother, pulling that thick mop of hair of hers back into a ponytail and wearing any old baggy clothes around the place. As for Gracie, while it was too early to tell for sure, Audrey thought her little sister might turn out quite striking when she was older, with her dark eyes and eyebrows, and that unusual white-blond hair. If it stayed blond and didn't go mousy, of course. Most annoyingly, it was Spencer who'd got the best looks in the family—a mass of blond curls that Audrey would have killed for, dark-blue eyes like their father's, and lashes so long they could have been false. Still, Audrey thought again now, leaning in toward the mirror and practicing arching her left eyebrow, the mark of true talent was making the best of your attributes, wasn't it? Growing into oneself. Having faith in oneself and one's place in the universe, staying grounded and yet confident at the one time.

"Breathe, Audrey, breathe," she said to her reflection in the low voice she was trying to cultivate. "Center yourself. Trust in yourself. Believe in yourself."

A noise outside made her jump. She swiftly blew out the candles and hurried back to bed. Charlotte had walked in on one of these private moments once, and after howling with laughter—"Who do you think you *are*, Audrey, Sophia Loren?"—had spent the next week mimicking her: "Breathe, Audrey, *breathe*, or else you will die, Audrey, *die*." Audrey knew it was counterproductive to waste valuable emotional energy on negative feelings, but sometimes she really did hate Charlotte. What would *she* know about the trials of having an artistic spirit? All Charlotte cared about was annoying teachers and spouting her ill-informed opinions. What would *any* of her family know about her hopes and dreams, if it came to that? Her parents barely gave her any attention when she was home on the weekends anymore. It was always all about the stupid Hall. Even Hope got more attention than she did these days. It wasn't fair, it really wasn't. She was truly starting to believe she was the cuckoo in the Templeton family nest.

To hell with them all, she decided now. Liking the sound of that sentence, she said it out loud, in a melodic deep voice. She tried it again, in an American accent. She was good at accents, her drama teacher had told her as much. Perhaps she could even try doing Ophelia in a foreign accent? What a great idea! Checking the schedule again, she was happy to see the next rehearsal was three days away. Plenty of time to prepare a convincing case about the accent. Already imagining the applause on opening night, she slipped the schedule under her pillow and fell asleep with a smile on her face.

SPENCER WAS too busy to sleep. What a great day that had been. He liked to think of a day's events as being divided into Good Things and Bad Things. Today had definitely been more Good Things. He made a list of them in his head as he rummaged around in the cupboard in search of ingredients for his current project.

The Good Things were:
1. Successful stink bomb
2. Gracie's crash
3. Police visit

The Bad Things were:
1. Crackdown on kids driving

That was exactly how his mother had put it. "There's going to be a crackdown on the children driving from now on." Spencer was hiding behind the curtains in the dining room after the police arrived with Gracie and he'd heard a big fight between his parents. Lots of soft shouting about whose fault it was, about the children running wild ever since Hope had started drinking again. That wasn't true, in Spencer's opinion. He'd been running pretty wild before Hope had started drinking again, it was just his parents didn't know about it. But it was a shame about Gracie's accident. Charlotte had promised to start teaching Spencer to drive now that he'd turned ten, but it looked like there wouldn't be much chance of that for a while, at least until all the fuss had died down about Gracie's crash.

In the meantime, there was still plenty of other stuff for him to do around the place. His new friend, Tom, who lived in a farmhouse a few paddocks away, thought Spencer had it made. No school. A huge house to roam around. Spencer had put him right on a few things. He did have school, it was just that he did it at home and his mother was his teacher. Tom had asked loads of questions about it, as if he'd never heard of homeschooling. What happened if Spencer misbehaved? Did his mother get him to stand outside the classroom? Did he still have to take exams? Wasn't it lonely sometimes? What if he woke up one morning and felt sick? Did he still have to go to school if his home was also his school? Spencer hadn't even thought about all that stuff before. He'd just always been taught at home and that was that.

"Is it because you're so rich?" Tom had asked.

"We're not rich."

"Everyone in town says you are. Look at the size of your house."

"Dad inherited it. We didn't buy it. His grandfather gave it to him. Or his uncle. Someone, anyway."

Spencer wasn't completely sure of the facts. He'd sort of listened when his father gave him the lessons about what to say when he was showing visitors around, but they couldn't expect him to remember everything. He'd never told his dad or his mum or Gracie—especially not Gracie, who would go crazy if she knew—but sometimes he just made up any old thing about where a painting or a piece of furniture had come from.

It didn't help that Spencer's dad was always arriving home with new clocks or paintings or small tables, all excited, saying they were "great finds." Spencer thought at first he was saying "grapevines" but Audrey put him right. A week or two later, some of those new "great finds" would turn up on top of the long cupboard in the big dining room, or in one of the glass cabinets in the morning room, or in one of the bedrooms they showed their visitors. Their father would give them a little speech about what to tell visitors: how valuable it was, how it had found its way into the Templeton family and been a treasure for generations now, blah blah blah. Spencer had found it all a bit strange at first. How could it have been in the family for generations if his father had just bought it in a shop?

He'd mentioned it to Gracie once, who got a bit funny, the way she did whenever any of them said anything about the Hall not being the most perfect place in the entire universe. "Dad knows what he's talking about," she'd said. Fine, Spencer thought. If Dad wanted to tell visitors that the blue jug he'd bought the week before in some junk shop was six hundred years old and had arrived in Australia on a ship with Captain Hook or Cook or whatever, then that was his business.

It had been funny one day recently when Spencer was showing a group around. His dad appeared in the dining room, all dressed up and with that cloth thing around his neck as if he was going to a wedding, putting on the really posh voice he used in front of visitors, calling Spencer "son." "That's right, son. I couldn't put it better myself." Spencer found it a bit weird. Of course he was his son. He was hardly the family dog.

His dad had taken over, telling all sorts of stories and making a fuss about the big glass vase on the table between the two windows. It was from the nineteenth century, he told everyone. It had been lying covered in dust in the Hall's pantry for years, until he, Henry Templeton, at the time living in England and working in antiques, had learnt of his inheritance of the Hall and arrived in Australia with his wife and four children.

The Hall had been full of hidden treasures like that, he told them. A treasure trove of wonders. People nodded a lot, Spencer remembered, although a boy his own age just stood there pulling faces at him and picking his nose. Then a man who'd been having a close look at the vase put up his hand and started talking really loudly. He was an expert in that sort of glass, he told Spencer's dad, and that vase wasn't even fifty years old, let alone one hundred.

"But this is terrible!" Spencer's dad had said. "Someone must have substituted a fake. The one that was there was certified by experts. I have the certificate somewhere. It's registered with Sotheby's. You're telling me it's a fake?"

"It's worthless," the man said. Spencer remembered him having quite red cheeks, as if he had run a race. "You've had a thief in the house. And if you don't mind me saying, your whole approach here is very risky and opens you up to exactly this kind of crime."

"But if we can't trust people in our home, where can we trust them?" his dad had said.

Since that day, any time any visitor announced they were an expert on something, or questioned an item's authenticity, there was a "new rule of behavior" to observe. They were to thank and congratulate the person, "quietly and firmly," their father said, for noticing, and also ask them to keep the news to themselves. They were right, it was a copy. They had been advised by their insurers and the local police that they'd been too relaxed about displaying treasured family heirlooms. So "regrettably" (it had taken Spencer a few attempts to pronounce that word) the family was forced to lock away the most valuable items, and put nearly identical but less valuable copies in their place.

"You shouldn't say it's original, then," a man said to Charlotte one afternoon, when Spencer was under the piano, listening. The man was cross about Charlotte telling his group that a painting over the fireplace in the drawing room was an original Gainsborough from the 1780s, commissioned by a member of the Templeton family. Charlotte had followed her father's directions to the letter, gently drawing the man aside and explaining that there was an original in a bank safe in Castlemaine but in the interests of protecting the family's assets, this copy had been hung in its place.

"That's false advertising, then. We paid good money for this tour and your brochure says all the interior decorations are authentic to the period."

"And so they are," Charlotte said. "This copy is from the 1860s. Thieves didn't just appear this century, you know. Our great-great-grandfather in Yorkshire had this copy made after coming home from a shooting party and disturbing a thief about to cut the original from its frame. In many ways, it's almost as valuable, don't you think?"

Spencer asked her about it afterward. He didn't remember his father telling him that story. Charlotte just laughed. "Of course it's not true, Spencer. What do I know about nineteenth-century forgery practices? Remember Dad's second golden rule? If in doubt, make it up. Do it quickly and then move on."

It was a lesson Spencer had taken to heart. He'd got away with it, too, so far. His aunt Hope had listened in one afternoon, standing in a corner of the room in that creepy way she did sometimes, hardly moving or even blinking. Her zombie mood, Spencer called it. He toned down his stories that day, but he probably needn't have bothered. Hope just stood there for a while, doing that thing where she scratched her arm over and over before wandering out again. He'd thought about saying something funny about her being the house's resident ghost but then his mother had come in and he was glad he hadn't. His mum got very fierce very quickly if any of them said anything about Hope.

Still, he didn't have to worry about doing the tours now for another week. He had his own projects to work on instead. The stink bomb had just been a practice run, but amazingly easy. Coming up next, just as soon as he'd saved up enough to buy all the ingredients he needed, would be the very best project of all.

He created a new list in his head. Future Good Things.

The fire-spewing volcano was at the top of the list.

IN HER ROOM, Hope was trying to make the inch of wine in her glass last as long as possible. The bottle on the floor beside her was empty. How could that be? she wondered, staring at it. It must have been half empty when she got it out of her wardrobe. She couldn't have drunk it all already, surely?

She took a small sip. Then another. Another. All tiny ones but as quickly as possible, trying to relax, trying to calm herself, trying to stop checking the door every two minutes to make sure no one was about to come bursting in. She hadn't meant to cause a fuss today, she truly hadn't, but when the police car turned up and she saw Gracie being carried in, she'd thought the worst, thought that Gracie had been killed. Even when she learnt the truth, that it was just a minor accident, it was too late, her nerves were jangling, the anxiety had set in, the tears, too.

Not that anyone understood, Eleanor especially, trying to shush her, saying that Gracie's accident had nothing to do with her. But of course it did. She knew what they were all saying. If Hope hadn't been there, causing problems, the Hall would be running like clockwork, the vases would have been filled with flowers, and Gracie wouldn't have had to drive into town. Did they think she didn't know what they were all thinking about her? Even as she'd tried to apologize for her tears, for getting so upset, even though she'd slipped away as quickly as she could back to her room, their voices had stayed with her. She'd sat on her bed for five minutes, telling herself that of course she could get through this without a drink, she just needed to calm down, to think of something else, all the things she'd been taught in different therapy rooms over the years. But her own voice wasn't strong enough. That other louder, stronger, nicer voice inside her started talking. She liked what it had to say. One drink wouldn't hurt, would it? It would take the edge off everything, make everything feel better, wouldn't it?

And it did. It always did. It just didn't last, that was the problem. It was a big, big problem, she thought, gazing again at the empty glass in her hand. Why did people make wine bottles so small? Why didn't someone invent an alcohol patch like a nicotine patch? Some sort of hidden device, like a morphine drip, that would keep a nice steady supply of alcohol drip-dripping into her vein, keep her nice and steady all day long, without anyone needing to know? She glanced over at the wardrobe, knowing she had another full bottle hidden behind her winter coats. No, she wouldn't get it. She'd be strong. She didn't need it. It wasn't good to mix her medication with alcohol. Besides, the way her luck was going lately, Eleanor would walk in just as she'd taken out the cork and there'd only be another lecture, another reminder of how awful it had been that time Eleanor had found her on the floor of her London flat.

"I thought you were dead, Hope. I thought you'd killed yourself. Can you even try to imagine how I felt?"

"How *you* felt? It wasn't exactly fun having my stomach pumped out."

She'd been trying to be funny, but of course Eleanor had got all high and mighty again. No sense of humor. She'd never had one. Anyway, for heaven's sake, why did she have to keep going on about that day? So she'd happened to drop round just in time. What did she want, a medal? Where was her Good Samaritan spirit? They were sisters, weren't they? Family? She would help Eleanor if she ever needed it, of course she would. If Eleanor ever stopped being so bloody perfect and showed some vulnerability or understanding once in a blue moon . . . Anyway, why was there such a *fuss* about her choosing to dull her pain with the occasional drink? Eleanor should be glad it was only alcohol and a few tablets. What if it had been heroin or another class-A drug?

"It's just *wine*, Eleanor," she'd said to her the last time Eleanor had started on one of her tedious lectures. "It's legal, isn't it?"

Even now, Hope could hear Eleanor's voice, at her, at her all the time, like a bloody machine gun. *I'm begging you, Hope, please don't do this to yourself again. Please, Hope, don't drink any more. Please, Hope, don't mix alcohol and tablets like that. Please, Hope, don't make a fuss. Please, Hope, change everything about yourself. Please, Hope, try to be as good and saintly and married and motherly as me. . . .*

Oh, *please,* Eleanor, shut up and mind your own fu . . . Just in time, Hope realized she was talking out loud.

It was all right for Eleanor, of course. It had *always* been all right for Eleanor. Always gone so perfectly: marriage, babies, career satisfaction. But had she ever shown her own sister any sympathy? No, of course not. Had she cared when Hope's heart had been broken, time and time again? Understood how she'd felt that time she thought she was pregnant, and the father had said he didn't want to know? So what if she'd been mistaken, that her period had just been late? Eleanor had shown her true colors that day, going on and on about her own problems, the children being unwell or something boring like that, actually saying to Hope that she "didn't have time for this right now." No time for her own sister's heartache and pain.

Hope stood up. Damn it. Damn her and damn all of them. She wanted a drink, so why couldn't she just *have* a drink? Who were they, any of them, to tell her how to live her life? *Her* life. The life she had given up for them. Hadn't she flown all the way across the world to give them a hand with this ridiculous Hall? Hadn't she spent hundreds, maybe even *thousands,* of unpaid hours helping Henry to design and plant the garden? Had Eleanor or Henry ever thanked her? No. Never. Too *busy,* all the time. Too busy *loving* each other, being so happily *married* all the time. As for the children. No gratitude from them either, ever. That brat Charlotte was the worst of them, the arrogant little cow. What she needed was a good kick up the . . . As for Audrey—had there ever been a more self-obsessed child in the world? The way she wafted around the house as if she were the bloody Lady in the Lake, it would make you sick. And Gracie? Well, all right, Gracie could be sweet, but if she didn't watch herself she'd end up *too* sweet. Thank God for Spencer. At least he had a bit of spirit. More to the point, thank God for that little arrangement she had with Spencer. . . .

The empty wine glass was annoying her now. Really annoying her. So was the empty wine bottle. Swaying only slightly, she tiptoed across the room to her wardrobe. It was so childish. So embarrassing. At her age, still hiding bottles as if she was back in boarding school. While downstairs she could just picture them all, Henry especially, pontificating, helping himself to another whisky, then another. What was the difference? Seriously, what was the difference between him having too many drinks and her drinking, every night? *But, Hope, I don't need to drink. I can stop anytime I like.* "Oh, shut up, Henry, and you shut up, too, Eleanor." She realized she'd shouted that and waited, poised at the wardrobe door, for movement in the hall. Nothing. Good.

Stuff it. She would have another drink. She'd never get to sleep now without it. Just a small one. Just to get her to sleep. As she opened the wardrobe door, she was smiling.

IN THEIR BEDROOM, Henry and Eleanor were fighting. Eleanor had come in from saying good night to Gracie to find Henry already in bed, reading a newly arrived copy of *Antiques Australia.*

"I thought you were going to do the accounts tonight?" Eleanor said.

"Too tired, I decided. No point doing them when I'm not at my best."

"You haven't been at your best for the past two months, then? Longer? Henry, this is getting serious."

"Eleanor," he said her name in a mocking tone, "your problem is you think everything is serious."

"No, my problem is I'm starting to think I am the only one in this house, in this family, who takes our problems seriously. You do nothing but stick your head in the sand."

"I'll do them when I'm feeling up to it."

She snatched the magazine away from him. "And when will that be, Henry? When the house falls down around our ears because we can't afford the most basic of repairs? When the visitor numbers dwindle to zero because you haven't felt like advertising or because you're too busy doing your family tree or entertaining yourself rather than anyone who happens to stumble upon us? Have you checked the bank statements lately? The money from that silverware sale is practically gone and you know the electricity bill is due any day. You're not even trying anymore, are you? Do you think all the vases and those chairs you were so thrilled to find are going to sell themselves?"

"I think I preferred it when you were in awe of me. The sweet little Eleanor I met twenty years ago would never have talked to me like this."

"Don't patronize me, Henry."

"I'm not patronizing you. I'm telling the truth. You were much easier to handle back then. Darling, you're just tired. Upset about Gracie."

"Yes, I'm tired. Yes, I'm upset about Gracie. But I am also completely and utterly tired and upset with you. How many more excuses, Henry? Do you know what Gracie's just asked me in there? Why people call us the mad bloody Templetons? Why we think we own the place?"

"We do. Well, most of it. I think the bank might have an interest in the stable roof."

"It's not a joke, Henry. I'm not joking."

"No, Eleanor, but you are shouting and I don't want you to wake the children any more than you do. You're tired, I'm tired, it's been a busy day. Come here. Come here and let me give you a kiss."

"I don't want a kiss. I want you to fix everything you promised you'd fix and haven't. I want you to bring in more money. I want you to do all the accounts you said you'd do months ago. I want Charlotte to start behaving, I want Audrey to stop all this acting nonsense, I want Gracie to stop being so anxious and earnest about everything, I want Spencer to stop plotting to blow us all up." She was now somewhere between laughter and tears, even as Henry patted the bed beside him, reached for her, and drew her closer. "I want a normal family life, Henry. Is that too much to ask?"

"Yes, darling. I'm sorry, but it is." He held her closely as she gave in to the tears. "That's not all, though, is it?"

She didn't raise her head from his shoulder but she shook her head. He stroked her back, her hair, held her tighter. Her words were muffled and he had to ask her to repeat them. She lifted her head and looked him straight in the eye.

"I want Hope to go. I want her to leave me alone. Leave all of us alone. She's ruining our lives. She tried to do it in England and nearly succeeded and she's trying to do it again."

"She can't help it, Eleanor. She's not well."

She shook his hands off her at the same time she shook her head against his words. "I don't care, Henry. I don't care anymore. I just want her to go."

Chapter Three

FOUR DAYS after Gracie's accident, in the kitchen of a farmhouse three paddocks away from Templeton Hall, thirty-five-year-old Nina Donovan was reading the local weekly newspaper. A large headline dominated the front page: UNDERAGE DRIVER WREAKS HAVOC.

Nina already knew all about it. She'd got the first call only minutes after the crash, as she came in from dropping her twelve-year-old son, Tom, at his junior cricket match, her head filled with the work she needed to finish, despite it being a Saturday. As a freelance illustrator, her income and reputation depended as much on her meeting her deadlines as her artistic talent. The caller was one of the school mums, breathless with excitement as she described the little girl in costume; the crash; the policeman.

"That family will do anything for attention, won't they?" the woman said as she finished her account. "The reporter from the local paper was there just now, too, taking photos—exactly what they'd want."

Another day Nina might have agreed with her friend, settled in for a spot of Templeton-criticizing, but she wasn't in the mood today. She surprised herself by defending them. "You really think they'd get a little kid to crash a car to get some publicity?"

"They've done that sort of thing before," her friend said, her tone huffy at Nina's refusal to play the game. Nina had found an excuse to hang up soon after.

It was a funny thing, Nina thought, as she finished reading the newspaper article now. Just because she was the Templeton family's closest neighbor, people assumed she either wanted to hear every bit of gossip about them, or already knew it. The truth was, she knew as much about the Templetons as anyone else in the area. She was happy to keep it that way. After what happened when she made the mistake of going to their first fete two years earlier, she'd deliberately kept her distance.

She'd heard talk of them long before the fete, of course. She'd even been taken to see Templeton Hall when she first moved to the goldfields area nearly three years previously, more than a year before the Templetons' arrival. Not that it had been called Templeton Hall then. The real estate agent showing her rental properties had been proud of the area's oldest colonial property. "Eighteen rooms, including eight bedrooms, three bathrooms, a huge kitchen, and a three-acre garden. A bit big for you, perhaps?" A bit beyond her budget, perhaps, she'd said wryly. It wasn't available anyway, he told her. "It's in a family trust of some sort. We've been waiting for a duke or duchess to arrive on a private Lear jet to claim their inheritance."

It wasn't royalty or a Lear jet, it turned out. It was the Templetons, a family of six or possibly seven, newly arrived from England. They were the talk of the town whenever Nina went shopping. "It's taken lawyers years to track them down, apparently." "They're spending a fortune on the renovations." "You must have seen them, Nina, surely?"

But she hadn't. Oh, she possibly could have if she'd rerouted her daily walk to go up their long driveway, walk across the extensive front garden, and peer in one of the house's twenty or so windows, but she chose not to. She'd been the focus of enough gossip herself over the years to know it was no fun being under scrutiny. Good luck to the Templetons, that's what she thought. They sounded like a perfectly nice family.

"They sound like weirdos," the man in the post office insisted.

Three months after their sudden arrival, the Templetons held a fete. They placed ads in the local paper. Flyers appeared stuck to the outside of shop windows early one morning. One of the children had been involved, the shopkeepers guessed. Most of the leaflets were glued at a child's eye level. All the neighbors within a fifty-kilometer radius of the old house found leaflets pushed under their doors as well, Nina included. Everyone insisted they hadn't heard anyone come to the door, that the dogs hadn't even barked. One child at Tom's school, overhearing his mother talking about the silent overnight leaflet drop, decided there were supernatural elements at work. The Templetons were ghosts, he announced, living in a haunted house. He did a great job convincing nearly all of his classmates of the fact. It didn't seem to matter what any of the parents said after that. The Templetons weren't just odd, weren't just foreign, weren't just mad to attempt to renovate that old house, they were also creatures from the underworld.

Those who didn't believe in ghosts found plenty else to be disgusted about.

"A fete? Who do they think they are? The royal family?"

The puzzling thing was that no one Nina knew, or even friends of people she knew, had actually talked to any of the Templetons. Someone said they'd seen the mother in the supermarket early one morning, her trolley filled with food, but she'd paid and left before anyone spoke to her. None of the children had joined any of the local sports clubs. Mr. Templeton had apparently been seen in a Castlemaine pub one Friday night, but it turned out to be a false alarm. He was always referred to as Mr. Templeton. It felt somehow wrong to call him by his first name, believed to be Henry.

On the morning of the fete, Nina wasn't surprised to hear far more traffic on the nearby roads. She glanced at her watch. Nine thirty. The fete was due to start at ten. It was a fine, sunny day. It wouldn't hurt for her and Tom to take a look.

Her first thought as she walked up the driveway, with the then ten-year-old Tom cycling beside her, was that perhaps the kids in the school had been right about the supernatural forces. The last time she was here with the real estate agent, the driveway had been overgrown with weeds and dry grass, rutted with potholes. The trees lining the road had badly needed pruning, the fences running beside in need of repair. Now, the fence lines were straight and new. The trees had been cut back expertly, to form a cool and attractive natural arch over the road. The driveway itself was still dirt, but it had been graded, and a path for pedestrians constructed along the right side.

If the driveway was impressive, the house itself was a miracle. There were already forty or more people milling on the front lawn when she reached it, and their talk was a hubbub of amazement. Not only was the garden immaculate, but the sandstone of the house looked polished, the window shutters freshly painted, the glass gleaming. It must have cost a fortune. How did they get it done so quickly? And one other question: what on earth were they doing here?

She heard a chime of a clock, from where she didn't know. Ten o'clock. The front door opened. There, standing beaming at them all, was Henry Templeton. He strode out, enthusiastically shaking people's hands, touching shoulders, leaning down and kissing babies. "Welcome! Welcome, all of you. Welcome to Templeton Hall."

His accent was upper-class English, his bearing was—yes—regal. He was in his late forties, perhaps early fifties. He had a thin face, tanned, creased. Dark hair, with a long fringe that he flicked away now and again. Above-average height. He was dressed in a dark frock-coat, a cravat, and shining black shoes with buckles, more suited to a ballroom than a dusty lawn.

"Oh my God," Nina heard someone mutter beside her. "He's a madman."

"What is this, some kind of film set?" someone else said.

That was it, Nina thought. That was the whole effect. It felt manufactured, as though it had appeared overnight and would disappear just as quickly. Henry Templeton himself was like an actor, playing the part of an English country-house gent under a bright Australian sun, surrounded by broad yellow paddocks instead of sweeping green fields.

After Henry Templeton introduced himself to everyone waiting on the front lawn, he returned to the front steps, shaded his eyes, and invited everyone into the house.

"Make yourselves at home. Look around. See what we've been doing. And then I hope you'll enjoy yourselves in the side garden where all the fun of the fete awaits."

It was then that Nina noticed bunting adorning a row of trees to the east of the house. Music was just audible now, too, a tinkling fairground sound, like a glockenspiel.

Henry Templeton spoke again. "Before you set forth, though, may I introduce my family. My wife, Eleanor." A petite dark-haired woman, easily his junior by ten years, stepped out of the house. "My oldest daughter, Charlotte." A plump girl aged fifteen or so, her thick brown hair tied back, a defiant expression on her face. "My middle daughter, Audrey." A pretty younger girl, tall and thin, with a dark-red bob. "Gracie, my youngest daughter." A smiling little girl, nine or ten, with a halo of white-blond hair that made Nina think of a dandelion. "And my one and only son, Spencer." A cross-looking little boy with a head of blond curls, perhaps seven or eight years old, stepped forward, scowled, then stepped back. "And, of course, my sister-in-law, Hope." An elegant brunette woman in her early thirties standing at the back of the group gave a small nod. She didn't smile or step forward.

The gathering crowd looked at the Templetons and the Templetons all looked back. There was silence for a moment as each took in the other. All five females were dressed in full colonial costume. Henry may have got away with it, his look formal but somehow in keeping with the house. There was no mistaking the women's clothing for daily dress. Eleanor was wearing a long, pale-blue gown and matching bonnet. Hope had a similar dress in bright-red satin. The three girls looked very pretty in their long dresses, gloves, and satin pumps, Nina thought. Even the little boy was dressed in old-fashioned clothing, breeches, braces, and a hat, which from his tugging seemed to be the cause of his scowls.

"Come now, don't be shy." Henry Templeton smiled at them all again, before throwing out his arms once more. "Welcome, all of you, to Templeton Hall!"

"What did he call it?" a man beside Nina said, too loudly.

"Templeton Hall," Henry Templeton repeated, beaming at them all once more. "Officially renamed today in honor of ourselves, but also, most fortuitously, in honor of William Templeton, one of the finest surveyors in Australian history and architect of many local settlements. His name already graces several of your streets, of course, but this is our additional personal tribute. I'll officially unveil the plaque this afternoon, but if you can't stay until then, please do take a peek in the meantime. In fact, why don't I read it out?"

He strode toward a velvet curtain covering a square of brass on the wall beside the front door and pulled it back with a flourish. *Templeton Hall, officially opened May 1860,* it read.

"Typo there, mate," someone called out. "It's 1991, not 1860."

"Oh no, it's not," Henry Templeton said with a warm smile. "The moment you drove past our gates you went back in time, didn't you realize? You think we would wear these clothes otherwise? Templeton Hall officially opens today as a perfect time capsule of life in the 1860s. I am honored and touched that so many of you are here to mark this special day with us. So please, come inside and make yourself at home with the Templetons with our compliments today, and for a nominal charge on all other weekends. And be sure to tell your family, your friends—even your enemies—about us." He laughed cheerily, then turned and went inside, followed by the rest of his family.

There was initial hesitation, then almost a stampede to the front door. Within minutes the house was filled with chatter, as people practically ran from room to room, exclaiming at the renovations, the furniture, the work that had been done, how authentic it looked, how much it must have cost, then, in more whispered tones, the *strangeness* of it all.

Henry Templeton was constantly on the move, smiling, pointing out this painting or that table, giving potted histories of the gold-rush days, answering questions, no matter how rude or invasive, with charm, grace, and humor. The five costumed females seemed to drift rather than walk—that ghostly feeling again, Nina thought—into different rooms, smiling at guests, each of them talking in confident, beautiful English accents.

"They'll go bust in a month," she heard people saying more than once.

"This will all get stolen within a month."

"He's nuts."

"The whole family is nuts."

Nina and Tom stayed for half an hour. They walked through each of the rooms, Nina marveling as much as the others milling around them, but keeping her thoughts to herself. She knew nothing about the interiors of grand homes during the goldrush era of the 1860s, but she'd have bet anything this was a faithful reproduction, with its gleaming wooden furniture, richly patterned floral wallpaper, thick rugs on polished floorboards, all the walls covered in portraits, land-scapes, and still lifes. Throughout the house everyday items like vases, lamps, hardback books, even an elegant hairbrush and mirror set, were arranged on top of chests of drawers and sideboards, as though they had just that moment been used. The kitchen had cut-lery, china bowls, wooden utensils, and what looked like freshly picked vegetables on the long table, old-fashioned jars and bottles on the shelves, even an apron and a flour-covered rolling pin lying waiting. It all looked right. It felt right. And somehow, despite the whole odd-ness of the situation, the Templeton family members were making her feel as though she'd just casually wandered into a day in their life.

As she toured the house, sometimes one of the costumed women would be in the room, playing the piano or sitting quietly, embroi-dering, looking up at her with a smile. In one of the front rooms—the morning room, she heard someone call it—the littlest girl was play-ing with a spinning top toy that also looked as though it was from the previous century.

It was in the dining room that the spell was broken. Nina thought at first it was Eleanor, Henry Templeton's wife, but she remembered the red dress, and realized it was the sister-in-law. Hope, was that her name? Another visitor, clearly throwing herself into the spirit of the occasion, had asked where all the servants were.

Hope looked a little bored by the question, but answered it all the same, in a languid, refined voice. "We had one maid, a young Irish woman, but she wasn't to be trusted. That's been the trouble with life here in the colonies, all sorts of riffraff made it here and of all of them the Irish are the least trustworthy. Quite dishonest, in fact. It's in their blood. The Italians are as bad."

Perhaps the woman was trying to be funny. Perhaps it was an au-thentic replica of the thinking of the time. But it burst a bubble for Nina. In that minute, the setting, the whole pantomime aspect of the house ceased to be entertainment for her. She wanted to object. *My name is Nina Therese Donovan, nee Kelly, and I find your comments of-fensive.* She could imagine her father urging her to speak up. He was proud of his Irish heritage.

Hope was still talking. "The Chinese are just as dishonest. Thieves, most of them."

Two women beside Nina, both of Asian appearance, looked as angry as she was feeling.

"If it was up to me, I'd bring all our staff out from England. Though that's as bad as anywhere else now. Immigration laws too lax. They let anyone in, more Indians around my house than in India these days. As for the blacks . . ."

Glancing around, Nina could see the group was a multicultural one.

"You might think I'm exaggerating," Hope was saying, "but you should see some of the streets in London near where I used to live. You wouldn't think you were in Engla—"

"That's enough." Nina spoke up then, conscious of the red flush flooding into her cheeks. "I don't care if you're playing a role here, but what you're saying is racist and offensive."

"I'm telling the truth and if you don't like it, then leave."

A man entered the dining room behind her. "You're asking one of our guests to leave? My dear Hope, what is happening here?" It was Henry Templeton.

"I'm just explaining the situation here and back home and this woman seems to be taking offense," Hope said, her voice sulky.

Henry turned his full attention to Nina. "My dear, I'm so sorry! Tell me, what's your name?"

"It doesn't matter what my name is," Nina said.

"Her name's Nina Donovan," Tom said beside her.

"Donovan? A fine Irish name."

"Don't you start, she was bad enough," a woman beside her said. Nina knew her. Carmel O'Leary from the library.

"Would you please tell me what happened?"

Nina told him, as Hope stood sullenly and other people in the group nodded in agreement.

"I do apologize," Henry Templeton said. "Hope, haven't I asked you to keep your thoughts to yourself?"

"My thoughts? My honesty, you mean."

"Eleanor," Henry called then, leaning out the door. "Could I see you here for a moment?" As he waited for his wife to appear, Henry turned his full attention back to Nina.

"My dear Anna—"

"Nina."

"My dear Nina, I do apologize. Sadly, that is how some people thought in the 1860s."

"I'm sure they did. What bothered me more is it's clearly how she feels in the 1990s."

"Please, don't be upset. Now, why don't you have a sit-down and we'll get you a cup of tea. I'm sure you'll calm down soon."

That was the last straw for Nina. "No, I won't actually. We're leaving and we won't be back. She's racist and you're condescending."

She and Tom had just collected his bike from beside the garden path when she heard a voice behind her. "Excuse me. Excuse me."

It was the woman from the dining room. Hope.

Nina stopped, waiting for the apology. Beside her, Tom watched quietly, pushing his bike back and forth.

Hope was staring at her with something like hatred in her eyes. "How dare you," she said.

"I beg your pardon?"

"How dare you humiliate me like that, in my house? Who do you think you are, coming into a family house like this and grubbying it with your rudeness."

"Excuse *me*. You were the one who was rude. I found what you had to say offensive."

"Offensive? You have difficulties with the truth, do you?" Hope was shouting now.

"Mum—" Tom said beside her.

Nina put her hand on Tom's shoulder to comfort him, still staring in disbelief at the other woman. She tried to be reasonable. "Look, I know this is all a joke, fun and games for tourists and to make money—"

Hope lifted her chin. "This is not a joke. This is living history. Something we all take very seriously. And I meant every word of what I said in there, and I mean every word of what I'm about to say to you. Get off this property this minute, you and your son, and never come back. You're not welcome. Do you hear me? Get out of here or I'll call the police."

Tom was now staring wide eyed at Hope, pressing even closer to his mother. People around the garden were starting to look across. Nina was tempted to call them over to listen. This place was supposed to be a tourist attraction?

The woman took a step closer. "Do I have to make myself any clearer? Leave. Go."

The walk back down the drive wasn't nearly as pleasant as the walk up had been. Despite Hope's ranting, Tom told her he hadn't wanted to leave yet.

"We had to. They're not nice people, Tom."

"But I wanted to see the fete."

"I know. I'm sorry, but we're leaving."

"Are you mad at me now?"

"Of course not. I'm mad at them, not you."

"Because their house is bigger than ours?"

That made her laugh. By the time they were home, ten minutes along the dry and dusty road, her son was back in good spirits again.

Nina wasn't, however. If anything, she was more upset. The unsettled feeling stayed with her all afternoon. She went to bed early that night, not long after Tom, and tried to distract herself with a book, then a magazine, before tossing them both aside. She turned the bedside lamp off, then on, then off again, moving restlessly in her bed, unable to sleep, annoyed at herself.

She sat up, switched on the full bedroom light, looking across at the photo on the wall opposite her bed. It was her wedding photo, taken eleven years before. She looked so young—she had been young, only twenty-two. So happy, too. Her hair had been completely black then, no gray hairs like now, her blue eyes so optimistic. Beside her, easily a foot taller, her husband, Nick, was looking down into her eyes and laughing, the camera catching the moment beautifully, his face full of love, his eyes crinkled, his tanned, open face proof of his happiness that day. Not just that day, either. Nick had been the most cheerful, most optimistic man she'd ever met. The perfect antidote to her own often anxious nature, constantly reassuring her. "Everything will turn out for the best, sweetheart, you just wait and see." In appearance, Tom was a perfect mix of them both—he had her olive skin, Nick's tall, lanky build, her black hair, and Nick's dark eyes. Even though he was still only a child, she could tell Tom had also inherited his father's determination, his calm nature, his gentle humor.

Back it came again, that yearning need for Nick to be there beside her, the longing to be able to turn to him in their bed, talk through her worries, take pride in their son together. The empty side of the bed seemed to mock her, as it always did. There was no telling when the grief might descend, even this many years later. The most ordinary of things could set it off: an unused pillow, an advertisement for family holidays on TV, or times like today, when she knew that if he had been here, Nick would have had her laughing in seconds about the crazy things that woman Hope had said; would have made everything all right again.

She knew she wouldn't sleep now. Instead, she got up and made herself a cup of warm milk. Sitting outside on the step, cradling the cup, she tried to sort through her thoughts and understand why today's events had upset her so much. Hope's racist comments, yes. Henry Templeton's condescending manner, yes. There was even a grain of truth in Tom's words. Sometimes she did wish they lived in a bigger house.

But as she sat out under the night sky, sipping slowly, listening but not bothered by the rustlings of birds and small animals in the bushland around their house, she realized they weren't the main reasons for her reaction.

As she'd walked around Templeton Hall, as she watched the family play their parts—not Hope, but the others—she'd become aware of a strange, unhappy feeling inside her. Jealousy. Not of the big house, the big garden, or the family's obvious wealth. She was jealous of the Templetons themselves. They were a family. A happy family. A happy mother and a happy father and four happy children.

The contrast between them couldn't have been starker. There she was in her small, rented farmhouse, trying her hardest, coping as best she could on her own, still desperately missing her husband, feeling lonely and sad and worrying about Tom, about money, about the future. And there they were, the perfect rich family, carefree and adventurous, with enough time and money on their hands to arrive out of the blue from the other side of the world, hire the best and quickest of builders and architects to open a living museum, and all with such style and confidence.

Another rush of envy overwhelmed her now. She tried to dismiss it, recalling what she'd heard people saying around her today as she and Tom moved through the house. Show ponies, she'd heard one man call them. Crazy. Mad. Eccentric.

They were all those things, Nina agreed. But their antics had also looked like fun. Any family that felt the need or had the desire to undertake a renovation like that and spend their weekends dressing up was having fun together. And that was exactly what she missed in her own life. The fun had gone missing the moment she was told about Nick's death.

She tried to concentrate on that exchange with Hope. Tried to summon the anger again. But even as the other woman was speaking, Nina had sensed that all wasn't quite right with her. Whether she'd been drinking, or had taken something else, her eyes hadn't been quite focused, her words too bizarre, as if she too had been playing a role, like the rest of the family, but in a much darker, stranger play.

Nina did what she often did at times like this. She went inside and rang her sister, hoping she was still awake. Her elder by just fourteen months, Hilary was her best friend and sounding board, sensible without being a stick-in-the-mud. After leaving school, she'd studied to be an accountant and worked for five years in a large Brisbane firm, before taking two years off to go traveling. She'd come home a changed woman, abandoned accountancy and retrained as a nurse. For the past four years she'd worked as a theater sister in a Cairns hospital, living with her husband of three years and happily playing stepmother to his two teenage daughters from a much earlier marriage.

Hilary was up, ready to listen, and, even more important, seemed to understand Nina's feelings immediately. "Just keep away from them. You've done your civic and neighborly duty now, haven't you? You're not a tenant on their land, legally bound to make regular weekend visits so you can be harangued by racist upper-class ladies or offered cups of tea by a man who quite frankly sounds as though he would surpass Basil Fawlty when it comes to interesting approaches to hospitality. . . ."

Nina laughed, feeling her tension lift and her mood change as she agreed completely with her sister that no, she need have nothing else to do with Templeton Hall or its new inhabitants.

"They'll try and seduce you, though, you know," Hilary continued. "Lure you into their world. Promise me, Nina Donovan. Swear on the nearest Bible or trashy paperback or school newsletter. Promise you won't be drawn into their debauched world of dress-ups and gala balls and garden fetes and cucumber sandwiches and croquet on the lawn and—"

"I promise," Nina said, smiling again.

Hilary's voice softened. "Maybe they looked perfect from the outside, Nina, but who knows what the truth is. You look like you have the perfect life yourself sometimes, you know. A beautiful son, a successful career."

"Oh, sure."

"I mean it, you do. Forget about them, honey. Don't visit the house again. Just try to put them and what happened today out of your mind. Promise?"

"Promise."

It was easy not to visit the Hall again. Not quite so easy to forget about it, however, when her route into Castlemaine to drop Tom to school each day took her past the entrance to their driveway, and her route back gave her a briefly perfect view of the Hall through the trees, but she made herself look away each time. It was even harder to insulate herself from news about the Templetons themselves. It quickly became obvious that anything the family did was prime gossip in the area. Over the next months, Nina heard countless anecdotes. There was the story of Henry Templeton marching into a council meeting to declare war on the mayor, insisting that a recent turning down of a planning permission application relating to Templeton Hall was vexatious and ill informed. A lawyer from Melbourne had followed him in, apparently, to state the case in far more civilized tones and language. A stormy exchange had taken place, Henry at the center, "carrying on as if he was in the House of Lords," one councilor described it. The application was passed a week later. "Bribery," people in town whispered. Money talks.

The local tourist association was equally disgusted several months later by the arrival of a letter from Henry Templeton, rejecting their "so kind invitation" to join the association. (The head of the association said she was surprised it wasn't signed "Esquire.") "We prefer to forge our own path but thank you for your valuable efforts to promote our beautiful area."

"The arrogance of him," one of the committee members said to Nina when they met in the town's main street one afternoon. "Who does he think he is? He *needs* us."

But it seemed he didn't. Henry Templeton and his costume-wearing, English-accented wife, daughters, son, and sister-in-law seemed able to attract all the publicity they could possibly need. There were regular articles in the local newspaper. Nina turned on the TV one night to see Henry beaming at the camera, as he led a crew from a current affairs program through Templeton Hall. "It's like stepping back in time to a more gracious era the moment you enter this wonderful living museum," the voiceover explained.

Two months later, another rush of media attention, this one sparked by the theft of a vase apparently worth thousands of dollars (thousands of pounds, originally, of course, as Henry explained in one of the many newspaper and radio interviews he gave). "We run Templeton Hall on a basis of trust," Nina heard him say. "This is our home and our visitors are our guests. It would be the height of rudeness to declare ourselves suspicious of their every move."

Nina's parents were enthralled by the whole case. They were visiting her at the time, and in Nina's opinion, far too intrigued by the Templetons. Nevertheless, she dropped them off at the driveway to the Hall, and also listened with more interest than she liked to admit when they returned, filled with stories. They'd been shown around by the little boy and one of the older girls, Audrey, they thought it was. Both very theatrical, they reported, and filled with facts and figures about the Hall. All very fascinating. And all very funny, too.

"They don't take themselves at all seriously, do they?" Nina's mother declared. "The little boy especially. We were nearly in tears laughing at the stories he was coming up with. Standing there in old-fashioned clothes, buttons undone, chewing gum as he talked to us," her mother continued, laughing again at the memory of it.

"The whole house was spotless, too," she'd also reported. Gleaming. How on earth did they manage it? she wanted to know. They either spent the entire week cleaning or had a tribe of maids or servants or whatever term was appropriate in an historic house like that. Her mother wasn't the first to ask the question. The mystery was solved when a delivery man reported seeing several Templetons in cleaning gear one weekday afternoon, scrubbing floors and washing windows. The little boy looked furious about it, he said.

There was also plenty of discussion locally about the family's unconventional school arrangements, particularly the homeschooling of the youngest children. Questions of legality were raised. Discussions on whether it was some sort of fundamentalist religious cult. Some people seemed quite disappointed when they heard, from reliable sources, that Eleanor Templeton had recently met with one of the local principals to organize access to the school library. It seemed she not only held a master's degree in education herself, not only had homeschooled all her children through their primary years, but had also coauthored a well-received handbook in the UK on the benefits of homeschooling younger children.

No matter how unorthodox their lives were, however, their business approach clearly worked. Within eighteen months of the fete, Templeton Hall had been named in the top five of the goldfields' premier tourist attractions, second only to the nearby Sovereign Hill, the replica goldrush settlement complete with operating mines, shops, and businesses.

"You must be curious to go and visit the Hall again," one of Nina's school-mum friends said to her once. "They're your neighbors, for heaven's sake."

"Let me guess what it's still like. An old house, people in costume, antiques, and history lessons?"

"Well, yes. But it's like living next door to Disneyland and never going to shake Mickey Mouse's hand."

"He'd have germs. Imagine how many people's hands he shakes every day."

"But their little boy is just a year or two younger than Tom. Wouldn't it be handy if they could play together?"

Nina had changed the subject then. Yes, it would be handy but it wasn't going to happen. Introducing Tom to the Templeton boy would mean walking up that long drive again, knocking at the door, and then what? Being overwhelmed by that feeling of envy and sadness again? Or being chased away by Hope? She didn't know which would be worse.

In the past month or two, however, the distance between their two houses had started narrowing again. From the moment Tom told her he'd met Spencer Templeton at the yabby dam that marked the halfway point between Templeton Hall and their house, Nina had felt uneasy.

Up until then, Tom had seemed content enough to spend hours playing on his own. It had worried her when they first moved here, that the house was too isolated, that there were no neighbors' kids for him to meet up with after school. But he'd always been independent, from the time he could walk, happy in his own company. Like his father had been. On weekends, Tom would organize a bag full of supplies for himself—a sandwich or two, a bottle of water, apples, chocolate if she had any in the house—and then set off to have what he'd tell her was "an adventure."

"Don't go far," she'd say. "You won't hurt yourself, will you?"

"Not deliberately," he said once, smiling at her. "Mum, come on. Why would I do that?"

She'd had to work hard to keep the relaxed smile on her face, too, to let him head off on his own without thinking she was home fretting every minute he was out of her sight. He was a sensible kid, she told herself. He won't do anything stupid. The problem was, she kept imagining the things he *could* do. She pictured him climbing a big gum tree and not being able to get down. Building a raft in the dam and having it sink moments after launching. Losing his sense of direction and being unable to find his way home, frightened as the sky grew dark, the air grew cold . . .

So far, Tom had proved her fears groundless every time. Just as she found herself growing anxious, she'd hear him whistling, or hear the sound of a stick he was carrying being banged against the fence that surrounded their small property. The whistling was what gave her the idea but it took her time to summon up the courage to ask him.

He hadn't laughed at her, or got upset. He'd just listened in that gentle, watchful way he had and then repeated what she'd said. "You want me to carry a proper whistle and blow it every now and then so you can hear I'm okay?"

"I shouldn't worry, but, Tom, I just do. Especially when you're out there on your own."

"I know my way home. I know every bit of the land around here."

"I know you do. And I don't want you to not go out there. It's just I find it hard to work if I think you might be lost or upset."

"What if I've broken my leg in five places, am lying on an anthill being devoured by fire ants while a pack of lizards is chewing my foot, and I blow the whistle. How will you know the difference between an 'I'm being attacked' call and a 'Don't worry, Mum, I'm alive and well' call?"

"Can you blow the whistle twice if there are broken legs, fire ants, and lizards involved?"

He grinned then, and took the whistle she'd bought for him. It was an antique one she'd found in a secondhand shop in Castlemaine, an old-fashioned silver cylinder with a ring on top and *Acme City: Made in England* engraved on the front. She'd felt bad about it the next time he'd gone out, too overprotective, until the faint sound of the whistle, just once an hour or so, soothed her worries completely, and let her relax into her own work. So relaxed, in fact, that it was almost a surprise when the whistle sounded outside her window and she glanced up from her canvas to see he was almost home. He'd guessed, too, laughing at her. "You forgot all about me, didn't you?"

"Of course not," she'd started to protest, before smiling back. "I just didn't worry about you, that's all. There's a big difference."

She'd been in the kitchen cooking dinner the evening Tom returned home from the dam with a bag full of yabbies and a tale to tell. "I met this kid Spencer at the dam. He's from England and he'd never even heard of yabbies before, so I told him they were sort of Australian crayfish, and then he ran home and got his own string and bait and—"

"Spencer? Spencer Templeton, you mean? From Templeton Hall?"

"You know him?"

"We saw him that day at the fete, do you remember? Dressed up and showing people around."

"He was that kid?" Tom said, as if it all made sense now. "He told me he's never been to school, not even for a day. His mum teaches him at home. Can you teach me? That would be so cool."

"No, I can't teach you and everything's cool to you at the moment." Nina was surprised at her bristling reaction to Tom's news. "We don't really know him or his family, Tom. I'd rather you didn't play with him again."

"But he's the only other kid around here."

"You can have your friends home from school anytime you like."

"But their parents have to drive them and pick them up or you have to drive me and pick me up. Spencer and I can just meet at the dam. I told him about the whistle. He's going to get one, too, so if he blows it I know he's at the dam and I can meet him there. He said I can go and visit his house anytime I like."

"No, you can't."

"Why not?"

It was taking some getting used to, this new, older Tom who questioned everything she said to him. "Because I'd rather you didn't. Because I don't know his family."

"So get to know them."

"Please don't talk to me like that."

Tom's face turned mutinous. "You don't let me do anything I want to do."

"I do, actually." She kept her voice calm, with difficulty. "You have a hundred times more freedom than I did when I was your age."

"This isn't freedom." He said the last word at the top of his voice as he left the room, slamming the door behind him.

Nina was shocked at her own anger. She wanted to ban him from meeting Spencer, tell him he wasn't to go near the Templetons' house again. She only just managed to stop herself following him into his room and shouting back at him. Again, she was overwhelmed by a rush of feeling, of wishing Nick were here, wishing that she could ask him to talk to Tom, ask him to deal with this new version of their previously sweet-natured son.

But if Nick were here, Tom wouldn't have needed a friend like this Spencer. Nick would have played cricket with him, kicked a football, taken him yabbying. She knew that line of thinking was counter-productive and also untrue. If Nick had still been alive, she and Tom wouldn't have even been in Victoria. They would have been living in Queensland, with her mother and father just down the road, their kids going to local schools.

Push it down, push it away, she'd told herself that night. Give Tom the fun he wants. Don't make a big deal of this. And she'd nearly succeeded. Since then, she'd managed to smile and try to look interested and relaxed and unaffected by Tom's stories about his new friend Spencer. They'd met only twice more, as far as she knew, at the dam each time. They hadn't caught any more yabbies, but they'd talked about building a raft together, using wood from one of the old Templeton Hall fences, corrugated iron left over from the new chicken coop at the Hall. They'd transport it all over in a wheelbarrow, Tom had told her. Again, Nina had to stop herself from warning Tom of all the dangers, from thinking too much herself about possible risks—rusty nails in the iron, splinters from the wood. The one thing she didn't have to worry about was drowning, at least. The water in the dam was only about six inches high at the moment.

The sound of the ten o'clock morning news jingle on the radio brought her back to the present. Time for work. As she put the local paper into the recycling bin, she imagined the excitement this latest Templeton antic would cause around town. And at home, too.

"Why haven't you taught *me* to drive?" she imagined Tom saying. "All the Templeton kids learnt to drive when they were babies. They all got mini-BMWs for their third birthdays. Baby-size ones. With their names monogrammed on the doors."

It felt good to laugh about it. She knew Hilary would enjoy hearing about it, too. She was just reaching for the phone to give her sister a quick prework call when it rang. She wasn't surprised. Their link was so strong they often rang each other at the same time.

"You're a mind reader," she said, settling down into the worn armchair.

"Am I? Why?" It was another of the school mums. "Did you see the newspaper this morning? That Templeton girl's crash? It has to be a publicity stunt, don't you think?"

Nina had to stop herself from laughing. She bit back all she wanted to say and put on a bright, casual voice instead. "A crash? Really? What happened?"

Chapter Four

THE NEXT TIME they met at the yabby dam, Spencer told Tom all about Gracie's crash.

"She was driving down the main street at a hundred kilometers an hour and she went into a skid and the car rolled four times and her arm nearly got torn off. The policeman had to carry her into our house and after he left, the entire floor was covered in blood."

"Is it still there?"

"A bit of it. Mum cleaned up the rest. Do you want to see it?" Spencer asked eagerly.

Tom remembered his mother saying he wasn't allowed to go beyond the boundary fence. He remembered her saying she didn't want him going to Templeton Hall again. He just couldn't remember why not. "What about the yabbies?"

Spencer shrugged. "They'll be there tomorrow, won't they?"

Thirty minutes later, Tom couldn't believe all he was seeing. He'd done a tour of the Hall the day of that fete, but he didn't remember it being anything like this. How come he'd never been back here before now? It was fantastic. Better than fantastic.

Spencer showed him through every room, upstairs and downstairs, into the dining room, the living room, the morning room. Tom hadn't known rooms could have so many names. He saw the big kitchen, the pantry, the three bathrooms, with enormous baths that could easily hold three people each. Eight bedrooms—eight of them! Spencer also proudly showed him the blood on the hallway floor. Tom thought it looked more like a speck of paint, but Spencer insisted it was blood. His mother must have done even more cleaning up that morning, he said.

Tom met some of Spencer's family, too. Spencer had told him to prepare himself: that his three sisters were revolting, especially the two home on holiday from boarding school. But Tom thought they were all nice, even if they looked a bit surprised to see him.

"Did your parents leave you behind after the weekend tour?" one of the older ones, Charlie, Tom thought her name was, asked him.

"He's a local," Spencer said, in a voice that made "local" sound like something unpleasant. "We met at the dam."

"Damned if you do, damned if you don't," the other sister said, which made the one called Charlie laugh loudly. Tom didn't get the joke but smiled anyway.

The sister around his age called Gracie, the one who'd been in the crash, was much more friendly and normal. She was in the drawing room. Tom wanted to ask if they did their drawing in there, but something stopped him. He was surprised to see she wasn't wearing a sling on her nearly torn-off arm but decided not to ask about it. She was polishing a row of silver jugs. Spencer picked one up and pulled a face into it, showing Tom his distorted reflection, urging Tom to try it. So he did. Then Gracie did it, too, and it was funny, all three of them poking their tongues at the jugs.

Spencer's dad came in then. "Welcome to Templeton Hall, boy-from-that-house-a-few-paddocks-away," he said, when Spencer introduced him as that. He left again, before Tom had a chance to say anything more than hello.

"His name's Tom," Spencer called after his father. "Come on, Tom, let's go upstairs. See you, Gracie. Happy polishing."

"See you, Gracie," Tom echoed.

"Lovely to meet you, Tom," she said, giving him a very nice smile.

For the next hour, he and Spencer took turns sliding down the long polished staircase banister. It was more fun than any adventure park Tom had ever visited. He forgot the time, forgot about his dinner, forgot about the whistle, forgot everything, as they slid, ran to the top again, slid, ran to the top, again and again, without anyone telling them off.

"You're actually allowed to do this?" he asked.

"I'm allowed to do whatever I want," Spencer said.

Tom had just completed a particularly fast slide down the banister to a loud cheer from Spencer, when the telephone started to ring and a knock sounded at the front door.

"Hide, quick," Spencer whispered.

"Why?"

"Just do it," Spencer said. "Here, quick."

Tom followed Spencer across the hall, into a big room with sofas and tables, and behind a screen in front of a fireplace, decorated with a picture of a deer.

"I hid here for two hours once," Spencer whispered as they both crouched down. "You can hear everything."

Spencer was right, Tom discovered. From their hiding place he was able to hear a man at the door identify himself as a policeman, hear his own name mentioned, hear, "his mother is frantic," "missing for more than two hours," "we've checked all the dams," "you haven't by any chance seen—"

"A twelve-year-old boy?" It was Mr. Templeton speaking. "Dark hair? Yes, he's here."

"He's here?" the policeman answered. "Here? Can I use your phone?"

"I'd better go out there," Tom said, standing up.

"Not yet," Spencer whispered, grabbing him. "Wait until they find us. Or until they get really desperate. Whichever happens first."

Tom felt strange, as if he'd been turned into two versions of himself. There was the Tom who did what his mother asked, who carried the whistle, who felt sad when she worried about him. But the other, new version of himself—the Tom he was at that moment—felt different. A policeman was looking for him! He'd spent the afternoon running wild in this big house! It felt bad, but it also felt good. Exciting. Adventurous. There was trouble ahead, he knew without a doubt. But he also realized something else. It was going to be worth it.

"Spencer? Tom? Spencer?" There were three voices calling their names now, and one of them was getting closer.

"We come out now," Spencer said firmly. He stepped out from behind the fireguard. "Sorry. Have you been looking for us? Here we are."

Tom stepped out beside Spencer, feeling that strange combination of defiance and excitement again.

"Here we are," he echoed.

TWO HOURS LATER, Tom's arm hurt from where his mother had gripped it, his back hurt from where she'd hugged him too tightly, his eyes hurt from blinking back his own tears after she'd started crying, and he was still shocked by the severity of his punishment.

"You're grounded for a month, Tom. Do you understand that? Completely grounded. We had a deal but you disobeyed everything I've ever asked you. I've never been so worried. I thought you were dead, drowned, kidnapped. You're grounded for a month, and no pocket money either. You can leave this house or this yard to go to school or to cricket practice but that's it. Do you understand? No outings, no treats, nothing."

"But Spencer invited me back tomorrow. He—"

"Forget Spencer. Forget that whole family and that whole house. You're never going back there again."

"But he's lonely, too. He hasn't got any friends around here either."

She stopped shouting then. "You've got plenty of friends, at school, on the cricket team. . . ."

Tom didn't say anything.

Her voice softened even more. "I'm only doing this because I love you, Tom. I thought something terrible had happened to you today. I couldn't bear it if it had."

"But it didn't happen. We were just having fun."

"I know that's how it looks to you, but you're still grounded. Good night. I love you."

He knew he should have said "I love you, too." He did love his mother. But he kept thinking about that huge house, the staircase, Spencer and his family. . . . It felt awful to think it, even for a minute, but a tiny part of him was wishing that was his house, his family, not this small house, with just him and his mother.

"Tom?" She was beside him again, hugging him, kissing his head.

She hadn't stopped touching him since the policeman had brought him back home. "I love you very much."

"I love you, too," he said, finally.

A WEEK AFTER the incident with the-boy-from-that-house-a-few-paddocks-away, as Tom had become known by the family, Henry was disturbed at his attempts to do the accounts (though he'd long put them away and was browsing through an antiques catalogue) by a knock at the office door.

"Come in," he called.

First Charlotte appeared, then Audrey, followed by Gracie and Spencer.

"A delegation," he said, pushing the magazine aside and looking up cheerfully. "Just what I'm in the mood for. To what do I owe this pleasure?"

The three youngest looked to Charlotte, who was wearing a defiant expression. "We've come to hand in our resignation."

"Resignation? From what exactly?"

"From our jobs here. From working for you and Mum. We don't want to do it anymore."

Henry stood up, leaned both arms on his desk, and sighed. "There are days when we're all unhappy with our lot, Charlotte. When we wish we could be anywhere but where we are. When we wish fate had dealt us a different hand. But resign from your family? I'm sorry, but there's the little matter of all of us being related to each other. You can't leave."

"We're not leaving the family. We're resigning from Templeton Hall."

"And moving where? Out to the chicken coop? Into Castlemaine? Or you're planning on living full-time at the boarding school? You'll love it there, Spencer. You can be everyone's little boy-pet."

"We're serious, Dad," Audrey said. She was wearing full makeup, her hair elaborately styled.

Gracie said nothing, but looked as if she was about to cry. Spencer just looked cross.

"I see," Henry said. "Then your mother should be here, too. Excuse me for a moment."

The four Templeton children stood motionless as their father walked out into the hallway. They heard him calling their mother's name.

"He won't accept it. I told you he wouldn't," Audrey hissed. "We should have done this my way."

"Gone on a hunger strike?" Charlotte hissed back. "Forget it. Anyway, he has to accept it. What's he going to do, force us into the costumes? Put guns to our heads as we lead groups around?"

Gracie looked even more tearful. "Maybe we should have discussed it with him first, not just come in and resigned."

The sound of their parents returning halted the conversation. The four children stood up straight, staring ahead.

Henry spoke first. "Here are our children, Eleanor, standing strangely and saying all sorts of peculiar things. Start again, Charlotte. Perhaps it will make more sense the second time around."

This time Charlotte directed her comments to her mother. "We're resigning. We don't want to be guides here anymore."

"Or dress up," Audrey added.

"Or have people coming into our house looking at us as if we were performing pigs."

"It's seals, Charlotte, not pigs," Audrey said.

"Shut up, Audrey. We mean it, Mum. We're going on strike. You'll have to find someone else to do the tours."

"Someone else?" Henry said, his voice mild. "Four other children who will have a much better sense of family loyalty, who will recognize that working together like this is the only way we can keep Templeton Hall running?"

"That's enough, Henry." Eleanor's voice was calm, her expression composed. "I presume you all have your reasons? Perhaps we could hear them, discuss them?"

Charlotte crossed her arms. "Our position is nonnegotiable."

"The only certain things in life are death and taxes," Henry said cheerfully. "Everything else is negotiable. Charlotte, I can see you're the ringleader here, though you seem to have some strong thoughts as well, Audrey. As for you, Spencer, you look like you'd rather be out catching pigeons. But, Gracie, my little Gracie, do you seriously mean it? You don't want to be part of our family fun anymore?"

A pinch from Charlotte provoked a squeaky response from Gracie. "No. No, I don't."

"And why is that?"

Gracie glanced at Charlotte again, who gave her a fierce nod. "It's embarrassing."

"Dressing up in colonial clothes and sharing your heritage and the history of this great country with eager tourists is embarrassing? Why is that?"

Another pinch from Charlotte. "We look silly," Gracie said in a small voice.

"I'm sure the tens of thousands of little girls and boys and their parents who wore these clothes in the 1860s didn't feel they looked silly. In fact, in my opinion, it's the people who visit us in their modern gear who look silly, all tank tops and T-shirts with slogans and ill-fitting shorts. But point taken. Audrey, your reason?"

"We never get any time to ourselves. Every weekend we have to do this. All our friends at school have normal lives."

"Normal lives? What is a normal life?"

"They watch TV, go shopping, play sport."

"And do they earn money doing that?"

"Well, no. They get pocket money."

"Are they gaining valuable work skills for the outside world watching TV, going shopping, and playing sport?"

"Well, no, but—"

"Are they amassing a fund of unique childhood memories that will give them food for hundreds of dinner party conversations in years to come?"

Audrey just shrugged.

"Do they make their parents as proud as you make your mother and me every weekend, when we see you all being so charming, so articulate, helping us get Templeton Hall on its feet? Making not just us proud, but surely your ancestors as well, from the distant great-uncle who built this beautiful property to all the family members involved over the years, each of us strengthening the bonds between England and Australia? Do they?"

Audrey, Gracie, and Spencer looked a bit lost. Charlotte stood her ground.

"It's slave labor, Dad. Is that really something to be proud of?"

"I'm hardly forcing you to hand-weave twenty carpets per day."

"You take us for granted. You just tell us to do things, you never ask us."

"I say please, don't I?"

"No," all four children chorused.

"Don't I, Eleanor?"

"No," five voices chorused this time.

"This strike is about me not saying please?"

Charlotte nodded. "That's one of our concerns. We'd also like to discuss our wage agreement."

"We don't have a wage agreement."

"Exactly," Audrey and Charlotte said. Gracie was now biting her lip. Spencer was sitting on the floor, tying his shoelaces together.

"You'll trip over, Spencer," Eleanor said.

Spencer kept tying.

"So this strike action, you're serious about it?" Henry asked.

"Unless you come back to us with fair and just working agreements," Charlotte said, "you and Mum are on your own."

"You and Mum and Hope," Gracie corrected.

Charlotte bit back a smile. "Of course. How silly of me. I forgot Hope. Helpful Hope. Happy Hope. Hiccuppy Hope."

"That's enough, Charlotte," Eleanor warned.

"So let me see your demands, Charlotte," Henry said. "I presume that's the paper you're holding. It's obviously not your homework, if your last report is anything to go by."

"That's not funny, Dad. I've told you, my teachers have serious attitude problems."

"How strange it is always the teachers' fault. Wouldn't you think that just once, Charlotte, your bad marks might have something to do with your bad behavior?"

"We're not talking about my schoolwork."

Henry suddenly straightened. "No, but I think we should. We're supposed to be a family here, all of us working together, for our common goal, to get Templeton Hall to the point where all of you will benefit from it. I know you think sometimes this is a vanity project for me, just some fun and games—wouldn't it be a lark to uproot us from

England, land halfway across the world for the sake of a few old for-gotten ancestors? And yes, I take your point that none of you signed up for this, that no, you didn't ask to be born a Templeton, that yes, sometimes there are better ways for you to spend your weekends than playing tour guides from the past." He was pacing the room now. All attention was on him. Spencer had untied his laces and was also standing up again.

"We all want what we don't have sometimes. I know I do. Shall I be honest? Charlotte, I would prefer it if you justified the high fees we're paying for your boarding school by working hard and making something of yourself, rather than wasting your substantial brain finding new ways to blame others for your own failings. Audrey, yes, I can see a career as an actress would be far more appealing than a ca-reer as a chemist, but I wish you would listen to our experience, gain a degree in something that will guarantee you employment, and then look into acting. Gracie, we love you, you know that, we love all four of you, but it really doesn't matter sometimes if every curtain in the house isn't drawn to exactly the same width, or if the forks on the dining-room table aren't perfectly aligned with the equator. We'd like you to learn to relax a little. And, Spencer—"

They all looked at Spencer. He seemed eager for his turn.

"You're ten years old," Henry said. "Keep doing whatever you're doing. We'll get on to you when you turn eleven." He gazed at his children again. "So there we have it. We all wish it were different, but it isn't. So what are we going to do about it? More money, is that really what this is about?"

"That would help," Charlotte said in a small voice.

"And decreased working hours? Sounds unfair to me, more money for less work."

"Can we at least have a whole weekend off now and then?"

"We can look at the rosters, of course. Anything else?"

Audrey spoke, but was looking at her feet as she did. "I'm sick of that pink gown you had made for me."

"I am, too. That color doesn't suit you. Fine, new costumes. For all of you. Would that make it better?"

Four nods.

"Splendid. Now, anything else, while we are having this wonderfully full and frank discussion?"

"I have a question," Charlotte said.

"That surprises me," Henry said. "Yes, Charlotte?"

"I'd like to know about your future plans for the Hall."

"I beg your pardon?"

"I'm wondering if you've given any thought to what will happen when—"

Henry started to laugh. "Am I hearing right? You, the oldest of my four young children, are asking me what I plan to do with this property when I leave this mortal coil?"

"Mosquito coil? What's he talking about?" Spencer hissed to Audrey.

"Mortal coil," Audrey whispered back. "He's talking about when he dies."

"He's dying?" Gracie hissed, alarmed.

"No, Gracie, I'm not dying," Henry said. "Not as far as I know, anyway. And not for a while yet, I hope. Charlotte, how delicate and diplomatic of you. Should I start checking my soup for rat poison? Watch out for you measuring for new carpets?"

Charlotte went a sudden shade of red. "I didn't mean it like that. I get asked about it all the time at school, whether all four of us will inherit the Hall equally, even if there's a title attached to it."

"From what you've just said, the most appropriate title for you is the Grim Reaper."

"I don't understand," Gracie said.

Eleanor stepped in. "There's plenty of time to talk about this another day."

"Exactly," Henry said. "Besides, I haven't finalized my will yet. I might leave the Hall to the chickens. Or Hope."

"That's not funny, Dad," Charlotte said, her expression stony.

"No, it isn't. I apologize. Believe me, Charlotte, once I get a valid premonition of my date of demise, I'll be sure to call you all in and inform you exactly what my plans are regarding the property. Are you happy to be patient?"

Charlotte nodded, still looking unhappy.

"Very good. Thank you. Gracie, please take that worried expression off your face, I promise you I'm not about to die. Spencer, leave your sister's shoelaces alone. As for all your other demands regarding the running of the Hall, sorry, your other *suggestions*, I'll draw up a contract. Thank you all for your time. See you at dinner tonight."

Eleanor waited until all four children had left the room before shutting the door and turning to her husband. "They don't know quite what hit them."

Henry smiled. "Talk fast enough and you can stop most uprisings in my experience."

"So you'll do what they ask? New rosters, new clothes, weekends off? When we can't afford to do any of that at the moment?"

"It's a delicate balancing act, Eleanor. Offer plenty, deliver some, forget about most of it. Governments and tyrants the world over live life by that creed. Who am I to start anew?"

"Perhaps we should do exactly that."

"Exactly what?"

"Start anew. All of us. Put the Hall on the market, pay off all our debts, move back to England again. Have a proper, fresh start."

"Do you really mean that?"

She nodded.

"Eleanor, my love, if it were possible, you know I would. But you know the limitations of the inheritance as well as I do. No selling the property for at least twenty years and even then only with legal permission. I know it's been hard and it might get harder still, but at least we're in it together, aren't we? All of us, a family, having an adventure on the other side of the world, giving our children special times to remember—"

Eleanor held up her hand. "Please, Henry, stop there. Your audience has gone."

"My audience? Eleanor, what are you talking about? I'm speaking from my heart, to you, the holder of my heart."

She shook her head, smiling now. "You really are a wily silver-tongued creature, Henry Templeton. Did you know that?"

"Of course." He walked across the room and touched her cheek. "I convinced you to marry me, didn't I?"

Chapter Five

IN THE FARMHOUSE, Nina turned away from the canvas she was working on, wiped the paint off her hands, and checked the time. Nearly six. Fifteen minutes before it was time to collect Tom from cricket practice. Instead of sticking to the rules of his now three-week-old grounding and bringing him straight home, she'd decided to allow tonight's long-scheduled outing to go ahead: dinner at one of the local Italian restaurants in Castlemaine, followed by a video of his choice back home. It was a tradition they'd started in recent years, taking place two months to the day after Tom's birthday, their own way of marking the anniversary of his father's death, wherever they were living.

Thinking of what lay ahead, Nina felt a flutter of nerves. Would she finally manage it tonight? Finally find the words to tell Tom the truth about his father's death? Each year that had been her plan. Each year she'd decided at the last minute that it wasn't the right time. Would tonight be any different? There'd been so much tension between her and Tom since she'd grounded him, they were barely talking about anything at the moment.

"Nina, you have to stop finding excuses," Hilary had said the previous year, when Nina rang to tell her another anniversary had gone by without her telling him the truth. "Otherwise he'll find out for himself one day and it'll cause even more heartache."

"How will he find out?"

"If he ever sees Nick's death certificate. Or if you ever let him visit his own father's grave. You think he won't notice the date is the same as his birthday?"

Hilary's tone made Nina immediately defensive. "It won't change anything. His father won't come back to life just because Tom knows the date he really died."

"You know that's not what we're talking about. You can't protect him from every hurt life throws at him, Nina. And he has to be able to trust you. The longer this goes on, the worse it will be when you do tell him the truth."

Nina knew Hilary was right. In their many discussions, Hilary had insisted that it was perfectly understandable why Nina had first lied to Tom, and yes, just as understandable that she had found it hard to tell the truth once the lie was there.

But Hilary only knew the half of it. As far as she knew, the only lie Nina had told Tom was about the year Nick had died. If only it were that simple.

Nina had met Nick on her first day at college in Brisbane, introduced in the cafeteria by a mutual friend. She was studying graphic design and illustration. Nick was doing a business administration degree. They were acquaintances for the first year, confidantes and study partners the next, until finally, four weeks before they did their final third-year exams, they went to an all-night party together, walked home hand in hand along the dawn-lit streets to his small flat in Fortitude Valley, and became lovers.

"At last!" all their friends had said. "We thought you two were *never* going to get it together." After graduation, Nina realized she didn't want to stop seeing him every day, and was relieved and happy to learn he felt the same way.

"I've loved you since the first day I saw you," he'd told her.

"You have? Why did it take you so long to tell me?"

"I wanted to be sure you'd improve with age," he'd said with a grin.

She'd hit him playfully and he'd grabbed her hand and kissed it, his face serious for once. "You did. You get better every single day."

They lived together in Brisbane for a year until he was offered a management job with a big sugar company in Mackay, just an hour from her hometown. He accepted it, they got engaged a month later, and they were married in her hometown church eight months after that. Their plan was to rent somewhere locally while they saved up for a deposit on a house and then think about trying for a baby. Tom, it seemed, had other ideas. She'd just turned twenty-three when she found out she was pregnant. Nick was twenty-five.

It was an easy, happy nine months, no morning sickness, only some tiredness. A textbook pregnancy, her doctor called it. She went into labor just after lunch on her due date, to her surprise as much as everyone else's. Even her mother had insisted first babies never arrive on time. Nick hadn't hesitated about going to work that morning as normal.

When the pains started, she rang him. They decided it was probably a false alarm and she talked him into staying at work. The second time she phoned he knew from her voice that it was serious. He made it back to their house in thirty minutes, a record even by his fast-driving standards. He knew every road like the back of his hand, he always reassured her, whenever she worried about him driving home exhausted after his twelve-hour days.

He fussed over her, took charge, rang the hospital another hour away in the other direction, rang her parents, his parents, her sister, his brother, his voice a rush of excitement and happiness, letting everyone know that *this* first baby was going to arrive on time, and was on its way already. He'd just started calling the rest of the people on their phone list—aunts, uncles, cousins, friends—when she gently reminded him that perhaps they should think about getting her to the hospital.

He drove more slowly than she'd ever seen him do, one hand on the wheel, the other tightly holding her hand, until she told him it really would be okay if he went faster than twenty kilometers an hour. He refused to let her walk into the hospital, stopping the car outside the front door, running into reception, begging the use of a wheelchair, despite her insistence that she was fine to walk.

"We're having a baby," he said to anyone they passed in the corridor. "My wife is having a baby."

"Good thing you're in a maternity hospital, then," an amused nurse replied.

Nina had just settled into her room and was lying back on her bed breathing deeply as she'd been taught, Nick doing the breathing alongside her a little too enthusiastically, when she remembered in all the fuss they'd left her suitcase at home. Nick checked with the doctor. Was there time for him to go back and get it?

Time to go there and back two or three times, the doctor assured them. "Your baby's just letting us know he or she's on the way. We've a long wait yet."

"I'll be back as soon as I can," Nick said, kissing her forehead. "I love you." They were his last words to her.

She was in full labor when she was told the news. She'd been scared by the sudden arrival and intensity of the pain, she needed Nick there, now, beside her, *now*. She couldn't understand where he was. She called his name, shouted it, began screaming it, asking the nurses to get him, shouting at her obstetrician, her mother, her father, *anyone*, begging them to find him. It was her mother who eventually came into the labor ward, her face ashen, her hands clenched. It was her hands Nina noticed, even through her own pain. Her mother never clenched her hands like that.

Later, she learnt there had been passionate arguments outside the delivery room about whether to tell her or not, and when to tell her. She reacted badly when she heard that. "You were just going to pretend Nick wasn't dead? That he'd gone out for a coffee while his child was being born? Taken a wrong turn and got lost?" She became hysterical, shouting at the doctor, at her parents, at her sister, at anyone who came into her room who wasn't Nick.

Three hours later, Tom was born, a strong, healthy baby. A beautiful baby. She learnt from Hilary much later that there was fear in the family she would reject Tom. That her shock about Nick's death would overwhelm any love she might feel for her son. It didn't happen like that. Her grief for Nick was the worst pain she'd ever felt—sharp, raw, frightening—yet her love for her baby son was as immediate and overwhelming. He was the only thing that was good in her life. He was now, suddenly, shockingly, the person she loved most in the world.

She managed to stay three days in the hospital before she discharged herself, against everyone's advice. "I know what I need to do," she said. It was a phrase she'd repeat many times over the next few weeks, the next few years, as too many people tried to tell her how to feel, what to do, how she should be behaving.

If it had been hard in the hospital, it was worse outside. Every moment of every day she missed Nick so much it was a physical pain. Each day she was confronted with the horrible, constant reality of his absence. She walked the streets they'd walked together, pushed the pram they'd chosen together, drove the roads they'd traveled together. After Tom went to sleep each night, she sat alone in their living room, slept alone in their bed. If she went to visit her mother and father, she had to drive through the intersection where Nick was killed.

Everyone in the town knew who she was and what had happened. She couldn't walk into the post office or the supermarket or the bakery without noticing conversations stop, seeing people rearrange the expressions on their faces or hearing murmurs and comments even before she'd walked outside again. "The poor things. What a tragedy." The closer it got to Tom's first birthday and Nick's first anniversary, the more she felt it.

Two weeks before Tom turned one she knew she had to leave. She ended the lease on the house they had rented, gave their furniture to the local charity shop, and said her good-byes. She ignored her parents' pleas, Hilary's phone calls, Nick's parents' advice. She had to. This wasn't about them. They weren't living with a constant sound track in their heads of what should have been, what could have been.

To begin with, she just drove. Simply packed as many clothes and toys into the car as she could and drove. Tom was a calm child even then, content in his chair in the backseat. They took the coast road south, staying in caravan parks and cheap motels. She made up stories if anyone asked her questions. She was going to meet up with her husband who worked on the oil rigs. She was bringing her baby to meet his grandparents for the first time, and no, unfortunately her husband hadn't been able to get time off work. She said anything she could to stop herself from saying the truth. My husband was killed in a car accident three hours before our son was born.

She stayed in Queensland at first. After a month driving aimlessly from town to town, she rented a furnished apartment by the sea in a town south of Brisbane and stayed there, with Tom, for a year. She didn't have to work. There was life insurance that she hadn't even known Nick had taken out. If she was careful, it was enough to live on for several years. Not that she felt she could ever work again. She hadn't turned on a computer or even picked up a pencil since the day Tom was born.

Her family visited, Nick's family visited. Everyone tried to talk her into coming back home, but no one succeeded. As Tom's second birthday and Nick's second anniversary approached, she became restless again. There was more pressure from home. "We're sad, too. Let us grieve with you," was the message from everyone. Somewhere inside her, buried deep, she recognized that, but it was no help to her and she couldn't help them. It was just her and Tom now.

The day before Tom's birthday, she decided to move again. She needed the distraction. As she drove, she sang songs to Tom, all the songs she could think of, except "Happy Birthday." It seemed too sad and unfair that he should share a date like that.

She spent the next twelve months in a small town in northern New South Wales. The next in Newcastle, five hours farther down the coast. A year in another town south of Sydney. Her family still worried. Her sister tried being mad at her. "Nina, you're just running away. It's not good for you or for Tom, to be uprooted every twelve months like this. We miss you. Come back to Queensland." But she couldn't. This constant movement was her life now. If she wasn't going to have the life she'd dreamed about—the permanent, settled, ordinary life she and Nick had planned—then she was going to have these different, temporary lives. She told herself she liked it that way. It suited her personality. Twelve months was the perfect amount of time to stay in one place, long enough to gather some impressions, short enough not to form too many friendships.

"But what do you do all day?" Hilary wanted to know.

At first, Nina did only what needed to be done. She looked after Tom. It took every minute she had. She wondered constantly how it would have been if Nick had been there with her. Sometimes it was a hardship, the constancy of it, the repetitiveness of it. But there was also a rhythm, a soothing sameness to being this close to another person, a child that she loved. They were a team. It was the two of them against the world.

The year Tom turned five, there was more pressure from her family. "You have to stay in one place now that Tom's starting school," her sister said. "He needs stability. Come home."

She considered it. She imagined Tom back in her hometown in Queensland, in the local school, playing alongside the sons and daughters of people she'd been to school with herself. Her thoughts stopped there. Each of those sons and daughters and their parents knew it all. From the first day Tom set foot in the playground, their story would follow him. Poor tragic Tom, born the day his father drove into a truck and killed himself.

"Nick didn't do it deliberately, Nina. It was an accident," Hilary said when Nina tried to explain her feelings.

"It doesn't matter. I hate that gossip about me and I don't want it for Tom."

"Then do whatever you need to do," Hilary said, finally.

Nina kept moving, three times in Tom's first three years of school. Not far each time, just to towns two or three hours away, but each move felt necessary. The school mothers always started to get too curious. She'd tried just not mentioning Tom's father, but there was always one who asked. Was she divorced? Separated? If she finally said that he had died, even more questions would follow. "I'd rather not talk about it," she'd end up answering, knowing it sounded stuck-up but preferring that to telling the truth.

Tom had also started asking questions. He'd always known his father was dead, but it was only when he started school that it became a constant talking point. "The other kids have all got dads and I haven't. Why not? Why did he die? Did the vet put him down?"

Nina related that particular conversation to Hilary one night after Tom had gone to bed. At least she knew what had sparked Tom's question. One of the teachers had told her the news that day of the school cat's untimely death.

"It's healthy that he's asking questions, Nina. It's a good thing. So did you tell him everything, at last?"

Nina hesitated before answering.

"Nina?"

"I changed the subject."

"You changed the *subject*? The subject being the truth about his own father's death? Nina, you have to stop lying to him."

But she'd *had* to lie to him, from the very beginning, for both their sakes. Not that everything she said had been a lie. Since the day he was old enough to understand, she'd told him the true things, too, over and over again: how wanted he was, how much she and Nick had loved him from the moment they knew she was pregnant. What a punctual baby he had been, arriving right on time. But she hadn't been able to stop there.

She'd told Tom how excited Nick had been that day in the delivery room. That his father had helped cut the umbilical cord, that Nick had been the one to shout—yes, *shout*—at the top of his voice, "It's a boy!" the moment Tom was born. Shout so loudly that her parents outside had been able to hear it! She'd told Tom how much Nick had loved holding him, playing with him, bathing him, dressing him. How Nick used to sing him to sleep. How good he had been at changing Tom's nappies. How he used to get up two or three times a night just to check his little son was sleeping well. How his favorite thing to do after work was sit out on the verandah of their small house, put his feet up on the rail, and nestle his baby son against his chest, telling him in the most serious of voices everything that had happened at work that day. "You were a great listener even back then, Tom," she'd tell her son.

She told him it was Nick who bought him his first football the year he turned one; his miniature cricket bat-and-ball set for his second birthday; the little bike with trainer wheels for his third. The child-size football jumper with his name on the back for Christmas that same year. Nick who first took him swimming at the local beach— "He told me you roared like a lion when your toes first touched the water." She'd painted every possible detail of the first three years of a father–son relationship, given Tom every memory she could, to spare him the knowledge that his father had never even seen him, let alone held him.

"You told Tom he was three years old when his father died?" Hilary said when Nina finally confessed. "Oh, Nina. Why?"

She tried to explain, to let Hilary know that she was fully aware of the mess she'd got herself into. Hilary, to her great credit, kept asking questions until she understood it all.

"But hasn't he ever asked to see pictures of himself with his dad?" she asked.

Nina hesitated. "I told him there was a flood in one of our houses. That all the photos of them together were destroyed."

"Oh, Nina," Hilary said again.

Hilary had made her promise to tell Tom soon. Each year as his birthday approached she'd vowed to herself she'd do it. Each year the date had passed without it happening.

The year Tom turned nine, their annual move felt like any of the others. She was back working part-time by then, not as a graphic designer but as a secretary in real estate offices, hardware firms, council offices, wherever a job was offered. As usual, on the day before the birthday-anniversary, she and Tom set off in her car, the trunk and the backseat crammed with their belongings. Tom rode in the front passenger seat these days, apparently as accepting as he'd always been about this nomadic life they led. She wondered how much longer that would last. She'd already seen signs of independence from him. Until now, he'd always cheerfully accepted her reasons for moving. She'd tell him work had dried up where they were. Or that she'd heard about a great town she wanted to show him. Or sometimes she'd simply turned it into a kind of story, describing them as two characters from a book, off having adventures.

"I'll miss this place," he'd said the previous day as she was packing what little they'd gathered around them in the latest rental apartment.

She'd looked up in surprise. "This place? What's special about this place?"

"I like my room. And my friends at school."

"Oh, Tom, you'll get a new room even better than this one. And new friends."

"Do I always have to keep making new friends? Can't I start keeping some old ones?"

As they drove away the next morning, his words echoed in her head. For a moment she considered staying on in that town, pretending her pretend job in a still-to-be-chosen new place had fallen through, reenrolling Tom in the small primary school. But something urged her to keep going. That town hadn't been the right place for them, she told herself. Perhaps the next one would be. Wherever that next place was. She still hadn't decided.

"I've got a great idea," she said, pulling over to the side of the road. They'd passed the last of the houses and buildings and there was now nothing around them but empty paddocks and gum trees, the highway stretching out in front of them. "You're the soon-to-be birthday boy. You choose where we're going to live next."

She handed him the map of Australia, silently hoping he wouldn't choose Perth, nearly four thousand kilometers to the west, or Tasmania, not just a long drive but a ferry journey away. He considered the map closely, and then pointed to the middle of Victoria, the neighboring state. She gently lifted his finger and read the name of the town he'd chosen.

"Castlemaine. Why Castlemaine, Tom?"

"I like castles," he said.

"Me too." Not that she'd ever seen one in real life and not that there'd be any in Castlemaine, she thought. "Castlemaine it is, birthday boy."

She'd never been to Castlemaine or the goldfields area before. She'd never even been to Victoria. But something happened as she and Tom drove into the town late the following afternoon. The light was beautiful, soft and golden, warming the old stone buildings that lined the wide main street. Following Tom's directions to turn left here, turn right there, go in this or that direction, the more she saw, the more she liked. The architecture was so varied, everything from a large market building with columns and statues that looked like it had been transplanted from Italy to an Art Deco theater, even several extraordinary gabled and Gothic churches. They drove down tree-lined side roads, past a cheerful-looking primary school, plenty of shops, a swimming pool, even an impressive art gallery.

After booking into a small hotel, they bought fish and chips from a shop on the main street and sat eating it out of the paper on a nearby bench. Two people smiled and said hello to them as they walked by. A small dog came running up, accepted a chip, and then ran away again. In a big tree across from them a flock of bright-pink galahs suddenly took flight, turning the air into a whirlpool of pink and gray to a sound track of harsh but vibrant squawks.

Tom watched it all, saying nothing, before eating his last chip and turning to her. "I like it here."

"Me too," she said.

They spent the next week touring the area in search of a rental property. She wanted space, privacy. After looking at dozens of places, they found a small, simply furnished farmhouse out in the countryside, twenty minutes from Castlemaine itself. It was perfect. She'd never have imagined herself settling thousands of kilometers from the tropical landscape she knew best, but from that first day she saw beauty in the wide paddocks, the big sky, the gentle lines of the surrounding hills. It was a small brick cottage, with a red door, a front and back garden, and nothing but space and clear views for miles around. They moved in that week. Two days after, Tom started at the local school.

The first weeks in the farmhouse were lonely, but she didn't let anyone, least of all Tom or her family, know it. With her Sydney-based landlord's permission, she painted every room a different color, choosing bright yellows, vibrant blues, warm reds. She drove to Castlemaine and the other nearby towns of Bendigo and Ballarat, trawling through secondhand shops for extra furniture, vases, curtain material. She visited markets for plant cuttings. She bought new linen, her one luxury.

She started drawing again. She hadn't expected that, either. She'd been painting the living-room wall, Tom beside her, doing a small section of his own. Bored, he drew what he insisted was a dog.

"Very good," she said. "Does your dog need a friend?" At his nod, she surprised him and herself by painting a quick, expert sketch of a cartoon dog, his mouth open and a bubble coming out in which she wrote "Woof!"

Tom's eyes opened wide. "Do another one," he said.

She drew another dog. Tom asked for a cat. A giraffe. A monkey. A kangaroo. She'd have kept drawing all night if Tom had his way. That night after he went to bed she painted over the drawings, finishing the room. The next morning he was sad to see they were gone. "I *loved* those animals."

She started again the moment she got back from the school run, mixing colors, preparing the background, in a kind of creative frenzy, almost dizzy with the joy of it. She didn't stop until it was time to collect him. She led him in that afternoon, insisting he keep his eyes shut until she gave the word. The ache in her arms faded the instant she saw the look on his face.

She'd covered the main wall in his bedroom with a mural of cartoon Australian animals: kangaroos, koalas, dingoes, echidnas, even a platypus. Not childish ones: cheeky ones, filled with personality. They were swimming in blue-hued creeks, playing on dark-red soil, climbing spiky-leafed trees, peeking from behind lush green bushes and shrubs. She'd even painted native birds on the ceiling: dusky-pink and gray galahs; red, yellow, and green parrots; plump kookaburras.

"About time," Hilary said, when Nina mentioned it. Two days later the postman delivered a large box filled with canvases, brushes, and fine-quality oil paints. There was no note inside. There didn't need to be one. Nina knew exactly what Hilary was telling her.

Her mother said what happened next was divine intervention, but Nina had long since given up on God. She knew it was just coincidence and good timing. Two months after she and Tom moved to Victoria, before she'd managed to find a secretarial job and just as her financial situation was getting worrisome, one of her old classmates from the Brisbane college tracked her down. He was now working for a commercial products company in Melbourne. They were launching a range of biscuits and needed a gimmick. He'd remembered a little cartoon kid she used to draw in class, to amuse herself and her classmates. Would she be interested? He couldn't promise anything, the company was looking at lots of other graphic artists' work as well. . . .

She faxed through a dozen sketches that same day. Her classmate rang with the good news that she'd got the contract, more excited about it than she was.

If the company loved them, the general public didn't. All the hope and relief she felt when she got the contract evaporated six months later when the company discontinued the line.

Those were her lowest days and nights. She and Tom alone in an isolated farmhouse, miles from anyone. She turned her fear and anger on to Nick again, forcing herself to forget how much she'd loved him, to forget his kindness, his gentleness, cursing him for crashing, for leaving her, for leaving them both. This wasn't what she'd imagined her life would be. She'd wanted a happy life. What had she done to deserve this?

She didn't tell her parents or her sister about her situation. They would have urged her to come home and that would have been even worse. Despite everything—her financial worries, her loneliness— she felt somehow she was right to be where she was, in that landscape. Slowly, tentatively, she started painting the views around her house. Her early efforts were too formal, too neat, her graphic art training taking over too strongly. While Tom slept, she kept painting, reusing canvases. Her hours sitting on the verandah gazing out across the paddocks began to reap rewards, as she slowly captured the muted colors, the glow of light on eucalyptus trunks, the subtle color changes in the grasses, the earth, the stones.

Her friend from college came to her rescue again. Visiting one afternoon with his wife, he noticed the canvases, the paints, the jars of brushes and asked to see the paintings. They were good, he told her. Very good. He felt guilty that the last deal hadn't worked out. Maybe she wouldn't trust him again, but he was doing some work for a company that produced generic souvenirs for tourists. Tins of biscuits, rulers, playing cards, anything that could be decorated with an Australian image. Could he show them her work?

They signed her up immediately. Her classmate negotiated it all. The money wasn't great, there would be no public recognition— she'd be handing over all the rights to the souvenir company. But the income would be steady and she could do it all from home.

She'd supported herself and Tom that way ever since. Her paintings had appeared on postcards, on tea towels, on guidebook covers, on biscuit tins. She painted whatever they asked her, from real life if they needed bush scenes, from photographs if they wanted wildlife. She never complained, never asked for more work than they offered. She wasn't ambitious. What she wanted was security.

She knew her parents still worried about her. So did her sister. But they'd also slowly realized that Nina was, not happy—perhaps that wasn't the right word—but content. Settled. That living down south suited her, even if it definitely wasn't for them. They visited often, picking the season carefully, finding the Victorian weather very cold after warm, tropical Queensland.

It was Hilary's visits that Nina most looked forward to. Hilary always seemed so calm, so unfazed by life's tribulations. Her most recent visit had been the week after Tom was grounded. Nina was glad of a third person in the house. She'd had to force herself to stick to the rules of the grounding, putting up with Tom's silences and the angry bowling of his cricket ball against the rainwater tank, over and over again, day after day, when he knew the sound of it drove Nina crazy as she was trying to paint.

Over dinner on Hilary's first night, Tom talked nonstop about Spencer and Templeton Hall.

"It sounds like it's a great place, Tom," Hilary said, shooting a glance across at her sister. "It's just a shame you went missing on your mum like that, and worried her sick."

After Tom had gone to bed, Nina and Hilary sat by the fire, sharing a bottle of local red.

"Thanks for backing me up," Nina said. "I was starting to wish I hadn't grounded him."

"He's just punishing you for punishing him. He'll get over it. Lesson learnt." She turned to check that Tom's bedroom door was completely closed and then spoke in a lower voice. "But what exactly's the problem with this Spencer Templeton? Is he a devil worshipper? Or do you just not want your son to have a friend?"

"He's got plenty of friends."

"Not friends who live a couple of paddocks away. Nina, Tom's a great, well-behaved kid. Don't let one mistake spoil what could be a good friendship for him."

"I just don't think he should spend too much time at Templeton Hall."

"Why not? I'd have loved a place like that to visit when I was Tom's age. What are you going to do, keep him in a cage until he's eighteen?"

"I don't want his head turned. And don't laugh, you know what I mean." She tried to make light of it. "Come on, Hilary. It's not as if the Templetons are a normal family living in a normal house. They couldn't be any more different. Me, the single mother, struggling to make ends meet, while the people in the big house throw parties and take baths in champagne—"

"Single mother? You're a widow, Nina, and I still don't understand why you feel the need to keep it a secret. And don't give me that 'don't want anyone's pity' excuse."

"It's not an excuse. It's a simple truth. And we're talking about the Templetons, not me. They're a much more fascinating subject than I am."

"You really are obsessed with them, aren't you?"

"I'm not *obsessed* with them. I'm mildly curious about them. That's different."

"So go and visit the Hall again. Get to know them. See if they're suitable for Tom."

"I can't. You made me promise after the fete to have nothing more to do with them."

"Two years ago. But I didn't realize you're still fretting about them. Go and lance the boil, Nina. Face your fears. You've come a long way since then. So have they, by the sound of things. Did you hear they won a big award?"

"Yes."

"And that they held a wedding there a month ago?"

Hilary had obviously been talking to people in Castlemaine. Local gossip was the Templetons had spray-painted the garden hedges green to look better in the photographs. The bride was now apparently suing for damage after discovering green streaks all over her dress.

Hilary smiled. "It could get tricky avoiding them if Tom becomes best friends with their son. They'll be dropping by for cups of tea and nice chats before you know it."

"Tom won't become best friends with their son and they won't start dropping by for cups of tea or even glasses of water."

"Want to bet on it?"

"No, I do not. Now, shut up and pass me the wine."

For the rest of Hilary's visit, Nina managed to avoid any more conversation about the Templetons.

Now, though, as she walked out to her car to go and collect Tom, she regretted not making that bet after all. She'd have definitely won it. In the days since Hilary's visit, Tom had stopped even mentioning Spencer Templeton. The Templetons certainly hadn't been beating a path to her front door to try to make friends, either.

Enough of the Templetons and Templeton Hall, she decided. It was time to focus on the night ahead with Tom. As she started the car and made her way out onto the highway and into Castlemaine, she made a promise to herself. Tonight would be the night she'd tell him everything about his father. She hoped.

Chapter Six

A MONTH INTO the new labor arrangement, peace of sorts reigned in Templeton Hall. Henry had met two of their demands: new costumes and a changed roster. He'd tracked down a company that specialized in period costume for TV companies and bought up a job lot of extras' costumes from a recent historical miniseries. He'd also tweaked the roster, giving them an extra day off per month. That was the good news, he told them. The bad news was there'd be no pay increase. Despite all the attention Gracie's accident had brought them, their visitor numbers were down again, for the second quarter in a row. Money was too tight at the moment for increased wages, he was sorry to say.

Back at school after another weekend spent marching groups of tourists around the Hall, Charlotte wasn't happy. She needed that pay rise. She wanted to travel, as far as possible and as soon as possible. The second she finished her schooling, hopefully. She'd decided against university. The truth was her results weren't good enough, anyway. But if she wanted to see the world, she'd need money soon, from somewhere.

She discussed the problem at length with her roommate at school. Celia was in a slightly better position than Charlotte, as the only child of elderly parents, an American father and Australian mother, though they were even more strict than Henry and Eleanor. They gave her only a small monthly allowance, and had also told her that were they to die soon, the bulk of their estate would be held in a trust until she was thirty.

"Thirty," Celia said, disgusted. "I could be dead by then myself. What makes me most sick about it is the hypocrisy. My mother only married my father because he was rich. They barely speak to each other."

"At least you've got the promise of money. And you're an only child. Whatever we get has to be divided between the four of us."

"But the Hall's worth a fortune, surely? It looks so amazing in the photographs."

Charlotte did her best to ignore the wistful tone in Celia's voice. She hadn't invited her roommate to visit Templeton Hall yet, despite repeated hints from Celia that she would like nothing more than a weekend there. Charlotte had so far produced all manner of excuses and lies: Spencer's recurring measles outbreaks; plumbing problems; water contamination scares . . . . It was humiliating enough for complete strangers to see her in that costume, let alone schoolfriends. She also didn't want any of her friends to witness Hope having one of her drunken "turns." They'd been happening too often lately.

She sighed. "Without sounding too ghoulish, Dad's in such good health it could be years before we get our hands on it. Even then, all four of us would have to agree to sell, and I can't see that happening. My little sister especially, she's *obsessed* with the place."

"Could you ask for some of your inheritance in advance, then?" Celia suggested, her voice muffled by the hot towel she was pressing into her face. Monday night was always beautify-yourself night in the girls' dormitories. "And didn't you tell me your father's an expert in antiques as well? There's great money in that, isn't there?"

"Any money Dad gets goes straight back into the property. It costs a fortune to run." It was only Celia she'd admit that to. All the other girls at their school seemed to have access to endlessly refilling bank accounts. What she wouldn't tell Celia, however, was just how *much* the Hall cost. Charlotte had happened to be in her father's office on a recent weekend and stumbled across a folder of outstanding bills, not just for the day-to-day running costs but dating back to the renovations as well. Shocked at the amounts, she'd then got another fright when Spencer crawled out from under the desk. She told him off for hiding, he told her off for snooping, and then their father came in and told them both off for being in his office.

Charlotte sighed again. "Maybe we'll just have to forget our feminist principles and marry for money," she said, pointing her newly painted toenails toward the ceiling. Not that a husband would solve her immediate problems. She wasn't even eighteen yet. Marriage could be years off.

"No need to rush into it," Celia said. "What comes before a rich husband?"

"A facelift?" Charlotte said, now peering at herself in the hand mirror as she prepared to pluck her thick dark eyebrows into something resembling current notions of feminine beauty. "A crash course in womanly wiles and alluring sexual antics?"

"A rich boyfriend, stupid," Celia said.

Charlotte put the mirror away, moved down to the floor, and started the fifty sit-ups she tried to do each night. She gave up after ten. She'd never be thin. What was the point wasting all this energy? "Oh, of course, stupid. I'll just pop down to the rich boyfriend shop next time I'm in town. Will I get one for you, too?"

"You're already in the rich boyfriend shop, *stupid*. This school. Just because the two of us are poverty stricken at the moment doesn't mean everyone else is. You know Margaret, two rooms down? Her father's on the list of Australia's ten richest people. She's got three brothers. And Paula, you know, with the red hair? Her father owns his own oil exploration company. Two older brothers. Samantha with the glasses? Huge mansion in South Yarra, a holiday home in the Whitsunday Islands, and three older brothers."

Charlotte was standing up now. "How do you know all this?"

"Because I listen and ask questions, not spend my time trying to annoy the teachers like you do."

"I don't try and annoy my teachers. I *do* annoy my teachers. All right, so we know who's got rich brothers. But how do we get to meet them?"

"You really have no idea, do you? Where were you brought up, the slums?"

"You know where I was brought up. In far too many English cities and then a strange colonial theme park in the back of beyond. Seriously, how do we meet these men?"

"It's simple," Celia said.

TWO WEEKS LATER, Charlotte stood in front of the dormitory's communal phone. For the first time ever, she was going to call Templeton Hall and tell a lie. A real lie. But it was an important one. Celia had gone to so much trouble in the past week, networking enthusiastically on Charlotte's behalf, beaming as proudly as a new mother when Paula-the-daughter-of-the-oil-baron invited Celia and Charlotte for a weekend with her family at their Mornington Peninsula holiday house.

"But we don't even know what her brothers are like," Charlotte said at first. "They might be hideous."

"It doesn't matter. If we don't like her first brother, we turn our radiant attention to her second brother. Or her father, if it comes to it. I'm joking, Charlotte. Her father's in his sixties."

"My father is ten years older than my mother. Maybe sugar daddies will run in my family."

"Start with the brothers, all right?"

Charlotte listened to the dial tone, trying to ignore her thumping heart. Her mother answered. Damn. It would be easier to lie to her father. He was usually more distracted.

There was an exchange of news, and then Charlotte set forth. "Mum, I'm really sorry to do this, you know I wouldn't if I could avoid it, but I'm not going to be able to come home this weekend. I know it's my turn to be head guide. I'm hoping Gracie won't mind stepping in. It's just my roommate, Celia, she's having some serious personal problems. I'd rather not go into it on the phone but she's got incredibly behind with her work. And we've got exams coming up, and she's asked, actually she begged me to stay and help her cram. Of course I'd rather be home, but she's been so good to me since I got here—"

Standing beside her, Celia made a mock gagging gesture.

"Thanks, Mum. Will you tell Gracie or will I? Thanks for that, too, and tell Gracie I owe her." Charlotte laughed. "I'm sure she will. Bye, Mum. Love to everyone."

She hung up and spun around, smiling widely. "Rich boyfriends, here we come."

IN HER ROOM two floors away from Charlotte's, Audrey was learning her lines. That was all she'd done in every moment of spare time for the past few weeks. Her drama teacher, Mr. Reynolds, had told her in what she considered a very sarcastic way that she should think about reentering the human race at some stage, but she had just laughed politely (not wanting to upset him) and returned to her room for some more study. She wasn't just reading the script. She was also poring over every book of stagecraft, acting tips, makeup tricks, and theatrical biography she'd been able to find in the school library.

Mr. Reynolds had expressed some concern that she was abandoning her other subjects. She was, but she wasn't going to admit it to him. Instead, she'd argued passionately that this was her one big chance, that if it didn't work for her, if the reviews were bad ("I'm not terribly sure we get reviewed, Audrey. It's a school production, not the West End"), if she didn't get the audience reaction she longed for ("We tend to be quite happy if they all stay awake"), she would realize a life on the stage wasn't for her.

"I just need to put all my energies into it, give it everything I have," she said passionately.

"Oh, yeah?" the drama teacher said. He was inclined to drawl when he was talking to his students, trying to sound cool, his students guessed. They thought he just sounded stupid. "You have to give it more than you have, Audrey. You have to give it everything that you don't even know you have."

She wasn't completely sure what he was talking about, but nodded and tried to look thoughtful at the same time.

She still hadn't told her parents about the role and had somehow managed to convince Charlotte to keep it a secret, too. She'd decided it was best if her mother and father didn't know she was spending so much time on her drama studies. They'd only nag her about her other subjects, she knew that. All she'd told them was that the school was holding a special presentation on the third Tuesday of October and she really wanted them to be there. All of them, Gracie and Spencer, too. Yes, even Hope.

"Are you getting an award, Audrey?" Gracie wanted to know when they spoke on the phone one night.

"I hope so," Audrey said, thinking of the Best Actress award the drama teacher could present if he felt one of the students merited it. "I won't know for sure until the night."

The rehearsals were going well, Audrey thought. At least she hoped they were. It was hard to tell. She was the only one who knew all her lines by heart, the only one who had read all the theory on the play, and especially the only one who had borrowed videos of other stage productions and a television production from a decade or so earlier. "You'll confuse yourself," her drama teacher warned her. "You have to reach into your own soul to find your performance, not become a simple echo of all that has gone before you."

The problem was that Audrey really didn't know what her own performance should be, no matter how hard she tried to picture it. Oh, some parts of the opening night she could clearly imagine. The hour before she went on stage, for example, sitting in the dressing room, staring at herself in the mirror, her pale face surrounded by the lights, as she slowly, expertly applied the makeup that would transform her from Audrey Templeton, student, into Ophelia, the tragic heroine. She could picture herself standing on the side of the stage—stage left, she reminded herself to call it—waiting for her cue. She could picture herself walking out onto the stage, her timing impeccable, her bearing regal, her stage presence electric. She could even visualize the moment after the play ended, the hall exploding into a billowing cloud of applause, the clapping coming at her in waves, herself graciously accepting an enormous bouquet of orchids (it was sometimes roses, but she preferred orchids) from the director, and then another from an anonymous admirer, hopefully the school's PE teacher, on whom she was harboring a bit of a crush.

The only thing she wasn't able to imagine was her actual performance. She knew that technically she couldn't be better prepared. She knew her lines. She'd studied the stage directions. In truth, she'd also learnt everyone else's lines and stage directions. If the cast was struck down by the flu, there was a fair chance she could pull off the entire production as a one-woman show. But could she actually act? Did she have what the role truly required? In every interview she'd read, famous actors and actresses spoke constantly about their insecurity, their self-doubt. She definitely had those negative qualities, but did she have the actual acting skills as well?

"You have the enthusiasm—I'm sure any talent will follow," Mr. Reynolds said unhelpfully, when she found the courage to ask him.

"Isn't it better to be talented first, and follow that with enthusiasm?" she dared to suggest.

"All I ask, Audrey, is that you learn your lines, turn up at every rehearsal, and don't put on any weight between now and opening night or our wardrobe lady will kill you and then kill me."

She'd taken all of his advice to heart and begun assiduously watching her weight, too. It was easy enough to do at boarding school. All the girls in her class and dormitory seemed to be obsessed with their figures. Audrey was naturally thin, and hadn't thought of dieting before, but perhaps her teacher was right. She started keeping a food diary as well.

In her room now, she tried to ignore the rumbling of her stomach, sighed, turned the script pages back to the beginning, and started, once again, to read through her lines.

AT TEMPLETON HALL, Eleanor, Gracie, and Spencer had come to an excellent arrangement with their schoolwork. In addition to their nightly homework and outdoor science and physical education projects, Eleanor insisted on four dedicated study hours per day. It was up to them if they spread it out through the day, or did it in one block in the morning, giving them the rest of the day off. Spencer had suggested doing one twenty-hour day and taking the rest of the week off, but to his disappointment, Eleanor didn't agree.

As usual, they were working in the morning room, sitting around the large round table that stood beside the bay window. Their lessons that day had been delayed slightly, after their mother was called away by their father to deal with what he called an "incident" with Hope.

"Poor Hope," Gracie said, as she busied herself sharpening her pencils so they were all exactly the same length. "She must have got upset about something again."

"She's not upset. She's just drunk."

"Spencer! Don't talk about her like that. You know what Mum says."

"But it's the truth. She *is* drunk again."

"How do you know?"

"I just do, all right?"

They were both silenced by the sound of their mother returning.

Spencer was soon occupied with his math exercises, while Gracie was thinking of possible topics for her history project.

"I can do a biography of anyone?" she asked her mother.

"Anyone you like."

"Do it on me," Spencer said, not looking up from his sums. "I'm really interesting."

Gracie ignored him. "Does the person have to be dead?" she asked her mother.

"No. It has to be someone you'd like to know more about. Someone who's played an active role in the history of Australia."

"Can I do it on Dad?" Gracie asked.

"He's not as interesting as me," Spencer said.

"Please, Mum? On Dad and his ancestors and Templeton Hall and the stories about Captain Cook?"

"What stories about Captain Cook?" Spencer put down his pencil. "Dad didn't know him, did he?"

"No, Spencer, they missed meeting each other by about two hundred years. Which Captain Cook stories, Gracie?"

"I heard Dad telling a tour group that one of his ancestors was from the same town in England as Captain Cook and they even learnt to sail together."

"Really? Gracie, wait here, would you? I'll be right back. Do your nine times table please, Spencer. And no, you haven't. I can see from here."

Gracie swung her legs under the table as she waited for her mother to return. Spencer started swinging his, too, much more enthusiastically than Gracie, kicking the underside of the table each time. Gracie knew that if she asked Spencer to stop, he would only do it twice as hard.

He stopped suddenly and turned to Gracie. "Captain Cook first saw Australia in 1770. His ship was called the *Endeavour*. There was a botanist with him called Joseph Banks. That's who the banksia flower is named after."

"I know," Gracie said, chewing her pencil.

"I know about Neil Armstrong, too. First man on the moon."

"So do I. I'm older than you, remember."

Spencer started kicking again. "Do you know about John F. Kennedy?"

"Yes."

"Phar Lap?"

"The racehorse? Yes."

"Ned Kelly?"

"The bushranger. Yes."

"Who don't you know about that I do, then?"

"I don't know. If I said their name, it would mean I know about them."

"But there must be things I know about that you don't."

"Not much."

Spencer threw his pencil at Gracie just as Eleanor returned. She nimbly caught it. "That's fine, Gracie. I'd like six hundred words on one of your father's ancestors by the end of today."

"That's not fair," Spencer said. "Can I do my essay on you, Mum?"

"No, Spencer. I'm too boring."

"Can I do it about myself, then?"

"When we're studying Great Criminal Minds of the Twentieth Century, yes."

GRACIE SPENT some time drawing up a list of questions before knocking on her father's study door.

"Gracie! What a surprise."

"No, it's not. Mum told you I was coming. I have some questions for you." She glanced down at her notebook. "Name?"

"Henry Charles Templeton."

"Age?"

"A youthful-looking forty-nine."

She was very businesslike now. "Please tell me something about your childhood."

"I grew up under the blazing African sun, rising each day to the sounds of the wildebeest. . . . Oh, Gracie," he said, laughing at her cross expression, "you really don't want me to have any fun, do you?"

"It's not me. It's Mum. She's very hard to please. I had to write my essay on the Tudors three times before she passed it. Can you please tell me all about your ancestors?"

"Gracie, I'd be honored. Pen ready?" At her nod, he began. "As I think you know from your many tours here, my great-great-grandfather on my mother's side was born and raised in Yorkshire, at a property twenty or so miles from the coastal village of Whitby—"

"Is that where he met Captain Cook?"

"I certainly believe so, Gracie. So it must have been destiny that a descendant of his decided to come to Australia, too. Your great-great-great-uncle Leonard, during the goldrush that began in 1851. Is he the one you want for your essay?"

Gracie nodded, opening her notebook to a new page.

Henry began reciting the facts, in a singsong voice at first, until Gracie gave him another stern look. "Leonard first came to Australia in 1855, Gracie, while employed by the Smithson and Son Trading Company. His drive and ambition placed him in an ideal position on the goldfields, as he imported all the goods a working miner, and more important, an officer and his family, might require. Fabrics, equipment, foodstuffs. Before many years passed, he was one of the richest businessmen in Victoria."

Henry stood up and leaned against his desk. "Leonard had all a young man could possibly desire. Untold wealth, a thriving business, standing in the community . . . All but love. Underneath all the trappings, Gracie, he was a lonely man, because back home he had left behind his sweetheart, Julia Smithson, the nineteen-year-old daughter of his employer. He was determined to bring her home to Australia with him and he set off to London with that express purpose in mind. Their reunion was romantic. He proposed to her, within an hour of arriving. To his great joy, she accepted. For twenty-four hours he was the happiest man in London."

Gracie sighed with enjoyment.

"He returned to Julia's house the next day to formally ask for her hand in marriage. When Mr. Smithson not only agreed, but also expressed his admiration for his future son-in-law's business acumen, Leonard went in search of his beloved with the happy news. They would marry swiftly, he told her. She could return to Australia with him, as his bride.

"And there the fairytale began to fall apart. 'Australia?' Julia said. 'Oh, no.' She'd heard only stories of horror and wildness and dirt and depravity from the colonies. 'If you truly loved me,' Julia said, 'then you would want to make me happy and live here with me in England.' But his life was in Australia, he told her. His business. His future. Back and forth they went, without agreement. It was with great sadness that his departure date came. He could put it off no longer. He assured Julia of his love, as she assured him of hers, and they farewelled passionately on the docks of Southampton.

"As the ship sailed, Leonard had plenty of thinking time. Julia had told him all she loved about England. Her family house, most of all. He made his decision before the ship was halfway across the seas. He would build his Julia her own piece of England in Australia. The perfect replica of her family house, gardens and all."

Gracie was now sitting completely still, barely breathing.

"Once he arrived back in Victoria, he took to work in a fever. His business continued to thrive, while he hired the finest architects, builders, and gardeners in the colony. Less than a year later, his beautiful new two-story mansion was completed. It was time to go back to England to fetch his fiancée, plan a lavish wedding, and begin their married life together in the home he had built especially for her." He paused. "And then tragedy struck."

"She died," Gracie said in a whisper.

"No, Gracie."

"She got scurvy." Gracie had recently done a project on scurvy and eaten barely anything but oranges for a fortnight afterward.

"Not scurvy, either. Sadly, Gracie, young Miss Julia Smithson broke the news to my poor great-great-uncle that while he was busy in Australia building her dream house and increasing his wealth tenfold so she could have all the fine dresses and jewelry and gloves that her little beating heart would desire, she had been busy, too." Another pause. "Falling in love with someone else."

Gracie stared, wide eyed. "Did he kill her?"

"I'm sure he wanted to. But no, he fought against his baser instincts like the fine gentleman he was. He demanded to meet his rival. He was a doctor, from a very well-known family in London. He was as wealthy as Leonard was. And perhaps more important to Julia, he had absolutely no desire, intention, or wish to up sticks and go sailing across the world to a hot, untamed wild land like Australia."

"Didn't he show her photos of the house? Try and change her mind that way?"

"There weren't photos back in those days, Gracie. Nothing like we have today, anyway. We'll discuss the technological advancements of the late nineteenth century another day. Try as he might, Leonard couldn't persuade Julia to change her mind."

"Poor Leonard."

"Poor Leonard, indeed. But then his luck changed."

"The doctor died?"

"You're keen to kill people today, Gracie. No, he met someone else in Julia's house."

"Her sister?"

"No, he met the governess. A young woman called Louisa, who had been taken on to teach Julia's much younger brother. You see, homeschooling has a rich and honorable tradition. And can you guess what happened next?"

Gracie shook her head.

"Gracie! Where is your sense of romance and drama? Leonard was so cross with Julia, that he decided to invite Louisa to dinner, knowing it would cause a scandal. And it did."

"Was she ugly?"

"No, she was quite beautiful, in fact. But she was from a different class than him."

"Like a local here?"

Henry's lips twitched. "Not exactly. In any case, Leonard soon decided those old rules didn't matter to him anymore. He also realized Louisa had far more spark, intelligence, and natural beauty than Julia had ever possessed. Six weeks later, Louisa sailed back to Melbourne with him, as his wife, and they took up residence in this beautiful building we now call home."

"She didn't mind it was based on Julia's house?"

"Not at all. She'd always loved Julia's house. It had been her home for many years, too, remember. And so Leonard and Louisa lived here, happily ever after, for many years."

From the doorway came the sound of a slow handclap. "What a beautiful story, Henry."

Henry turned and gave his wife a small bow. "I aim to please, darling."

"I can't wait for you to tell Gracie how you and I met," Eleanor said.

Gracie looked up eagerly. "Can you tell me now, Dad?"

"When you turn twelve."

"That's not for months."

"It will be even better for the waiting. So, any questions, Gracie? Did you get all of that?"

Gracie glanced down at her page. It was blank. Eleanor walked away, shaking her head, as Henry pulled up a chair and started to tell the story again.

LATER THAT NIGHT, Eleanor knocked gently on the door of Henry's study. He was sitting at his desk, a glass of whisky beside him, a pile of magazines to his side, a folder of accounts in front of him.

He glanced up and smiled. "Look, darling, I'm working. Doing the accounts. Being responsible."

"So you are. Can I interrupt you?"

"I wish you'd interrupted me an hour ago. I'm bored rigid. Drink?"

She shook her head. "Henry, you have to stop telling Gracie those stories. She believes every word of them, you know."

"Of course she doesn't. How could she?"

"Gracie is eleven years old. A well-educated but also gullible, earnest eleven-year-old. She desperately wants to believe that every story she hears about Templeton Hall is true."

"Perhaps I shouldn't have gone quite so far with Leonard's story?"

"No, perhaps not."

"I didn't seriously think she'd believe it. I mean, a merchant flitting back and forth between England and Australia like that? On those ships?"

"It's your fault. You made it sound so authentic and romantic. She's up in her room right now writing the best essay of her life."

"Then make sure you give her an A, won't you?"

"For fiction or essay writing?"

"Well, now, that moral call is up to you." He took a sip of his whisky. "The other children don't believe every story they've heard me tell, do they?"

"No, of course not. Yes, perhaps. I don't know. You can be very persuasive. And the basic facts of them are true, at least, aren't they? All that family research you did before we arrived here?" She laughed briefly. "Now, that would be funny, if you've pulled the wool over all our eyes, mine included."

"Eleanor! How devious do you think I am?"

"I don't think I'll answer that." Eleanor sunk gratefully into the plush antique chair opposite his desk, closing her eyes for a moment. "The sooner today is over, the better."

"How is she now?"

"Locked in her room still, thank God."

"Have you managed to talk to her yet?"

She shook her head. "I've been trying all day. This morning she was too drunk, when she sobered up she was too angry, and last time I tried she was too tearful. I'll try again tomorrow. It can't go on like this, Henry. It's affecting Gracie and Spencer's schoolwork again, all of us tiptoeing around her. I have to try to get her to see—"

"You *have* tried. You've been nothing but a good sister to her."

"I've been nothing but a foolish sister. I've put up with it for too long, yet again." She sighed as she stood up. "Are you coming up to bed?"

"Not yet. I'll finish the accounts first. Make a start on next year's business plan, too. Look at our visitor numbers. They're down again, unfortunately. Nothing I can't fix, I'm sure."

She came across and kissed the top of his head. "You're a saint, Henry Templeton."

"And you, my love, are an angel."

He didn't go back to his accounts after she left. He sat staring out the window instead.

THE NEXT AFTERNOON, Gracie was in her bedroom. She'd just finished her essay and if she did say so herself, it was fantastic. Her mother had asked for six hundred words. Gracie had found it hard to stop at two thousand. She would have kept going only she'd reached the last page of her copybook. So she'd written *To be continued* in her neatest handwriting. It was amazing to think that all the stories her father had told her about his ancestors were *her* stories, too. And she hadn't even started on her mother's side of the family tree yet. Her mother had said there was plenty of time for that. "One branch at a time, Gracie," she'd said. "And there's the small matter of your other subjects, too."

Gracie had just started on her geography homework when there was a knock at the door.

It was Spencer. "Quick, Gracie. Come with me. I need to show you something."

"What is it? What's wrong?"

"I'll show you when we get there. Come on, quick."

Fifteen minutes later Gracie was standing beside the dam several paddocks away from Templeton Hall. She wasn't happy about it. "That was a mean trick, Spencer. I don't want to go fishing for yabbies. Do it yourself. I've got homework to do."

"It's easy. Look. You just tie a bit of meat to the end of the string and wait."

"It's disgusting. The meat and the yabbies. What's the point of catching them, anyway? They sound horrible. You may as well eat cockroaches."

"There's no meat on cockroaches. Come on, Gracie. It's fun."

"It's not. I'm going home. Why don't you ask Hope to come and play with you?"

"She's still locked in her room, that's why." He threw a rock into the water, deliberately splashing her. "Why did I have to be the only boy in this family?"

"Because two of you would have been even worse. Why don't you get that boy Tom to come over again? He was nice."

"He's banned. We're a bad influence on him, apparently."

"We're not!" Gracie said, indignant. "His mother was just upset that he went missing." Gracie had heard the fuss with the policeman. "She didn't even meet us."

"She didn't need to. She rang after she got Tom back. Dad told me. She wasn't happy."

"So get Dad to go and talk to her again. Go with him. Try and pretend you're normal for a few minutes."

Spencer pulled a face. "Adults don't usually like me."

"She might be the exception." Gracie stood up. "I'm going, Spencer. This is boring."

Spencer didn't try to stop her that time. Yabby catching wasn't boring. It was sisters who were boring. As he sat impatiently watching for a tug on the line, throwing pebbles across the dam, he thought back to what Gracie had said. He sighed. Maybe it was worth a try. It couldn't be any worse than sitting around on his own like this for days on end.

Chapter Seven

NINA RARELY HAD a night to herself. Not completely to herself, when she was alone in the farmhouse, a whole evening stretching out in front of her, the prospect of a lie-in in the morning a reality rather than a longing. Now, as she drove back along the highway from Castlemaine, she realized it was an unfamiliar, almost unsettling feeling. When he was younger, Tom had hated spending a night away from her. Now, he seemed to take any opportunity he could to stay in town with one of his friends.

She knew she wasn't the only mother of a twelve-year-old son finding the relationship between them changing. What had happened to the Tom who would tell her in great detail everything he had done, was doing, or planned to do? She missed him. She didn't know this new Tom yet. He was becoming secretive. Independent. Grown-up.

"He's not turning against you or suddenly hating you," Hilary had said. It had been just the same with her two stepdaughters, she told Nina. "He's just stretching his wings. Testing the boundaries. He has to change sometime. He's nearly a teenager, remember."

Nearly a teenager, yes. And she still hadn't told him the truth about his father. She'd had every intention of doing it that night in Castlemaine a few weeks previously. Throughout the drive to collect him, she'd rehearsed what she would say, even decided at what stage of the dinner she would raise the subject. When it came to that moment, though, after their main course and before dessert, she simply hadn't been able to do it. Hilary had been angry with her, as she'd expected. "The longer you leave it, the worse it will be. Don't make an occasion of it. Just *tell* him." But she was too nervous now, Nina realized. Too worried it would change things even more. Create a bigger gulf between them.

Even tonight, as she dropped him off at his best friend's house to stay for the night, she noticed the difference in him. He barely said good-bye to her. Just thanked her for the lift and went straight in the front door to Ben's room.

At the car her friend Jenny sympathized. "You'd swear they've been taken over by aliens, wouldn't you? Our beautiful boys replaced by these strange creatures. He's still in there, don't worry. Ben's my fourth and it's been exactly the same with each one."

Home alone now, Nina decided to try and be positive about it. Enjoy the night to herself. Have a glass or two of wine. Play the music she wanted. Watch the TV programs she wanted. Paint until three a.m. if she wanted, in the knowledge that she didn't have to wake up at seven to get Tom organized for school or cricket.

The phone rang and she actually ran to answer it. It would be Tom, homesick, wanting her to come in and get him. It wasn't Tom. It was another of the school mums, confirming an arrangement for school-shop duty the following week. It was a friendly, brief, and businesslike conversation and it didn't last long enough for Nina.

Two glasses of wine later, she was finally starting to relax. She'd eaten a simple dinner of tuna salad. She'd read a glossy magazine from cover to cover. She was just deciding whether to turn off the TV or watch a video when she heard the sound of footsteps outside. On the gravel and then on her verandah.

She froze. She hadn't heard a car and people didn't visit her on foot, not this far out of town. There was a knock at the door. A fast, efficient knock. A burglar wouldn't knock, would he? She stood up. This was ridiculous. Why was she so jumpy? If Tom had been here, she would have been fine.

"Hello? Is there anyone home?" It was a woman's voice.

Nina instantly relaxed. Women didn't tend to be burglars, rapists, or escaped prisoners. She opened the door, a welcoming smile on her face, and then stopped. Standing on her front verandah was Hope. Hope from Templeton Hall.

"Good evening," Hope said graciously, as if she were the one welcoming Nina. She gave no indication that they'd met before. "I'm Hope Endersley. From Templeton Hall."

"Yes. Yes, I know."

"And you are?"

Nina blinked. "Nina Donovan."

"May I come in?" Hope said.

For a moment Nina hesitated. If this woman didn't know who she was, why was she visiting?

"It's quite cold out here," Hope said.

"I'm sorry. Please, come in."

Nina had heard plenty of stories about Hope since the fete. Antics during tours, gossip that she had a drinking problem, a drug problem, a drinking *and* drug problem. That she was inclined to swan around Templeton Hall in ridiculously over-the-top clothes. She seemed sober tonight, and she was wearing quite an ordinary sundress. Not so ordinary, perhaps, Nina thought again, noting the beautiful fabric and cut. She suddenly felt too aware of her own faded T-shirt and jeans. Hope was also wearing a beautiful pair of red, high-heeled shoes. They were covered in dust. She'd obviously walked over. Nina's own feet were bare. As she opened the door and let Hope go past her, she hurriedly slipped her feet into a pair of Chinese slippers.

Hope stood in the hall, gazing around her, relaxed, confident.

Nina found her voice again. "Please, come through to the living room."

The TV was still playing. The side table was covered in the remains of her dinner-for-one. A plate. A half-full bottle of wine. A half-empty glass. Nina felt strangely guilty, as if she'd been caught misbehaving.

"Can I get you a cup of tea? A glass of wine? Water?" she asked as she straightened the cushion on their one good armchair and gestured to Hope to take a seat. At the last second she grabbed a sneaker that was wedged halfway down the back of the chair. "Sorry," she said, smiling for the first time. "My son's."

"You have a son? That's right, someone mentioned that."

Nina knew then that Hope definitely had no memory of their altercation at the fete. She decided to at least try to be polite. "So, wine, water? Juice? Tea?"

"Do you have whisky?"

Did she? Some brandy maybe, left over from last Christmas's plum pudding. She offered that instead.

"Fine, yes. With a little water."

Nina got the servant feeling again. How did this woman manage to make her feel like this? she asked herself as she stood in the kitchen, getting the drink, making doubly sure the glass was clean, running the rainwater tap for much longer than usual to make sure it was as clear as possible. Her imperious manner? Her confidence? Or was it just the upper-class accent?

"Your drink," she said as she delivered it, tempted to add the word "madam."

Hope took a sip, closed her eyes as if in pleasure, and then thanked Nina, very graciously.

Nina settled herself in her chair, picked up her own glass of wine and waited.

Hope began to speak moments after taking her second sip. "I'm sure you're wondering why I'm here. I've often seen your lights on as I take my evening walk."

Nina couldn't stop herself from glancing down at Hope's shoes again. Bright-red silk. They were most definitely not walking shoes.

"And it seemed rude of me to walk by one more time."

"You take a walk past here every night?"

"Most nights. My doctor in London advised regular exercise. Of course, I'm rattling with pills and tranquilizers as well, so why she thinks a pleasant stroll now and again will do any more good than all those chemicals, I don't know, but it gets me out of the house and I suppose it gets me out from under their feet or in their hair as well. Which is it? Under their feet or in their hair? Or in their clutches?"

Nina found that hard to answer. She tried nodding instead.

"It's very difficult for me, you know," Hope continued. "I often feel like one of those condemned prisoners you see in photographs from death row. A human can sense when they're not wanted. Sense when people wish them ill will. I know they wish that I were any-where but where I am. Do they not think I don't feel that way myself, sometimes? Do they really think I wanted to spend this much of my life here? 'We need you,' they said. 'Come with us,' Eleanor begged. 'It's not charity. There's no one better qualified to do the Templeton Hall garden than you, Hope.' "

"The garden? You're a gardener?"

"I'm a garden designer," Hope said, enunciating the words very clearly. "Though how I'm supposed to create an oasis of verdant beauty here when that ridiculous sun you have threatens to burn it to a crisp most of the year, I don't know. Still, they insisted. 'Give us a garden that would make our ancestors proud, Hope,' Henry kept saying to me. 'Fuck the ancestors,' I said to him. 'I'll give you a garden that will make *me* proud.' I'm good at my job, you see. Oh, people always said it was Eleanor who was the bright one, with her degrees and her campaigning for home education and the rest of it, but I'm the one who did the hard graft. It's not just a matter of picking nice-smelling flowers or pretty shrubs. It's about color all year round. It's about selecting the right plants. Not that any of the oafs—" she almost spat the word, "that come to drag themselves around the Hall and the gardens would notice even a leaf of it. You know I catch people cutting the roses every weekend? Pulling out whole plants? Taking cuttings? Thieves, all of them. Why don't we just dig it all up and hand it to them as they leave? I said to Henry once. Give everyone a wheelbarrow and they can take a few trees as well. Do you have any cigarettes?"

Nina blinked. "I'm sorry, no. I don't smoke."

"Too bad. Do you know not a weekend goes by without something being stolen from the Hall? If it's not pieces of my garden being dragged out of the soil, after all my hard work and imagination, it's candles. Vases. A doormat one weekend. My sunglasses another time. I'd only put them down for a moment. I hadn't even realized the Hall was open."

Nina tried to think of something to say. "You could always put those red ropes up, I suppose. Like they do in museums."

Hope gave her a scornful look. "You think I haven't suggested that to Henry? Suggested he might think about securing some of the family heirlooms before they all vanish? Oh, but there's no convincing Henry when he's made up his mind. 'If we do that, Hope,' he says," she switched to a deeper voice, " 'we may as well forget the whole idea. That is what makes us so appealing. That is why people come in droves to visit us.' "

"So they can steal things?"

Another scornful look. "No. Because Henry believes the visitors think they're getting an authentic experience. That they're stepping back in time."

"It's a very popular attraction," Nina dared to offer.

"It's ludicrous. The whole thing is ludicrous. When he first inherited it, my advice was to sell it. Sell it all. But, oh no, not Henry. Even if there hadn't been that twenty-year no-selling clause with the inheritance, he wouldn't have sold. It was an adventure, he said. A once-in-a-lifetime opportunity. What fun! What games! And of course Eleanor just went along with him. I warned her, you know. About the age difference. When they first met, when she told me about this man she'd found to value our poor deceased grandparents' belongings, how charming he was, how funny, I asked her how old he was. She was deliberately vague. She didn't tell me the truth until they were engaged and it was too late. Our parents were unhappy enough. If our grandparents had been alive, they'd have turned in their graves."

Nina bit her lip to stop herself from smiling. She didn't think Hope was trying to be funny.

"Oh, it's romantic at first. The older boyfriend. I know from experience myself. But it's later that the problems begin. He gets used to being in charge, you see. And that's exactly what happened. Eleanor became completely and utterly subjugated to him. Not only was she a child bride, barely twenty, but she was pregnant within seconds of signing the marriage certificate, as far as I could tell. She'd always told me she didn't want to have children. Now look at her, four of them. And she's not only mothering them, she's educating them. Where's the independence in that? It's what Henry wanted, of course. For all his talk about women's rights and love of her spirit, he's got her exactly where he wants, under his thumb, under his control, and now trapped on the other side of the world in a ridiculous museum." She nearly spat the final word.

Nina was in a difficult position, enjoying every word while knowing she shouldn't be hearing such personal information. She tried to change the subject. "And have you seen much of Australia yourself?"

Hope was having none of it. "I mean, what did we even know about him, apart from the fact he was an expert in antiques? It's shopkeeping, isn't it, at the end of the day? He's a salesman. I asked around. The same story every time. 'Henry Templeton? Oh, we *adore* him. So charming. So handsome. Such good manners. So generous.' Too good to be true, in my opinion. And I was right. He took his time, but I knew it would happen."

"Knew what would happen?"

Hope gave a sinuous stretch, reminding Nina immediately of a cat. An exotic cat, like a Siamese. Hope took another large sip of her drink before staring at Nina. "There's no delicate way to put it. He made a pass at me."

"Henry did?"

"Don't look so innocent. You're a grown woman with a child. You didn't find it in the cabbage patch, did you? You must know what happens to a couple's sex life after children arrive. Where *is* your husband? Don't bother. I don't want to hear. You grew apart, he left you for another woman, blah blah blah, the usual old story. Or the other even more tedious reply. 'We decided to stick together for the sake of the children.' You decided not to go down that boring old road, obviously. Well done. Once the trust is gone, there's no regaining it, you know." She gave a low laugh. "I should know. And Eleanor must know now. How could she not know? Answer me that."

"I'm sorry. Know what?"

"That Henry and I have been having an affair for years."

Nina couldn't hide her shock.

"Oh, for God's sake, don't be so surprised. Eleanor was never as interested in sex as me. I'd hear them arguing about it. The first time Henry and I slept together, we were both drunk. That was our excuse, but it was lust as much as wine. Too fast the first time. Better the second. And after that, quite marvelous. It's the guilt, of course. The world's best aphrodisiac. That's why so many people have affairs. Sex is sex when you come down to it. It's what happens before and afterward that provides the thrill. How could I do it to my own sister? That's what you're thinking, isn't it?"

Nina blinked. Yes, that was one of the many things she was thinking. She opened her mouth, about to say that what had happened between Hope and her sister was their business, when Hope began
talking again.

"I used to meet him in London mostly. They lived in Brighton at
the time. Or was it Yorkshire? They were always moving, two years
here, three years there. Hard enough on one's own, let alone with
children. Though that's why she became interested in the whole no-
tion of home education. I'm talking about the two older children.
The two youngest hadn't arrived yet." Hope gave an unpleasant
laugh. "Unsurprising there was a long break between them. Henry
used to tell me only a miracle would get Eleanor pregnant again.
She was always too tired. Too busy. Who can blame him for going
elsewhere? I wasn't the only one in his extracurricular life, either. His
work was such great cover, you see—" She glared at Nina, in a way
that made Nina feel as though she were on her property, not the other
way around. "What was your name again?"

Nina told her.

Hope nodded, as if it confirmed something she'd suspectèd. "He
spent all his days in grand houses, charming widows and innocent
young women. They were his best customers. He can be so persuasive, you see. He has a way of talking that makes you feel as though
you're the most interesting, most beautiful, most important person to
enter his life. And he really knows his subject, too. That's very attractive in a man."

"His subject?"

"The antique business. Henry's great skill is his eye for beauty.
Beauty of value, of course. I went with him once on a buying trip to
Scotland. Not that Eleanor knew I was there. Henry and I pretended
I was his secretary. All the more spice later. I followed him around this
drafty old house, up and down staircases, and by the end of it the ad-
dled old woman who owned it would have handed the whole place
and all it contained to him. But do you know what he bought from
her? Two items. A big old wardrobe that he exclaimed over and then
a small vase that he barely seemed to notice, almost as if it was an
afterthought. And of course it was the vase that was valuable. Worth
tens of thousands of pounds, while the wardrobe was worthless. I

think he used it for firewood. Our first affair didn't last long. A year, less perhaps. I called a halt to it. I didn't want what he was offering, if the truth be told. He talked of divorcing Eleanor, the two of us running away together. Completely ridiculous. He knew I was going cold on him. Eleanor had started to guess around then, too, I'm sure of it. She started coming with him on all his visits. I certainly never told her what had happened between Henry and me. It was a mistake, as far as I was concerned. And years went by, as I said, before it happened again, just a few weeks after I arrived here. I wonder, was it a fear of death that made Henry approach me again? They say that men in their forties think of death more often than they used to think of sex." She laughed then, a sudden noise, too loud. "Henry clearly thinks about both. Eleanor was away in Melbourne, down trying to convince that boarding school to take on Charlotte. Best place for her. She's an arrogant brat, has been from the moment she could speak. As for Audrey, all she cares about is herself—but I was telling you about Henry, wasn't I?"

Nina nodded, not daring to speak.

"Henry begged me to come here, you know. Begged me. 'I need you, Hope,' he said. And it wasn't about the garden. He knew that. I knew that. An attraction as strong as ours doesn't die. It stays dormant. That's the word, isn't it?"

Again, Nina dared only to nod.

"There's a curiosity, isn't there, about someone you've slept with in your younger days. Especially if it was good. Wonderful, in fact. You always wonder, what would it be like to try it one more time? For old times' sake? Especially if that spark of attraction is still there. And it was, from the second I arrived here. The two of us in the Hall together, me doing all I could in the garden, while Henry had I don't know how many builders working around the clock. He needed me. And of course all that time the sexual tension was building between us. So delicious. It started with stolen kisses. It's always sexier like that, don't you think? Like a series of courses in an elaborate banquet, little bite-size pieces, the pleasure building and building between—"

Nina didn't want to hear any more. Out of nowhere, she remembered her first and only sighting of Eleanor, recalled liking her face, her expression, the look of humor in her eyes. What had seemed like good gossip to pass on to Hilary now felt tawdry and salacious. She stood up. "Would you like me to drive you home?"

"Home?" The haughty tone returned instantly. "I'm not going back there yet."

You're not staying here either, Nina thought. "My car's just outside. I'll have you home in five minutes. Or I can ring the Hall and they can collect you if you like." Nina didn't really want either situation. She wasn't sure if she'd manage to get Hope into her car. As for one of the Templetons coming here to collect Hope . . . no, Nina didn't want that either, especially now that she knew so much about them.

Hope surprised her then by suddenly sitting upright. "Do you have a bath?"

"A bath?"

"Yes, a bath. I'm sorry. I'm upset. If I could just have a bath, I'll be fine."

Nina pictured Hope slipping under the water. Falling asleep in the tub. Being there in the morning when Tom arrived back. "There's something wrong with it," she improvised.

"A shower, then?"

"A shower?"

"I have to go home. But I think if I freshen up before I go, I'll feel much better. Please."

Nina was thrown by this new reasonable Hope. In truth, she'd rather Hope didn't see the bathroom. It badly needed renovating and Tom's cricket whites were soaking in the bath. Not that she thought Hope would notice.

"Where is it? I'll be quick," Hope said, standing up and steadying herself after just the briefest of sways.

Nina made her decision. "Let me just get it ready."

"Thank you. You're very kind." Hope sat herself down again, once more with a controlled combination of grace and tipsy unsteadiness.

In the bathroom, Nina quickly emptied the bath of Tom's clothes, sluiced the shower, grabbed fresh towels, wiped the mirror, put out new soap. It took her less than five minutes. When she went back to the living room, Hope was gone.

"Hope?" she called.

She checked the kitchen. The bedrooms. Under the beds. The laundry. No sign of her. She went outside, calling Hope's name. Nothing. Where could she have gone? As she came around the side garden, Nina thought of her car. She had a bad habit of leaving her keys in the ignition. She ran to the driveway. The car was still there.

"Hope?" she called again. She had to be nearby. She couldn't have gotten far in those heels.

Nina saw her then, barely visible in the moonlight, walking unsteadily down the road that led to the main highway. There wasn't time to worry whether she was over the limit herself. She got into the car and was pulling alongside Hope less than a minute later. She opened her door and ran around, catching up with Hope, half expecting her to lash out or collapse on the ground.

Hope did neither. She directed a confident stare at Nina, as if she hadn't just made a run for it in the middle of the night wearing high red shoes. "I want you to take me to the police station. I've decided to make a formal complaint."

"Against me?"

"Against the thieves who've been taking all my plants."

"Please, Hope, get in the car. I'll take you home."

"No. Take me to the police station."

"I don't think that's a good id—"

"Please. Please, Nina. I need your help."

It was the use of her name that softened Nina's resolve. With one hand on the other woman's sleeve, she guided Hope toward the passenger seat, maneuvered her in with some difficulty, and fastened her seat belt. Hope was now sobbing.

"I really think it would be better to drive you home," Nina tried again. "You could go to the police another time. When you're . . ." How to put it? Sober? "A little less tired."

The sobs stopped. "Forget it. I'll find my own way."

Hope reached for the door handle as Nina was starting the engine. Just as quickly, Nina reached across and pulled it shut. To her relief, Hope didn't fight her, just began crying again, covering her face with her hands.

Nina hesitated again. If she took Hope to the police station now, word would be all around the area within hours. But then, when weren't people in the local area talking about the Templetons? And what was the alternative? If she did start driving her home, there was every chance Hope would leap out while the car was moving. If they did make it safely, Nina wasn't sure she wanted to be witness to the homecoming scene either.

"The police station it is, then," she said, more cheerfully than she felt.

Chapter Eight

WHY AM I coming, too?" Gracie said, a week later, as she, Henry, and Spencer walked down the driveway toward the farmhouse several paddocks away.

"To make a good impression," Henry said. "That face of yours could melt icebergs."

"But I only met Tom once."

"And now you'll have met him twice. Remember to smile, Gracie. You too, Spencer. Use every drop of family charm and before the end of the day, we'll have a friend for you, Spencer, or my name isn't Henry Charles Templeton."

"The third," Gracie said.

"The third," Henry agreed.

IN HER HOUSE, Nina was panicking. There was no other word for it. Answering the phone to Henry Templeton was one thing, but before she'd got over that shock, he'd invited himself over. There was something he needed to discuss, he said to her, in the deep, cultured tone she remembered from the day of the fete. Realizing it was about Hope, she agreed to a visit.

"Thank you, Nina," he said. "These things are much better face to face. We'll see you shortly."

She didn't have time to ask who he meant by "we" before he hung up. Himself and Eleanor? Henry and Eleanor and Hope, dragged along to apologize? How was Nina going to be able to sit with all three of them and act as if everything was normal? Pretend she heard stories of affairs like theirs every week and they didn't bother her in the slightest?

There wasn't time to ring Hilary to ask her advice. She was too busy tidying the house, sweeping the kitchen floor and cursing the fact she worked from home, which meant the living room was taken up with her easels and canvases and paints.

She called Tom three times from the front verandah but he didn't answer. She went to the very bottom of their garden and called again. He was building a tree house, he'd told her that morning. She just didn't know in which tree. There were hundreds of them in the paddocks around their house. He finally heard her the fourth time.

"Tom, come home. Quick!"

"What's wrong?"

"The Templetons are coming. The father and some others."

A minute passed before Tom came into sight. He looked like he'd been rolling in dust. "So what? They're just people."

"No, they're not."

"They are. I've met them."

He ambled toward her. She had to stop herself from shouting at him to hurry up. "Quick. Go inside and comb your hair."

He ran his hands through his hair, sending up spikes. "No. And I'm not changing either." He grinned. "Mum, calm down."

"I am calm."

In her room, Nina caught sight of herself in the wardrobe mirror. She wasn't in the least bit calm. She was a cross between overexcited and wild eyed. What had got into her? Why was she in such a state? She stopped, told herself to breathe deeply and relax. It was just her neighbors calling by. The neighbors she'd done her best to avoid. The neighbors she'd rung and shouted at just a month before when Tom went missing. The neighbors she'd learned far too much about from a drunken Hope . . . She heard the sound of footsteps on the verandah.

The neighbors who were now at her front door.

Tom got to them first. He was very relaxed. "Hi, Spencer. Hi, Gracie. Hi, Henry."

"Mr. Templeton, Tom, not Henry," Nina said behind him, trying to hide her surprise that he'd brought his children with him to discuss a subject like Hope.

"Oh no, Henry is fine," Henry Templeton said, extending a hand, smiling broadly. He introduced his two children. "And you must be Nina. It's a pleasure to meet you."

"Again."

"Again?"

"We met at your first fete. In the dining room with Tom and your sister-in-law."

"With Hope?"

"Yes, Hope."

"Uh-oh," Spencer said.

Henry frowned. "I'm sorry. I don't remember that occasion. We've had quite a few people through the house since then."

"Was Hope dressed? Drunk? Throwing herself down the stairs?" Spencer asked in a bored voice.

Henry placed a hand on his son's shoulder but didn't seem too concerned. "That's enough, Spencer. I'm sorry, Nina. Can you remind me what happened? It clearly upset you if you can remember it more than two years later."

"Your sister-in-law made some racist comments. You came in and spoke to me then."

"Was I masterful? Did I deal promptly with the awkward situation?"

She stood up straighter. "It wasn't a laughing matter, actually."

"I can see that now. I do apologize again." He paused. "May we come in, all the same?"

"Yes. Yes, of course."

As she led them inside, Nina could see all three Templetons taking in every detail of her living room, from the non-matching furniture to the secondhand curtains to her painting paraphernalia in one corner. The whole room suddenly looked too small, too crowded, too colorful, lacking in any real style. She was embarrassed for herself and Tom.

"It's beautiful," Gracie said, gazing around. "I'd love to live here."

Nina couldn't stop a laugh. "I'm sure. Swap your house for this one?"

"But it feels so warm and it looks so inviting. Doesn't it, Dad?"

Inviting? Where had a child of that age learnt a word like that? Calling her father "Dad" surprised Nina, too. What had she expected, though? Your Majesty?

"You're an artist?" Henry Templeton said. "Well, of course you are. Unless this is all your work, Tom, is it?"

"I taught her everything she knows," Tom said.

They all laughed.

"Please, sit down," Nina said, hoping to distract them from her paintings. "Can I get you a cold drink? Coffee? Tea?"

"Tea would be lovely for all three of us."

Of course, Nina thought, kicking herself for offering. What did she have? Six chipped mugs, teabags, and a packet of plain biscuits. What were they used to? Fine china, imported tea, wafer-thin cucumber sandwiches?

"Can I help?" Gracie asked. "I love making tea."

"Thanks, but no, I'm fine," Nina said. The living room was chaotic enough. She didn't need the Templetons seeing her kitchen as well.

"She's a very good helper," Henry said. "She's also not good at taking no for an answer. Are you, Gracie?"

"Only when I really want to do something. And I do love making tea."

Nina gave in. Gracie followed her into the kitchen, then stopped, looking around at the brightly painted walls, the open shelves of colored plates and mugs, the large window overlooking the back paddock. As Nina put the kettle on to boil, the little girl turned in a full circle, gazing at the opposite wall covered in small framed landscape paintings, before sighing softly. "Your kitchen is lovely, too. Did you really do all these paintings? How long have you lived here, Nina? Do you have a husband?"

Nina's surprise at the sudden rush of questions must have showed.

Gracie blushed. "I'm sorry. Mum always tells me off for being too curious. You don't have to answer me. That was just to give you an idea of the sorts of things I would ask if it wasn't so rude."

Nina smiled then. "You weren't being rude. It's good to be curious. Let me ask you a question first, though. How old are you?"

"I'm eleven," Gracie said, beaming. "Spencer is ten. Audrey is sixteen. Charlotte is seventeen, nearly eighteen. Mum is thirty-nine. Dad's about to turn fifty. We've lived here at Templeton Hall for two years. Before that we moved all over England because of Dad's job. Is Tom your only child?"

As the kettle boiled with a loud whistle, Nina nodded, glad of the interruption. She watched as Gracie expertly warmed the teapot, put in the teabags, and poured in the water, talking all the while. "I hope you don't mind us arriving out of the blue like this. We've been discussing it for the past few days. We need your help, you see."

"With Hope?"

"Hope?" Gracie looked puzzled. "No. Why would we need your help with her? She's gone."

"Gone?"

Gracie nodded. "Back to England, last week. It was the best for everybody. Mum's gone with her, just to get her settled. Hope has problems with her moods. And her nerves. And drink. And tablets. Lots of problems, really. Charlotte and Audrey, my sisters—have you met them yet? No. Well, they call her Hopeless, which is funny but mean, Dad says. Mum says we have to be understanding, that Hope isn't well. Do you have a sister?"

Nina was trying to keep up. "Yes, one. Her name's Hilary."

"Is she sane?"

"Yes, perfectly."

"Good," Gracie said solemnly.

"But if you're not here about Hope, why are you here?"

Gracie lowered her voice. "It's about Spencer. He's getting out of hand again."

"Your parents want *my* help with Spencer?"

"Not yours, your son's," Gracie said, speaking at a normal volume again. "Mum and Dad think Spencer is bored on his own so much, so they've decided it might be a good idea if your son comes and plays with him sometimes. Especially over the next week or two while we're unofficially on school holidays, with Mum being away. She home-schools us, you see. In the drawing room. But we're on a break and Spencer is at a loose end. That's why we're here. To ask your permission about your son. Will you let him?"

Nina was again having trouble keeping up. "Let who?"

"Let Tom play with Spencer. Though I'd say it will be Spencer playing with Tom here, with that dam you have. Spencer took me there to catch yabbies but I didn't want to. It's more of a boy thing to do, don't you think? Shall we take the tea in now?"

When they came in, Henry was alone in the living room, looking at Nina's paintings. He turned, came across, and took the tray from her. "Lovely, thank you so much. I can't pretend it was an arduous journey over. What is it, ten minutes' walk at the most? So I'm hardly dying of thirst but I could drink tea all day long."

"You don't, though," Gracie said, reaching for the teapot and beginning to pour. "You drink it in the day and then you have wine at night. Or whisky."

"That's right, Gracie. So I do." He nodded toward the paintings. "Your work is charming, Nina. So evocative. You capture the mood of the landscape perfectly."

Thrown by the praise, Nina thanked him, then changed the subject. "Where are the boys?"

"Tom said something about a cubbyhouse," Henry said. "Spencer said something like 'Cool.' Then they were gone, faster than the speed of light. Never mind. It might be easier to talk about them while they're not here."

Nina was wondering if she could feign ignorance about what she'd just been told in the kitchen, when Gracie made the decision for her.

"I was just telling Nina the reason we're here, Dad," Gracie said in a composed voice. "I hope I didn't make Spencer sound too wild or out of control, did I, Nina?"

"No, no, you didn't."

"He is, though, isn't he, Dad?" She turned back to Nina. "We gave him chemistry set for his birthday and it was a big mistake. Stink bombs. Explosions. He mixed up some powders once and put them in all the toilets—sorry, the lavatories—and you've never seen such a mess. You see, it reacted with—"

"That's probably enough detail, Gracie, thank you. We're here to make a good impression, not scare Nina."

"I just thought it was best to be as candid as possible."

"Candid?" Nina said.

Gracie gave her a sympathetic look. "It means truthful, straight-forward. Nina thought we were here to talk about Hope, Dad. So I informed her that Hope and Mum were in England—"

Henry put his mug back on the tray. "Gracie, would you like to go and find the boys?"

"No, thank you."

"Gracie, would you like to go and find the boys?"

"You mean you want me to leave so you and Nina can talk in private?" At Henry's nod, she stood up. "How long will I give you?"

"Five minutes should be fine. I don't want to take up any more of Nina's time. I'm sure we've interrupted her work as it is."

"Five minutes. Good, see you then." At the door, Gracie turned back. "Do I have to play with the boys? Have you any pets, Nina?"

Nina was now finding it hard not to smile. "We have hens, a lizard that lives under the tank, and a fairly wild cat. He's called Tiger."

"I'll take my chances with Tiger. See you in five minutes."

They could hear her calling the cat's name even before they heard the back door open.

Nina turned to Henry Templeton, once again fighting a feeling of unreality. Henry Templeton of Templeton Hall was here in her living room, drinking tea out of her mug and looking like there was nowhere he'd rather be. He also seemed to be in no hurry to begin the conversation about Spencer.

Nina was quick to fill the silence. "She's quite something, that daughter of yours."

He smiled. "She is, isn't she? Precocious, really, though I'm sure she'd give us four other words with a similar meaning. Our own fault, of course. She is constantly stimulated and constantly curious, which we thought was marvelous until we realized there's no off button. You don't have to answer all her questions. I find it works well to tell her she needs to be patient. That she can't learn everything all at once or her brain might explode. But then of course she asked me were there any documented examples of a brain exploding due to too much in-formation."

Nina laughed, about to share a similar story about Tom, when she stopped herself. "So, you wanted to talk to me about Spencer?"

"I did, yes. Let me explain, Nina. The two children are usually homeschooled, but with their mother away at the moment, I've realized Spencer is lacking any structure to his day. Gracie's happy to keep studying but Spencer definitely needs company. He has so much energy, you see. And the other problem is he's fearless. If you tell him something's dangerous, he wants to try it then and there."

"He sounds like most boys."

"Does he? After three daughters, we still don't know what's hit us. That's why we're here to ask your help. Or your son's help, at least. We are wondering if we could come to some sort of arrangement regarding Tom spending time with Spencer?"

"Arrangement? As in a timetable?"

"We can have a timetable, of course. What I meant was a financial arrangement."

"You want to *pay* Tom to play with your son?"

"Yes, of course. We got off to such a bad start with you when Tom went missing that day. We can't just march in here and say, 'Our son needs company. Can we borrow your son for a few hours a week to try and run some of the energy out of ours?' "

"Why can't you? Isn't that how friendships are made the world over?"

"But we didn't want to seem presumptuous. If you'd been at all interested in your son becoming friends with our son, you'd have visited us long before now. Long before Tom and Spencer came across each other themselves."

Nina was wavering between being taken aback and annoyed. She decided on annoyed. "How do you think Spencer would feel if he heard his father had to buy friends for him?"

"Spencer already knows. It was his idea."

Nina blinked. "Is he really that bad? He can't make friends on his own?"

"I'm not sure if bad is the right word. A little dangerous to be around, but he's great company. You just have to keep your wits about you. He hides. Climbs. Makes things. Then destroys them. He was active enough in the UK. He moves at twice the speed here. All this space, I suppose."

"Moving countries when he was so young was probably disruptive for him." Nina couldn't believe she was calmly offering her opinion.

"It was disruptive for us all, yes. But exciting, too. You've never been back to the Hall since the fete, have you? And all because of Hope. Nina, I do apologize again. She's—let me think how best to put it—a very fragile person. A difficult person in many ways. But what a shame that she turned you against us."

Nina couldn't stop herself. "It wasn't just that."

"Oh, dear. There was more?"

She wanted to tell him, she realized. After being so private for so long, she suddenly wanted to tell someone—to tell him—everything. About Nick's death, about running away, time after time, until she found this place, thinking it was a sanctuary of sorts. Until the Templetons arrived and somehow began to unsettle her. Henry Templeton was watching her. Giving her his full attention. It made her feel . . . good. Yes, good. Interesting. Worthy of attention. She would tell him. It was only fair. She had judged him, it seemed, from afar and too quickly. She could almost hear Hilary urging her on. *Clear the air, Nina. It'll do you good.* She took a breath, about to speak—

"Has that been five minutes?" It was Gracie, back in the doorway, holding an annoyed-looking ginger cat. "He was sleeping in the sun," she said. "Is he a house cat or an outside cat?"

"He's an indoor and an outdoor cat," Nina said, glad and sorry for the interruption.

"Test that, Gracie, would you?" Henry said. "Take him outside for five more minutes and see if he's happier there."

"You haven't finished talking yet?"

"That's it." He waited until the door closed and then turned his attention back to Nina. "My apologies. You were about to tell me why you decided you didn't like us."

"I'm sorry. I don't even know you. It's unfair."

"Life can be unfair. But I'm curious now. We don't have much to do with local people."

"No, that causes some problems."

"It does? But why?"

"Gossip abhors a vacuum, I suppose. What people don't know about you they make up. You chose to keep your distance, so people decided—"

"That we think we're better than them?" At Nina's nod, he continued. "So the fete didn't work? That's why we decided to hold it, you know. To show everyone locally what we were doing."

"They thought you were just showing off."

"I suppose we were."

"It worked, then."

He smiled. "Nina, I really should have called over to you earlier. This is fascinating. We'll get back to you and Tom in a moment, I promise. I want to find out more about ourselves first, before Gracie comes back. Tell me, why else do people dislike us?"

After today she'd probably never speak to Henry Templeton again. She may as well tell the truth. "Initially it was because you didn't hire locals to help with the renovations."

"But we needed experts. We needed the work done quickly. You mean there were qualified stained-glass repair people nearby? Interior designers experienced in the re-creation and sourcing of colonial-style wallpapers, carpets, and linen? Authentic 1860s furniture suppliers? So we were condemned for using imported experts. I'd argue that point, but never mind for the moment. Why else don't people like us?"

"Because you haven't joined any of the local associations or business groups."

"But why should we?"

"Good manners? Curiosity? Good business practice?"

"But it's good business practice to keep ourselves apart. That's the whole mystique of us, surely? Why would people pay good money to visit the Hall, to hear us talk, to go on our tours if they'd already met us for coffee or stood next to me at a local sausage sizzle?"

The casual term made Nina smile. "What do you know about sausage sizzles?"

"We read the local paper from cover to cover. We like to keep in touch. I'm not being sarcastic. I mean it. Nina, one of the best forms of business promotion is word-of-mouth. Let me put it like this. If you were a visitor to the area, and someone said to you (a) there's a family of English people living in a big house near here who run a kind of museum. In fact, there's one of them now, in a tracksuit, or (b) there's a very peculiar English family who seem to think they're living in colonial times and we hardly ever see them in town. There's something very odd about them. Which would intrigue you the most? Which would make you determined to go and investigate for yourself?"

"B, of course. That's why you keep yourself so apart?"

"That, and the fact that the blasted Hall takes so much work that Eleanor and I barely have time to talk to each other and the children, let alone any already hostile and suspicious local people. Also, I don't like meetings. Can't bear them." He smiled. "Thank you. For someone tucked away in the middle of a paddock like this, Nina, you have your finger on the pulse. This is wonderful, like market research without all the bother."

"I'm not telling you anything you wouldn't hear from anyone else. You could walk down the main street of Castlemaine and you'd hear far more than I could tell you."

"Ah, but none of them would be as friendly as you. Or such a good listener. I feel like I could talk to you for hours." He laughed then. "Perhaps it helps that you've not been married to me for nearly twenty years. Eleanor always tells me I am too vain, but it's not vanity talking about yourself, is it? It's curiosity, I think. I find it helps to talk aloud when one is trying to understand one's motives, beliefs, and experiences. Now you, Nina. Tell me about you. Who you are. Why you're here. About your painting."

She tried not to react to the sudden switch in subject. Hilary appeared in her mind's eye again. *Have fun. Enjoy this. How often do you talk to attractive men?* An admission in itself that she found Henry Templeton attractive? But he was, in a tall, lean, English way. She changed position in her seat, trying to appear relaxed and poised, all at once. It was quite difficult. "I'm not from here either. That's the starting point, I suppose."

"Ah, so you're one of us. A blow-in. Isn't that the term?"

"That's it, though my arrival was a little less flamboyant than yours, I think."

"Oh, I don't know about that. I'm sure you would stand out in any crowd. Your coloring is very striking, by the way, that dark hair and those lovely eyes."

He didn't say it in a sleazy way. He just sounded matter-of-fact, which made it all the more affecting. Nina found herself abruptly changing the subject and asking after Eleanor, whether she'd be away long.

"We don't know yet. Eleanor's taken her sister home, back to friends who have a house in Surrey. The difficulty with Hope, you see, is—"

"Can I come back in yet? I've run out of distractions and I can't find Spencer or Tom anywhere." It was Gracie, back again.

Henry smiled at his daughter. "Gracie, perfect timing. Come in. I've just finished telling Nina all about our family. But it turns out she knew most of it already."

Gracie looked pleased. "We can tell you even more things once you start visiting us, Nina. You can come too, you know. It's not just Tom we want to hire."

"Ah, yes, the financial arrangement. Thank you, Gracie, for subtly moving the subject in that direction. And once again, Gracie, I need you to make yourself scarce. I'm sure Nina would rather have a conversation about money with just one of us, not the whole family."

"Gracie, you don't need to leave. I don't need to be paid, Henry, nor does Tom. I'd be insulted if you paid us."

Gracie frowned. "But you banned Tom from seeing Spencer again. You rang in a fury. I heard Mum and Dad talking about it. That's why we thought we'd have to offer you money. Mum said things had come to a pretty pass when she had to start buying friends for Spencer, but if that was the only option, so be it. That's what she said, Dad, isn't it?"

Henry shot Nina a brief, amused glance before turning to his daughter. "Thank you, Gracie, but please, off you go again. Five more minutes."

"But where do I go this time?"

"The boys are probably down at Tom's new tree house," Nina said. "In the paddock near the main road."

"A tree house? Not just a cubbyhouse? I love tree houses." She ran outside.

Henry turned his attention back to Nina. "I'm sorry not to couch this in any more elegant or less desperate terms, but can we call on your neighborly assistance with Spencer? Perhaps Tom might even enjoy Spencer's company, or all our company over at the Hall? You might even enjoy some peaceful time yourself?"

"Peaceful? After what you've told me Spencer gets up to and what I know Tom would like to get up to?"

Henry smiled. "Perhaps it will be a case of like meeting like, the two of them burning themselves out and immediately turning into studious, book-reading, stay-at-home boys?"

"Either that or you and I could take turns checking them for explosives."

Henry smiled again. A genuine, proper smile. Not the practiced, persuasive one she'd seen several times that afternoon already. This was different. The angular lines of his face softened, his eyes creased. He changed from being remotely attractive to being completely attractive, the soft laugh he gave only adding to it all. She suddenly understood why Hope could have done everything she had.

"You're sure we can't pay you, Nina? Pay Tom, even? Put this on a business footing?"

"No. I mean it. I'd be insulted."

"Then I'll have to think of some other way to show my gratitude." He gave her that smile again. The real one. "Nina, thank you again. So we have a deal?"

"We have a deal," she said.

They were just reaching across to shake one another's hand when they heard the sound of running feet. Gracie appeared in the doorway, white faced. "Dad, quick. Call an ambulance. Spencer's cut off his arm!"

TWO HOURS LATER, all five of them made their way from the local hospital's emergency department back to Nina's car. Spencer hadn't cut off his arm, but had fallen from the tree house, badly cutting his hand on the barbed-wire fence on the way down. Nina had hurriedly got everyone into her car, while Henry used his shirt to staunch the blood. After a fortunately short wait at the hospital, Spencer's wound had been disinfected, stitched up, bandaged, and his arm put in a sling. The bravado or recklessness Henry had described earlier wasn't evident. Spencer was now just a little boy who needed his father.

As she drove along the main road for the twenty-minute journey back to the Hall, Nina kept glancing in the rear-vision mirror. Henry and Spencer were in the back seat with Gracie. She noticed how gently Henry was holding Spencer, the constant checking that he was okay. She'd seen that same display of love when they'd run to the scene of the accident, seen it as Henry picked up his son and carried him across the paddock.

It hurt. She'd thought her jealous feelings were gone and yet here they were back again, bigger than ever, come to life in her car. It was as if they were all acting out some kind of family scene, mum and dad and their three children, heading home together after an eventful afternoon. She forced herself to look only at the road, to listen to Gracie's constant chatter about the wards in the hospital, to smile at her perfect pronunciation of different operations, appendectomies, tonsillectomies. . . .

Driving up the avenue to Templeton Hall made her feel even stranger. She pulled in beside the front door, as if this were normal, as if it wasn't the first time she'd been there in two years. And even though she wanted to just wave good-bye and drive away, she got out too and followed them inside: Henry, with Spencer in his arms, Gracie, and Tom.

Henry stopped in the hallway. "I'll be right back," he said to Nina. "I'll just get him settled upstairs. Gracie, fix Nina a drink, please."

"Henry, thanks, but we won't stay."

"Of course you will. We've all had a shock. Please, Nina, stay."

"I don't think so. Tom's very tired."

"I'm not," Tom said immediately. "I'm fine."

"We'll go home," she said firmly, not looking at her son. "It's been a big day for you all."

"But you'll be back tomorrow?" Gracie said. "Don't we have an arrangement now?"

"We'll put that on hold, won't we?" Nina asked Henry. "Until Spencer is better?"

"I'm fine," Spencer said, suddenly reviving. "Tom, can you come over tomorrow?"

"Mum, can I? First thing in the morning?"

How could she say no? When not just her son, but three of the

Templetons were gazing at her, so sure of themselves, sure of their appeal.

They agreed on nine a.m.

IT WASN'T UNTIL ten o'clock that night, after Tom had taken more convincing than usual to go to bed, that she was able to phone her sister and fill her in.

"But this is all great," Hilary said. "Why do you sound so worried?"

"Because I liked them too much. Gracie, Henry, even Spencer—"

"Well, that's something to worry about. It would be much better if you were sending your son over to play with a family you hated. Nina, what's got into you? First you decide you don't like them before you know anything about them, and now you decide you don't like them because you do like them. If that makes sense."

"About as much sense as I'm making, I guess. But it was just so unexpected, Hilary. How easy it was to talk to Henry, especially."

"Your problem is—"

"It's been too long since I've spoken to any man apart from the butcher, the baker, and the candlestick maker. Yes, I know. He's also married, Hilary."

Hilary laughed. "Nina, I'm not saying you should run off with Henry Templeton. I'm just saying relax, enjoy his company, enjoy the whole family's company. It'll do you good to meet new people, get out a bit more. They must have all sorts of parties and soirees."

"They don't. He said they're so busy he and his wife barely get time to talk to each other let alone anyone else."

"Oh, no. The old 'My wife doesn't understand me' line. So he *was* making a pass at you?"

"He wasn't. I'm overreacting."

"Yes, you are. Just go with it. See what happens. It'll be good for Tom and good for Wild Boy or whatever his name is."

"Spencer."

"That's their main problem, if you ask me. Tell your darling Henry to give him a different name, a manly name like Wolfgang or Hank, and his problems will be solved immediately."

Nina felt calmer after she hung up. She always did after she'd spoken to Hilary. But she still found it hard to sleep. There was no going back now. A connection had been made between herself and Tom and the Templetons, whether she wanted it or not. She knew the next day would be just the start of Tom visiting the Hall. Why would he be happy with just her company when there was a huge place like the Hall to play in, a family as interesting and as unusual as them to get to know? She'd found them fascinating enough herself. She could only imagine how they seemed to a twelve-year-old boy.

It was after two before she slept. Even then, she was plagued by bad dreams. One in particular. Tom, standing on the front steps of the Hall, surrounded by the Templetons, telling her he'd decided he wanted to live with them from now on.

Chapter Nine

AT TEMPLETON HALL three days later, Henry had just hung up from talking to Eleanor in London and was looking for his youngest daughter. He found her in the morning room, curled up on the window seat, apparently reading but clearly waiting for him. Her expression was eager as she looked up.

He smiled. "It's a yes, Miss Gracie, I'm pleased to say. Your mother agrees it's not fair that you should be doing any work while your brother is making merry with his new friend, so you're on holidays now too until she gets back on the weekend."

"Hurrah!" Gracie said. She hopped up, put down her book, and followed her father downstairs. "It's all working out, isn't it? Spencer's so much better since Tom's been allowed to come and play."

"Better? Out of sight, perhaps. I'm still waiting for the sound of something exploding."

"Don't worry. They're only using bicarbonate of soda."

Henry stopped midstep. "What do you mean 'only using'? Using for what?"

"Their volcano. They're building it out in the stables apartment. Spencer said it will send lava spewing more than ten meters into the air. But he's going to add twice as much petrol to the soda, to see if it will go twenty meters. Dad? Dad, where are you going?"

———

THE NEXT MORNING, Gracie relayed the entire story to Nina. "It wasn't as bad as Dad thought it would be. I'd got it wrong about the petrol. It was just bicarbonate of soda and kerosene."

"It still could have exploded," Nina said. "It's lucky you told him when you did."

"Spencer was furious at me. I think Tom was, too. Spencer called me a squealer. That's why I came here. There was no one to talk to at the Hall. You don't mind, do you?"

"No, Gracie. It's nice to see you."

Nice, if surprising. Nina had planned to spend the day priming canvases. She'd got a faxed order for a dozen landscape paintings. It was as broad a brief as that. The company had received an order from a colonial-style restaurant. Gum trees, dams, hazy blue mountain range in the background, that kind of thing. It was as well she didn't harbor a huge artistic ego, Nina thought. Painting by numbers, painting to order. It had kept her and Tom going for nearly three years, though. She wasn't going to complain.

"Can I help?" Gracie asked. "You'll need to tell me what it is you're actually doing, but then I'll happily lend you a hand."

Nina fought a smile. Gracie spoke as though she'd learnt English from watching too many BBC period dramas, a funny mixture of stiff formality and excellent vocabulary. Nina explained what she was doing, applying undercoat to the canvases to give her a clean working surface. She got Gracie an old shirt and set her up with the paint and brushes. They worked in silence for less than a minute before Gracie spoke.

"Nina, how did you know you wanted to be a painter?"

"I didn't. I thought I wanted to be a gymnast. I used to watch the gymnastics at the Olympics and longed to be one of them. I tried swinging from our clothesline once, fell, broke my arm, and gave it up then. While I was waiting for the plaster to come off, my sister bought me a coloring book and pencils and that got me started."

"But how did you know you were any good?"

"I didn't at first. I had to learn how to do it. And I'm still not that good. These aren't works of art, Gracie. I paint whatever it is people ask me to paint."

"I think they're beautiful. I think you have a great talent."

"Thank you very much."

"And where is your husband, Nina, if you don't mind me asking?"

The question took Nina by surprise. All the answers she normally gave suddenly seemed inappropriate to say to a child like Gracie. *It didn't work out between us. We're no longer together.* She also knew that if she said those things, Gracie would only ask another question. *Why not? Where is he now?* She hesitated for just a moment before answering.

"He died, Gracie." The truth felt strange in her mouth.

Gracie put down her paintbrush. "He died? He's dead? How?"

"It was a car accident."

"Oh, Nina." To her amazement, Gracie's eyes filled with tears. "But that's so sad. When did it happen?"

That feeling again, of being about to take a big plunge into the unknown. "Twelve years ago."

Gracie frowned. "Tom's twelve, isn't he?" At Nina's nod, she was quiet for a moment before speaking again. "So he died when Tom was just a baby?"

Say it, Nina, say it. "He died the same day Tom was born, Gracie. He was on his way to the hospital."

"Oh, Nina. So he never met Tom?"

"No, he didn't." Damn it. Damn. She was starting to cry now, too.

"That's so sad. He would have loved Tom."

Nina gave a hard blink to force away the tears. "You think so?"

"I'm sure of it."

Nina now couldn't believe she had told an eleven-year-old girl something she'd been unable to tell anyone else for years. It was a mistake. She should never have mentioned it.

"Gracie, I need to ask you a big favor. What I just told you, it's something not many people know. Please, can I trust you not to tell anyone else? Not your family. Especially not Tom."

"But he knows his dad is dead, doesn't he?"

"Yes. Yes, he does. He just doesn't know everything."

"Are you waiting until he's old enough?"

"That's it."

Gracie nodded solemnly. "I won't breathe a word. To Tom, especially. He's a very nice boy. You've done a very good job raising him on your own."

That changed the mood. Nina found herself trying not to smile. "Thank you, Gracie."

They worked in silence for five more minutes, before Gracie glanced across at the clock above the mantelpiece. "Time for me to go. I'm cooking dinner while Mum's away and I need to decide tonight's menu. Dad's giving me two dollars a meal."

"You're feeding three people on two dollars a meal?"

"No, he's paying me two dollars. I'm doing it alphabetically using Mum's favorite recipe book. It makes it much easier to decide. I'm up to the J section but I've only found things like jellied eel or jam and Spencer won't touch those. I might start on K tonight instead. Thanks for letting me help you, Nina. Bye for now."

"Bye, Gracie," Nina said, relieved and sorry at the same time to see her go. Was that what having a daughter was like? A mixture of entertainment and exhaustion? Perhaps she should be glad she only got to have Tom.

AN HOUR LATER, Gracie was crouched in the shadows of the hallway just outside her father's study. She knew she shouldn't have been listening. But that was just the way it happened in this house sometimes. It was so big, with so many tucked-away spots behind curtains and under the staircase, that sometimes you could just be sitting still, thinking about something, and you'd find yourself overhearing a conversation or a row.

In this case it was definitely a row, over the phone, between her father and her mother, still in England. It was about money, Gracie soon realized. Bills that needed to be paid. Work that needed to be done. And money they didn't have.

"It's a catch-22, Eleanor," Henry said, raising his voice. Gracie didn't like the sound of that. Her father usually had a quiet voice. "Can I remind you how expensive it is to advertise? Yes, yes. If we don't get more visitors, we lose even more money, more bills don't get paid, and more repairs don't get done. I already know everything you're telling me."

Gracie stood, barely breathing, listening to the silence in her father's office as her mother told her side of the story. It was a long silence. Her mother obviously had a lot to say.

Her father's voice sounded again, even more loudly this time. "No, I won't accept that. You agreed that we were better to do it ourselves, stay separate, and it worked very— No. Please don't interrupt, Eleanor. Yes, it did work at the start and it will again. Please, let me finish." Another long pause. "I know. I know. Of course I can't go and make a sale. Who would look after Gracie and Spencer? Well, tell her you can't stay any longer. You have a family here that needs you."

Gracie realized she was holding her breath. She knew who they were talking about now. Hope. It was nearly two weeks since her mother and Hope had left, and while she didn't miss Hope at all (even if she felt a bit guilty admitting it), she really missed her mother. If she was home again, life would almost be perfect, just the six of them, no Hope in her room, no feeling sick in her stomach every time she came down to the living room or kitchen in case Hope was there, drinking on her own, waiting for whichever one of them happened to come in. In the days before Hope and her mother left, Gracie had perfected a kind of slinking movement past the doors so that it looked as though she was going somewhere else, even if she wasn't, just in case Hope caught sight of her.

Gracie loved her dad, but he was always busy these days, spending a lot of time in his study, sighing, and looking through magazines about furniture and picking up folders filled with bits of paper. He'd also started making lots of phone calls, at odd times of the day or night. She'd dared to ask him about them once, and he'd said, a little bit too crossly, she thought, that there was such a thing as an over-observant child, and in his opinion Gracie was heading in that direction.

"Are you phoning Mum all those times, though? Can I talk to her next time?"

"Gracie, you can't always get all the answers you want, you know. As it happens, I've been ringing some old work colleagues of mine."

"In the antique shop in Brighton?"

"No, Gracie, not Brighton, and that's all you need to know for now, all right?"

Gracie wondered whether she should appear in her father's doorway now and ask to talk to her mother. She'd have the pleasure of talking to her and stopping their almost-fight, too. She leaned in more closely. They were still arguing about money. Her father was sounding quite angry now.

"No, we can't cut costs any more, unless you want to pull the girls out of school. Exactly. Look, I'll think of something." She heard him say good-bye to her mother abruptly, hang up loudly, and then sigh.

Gracie waited for just a few moments and then knocked gently on his door. "Dad?" No answer. She tried again. "Dad? Is everything all right?"

Henry looked up from his desk, ran his fingers through his hair, then beckoned her in. "Gracie, are you lurking in the shadows again? You're getting worse than Spencer."

"Spencer's stopped doing that now he's got Tom to play with."

"Perhaps we need to get you a friend, too."

"I don't want one. I'm happy here on my own." She was. She had her books and puzzles and every weekend to look forward to, when the house was filled with visitors. But not enough visitors, from what she'd just heard. "Dad, can I do anything?"

"Now? No, darling, you go and read or whatever it is you usually do at"—he checked his watch—"seven o'clock at night."

"I mean about the money."

"You heard me?" At Gracie's nod, he smiled. "Gracie, don't worry. Everything is fine. We're just going through what business-people throughout the ages have called a rough patch. A lot of bills coming in, not enough money to cover them for the time being, but we'll find what we need and you're not to worry."

"I can show more groups around if you need me to."

"You already show more groups around than any of us. No, Gracie, we just need the groups to be bigger, that's all."

"Could we run tours during the week as well?"

"It's too expensive, darling. We'd have to advertise for a start, and we'd have to turn all the lights on for longer, clean more often. It wouldn't be worth any extra money we might make, not for a long time, at least."

"What about night tours on the weekend?"

Henry smiled then. "You stay in character long enough every weekend as it is, Gracie. I'm already in fear of the child protection agency. Please stop worrying. Everything is fine, I promise. Repeat after me. Everything is fine."

She repeated it. But she wasn't sure she believed it.

LATER THAT EVENING, a now slightly more cheerful Gracie was setting the table for dinner. Spencer hadn't appeared yet. He'd been missing in action since Tom called over after school. There'd been a lot of whooping and shouting out in the stables, but when she'd gone to investigate, they'd either disappeared or were hiding from her. Her father was still in his study. She'd sneaked out once to press her ear against his door, heard only a low tone of voice, and tiptoed back to the kitchen, relieved. According to her calculations, her mother was on her way to the airport now, so she knew her father couldn't be talking to her. But as long as there were no raised voices, Gracie knew everything was all right.

She smiled now as her father came into the kitchen. "Dinner's nearly ready. It doesn't look like the picture very much"—she held up a luridly colored photograph of what the caption said was kedgeree—"but I think it will taste all right if we put lots of gravy on it."

"I'm sure it's delicious, Gracie. And your mother sends you lots of love and said to tell you your meals sound lovely and she hopes you'll keep cooking when she gets home."

Gracie frowned as she turned to get the dish out of the oven. "You were talking to Mum? How? I thought she'd be at the airport by now."

"Ah, yes. Well, she nearly was. Unfortunately there's been a last-minute hitch with her flight and she's coming back early next week instead."

"Next week? But why? What happened? Is she all right?"

"She's fine. But as it happens, there's another bit of news. About your aunt Hope."

"She doesn't like her new place?"

Henry paused. "Hope got very upset about your mother leaving her alone. Extremely upset. So she's coming back here with her again."

"Oh, Daddy, no!"

Henry only just stepped out of the way as the kedgeree landed on the floor.

NOT LONG AFTER, Charlotte didn't take the news any better.

"No way, Dad. She can't. Forget it."

Henry moved the phone from one ear to another. "Charlotte, she can and she is. Audrey understood the situation. Why can't you? In any case, we don't have a choice."

"Audrey understood because she's a drama queen, too, and we *do* have a choice. So does Hope. Hasn't she got any friends left over there who will take her in?"

"She does have friends, and they did their best, but unfortunately Hope had one of her episodes the second night she was there and—"

"*Episodes?* Got raging drunk or raided their medicine chest or tried to seduce their gardener, is that what you mean? Just say it as it is, Dad. Stop tiptoeing around it with all this talk of 'episodes' or 'events,' would you?"

"She's your mother's sister, Charlotte, your aunt, part of our family, and as I have said to you a thousand times, we have a responsibility to help her."

"You do. Mum does. We don't. But it's us she affects. We're the ones who can't watch TV some nights because she's obsessively playing the piano. Or we can't have friends to stay in case she raids the wine cellar and makes a show of herself. We can't care about her just because she's related to us. It doesn't work like that."

"So what are you suggesting, Charlotte? That we look up the Yellow Pages under A for Asylum and get her locked up in London somewhere?"

"If someone would take her, yes, that's exactly what I'm saying."

"Charlotte, she's a fragile human being, who needs—"

"She's not fragile! That's exactly what she isn't. She's just a selfish, self-centered, self-obsessed alcoholic and she's got you and Mum completely hoodwinked. You'll do anything for her, while all of us suffer."

"Suffer? Which part of your privileged upbringing and comfortable existence could be described as suffering, Charlotte? Did I miss the years you were locked in a dungeon?"

"You just don't get it, do you? It's never been just us, our family, the six of us. She's always been there, making it awful for the rest of us. No matter where we went, she'd turn up, messing it up for all of us. And it's not just me she upsets—"

"It mostly is you."

"You don't know half the lies she tells, Dad. The things she says about all of us."

"Most people can recognize fairly quickly that she's troubled."

"Actually, no, they can't. I've heard her, Dad. She talks about you, as well, did you know that? About you and her having an affair?" Charlotte's voice was getting louder.

"There's no need to shout, Charlotte, and yes, I have heard those stories. Quite a few times over the years, as it happens."

"Good. Great. So can you please tell Gracie and Spencer they're not true, because any day now they'll start asking me about them."

"She's your mother's sister, Charlotte. You'd do the same for you sisters and brother."

"Would I? If I hadn't already done it for Hope all my life, ma but now, forget it. If she's going to be back at the Hall, Dad, I'm coming home again."

"Don't be ridiculous. You're in charge this weekend."

"I mean it. If Hope's there, I won't be back this week weekend, or ever again."

"You're just going to live at the boarding school forev at university?"

"I'm not going to stay here and I'm not going to ur

"So what are you going to do?"

"I'll work."

"Doing what? You haven't got any qualificatic

"I'll think of something. Do something. Go back to England. I'll do whatever I have to do, Dad, but I won't come back to the Hall while she's there."

"You'll feel differently in a day or two. Wait until your mother is home and talk to her."

"Mum already knows how I feel about this. I mean it, Dad. It's Hope or it's me."

Henry laughed. "Because there's not room here for the two of you?"

"Don't try and joke your way out of this one. Good-bye, Dad."

Henry was left staring at the receiver as Charlotte hung up on him.

AS THEY ATE a dinner of toasted cheese sandwiches later that evening, Spencer didn't seem bothered by the news of Hope's return. He simply shrugged when Henry told him.

"You don't mind, Spencer? She doesn't upset you as much as she upsets the others?" Henry glanced at Gracie. She'd gone silent since he'd told her about Charlotte's threat.

Spencer shrugged again. "She's okay. A bit mad, but I like the way she gives me money."

"Gives you money?"

"Well, not just gives it to me. I have to do things for her."

Henry went still. "Like what?"

"Nothing too hard. Take the bottles out of her room. And take more bottles in."

"What bottles, Spencer?"

"The bottles of wine. She pays me a dollar a bottle."

Henry's voice was casual. "And where do you get these bottles?"

"From that cupboard under the stairs. There's always loads in here. We have a system. I take up a full one, she gives me an empty one and two dollars."

"How do you get past the lock?"

"Your keys," Spencer said matter-of-factly.

"And what do you do with the empty bottles?"

Spencer was looking a bit fed up with the questions. "I throw them in the dam. Or under the bushes on the driveway. Or in the rain tank. Loads of places."

Before Henry could reply to that, Gracie spoke.

"I've had an idea, Dad. Maybe you could pay Nina to look after Hope at her house. That way she's close by but not living here and Charlotte could come home."

Henry was distracted. "I don't think so, Gracie. We'll work something out. Don't worry."

"We have to, Dad," Gracie said, now nearly in tears. "Or Charlotte is lost to us forever."

THE NEXT DAY Gracie reported it all to Nina in great detail.

"Charlotte means it, Nina, I know she does. But Mum won't send Hope away again. It's a very awkward situation."

"I'm sure it must be," Nina said, still trying to take in all that Gracie had told her since she'd arrived without notice that afternoon. She now didn't even bother knocking, simply calling out a greeting before walking straight in. "Your parents will sort it out, I'm sure."

"I just hope they can." Gracie hopped up from her seat. "I'd better go home. Thanks for the tea, Nina, and for having me. See you tomorrow."

It was some time after Gracie's departure before Nina was able to start working again.

Chapter Ten

THREE WEEKS AFTER Eleanor and Hope arrived back at Templeton Hall, Charlotte still hadn't come home for a weekend. Eleanor's reasoning, then arguing, then pleading, then insistence had fallen on deaf ears. Charlotte refused to change her mind.

"And you'd better not bring her to Audrey's special night, either," Charlotte told her mother during the latest call. "She'll only wreck it for Audrey and for everyone else."

"Hope's much better now, I told you," Eleanor said. "She's not drinking, she's out working in the garden every day, joining us for dinner, helping Gracie and Spencer with their schoolwork."

"Oh, I'm sure she's an absolute pussycat. Especially now that I'm out of the way."

"You're not out of the way. You're refusing to come home and I still don't understand why and I'm very disappointed in you. I thought you had more—"

"If you say 'compassion,' I'll scream, Mum. What stores of compassion I might have been born with were used up years ago. I've already lost enough of my childhood because of Hope. I don't want to lose what's left of my teenage years either."

"Stop being so melodramatic."

"I mean it about Audrey's special night, Mum. She's nervous enough as it is. If she knows Hope is there and liable to do anything, get drunk and take off her clothes or start screaming at the stage, it will make it even worse for her. Get a babysitter in if you don't dare leave her for an evening. But I'm begging you, don't let her come or I won't be held responsible for my own actions toward her."

"It's only an award presentation, isn't it? Why would Audrey be so nervous about that?"

Charlotte nearly kicked herself. She'd forgotten that Audrey—for some inexplicable but undoubtedly dramatic, self-obsessed reason—was still keeping her acting debut secret from the rest of the family.

"She just is," she improvised. "And I'm backing her all the way. If Audrey's big night is upset in any way, I swear I'll stop her from going home ever again too."

HENRY LAUGHED that night when Eleanor recounted her conversation with Charlotte. "Get a babysitter? She was joking, Eleanor. Hope is thirty-six years old. She's not a toddler we're trying to keep away from the poisons cupboard."

"No? She's not far off from being a toddler sometimes. The tantrums. The selfishness. The noise." Eleanor ran her fingers through her hair. "Oh, she's better, Henry, she is. The new tablets, being sober, all the talking we did, but she's still angry at me."

"Why? Because you let her come back here? You should be angry with *her*."

"You know she's always felt I got all the good things in life and she was left with the dregs. That I have it easy. Oh, yes, very easy, trying to stay above all that is going on, keep this business afloat, teach Spencer and Gracie, handle Charlotte and her temper, Audrey and her pipedreams. I really have it easy. How dare she, Henry? Hasn't she taken even a second to see what my life is like, how she makes it even more difficult? Of course she hasn't. Because since the moment she was born it's only ever been about her and I'm so sick and tired of it."

"Then why did you bring her back here, Eleanor?" His voice was quiet.

"Because she begged me, Henry. Begged me. And because I never want anyone else to go through the guilt I went through, finding her passed out after that overdose, thinking she was dead and it was my fault. She's my sister. My only sister. How could I say no?"

Henry didn't answer, just took his wife's hand and absentmindedly stroked it. There was silence for a few minutes before he spoke. "Charlotte's right, though. I don't think it's a good idea if Hope comes to Audrey's presentation. I'll stay here with her."

"You can't. Audrey would be devastated. She's insisting we all be there."

"Surely we could leave Hope on her own just for one night? It's mid-week. There shouldn't be any visitors. We could lock the front gate if we had to."

"And make it harder for the police or the ambulance to get through if she did something stupid again, like cut herself or throw herself down the stairs? We can't do that either."

"I do have a small idea. Maybe it's asking too much, maybe it's out of the question, but maybe not, just for one night."

Eleanor protested about his suggestion at first, then listened some more, then finally agreed that it was worth exploring, if nothing else.

"But I'll go and do the asking," Eleanor said, looking tired and sad. "It's only fair. She's my sister."

AT LEAST this time there'd been a chance to tidy up a little bit, Nina thought the following morning. Eleanor Templeton had phoned the night before to ask if she could call over. The house was now tidy, there was a tray of tea things ready in the kitchen, and Nina had changed into a dress rather than the painting outfit she normally wore each day.

Eleanor arrived at exactly ten o'clock. Nina noticed immediately that she shared none of her younger sister's imperious behavior. There was something gentle about her. Even her looks were softer than her sister's. Hope was all sharp angles, tilted chin, fast movements, her clothes tailored and expensive. Eleanor's face was rounder, prettier, her expression more guarded, her summer dress elegant but clearly well-worn. Nina glanced down. Eleanor was wearing an ordinary pair of sandals, stylish but showing wear, a long way from her sister's impractical red shoes.

"Thank you, Nina. I appreciate this." Eleanor's voice was also different from Hope's: low, even, without Hope's dramatic tones. She'd barely taken her seat before she began talking. "Nina, we don't know each other well enough, or know each other at all, so there's no point in me making polite conversation or pretending this is a social call." Eleanor laughed softly. "Well, it is a social call, and I'm trying to make it as normal as possible, because it's quite an awkward situation. I'm also sorry I haven't called over to thank you before now."

At Nina's clearly puzzled expression, she hurried on. "About us borrowing your Tom. I can't tell you the difference it's made to Spencer. It's been different with each of the children, you see. We lived in cities with Charlotte and Audrey when they were being homeschooled, and so they were able to make friends with their neighbors. And Gracie, well, as you may have discovered, Gracie is an unusual child. If she hasn't a friend nearby, she's just as happy to talk to a leaf or a passing cloud. And we assumed it would be the same with Spencer, that he'd be happy in his own company, especially once we arrived here with so much space and land. But it's true, isn't it, that the devil makes work for idle hands? Did you find that with Tom? But of course you didn't. Tom has beautiful manners. He's a credit to you. I only hope Spencer isn't having a bad effect on him. You haven't noticed Tom becoming wilder by the day?"

It was quite a speech and Nina liked her more for every word. "Not so far, no. He's always too full of praise for Spencer and Templeton Hall. It's when they go quiet on us that we should worry, I think."

Eleanor smiled, then shifted position. "Nina, I'm actually here to talk to you about Hope. My sister. I'm not sure what, if anything, you know about her."

Nina tensed, hoping immediately it hadn't been too obvious. "Not much. Only what she told me herself, and a little from Henry and Gra—"

"What she told you herself?"

"She came here one night. About a month ago. Just before she went to England with you."

Eleanor ran her hand through her hair. A piece was left standing up. Another time Nina might have found it comical but now it just made Eleanor seem more vulnerable.

"I'm so sorry, Nina. Do you mind telling me what she said? How she was?"

Nina hesitated, not sure where to start. She explained how Hope had appeared at her door, how she'd asked for a drink and begun to talk. "She seemed to have a few . . ." She tried to find the right word. ". . . grievances she needed to get off her chest."

"Nina, please don't feel awkward. I know that Hope gets it into her head sometimes that she and Henry had a long and torrid affair. It's not true. I'd be quite sure that nothing she told you was true. That time, before we went back to England, was a particularly—how can I put it?—troubled period for her. Can I also assure you that no, she isn't Gracie's real mother, that no, Spencer isn't adopted, Charlotte isn't a recovering drug addict, and Audrey doesn't have a fatal disease and less than two months to live." Eleanor registered Nina's expression and gave a soft laugh. "Oh, dear. Am I right in guessing that Hope didn't get to those and I've just opened a Pandora's box myself?"

At Nina's nod, Eleanor ran her fingers through her hair again. The errant lock dropped into place. "At least now you'll be prepared for it if you do hear it. Can I ask how you managed to get her home that night? None of us were even aware she'd gone missing."

"I didn't take her home," Nina said, surprised that Eleanor didn't know. Surely she'd have heard about a visit from a police sergeant. Nina had delivered Hope into his not-exactly-welcoming care that evening. "I did as she asked, drove her to the Castlemaine police station. She'd got quite, um, agitated about people stealing her plants and wanted to press charges. The sergeant told me he'd take care of things."

"Oh, God, so now the whole town knows. It's hard enough—" She stopped. "Sorry, Nina. I'm sorry you had to put up with that. I wish I'd known. Henry said he visited here while I was away to talk about Tom but he didn't mention anything about Hope visiting you."

"I didn't tell him. It didn't seem right, in front of the children and then—"

"Of course. Spencer cut his hand. Thank you for your discretion. In light of that, I think I may as well go home without asking you what I'd come to ask. You've already seen Hope in full flight. I'm sure it's not an experience you're in any hurry to repeat."

"I'm sorry?"

Eleanor looked exhausted. "I was here to ask an enormous favor that we as a family have no right to ask. We've lived beside you for two years and have never made an effort to call over and meet you before now, so it's beyond reason that you would even consider it, but we were desperate on behalf of one of our daughters and acted without thinking."

Nina listened as Eleanor explained about Audrey's school event in Melbourne and the family's fear about bringing Hope with them.

"There are times when we wouldn't worry about leaving Hope on her own for a night. . . ."

"But this isn't one of those times?"

"I'm embarrassed to even ask, and 'babysitting' isn't the right word."

"Would I just keep an eye on her for the night, do you mean?"

"That's it, exactly. But, Nina, I can see from your face how you feel, and I understand, and I hope this won't have any bearing on Tom's visits to us—"

"Would you want me to watch her at Templeton Hall or here?"

"You'd even consider it?"

"I spent my teenage years working as a babysitter. I'm guessing Hope and I don't both get to stay up until midnight and eat as many snacks as I did back then, though?"

"You'd do it? Really?" Eleanor's face changed, became younger, more carefree, in an instant. "Oh, Nina. Thank you."

GRACIE WAS OVER within the hour. "Nina, thank you! Mum couldn't believe it. I heard her calling to Dad as soon as she got home. 'She said yes! She'll do it!' Hope heard her, of course, and there was a huge row, but Dad was so quick thinking, he said it wasn't Hope you would be minding, it was Templeton Hall. They said that they felt it wasn't fair to leave her with so much responsibility, that if she wanted to have an early night, it was better to have someone else there. So when you come, Mum is going to ask you to pretend that it's all about the Hall, not Hope. I thought I'd warn you now so that you could get your expression ready. Thanks again, Nina!" With a cheery farewell wave, Gracie let herself out again.

AT THEIR boarding school in Melbourne, Audrey and Charlotte were in Charlotte's room, arguing. They'd been arguing about the same subject for the past two days.

"But it's not fair. You have to let me come," Audrey said again, close to tears now.

"No, I don't, actually," Charlotte answered. "And it's not about being fair. I've got your well-being at heart, Audrey. You told me yourself you need to learn your lines. That this is the performance that might change the course of your life. A weekend away with my friends is the very last thing you should be doing."

"I know my lines perfectly already. Oh, please, let me come."

"There's no point begging. I'm not going to change my mind. This isn't just an outing. I need to do some serious networking. Now that I can't go back to Templeton Hall for weekends, I need a lot of friends with large weekender homes, very quickly."

"You are *so* selfish. It's always about you, isn't it?"

"If it wasn't about me, it would have to be about you, and quite frankly I'm much more interesting," Charlotte said, lifting down her suitcase from the wardrobe.

"You're a bitch, Charlotte Templeton. A selfish, self-centered bitch."

Charlotte put her hands on her hips. "You're one to talk. Who brags about nothing but her so-far-unproven acting career or her stupid artistic spirit, spends hours each day gazing in the mirror, and is, in my opinion, becoming completely and utterly obsessed with herself?"

"You just don't understand how it feels to be sensitive, do you? How much I hurt inside sometimes. You're just mean, you know that? Mean. Mean and bitter and a horrible selfish cow."

"And I love you, too," Charlotte said, not looking up as her sister flounced out of the room.

BY NINE O'CLOCK the next night Charlotte was wishing she *had* let Audrey come with her. At least she could have bribed her sister to use her alleged acting skills to fake a stomachache or migraine and given her an excuse to leave this excruciatingly boring party.

It was being held in a large, luxurious split-level house in the exclusive Melbourne beachside suburb of Brighton. Celia's cousin from America was subletting the property while he was here on holiday, or something like that. Charlotte hadn't really been listening. Celia had promised her it would be filled to the brim with family friends and eligible bachelors, the wealthy sons of even wealthier property barons. Farm boys, in other words. All Charlotte had seen so far was an endless parade of cartoon cut-out boys. Boys, not men. They were all dressed alike, in moleskin trousers, pale-blue shirts, sweaters tied casually around their necks. They had ruddy faces, sunburnt arms, and zero conversational skills. If she'd wanted to learn so much about the Australian farming industry, she'd have gone to agricultural college. At least there'd have been a degree at the end of it. If the amount she was drinking to stave away the boredom tonight was any indication, the only thing she'd have to show for this tedious evening was a bad hangover tomorrow.

". . . largest in the state, ten thousand head of cattle and cropping, too, of course."

Of course, Charlotte thought, so bored she was astonished she was keeping her eyes open. She glanced around for Celia. She was in a corner of the room, gazing up at another young man, either very interested in everything he was saying or very good at pretending.

"And your family?"

"Sorry?" Charlotte said, dragging her attention back to the man beside her.

"Your family's on the land?"

"We walk on it every day, yes."

He didn't get her joke. "Where's your property?"

"North."

"Of where?"

"Here," Charlotte said. "Excuse me, would you?" She crossed the room, moving swiftly between the different groups, catching snippets of conversation, each more land-obsessed than the other. She didn't even try to be polite by the time she reached Celia, taking her forcibly by the arm and moving her away from her still-talking new friend.

"Charlotte! What are you—"

"Sorry, Celia, but I've never been so bored in my life."

"He's just asked me out! Next weekend!"

"To what, a shearing demonstration?"

"Yes, actually. Are you coming, too?"

"Forget it," Charlotte said. "Go back to him. I'll talk to you later."

If only this were the movies, Charlotte thought, as she stood outside on the balcony on her own. If this were on-screen, a handsome man, her intellectual equal, would follow her out now, light her cigarette with an expensive silver lighter and an expert touch, engage her in witty, flirtatious conversation, and the two of them would fall instantly in love.

"Are you here on your own?"

She spun around. There was no one there. She looked down. Yes, there was. A boy. Seven or eight years old. Younger than Spencer, anyway. He was holding something in his right hand. For a moment she thought it was a cigarette lighter and nearly laughed.

"Yes, I am," she said. "Are you?"

He gestured back into the room. "My dad's in there somewhere."

"What's that accent of yours?" Charlotte said. "American or Canadian?"

"American," the boy said. "Want to play Space Invaders with me?"

Oh, why not? Charlotte thought. It was better than anything else on offer here tonight.

"Sure," she said. "But you better watch out. I'll *murder* you."

IN THE TRAIN on the way back to their boarding school the next day, Celia didn't hesitate to let Charlotte know how unhappy she was. "I invited you to do some serious matchmaking with the right sort of person, not fix you up with my ancient cousin's seven-year-old son," Celia said. "What a waste of a weekend. I was looking for you everywhere last night. And where do I find you? Stuck in front of a TV set with a kid half your age."

"Nearly a third of my age, actually. Ethan's a great kid. You should

be proud of him. He beat the pants off me at Space Invaders as well."
Charlotte looked more closely at her friend. "You're seriously mad at
me, aren't you?"

"Of course I am. All the trouble I went to, inviting all the right
people, the right guys, and you didn't even try to talk to them."

"It wasn't a waste for you, meeting Mr. Sheepdip 1993. And it
wasn't a waste for me either. I think Ethan and I have a very happy future ahead of us."

Celia started to thaw. "He's fallen in love with you, you know. I was
talking to his father this morning. Apparently Ethan didn't shut up
about you all night."

Charlotte grinned. "There. See? I was a hit."

"With a kid, Charlotte. A little kid." Celia pulled out a magazine,
opening it with a sharp, cross flick. "Next time, lift your sights a little
higher, would you? A little older, even."

"Next time? I thought you'd washed your hands of me."

"Not yet. You get one more chance."

"I do? When?"

"Next weekend. I can't believe I'm saying this, but Ethan's invited
you to his eighth birthday party. As his guest of honor."

Chapter Eleven

She was going to be sick, Audrey knew it. She was going to be physically sick, on her costume, on her shoes, on the floor. She couldn't do it. She couldn't go out there.

From her position in the wings, she could hear the other actors saying their lines, word-perfect, their timing spot on. The scene was moving swiftly, leading up to the moment of her entrance. She wanted to run away. She would run except she was suddenly frozen. She knew with complete certainty that if she stepped from here to there, onto that stage, in front of that audience, she would not be able to speak. All her preparation had been for nothing. There were no lines in her head, just white noise, the sound of her fear. Her breathing was shallow and noisy, too noisy. She felt a touch on her hand, the drama teacher, there beside her, an encouraging smile on his face, but it was too late. She couldn't do it. She thought of her family in the audience. Her friends and classmates. No one would applaud her, she knew it. They'd laugh at her, talk about her dismal performance. She couldn't go out there. She couldn't.

Her entrance line came. Once. Twice. She heard the actor say it a third time, her expression changing, alarm registering, knew she was thinking, *What's wrong? Get out here.* Audrey couldn't move. Her teacher touched her arm. "Audrey, that's your cue. Go." She couldn't. Something had happened to her body. It had turned to stone.

"Audrey, go!"

She went. His push—not gentle that time—propelled her. Before she knew what had happened she was on the stage. The spotlights were shining on her. She could feel the sweat beading on her fore-head, under her arms, in the small of her back. The other girls on the stage were staring at her. Waiting for her. She took a step back. She heard her line being hissed from the prompter at the side of the stage. It sounded like more white noise.

She took another step back and bumped against a piece of scenery. Her eyes adjusted to the lights. She could see the audience now. Hundreds of people. Rows of them, staring at her. Waiting for her. Wanting to hear her talk. But there was nothing in her head, no words on her tongue. She was speechless, movement-less, filled with only terror.

A hiss from offstage. "Come *on*, Audrey. Do something. Say something."

Do what? Say what? She couldn't remember anything. Anything at all. She heard the laughter and the chatter start from the back of the hall. It was like a wave coming at her, building into a flood. They were laughing at her. All of them. She heard voices from close by, the other actors, hissing at her. She could see the hatred in their faces. They'd always hated her. They'd made that clear in the final rehearsals, gossiping about her, jealous of her. She'd known that, but now they were furious with her, too. More laughter from the audience. How long had she been standing there? A minute? More? Less?

She opened her mouth. Nothing. No sound. She tried again. A squeak. A squeak like a mouse, like a door needing oil. A stupid, silly, ridiculous sound. This time there was no mistaking the laughter. One of the other girls on the stage had the giggles now, too. Audrey could hear her, mocking her, laughing at her. Everyone in the auditorium was staring at her now, laughing at her, *laughing* at her. She couldn't bear it. Didn't anyone understand what this meant to her? This was everything to her. She turned, eyes panicked, to see the teacher preparing the understudy, to see the other girl struggling into a costume. . . .

No, it couldn't happen. They had to let her stay on. She'd find her voice, she would. She was trying. Couldn't they see that? She opened her mouth. Another squeak.

She felt a hand on her arm, one of the other actors. Her face was angry, her grip tight, her nails digging into Audrey's arm, as if she was going to drag her off the stage, there, now, in front of everyone. No. No! She wouldn't let her. How dare she even try. Audrey took a step back, wrenching her arm away, bumping into another actor she hadn't seen. She turned to apologize, no sound, still nothing, turned again, tripped on her long dress and started to fall. For a second she found her balance, but as quickly she lost it again. The sound she made as she crashed to the floor, her dress riding up around her bare legs, sounded like a thunderclap.

"Is she drunk?" she heard someone ask, his voice loud, too loud. More ripples of sound from the audience, whispering, giggling, laughing. She tried to get up. She couldn't. She couldn't. Her dress was tangled around her body, her limbs felt numb. She wanted to talk, she wanted to say her lines, she wanted to insist she wasn't drunk, of course she wasn't drunk, but she couldn't seem to move, to talk, to find even a single word.

She started crying, the tears spilling from her eyes. Somehow dragging herself to the edge of the stage, she curled into a tight ball, her head tucked against her knees, wishing, hoping, feeling as though she were going to die. She could barely hear the commotion around her—hisses, brief arguments—until somehow she registered that the play was continuing. Against a murmur of voices, even laughs from the audience, she saw from her huddled position on the floor that the understudy was now on stage, her dress only half done up, reading from a battered script, her voice like a monotone, instead of Audrey, in her costume, her lines perfect, delivering a moving and triumphant performance. . . .

The rest of the play passed in a daze for her. Within minutes of the curtain falling, she was surrounded by the actors, the stagehands, anyone who'd had anything to do with the play. The play she had just ruined. She still couldn't talk, couldn't explain, couldn't untangle her limbs, couldn't stand up. All she could do was stay curled in that ball, unable to stop crying silent tears, sick and heartbroken and as lonely as she had ever felt. She had not just ruined her acting career. She had ruined her life.

Charlotte appeared, pushing through the crowd, grabbing her arm. "What is it? Are you sick?"

Audrey could only shake her head.

"What is it, then? Audrey, what happened?"

A girl beside them spoke up, her voice angry. "Stage fright, allegedly."

Another girl scoffed. "She's the one who said she knew this whole play backward. She's been telling us all for weeks how to do our parts."

Charlotte dragged Audrey up from the ground with difficulty and began to pull her through the crowd. "Let us through, please. Let us through."

Audrey was now powerless. She'd rehearsed every moment in her head, imagining herself on the stage bowing after a victorious performance, accepting the bouquets of flowers. Not this, something so terrible. A river she couldn't cross, a black chasm, so wide and so deep and so frightening. It could never happen again. She could never again set foot in that school, talk about acting, talk about anything, ever, ever again.

At Templeton Hall, Nina's "housesitting" with Hope was not going well. She had guessed it wouldn't, within minutes of arriving at the Hall with Tom that afternoon.

"I'm so sorry, Nina," Eleanor had said. "Hope was fine this morning, fine at lunch, but she hasn't come out of her room since just after two o'clock."

"Should I go and say something through the door? Just let her know I'm here? She does know I'm here, doesn't she?"

"She does. Yes." Eleanor hesitated. "We reminded her today you were coming. That's when she locked herself in her room."

"Don't worry about it," Nina said as cheerily as possible. "If she wants to come down and join us, that's great, and if she doesn't, that's fine, too."

"We'll leave Melbourne straight after breakfast tomorrow," Eleanor said. "We'll be back before lunchtime. Before eleven, hopefully."

"Take your time. Don't rush. We'll be fine."

Fine? If only, Nina thought now as she walked up the stairs again, calling Hope's name once more. Since Tom had casually told her that Hope's bedroom door was open but the room empty, they'd been roaming the house, calling her name. There was no reply.

"She must have gone outside," Tom said. "We've looked in every room."

"I didn't hear the front door open, did you?" Nina checked the time. Only nine p.m. It was going to be a long night. "Hope?" she called again. "Hope, please, come out."

It was during their second search of the house that she appeared. Nina and Tom had just come down the stairs once again when the front door opened and Hope walked in. She was wearing a dressing-gown and a shawl. Her feet were bare.

"Hope, thank God," Nina said, unable to hide her relief. "I've been so worried."

Hope barely looked at her. There was no acknowledgment that they'd met before, either. "Really? Why?"

"Because Eleanor asked me—" She stopped, as Hope gave her a very unpleasant smile.

"Asked you what?" Hope said. "To look after me? How amusing. Because Eleanor told me that you and your son were here to look after the Hall. And that being the case, I decided it made sense to leave you both to it and take a nice evening walk."

She smiled as she saw Nina glance toward the phone. "Go on, ring Eleanor. Right in the middle of Audrey's special night. You think I don't know where they are? I'm her godmother, you know. Nice of them to invite me, wasn't it?"

"They didn't think you were . . ." Nina tried to choose the right words. ". . . well enough."

Hope scoffed. "You have absolutely no idea what they think, and if you do, you shouldn't. You're our neighbor by accident of geography. It doesn't give you any right to know me, to babysit me"—she nearly spat the word—"or to know our family business."

Nina kept her voice neutral with some difficulty. "I don't want to know your family business. Eleanor simply asked me for a favor and I was happy to help out."

"Oh, I can just see how she would have done that." Hope changed her voice, put on a sweet expression, " 'We do all we can for poor Hope, but I'm afraid it's just take-take-take with her.' It's lies. All of it. I gave up my own life for her, for all of them, to come here, design their entire property. Do I get any thanks? Do I get to show people around anymore? No!"

Nina turned and gestured to Tom to go into the living room. She didn't want him to hear this. He wasn't happy to go, but he did. After he'd shut the door, she turned back to Hope. "Hope, I'm sure Henry and Eleanor would be happy to let you take some groups—"

"You aren't sure. You have no idea. You don't know us. Stop pretending that you do. She's just using you, like they used me. They started with your son, trying to keep Spencer out of juvenile detention, but it won't work, and it's your son that will be spoiled. You don't know half of what the two of them get up to, do you? He's a bad child, that Spencer. Oh, he's high-spirited, they say. He's not. He's bad. Evil. And he'll damage your son, too. I mean it."

Nina refused to rise to Hope's bait.

The other woman kept talking. "You'll regret getting mixed up with this family, you know. They'll suck you dry like they sucked me dry. But don't say you weren't warned. You or your son. Get away while you still can. I wish I had."

Nina could only stand open-mouthed as Hope stalked past her and up the stairs.

Tom went up to bed not long after. Nina talked down her own nerves as she walked around turning off the lights, ignoring the creaks as the Hall settled itself at the end of the day. The altercation with Hope echoed around her. Her words had struck too many chords with Nina.

She suddenly didn't want to be at the Hall anymore. She wanted to be home, just her and Tom, in their own small house, as far from the whole Templeton family as possible. Hope was right. It had been a mistake to let Tom play with Spencer, a mistake to let Gracie visit her so often, a mistake to allow herself to be pulled into their orbit. She should have trusted her instincts and kept her distance.

By the time she'd finally locked all the doors and climbed into bed in one of the spare rooms—twice the size of her own room at home and furnished with so many antiques she was nervous to touch anything—her mind was made up. It was time to pull away from them all. It was the best thing, for her and for Tom.

A noise woke her at three a.m. Her heart started beating faster as she lay trying to work out what it was. A door opening. Footsteps. Low voices. Instantly wide awake, she got out of bed, tiptoed to the doorway, and glanced down the hallway. Hope's door was shut. She quickly checked Tom, in Spencer's room, also furnished—incongruously—with antiques. He was asleep. She heard more whispers downstairs, the creak of a floorboard. Then a deeper voice. Henry Templeton's voice.

She came to the top of the stairs and looked down just as the lights came on. In the entrance hall were Eleanor, Gracie, Spencer, Henry, and a young woman Nina knew had to be Audrey. Nina hadn't realized she was coming back with them. She moved quickly down the stairs, pulling her dressing gown around her. "You're back already?"

"An unexpected change of plan," Eleanor said, with the quickest of glances in Audrey's direction. "Did everything go all right here?"

Nina noticed Audrey's miserable face. Gracie looked like she'd been crying. Henry and Eleanor were tense, Spencer tired and mutinous. Something bad must have happened, with Charlotte, perhaps. Something Eleanor couldn't share yet. Fine, Nina thought. If she was going to try keeping her distance from this family, she'd start now.

She found a smile from somewhere. "Everything was just fine," she lied.

LESS THAN twelve hours later, Nina was back in her own living room, trying and failing to do some work, tired and nervy from lack of sleep. She and Tom had left the Hall before the others woke, leaving a note on the kitchen table. Tom wasn't happy, even when she explained that something had happened in Melbourne and the family needed time alone.

"But Spencer and I had plans for this morning. I don't have to be at cricket until after lunch."

Nina stood her ground. He took out his anger on her by spending an hour throwing a cricket ball against the rainwater tank. Good for his cricket practice, bad for her nerves. It would have to be like this to begin with, she told herself. He'd forget about Spencer and the Templetons eventually. She was quietly relieved when he was collected for the match by her friend Jenny, leaving her in peace to do some work at last.

It was short-lived. She'd just started work when she heard her name being called. Moments later, the front door opened and Gracie walked in without knocking, immediately launching into a detailed account of the night's events in Melbourne.

". . . so it's just a tragedy, Nina," Gracie said as she finished. "Audrey's big dream to be an actress is in ruins and she's inconsolable. Mum has tried bringing her breakfast in bed, magazines; Dad even brought a TV into her room to distract her, but nothing has worked. She won't speak, she won't eat, she won't stop crying. I can see why, the poor thing. As I said to her, what can she do with her life now that her dream has been shattered?"

Nina kept her reply matter-of-fact. "Gracie, her dream isn't shattered. It was just a bad case of stage fright. She'll have another chance in another play at school."

"She won't. She wrote Mum a note to say she can never go back there again. They all hate her now. It's a very competitive school, you see. Cutthroat. Charlotte told me all about it today."

"Charlotte's home, too?" Nina asked. She didn't remember seeing her with the others.

"Oh, no. We spoke on the phone this morning. She's still insisting she won't come back while Hope's here." Gracie lowered her voice. "Can I tell you a secret?"

Nina's vow not to get caught up in the Templetons' lives anymore wasn't going well. She nodded.

"I think Charlotte's up to something," Gracie said. "Something exciting. I asked her what she was going to do when she finishes school this year, once she turns eighteen, and she whispered that everything was organized, it was a very exciting plan, and she'd tell me as soon as she could. I think it might have something to do with going away. She said to me in a very mysterious voice, 'Have passport, will travel, Gracie.' What do you think she means? She hasn't got any money, none of us do, so where could she afford to go?"

"I don't know, Gracie."

Gracie looked up at Nina with a sad expression. "I think we need a cup of tea, don't you? Can I make you one, Nina? You must be tired after your late night, too?"

Nina's resolve faltered. Gracie was right. She *was* tired and she *would* like a cup of tea. It looked like she'd have to put off her withdrawal from the Templetons for one more day.

THEY WERE just finishing their tea when they heard the sound of a car. Seconds later the back door opened and Tom ran in, dressed in his cricket whites. Nina glanced at the clock. He was home early. Before she had a chance to ask why, he threw his arms around her and to her astonishment tried and nearly succeeded in lifting her up off the ground.

"I'm in, Mum. I'm on the team!"

"You are?" For a second she didn't know what he was talking about, until she remembered that he and his friend Ben had been involved in cricket trials today. With everything happening at Templeton Hall, it had slipped her mind.

"Ben got picked, too! Both of us!" He threw his cricket gloves up into the air and caught them with a leap.

"Tom, that's fantastic! Congratulations!" Nina pulled her son into another, proper hug. He let her, any tension between them now gone.

He turned and noticed their visitor then, stepping back from the hug immediately. "Gracie, hi. I didn't see you there."

"Congratulations, Tom!" Gracie beamed at him. "You've made a team for something?"

He nodded, shy and proud at once. "It's part of a national competition. I've been picked for the junior country team. If we win against the city team next month, we get to play against all the other states, maybe even internationally."

"Tom, that's fantastic!" She threw her arms around him, too. "What sport is it?"

"*Gracie,*" Tom said, all shyness now gone. "Cricket, of course. I'm a fast bowler."

"Oh, I love cricket! We all do, Dad especially. When's your big match? Can we come and watch, too? Will you come over to the Hall now and tell everyone? We need cheering up."

Nina stepped in. "He can't, Gracie. Sorry."

"Sure," Tom said, at the same time.

Nina tried again. "I don't think so, Tom. Not now. And perhaps you should head home, too, Gracie. Your mother must be wondering where you are."

Gracie's face fell. "She knows I'm here. Don't you like me visiting? I won't come again if you don't want me to."

"Gracie, I didn't mean that."

"What did you mean, then?" Tom said.

Nina was now floundering. "I meant to say that just because we're neighbors doesn't mean we should spend too much time in each other's pockets. We all need our own space now and then." She was echoing Hope's words, she realized. But the other woman had been right. It was only geographical coincidence that they'd all met.

"You just want a bit of a break from us, is that what you mean?" Gracie said. "A few days? Longer? Would you prefer I made my visits more formal? If I rang first?"

"Gracie, no, you've misunderstood." Both children were now looking at Nina with great interest. Where was the sense of adult wisdom and superiority she was supposed to feel in situations like this? "We're all so busy, perhaps it might be better if we don't—"

Gracie's face cleared. "It's Hope, isn't it? Do you feel like Charlotte does? You don't want anything to do with us while she's there?"

Oh, why not accept the lifeline, Nina thought. "Yes, that's part of it. I think we—Tom and I—might have upset her in some way last night and that's not fair on the rest of you."

"It wasn't your fault, I promise. Everyone upsets her. She upsets everyone. That's just the way it is with her." She beamed at Nina. "And I'd hate to have to book ahead to see you. I love visiting whenever I feel like it. Everything's more fun if it's sponta—" She frowned.

"Spontaneous?" Tom suggested.

"That's it!" Gracie said.

"You're right," Tom said. "I'm spontaneously going out to practice my bowling."

Gracie turned eagerly to him. "Can I help?"

"Are you a good batsman?"

"I might be. I don't know. I could try."

"Okay, then. But if I hit you with the ball, you're not allowed to cry."

An hour later, they were still outside playing. Nina had returned to her painting, periodically glancing out the open window to see Gracie bravely standing in front of the rainwater tank brandishing the cricket bat, while Tom pelted ball after ball at her. As Nina watched, a particularly fast delivery missed the bat and hit Gracie on the leg. Nina held her breath, waiting for the scream. It didn't come, even though Gracie's face was bright red and her hands clenched tight on the bat, obviously in pain.

Tom ran up to her. "Are you okay, Gracie?"

"Fine," Gracie said brightly. "I didn't feel a thing. Ready for the next one when you are."

Nina saw Tom give her an admiring smile, before he picked up the ball again. "You're almost as much fun as Spencer," she heard him say over his shoulder as he walked back to his mark.

Gracie's smile nearly lit up the backyard.

Chapter Twelve

FOR THE NEXT WEEK, Nina avoided any more contact with the residents of Templeton Hall. It wasn't deliberate, she told herself. She just happened to be out during the hours Gracie normally visited. Tom was so busy with extra cricket practice that he'd stopped asking if he could go and visit Spencer. And there'd been no phone calls from any of the Templeton Hall adults either. They were obviously busy dealing with Audrey and Hope. It was a good thing. She refused to let herself wonder what was going on in the Hall, and refused to rise to Hilary's bait when they spoke one night.

"A whole week without contact? Have you been banished from the kingdom?"

"Of course not. I'm glad of the peace, to be honest."

"When people say 'to be honest,' I always think they're lying, don't you?"

Nina ignored that. "I'm too busy getting Tom ready for the match to worry about the Templetons."

"How is he?" Hilary asked. "Excited? Nervous?"

"Both, I think. I don't know. I've never seen him like this before."

Since the day he'd made the team he'd been preoccupied, distracted, distant even. He spent all his spare time outside bowling against the tank, coming in only to eat dinner, barely speaking to her, going straight to his room after he'd done the dishes, not even staying up to watch TV. He'd asked if he could go into school earlier, telling her he wanted to make use of the cricket nets at the school oval. She'd tried chatting as they drove in each morning, but he spent the journeys gazing out the window. She was finding it hard to get even two words out of him, she told her sister.

"No wonder," Hilary said. "Think of the pressure. Give him my love, won't you?"

At practice one evening, Nina casually asked Ben's mum if she'd noticed any change in her son since he'd got the news. Jenny laughed. "Any change? He's a brand-new kid. Focused. Obedient. Eating every vegetable I put in front of him. Out doing push-ups every minute of the day. It's a big deal for them both, Nina."

Nina began to realize how big. The local paper ran a story on page one about Tom and Ben. The school hung a banner on the front gate. People in Castlemaine suddenly seemed to know who she was. "You're Tom-the-cricketer's mum, aren't you?"

The match was taking place the following Thursday in Ballarat, just over an hour's drive away. The night before, Nina checked Tom's bag for the third time. His whites couldn't be any whiter. She cleaned his shoes, then he cleaned them again, and then, secretly, she did them one more time. She cooked a special meal, his favorite, lasagna, telling him how good it was for him, all the energy it would give him the next day. She told him one more time how proud she was. He barely acknowledged her.

She tried to find the words to tell him how proud his father would have been of him, too. Something kept stopping her, though, some instinct that it would be a mistake to mention Nick. Was it a sign? she wondered. A good sign, proof that she had come to an acceptance at last about Nick? That it was enough that *she* was proud of Tom? That Nick's absence didn't have to rule over them for the rest of their lives? She dared to hope it was true, feeling somehow lighter than she'd felt in a long time.

Just before nine o'clock, Tom announced he was going to bed. She forced herself not to kiss him good night, reminding herself that he was twelve years old now. At his bedroom door, she settled on wishing him a good night's sleep and reassuring him that she would set both her alarm clocks, before finally turning off his light and gently closing his bedroom door. She wouldn't let herself be hurt by the fact that he didn't answer her.

An hour later, she'd just turned off the TV and was about to go to bed when she heard his voice behind her. "Mum?" He was standing in the doorway.

"Tom! Can't you sleep?" She patted the couch beside her, smiling. "No wonder. I'm very, very proud of you, did you know that? Have I told you recently?"

He didn't move.

"Tom? Are you all right?"

"Gracie said she was sorry about my father dying."

Nina stopped patting the couch. "What?"

His voice was very low. She had to strain to hear. "After we were playing cricket here last week. She said she was sorry my dad had died and that he'd never met me but she was sure he'd have been proud of me for getting on the team. But he did meet me, didn't he?"

Nina felt her face flush red. This was it. The conversation she'd dreaded. The scene Hilary had warned her would happen. But now? Like this, the night before the match? No. She couldn't do it to him. Pushing away angry thoughts toward Gracie, she tried to buy herself some time, tried to keep her voice casual. "Gracie said that?"

"She said you'd told her all about Dad's accident. That it happened the day I was born, not three years later. That he died on the way to the hospital."

Nina heard Hilary's voice in her head. *You have to tell him yourself. It will be worse for you and for him if he finds out any other way.* She swallowed. "Let's talk about this tomorrow, Tom. After the match."

"I need to know now. Did Dad meet me or not?"

Tell him the truth, Nina. You have to.

She gazed across at her son, hating herself for what she was about to do and say to him.

"Tom, can you come and sit here, please? There's something I need to tell you."

THE NEXT DAY Nina needed three cups of coffee before she felt even half awake. She knew that Tom hadn't slept any better. On the surface, it looked like a normal day in their house. He ate his breakfast, watched a cartoon on TV, fed the cat, did the dishes. But he was angry with her, she knew that. Filled with anger. She could see it in the set of his jaw, in the flash of his eyes, in the way he looked at everything in the room except her. He hadn't looked directly at her since she'd told him the truth about his father's death.

She wanted Hilary to witness this. *See why I was right to keep it a lie?* But she knew she had no one to blame but herself. She was the one who'd set it all in train, by lying in the first place. She was the one who'd told Gracie—Gracie, of all people—the real story. She could never have expected Gracie to keep it to herself. She was just a child. So why *had* she told her everything? What would one more lie have mattered? She knew the answer, deep inside herself. She'd been trialing it, carefully bringing the truth out into the air, to see what would happen.

Now she knew. Tom was devastated. She had ruined their relationship. Spoiled one of the biggest days of his life.

She glanced at the clock. "Tom, we'd better get going." She didn't try to make her voice sound cheery. She felt as wretched as she knew he did.

NINETY MINUTES LATER she was sitting in the grandstand of the Ballarat cricket ground, watching her son warm up. Even from a distance, she could sense the energy coming off him. More than energy. A fierceness.

Beside her, Ben's mother, Jenny, obviously noticed something, too. "Good God, Nina, what did you give Tom for breakfast? Nuclear-powered cornflakes?"

Nina could only half smile. If only Jenny knew. As she watched her son throw ball after ball with great force, she knew exactly what was powering him. Fury at her.

She'd felt it coming off him the whole way to Ballarat. He stared out the window and wouldn't talk to her. He got out of the car the second they arrived and ran over toward the change rooms where his teammates were assembling, his bag bouncing on his back. She could only watch him go, and make her own way across to the grandstand. Jenny had waved up at her soon after, arriving minutes later with two cups of coffee.

"Need this as much as I do?" Jenny settled into her seat. "How was

Tom this morning? Ben was literally sick with nerves, poor kid. He spent the whole trip here babbling, 'What if I miss every shot?' 'What if I get out for a duck?' . . ."

As Jenny continued describing the scene in her house that morning, and how her husband had helped calm Ben down, Nina's thoughts turned to Nick again. Today of all days she'd never felt his absence so strongly. Seeing Tom out on the field, so like his father with his tall, lanky build, his quick movements . . . It should have been Nick here beside her, not Jenny, the two of them cheering for their son, so proud of him, together.

The country team batted first. Ben played well, forty-two runs not out. Tom, on the team for his bowling rather than batting skills, still managed to score twelve runs, including a four. He hit the ball with a huge swing, sending it across to the boundary, receiving loud applause.

"Wow," Jenny said to Nina. "I didn't know he could bat, too."

Nina didn't either.

Tom's team was two overs into their first bowling innings when the Templetons arrived.

Jenny saw them first. "Good God. It's the Addams family."

Nina knew it was the current local nickname for the Templetons, a play on their pale skin as well as the big house. She turned to look, sure Jenny was mistaken. She wasn't. There they all were, carrying rugs and baskets, making their way to the edge of the oval. Henry, Eleanor, Hope, Gracie, Audrey—in a pair of large sunglasses—and a very excited Spencer, who was already leaning over the boundary fence, cupping his hands to his mouth and shouting out to Tom on the field. Nina saw Tom give a flash of a smile and the briefest of acknowledgments.

Jenny stared in amazement. "What's lured them into the real world?"

Nina didn't reply. She didn't need to. Gracie gave everyone the answer as she reached into the bag beside her and unfurled a white banner that read: *Tom to Win!!!!*

"They're Tom's fan club?" Jenny said. "Nina, you dark horse! I didn't realize you knew them."

"I don't. We don't. Not really."

Jenny obviously wanted to ask more but it was Tom's first turn to bowl. Nina sat, holding her breath. It was a regional competition. She'd watched Tom bowl many times before. This wasn't the Ashes and they weren't playing at Lord's, but she had never been as nervous as this. It felt like her whole relationship with her son hinged on this first ball.

Afterward, she couldn't even tell Tom she saw it happen. The ball left his hand so quickly that she, as well as all the spectators and most especially the poor batsman, didn't see it. It clean-bowled all three stumps of the wicket. There was no protest from the batsman, just a huge roar from Tom's teammates, even louder cheering from the crowd.

Tom took five wickets that afternoon. In the clamor after the match, Nina received so many congratulatory hugs it was as if she'd been on the pitch herself.

"You must be so proud," the other school mums kept saying to her. People who didn't know her had things to say as well. "You and your husband have a star on your hands."

It took her ten minutes to make her way from the stand to where everyone was gathering in preparation for the cup presentation. Tom was still surrounded by teammates and new fans. He was smiling, his face alight, dirty with sweat, his shirt half buttoned. She'd never seen him look so happy. She had to stop herself from running across and pulling him into a hug. As she came closer, Spencer ran past her, shouting Tom's name.

"Champion! It was all my coaching, wasn't it?"

Behind him were Henry, Eleanor, Hope, then Audrey and Gracie. Nina's private moment with Tom lasted five seconds—she only had time to hug him tightly and whisper, "I'm so proud of you," before the Templetons surrounded him, shaking his hand. She tried to ignore the fact that Tom hadn't hugged her back and that he seemed happier sharing his success with Spencer and his family than her. She exchanged greetings with Henry and Eleanor, conscious the other parents were watching them curiously.

"Big celebrations at your house tonight?" Jenny said beside her, as the presentation began.

Nina nodded, already trying to plan the best night for Tom. His favorite pizza? His pick of videos? Maybe Ben would like to come and sleep over? She was about to ask Jenny, when the speeches began. Afterward, just as she was looking for Jenny again, Tom came up to her. He still wouldn't look her in the eyes. It hurt her to notice. But his excitement was still high, the thrill of the win spilling color into his cheeks. "Mum, Spencer's invited me to sleep over at Templeton Hall tonight. Is that okay?"

Tonight? she wanted to say. No! She wanted it to be the two of them tonight, celebrating together. She wanted to tell him again and again how proud she was, even if he was so angry with her that he couldn't bear to look at her.

Spencer appeared beside them. "Can you?" he said. "Nina, can he?"

She felt ambushed. She also knew she couldn't say no. Somehow, from somewhere, she found a big happy smile. She casually tousled her son's hair. "Of course he can. If that's what he wants."

Tom turned and left with Spencer and his family without saying good-bye to her.

HE WON'T EVEN talk to me, Hilary." Nina was crying as she spoke. "He won't look at me. I should never have told him. I told you it was the wrong thing to do."

"It wasn't, Nina. He had to know someday. The timing would never have been good."

"But it should have been a great day for the two of us, and it was ruined. I ruined it."

"Nina, he'll come round. He will. You're his mother. He loves you."

"He likes them more. You should have seen him today, Hilary. He couldn't get over to the Hall quickly enough. I'm sitting here on my own and they're the ones throwing a party for him."

"So go over there, too."

"He doesn't want me to."

"Nina, you're his mother. He's hurt and confused. Go over there."

"I'd feel pathetic just turning up."

"Any more pathetic than you feel sitting on your own now? Take over his favorite snacks. Leave again if you want, but at least he'll know you love him."

It was good advice. Nina took a deep breath, feeling herself become calmer, having something to do. "What would I do without you, Hilary?"

"Shrivel up and die? Now get off the phone and go and see your son."

Nina thought about ringing the Templetons first, before she realized she would be asking permission to come and see her own son. She went to the kitchen, found a packet of Tom's favorite biscuits, his favorite soft drink. She got a clean pair of his pajamas. Five minutes later she was knocking at the front door of Templeton Hall.

Audrey answered the door without a word. She was still wearing the sunglasses.

Nina smiled and held up the bag. "I just thought I'd drop these off for Tom."

Audrey turned away. Nina had no choice but to follow her silently down the hallway.

She was relieved to see that when the Hall wasn't on show, it was as cluttered as any normal family house. There were football boots beside the grand staircase, newspapers on the dining-room table, and what was clearly the week's clean washing half sorted on one of the side cupboards. The sight relaxed Nina a little.

As they came into the kitchen, Gracie saw her first. "Nina! Now everything's perfect!"

Nina glanced around. There were balloons in every corner and streamers hanging from the ceiling. The large table was covered with glasses, soft drinks, sandwiches. It was a celebration party. The Templetons were giving Tom the party she should have given him.

Tom didn't acknowledge her. He was at the head of the table, still in his cricket clothes, his hair in spikes. Spencer was sitting beside him. Would Tom have told Spencer about his father? Nina wondered. Had he told all the Templetons?

"I brought these for you, Tom," she said, holding out the biscuits and drink. When he still didn't look at her, she tried her hardest to find an even cheerier voice, suddenly unable to bear how much she had hurt him. "Your favorites."

"This is a big mistake, Nina," Henry Templeton said then, coming over and casually greeting her with a kiss to her cheek, perfect host style. "We shouldn't be celebrating Tom's success. We should scupper him while we have the chance, while he's still young. In years to come, when he's playing for Australia and mowing down England's finest batsmen, we'll know it's all our fault. Isn't that right, Tom?"

"One day, maybe," Tom said shyly.

"Of course it will happen, Tom," she said, hating the too-bright tone in her voice. She wanted him to get up and say, "I'm glad you're here too, Mum." He didn't.

Eleanor seemed to sense something was amiss. "Nina, please have a seat. I was about to ring you to invite you over to eat with us. You've saved me a phone call."

Nina took a seat beside Audrey, across from Gracie, who was now humming happily under her breath as she arranged Nina's biscuits on a large and valuable-looking platter. Spencer was talking to Tom about the match, gazing at him in something like awe. There was no sign of Hope, Nina was glad to see.

There was noisy chatter for the next few minutes, everyone helping themselves to something to eat, Gracie keeping a special eye on her, Nina was touched to notice.

"Audrey knows you know what happened to her, by the way," Gracie said in a loud whisper, as she sat beside Nina. "So please don't feel shy about mentioning it. And just ignore her sunglasses. She's been crying so much, they're to hide her puffy eyes."

Nina took the hint. "I'm sorry, Audrey," she said, turning to the young woman. "I've heard stage fright is an awful thing. So many—"

Audrey just crossed her arms and studiedly turned away.

Gracie smiled. "It's all right, Audrey. We can talk about this in front of Nina. She's almost family."

Tom and Spencer stood up then. "Mum, will you excuse us?" Spencer said to Eleanor.

"Where are you going?" Eleanor said.

"Tom, have you had enough to eat?" Nina asked.

They'd spoken at the same time. They looked at each other and smiled.

"Sorry," Nina said. "Force of habit. It's your house, your rules."

Eleanor turned to the boys. "Yes, you're both excused. Where are you going?"

They both shrugged at exactly the same time. Everyone laughed.

"Twins, separated at birth," Henry said with a grin.

Nina forced herself not to watch Tom as he left the room, stopped herself from following him to say sorry again. She focused instead on trying to look calm and relaxed, as if sitting here at a party with the Templetons was something she did every day.

"You must have been so proud today, Nina," Eleanor said. "He's so talented. My cousins in England were great bowlers. I suffered through many games myself when I was younger, but they never had the energy Tom has. Was his father a good cricketer? It often runs in families, doesn't it?"

Nina glanced back and forth between Gracie and Eleanor. Did Eleanor know? Had Gracie told her? It was as if Gracie knew what she was thinking.

"I haven't told them about your husband, Nina," she said. "I wanted to, but when I mentioned it to Tom last week he went so strange that I thought I better not tell anyone else." She suddenly went red and put her hand to her mouth. "Nina, I'm sorry. I told Tom. I'm so sorry. I forgot it was a secret."

Eleanor was alarmed. "Gracie, what are you talking about?"

"It's all right, Eleanor," Nina said. "And it's all right, Gracie." The words she was about to say still felt foreign in her mouth but it was important to repeat them now. She tried to buy herself some time, to think of the best way to do it. "My husband was a good sportsman, Eleanor, yes. He played football rather than cricket, but he was very fit."

"Was? Are you divorced?" Henry asked. "If you'll excuse me being so curious."

Nina took a breath. "No, I'm not, Henry. I'm a widow. Tom's father, my husband, was killed in a car accident."

"Just a few hours before Tom was born," Gracie added softly. "Tom never met him."

"Gracie!" Eleanor said again. "Nina, I'm so sorry. I didn't realize. I wouldn't have asked."

"It's all right." It was. It was actually easier to say it than to invent a tale, to try to step gingerly between truth and make-believe. "Nick was killed on his way to the hospital."

"Oh, Nina." Eleanor's eyes filled with tears.

Nina wouldn't cry again. She wouldn't. Not here, not now, in front of the Templetons. Not when there was a chance that Tom would come in to find her, here, ruining his alternative life as well. She stood up suddenly. "I should go."

"Nina, no." Henry reached across and touched her arm. "You can't. It's too sad for you to be on your own. A day like today, of course you'd have loved Tom's father to be there to celebrate with you." He stood up. "I believe this calls for a toast, to you and to Tom. Not only are you a woman of courage and fortitude, but you have a son to be proud of and we're honored to know you both. Eleanor, please, fill the glasses."

"What a great idea," a voice from the doorway said, too loudly. "Make mine a double."

They all turned. Hope was there, swaying. As they watched, she slowly fell forward.

I DON'T *CARE* that she was drunk," Tom said. Moments after Hope's sudden arrival and collapse, a hurried conversation between Nina and Eleanor led to her calling Tom in from playing with Spencer. They were now driving home and Tom was extremely unhappy about it. "Why did we have to leave? Spencer sees her like that all the time."

"Spencer's her nephew. It's better we left, if Hope's in one of her moods."

"It's not a mood. She's just drunk. She does a few bad things, then she just falls asleep. You don't have to hide me from it. I've seen you drink."

"You've seen me have a few glasses of wine, not collapse like that, or climb out on the roof like Hope does."

"Spencer said it's great up there. We're going to try—" Tom stopped whatever it was he was going to say. "Forget it. Thanks for spoiling everything again."

Nina pulled the car to the side of the road. She'd planned to delay this conversation until they were home again, but she had to do it now. She turned toward him, filled with a sudden fury herself, determined to speak, determined to ignore the fact he was staring out the window and she was speaking only to his profile.

"Tom, I am so sorry and I am so proud and I love you so much and it's breaking my heart that I've upset you, that you found out the truth about your dad's death the way you did, from Gracie and not from me. But I want you to understand why I did it."

"You lied to me."

"Yes, I did. Because I wanted to protect you."

"From what? The truth?"

"Yes, Tom. The truth. Because I've always hated the truth. I've always hated the fact that your dad didn't meet you, that he never knew what a beautiful son he helped make, what a great kid you are. I hate it every day that he isn't here with us, watching you grow, enjoying every minute of you the way I do. I didn't want you to ever think for a minute that your dad hadn't had a chance to hold you, to kiss you, to tell you how much he loved you. So I made up a different story. What I thought was a better story."

"You said he was there when I was born."

"And he was. I still believe that. If it was possible for him to be there, I know he would have been. In spirit, in whatever way he could."

"I don't believe in ghosts."

"In whatever way possible, Tom, your father was there. He wanted you so much and loved you so much, as much as I love you, every single day. Please, Tom. Please forgive me."

A shrug.

That hurt, more than anything he could have said to her. She wanted to shout at him then, to tell him to stop picking up Spencer Templeton's habits, to stop going to Templeton Hall, to stop making it so obvious that he preferred life with the Templetons to his lonely life with her, without his dad and without any brothers or sisters. Did he think she didn't realize he should have had a different life? A better life than the one she'd been able to give him?

She managed to stop the words but she couldn't stop the tears. To Tom's obvious horror, she was suddenly crying. She tried to stop the tears, but it was impossible. Her whole body ached with the hurt.

He turned toward her then. "Mum, don't. Please don't."

She could see he was upset now, too, that he needed comforting as well, but there was no stopping her own feelings now, all the anger, the hiding, the guilt of lying to him spilling up and out of her, the sound of her sobs filling the car. She tried to speak, tried to explain to Tom all over again, but it was as if she'd run out of words. All she seemed to have now were tears.

Tom reached over to her, reached for her hand. "Mum, I'm sorry. I'm sorry I've been mean to you today. Please, stop crying."

That stopped her. She took a shuddering breath, wiped her eyes, tried to fix it all. "Tom, you weren't mean. You weren't. I deserved it. I should have told you years ago. I should have told everyone before now. Let you tell people whatever you wanted to tell them. It's my own fault."

"It's not your fault."

"It is. I wanted you to have a perfect life, Tom. The best you could." Out it all came. All the plans she and Nick had made, the four children, going into business together. An idea, a dream they'd had, that when their kids were still under ten, they would buy a camper-van, take a year off work and school, and simply travel around Australia together. She talked about the day she'd found out she was pregnant with Tom, how thrilled they'd been. She talked about how they'd decided they didn't want to find out if he was a boy or a girl. She told him about Nick driving her at snail's pace to the hospital, how excited he'd been, how happy. How loved Tom had been before he was born. How loved he was now.

They were both quiet for a long moment afterward, Nina's shuddering breaths the only sound in the car.

It was Tom who broke the silence, as he turned in his seat again and looked at her. Directly at her, for the first time that day. "I took five wickets today, Mum. It's a school record. Five of them."

Her tears came again then, different tears, soothing this time. "You sure did, Tom." She pulled him into her arms and he wrapped his arms back around her. "My wonderful, clever Tom. Five fantastic wickets."

Chapter Thirteen

Back at Templeton Hall, as far as Gracie could tell, things were going from bad to worse.

It was all Hope's fault. The fun had ended the moment she appeared in the doorway, muttered something about a double something, and then collapsed. There'd been such a fuss then, everyone leaping up from the table, shouting and talking across one another, before Hope woke up again and let Gracie's dad half drag her across to the chair at the end of the table. Barely a minute later, Nina went out into the hall and called Tom, and suddenly everyone was saying good-bye and it was just the family left in the kitchen.

Now, as her parents still fussed over Hope, who at least was sitting up again, Gracie slipped silently away from the table and into the farthest corner of the kitchen to take down the balloons. It kept her busy, and out of her parents' sight, which hopefully meant they would talk to Hope in an adult way, forgetting she was there, listening. She noticed that Audrey had also moved away from the table to the chair by the stove. Audrey had got very good at sitting still, so that you sometimes didn't notice she was there. Gracie had tried to stay still herself for an hour one day but it had proved impossible.

Eleanor was furious at Hope. Gracie had never heard her talk to her sister like that.

"How *dare* you, Hope! You *promised*! That was the deal. You could come back here if you didn't drink anymore and you respected our family life. Don't you think I have enough on my plate, *we* have enough on our plate, without having to worry about you? Have you even noticed the mess we are all in? Charlotte refusing to come home while you're here. The bills coming in without any way to pay them. Worry after worry, and *this* is how you help? *This* is how you break your promise?"

In the corner, Gracie stopped taking down the balloons. She hated hearing her mother shouting but nor did she want to miss any of this. She watched as her aunt straightened in her seat, lifted her head, and then, very strangely and much too loudly, started to laugh.

"What a speech, Eleanor," she said, in a low, slurred voice, before laughing again, the high-pitched laugh that always made Gracie feel sick inside. "What an outburst. What passion. What horseshit."

Gracie wasn't the only person who looked shocked at what happened next. Gracie's mother slapped Hope across the face.

"Eleanor, no!" Henry moved quickly, holding his wife back as though expecting her to lunge again.

"It's all right, Henry," Eleanor said, moving out of his arms, her voice calm and cold. "I won't do it again. Not tonight."

Hope laughed again, her hand to her cheek, her eyes flashing. "Well, well, so the little angelic mouse has claws. Feel better now, Eleanor?" Her voice had a strange tone to it, Gracie noticed. It was too high and the words were running into one another.

Eleanor laughed then, a too-quick laugh that sounded just as bad to Gracie. "How much more do you think I can take, Hope? And don't you dare say I have a perfect life. I never will have one, not while you're around ruining it for me."

Henry suddenly turned and noticed Audrey and Gracie. "Eleanor, please. Not now."

Hope noticed them then, too, laughing again. "I don't know, dear Henry. Carpe diem, don't you think?" she said, sitting up even straighter and gazing around the room again, her eyes smudged dark with mascara, yet strangely bright. She stared directly at Gracie before shifting her gaze to Audrey, motionless in the corner.

"For God's sake, Audrey," Hope said, pointing a finger at her niece, laughing even louder. "Would you take those sunglasses off? You look ridiculous."

"Leave her alone, Hope." Eleanor's voice was like steel.

Hope ignored her and continued talking directly to Audrey. "So you made a fool of yourself at school. Became a laughingstock. So what? Welcome to the world. Welcome to real life. Who the hell do you think you are? Something special? Someone talented who will miss out on disappointments or heartbreak or failure, just rise straight to the top, land on her feet, like your darling sweet mother? Well, you're not. That stage fright business was just the start, miss. Just wait and see how awful the rest of your life might turn out to be. Take it from me. It can be shit. Shittier than shit. Kill yourself while you still can, that's my advice." She started laughing again.

"That's *enough*, Hope." This time Henry stepped in. "Gracie, Audrey, go to your rooms, please. You've heard more than enough nonsense tonight."

Gracie didn't want to leave. "But can't I—"

"Go, Gracie. Now. And take Audrey with you. And if you see Spencer, tell him to go straight to his room as well."

It took Gracie all her strength to help her sister to her room. Audrey had started sobbing midway through Hope's speech, and as Gracie went up the stairs with her, patting her back in what she hoped was a consoling way, Audrey's sobs turned to something more like wails. From downstairs, Gracie could hear more shouting: her mother, then Hope, then her father. Their raised voices filled her with a strange panicky feeling.

"Shh, Audrey," she said, trying to sound firm but kind, the way her mother did when she was trying to calm one of them down. "Ignore Hope. She's not well, remember."

A shudder went through Audrey's body, followed by another sob.

"You're not a failure, Audrey. You're not. Or a laughingstock. It was more awful than funny that night." She couldn't understand why that made Audrey cry even harder.

They finally reached Audrey's bedroom. Gracie stayed with her, taking off her sunglasses, helping her sister into bed, pulling up the covers, clumsily patting Audrey's heaving shoulders, trying to soothe her but finding it hard to know what else to say.

"Can I get you anything?" she said after a while, when Audrey's tears seemed to have stopped a little.

The sobs became more like a wail again.

Gracie decided that perhaps it might be best if she left Audrey alone for now. "Will I turn out the light or do you want to read?"

Another wail.

Gracie took that as a sign to leave.

She couldn't go to bed yet, though. She was too upset now herself. She roamed around upstairs for a few minutes instead, going into her parents' bedroom and switching on their bedside lamps, then poking her head into Spencer's bedroom. He was already in bed, curled up under his quilt and not answering when she called his name. That was just like him, putting himself to bed without even saying good night to everyone. Carefully closing his door, she went into Charlotte's room next, sitting on her bed, smoothing down her bedcovers and getting a sad rush of missing her big sister. No matter how hard Gracie had tried to convince her otherwise, Charlotte kept insisting there was no way, "Absolutely no way, Gracie," that she was coming home again while Hope was there. "I know I've left you in the lurch tour-guide-wise, Gracie, but I'm sorry. That's just the way it has to be," she'd said during their last phone conversation.

"But aren't you lonely there on your own?"

"Lonely? Far from it. I've never been busier."

A thought occurred to her. "Charlotte, have you got a boyfriend?"

Charlotte had laughed. "A boyfriend? I guess I have, as it happens. In a manner of speaking, at least." Before Gracie had a chance to ask more, Charlotte said she had to go.

Gracie thought for a minute about ringing Charlotte now, but the phone was downstairs and she didn't want her parents catching her. She spent a minute or two sitting on the top stair instead, hoping and even crossing her fingers for luck that her mother or father would come out of the kitchen, look up, see her, tell her Hope was fine again, and invite her down to have a cup of hot chocolate. But nobody appeared. Gracie could hear the three of them in the kitchen, their voices shouting one minute, quiet the next. She wanted them to talk to one another in their normal voices, about normal things.

It seemed she had no choice left but to go to bed. She'd just stood up when a shadow down in the entrance hall made her jump. Three fast heartbeats later, the figure moved into a patch of moonlight and she realized it was Spencer. She waited until he'd crept up the first flight of stairs before moving into the light herself, glad to see him get a fright.

"Gracie! What are you doing hiding like a weirdo?"

"Did I scare you?"

"Nothing scares me."

"I thought you were in your room. Where have you been?"

"Out."

"Out where?"

"Just out."

"Doing what?"

"Just stuff. Tom-and-I stuff. What's going on here?" He sat down on the stairs.

Gracie sat down again beside him. "Mum and Dad and Hope are in the kitchen fighting and Audrey's in her room crying but still not speaking."

"Oh. Okay."

She noticed then he had a black mark on his shirt sleeve. "Is that a burn? Spencer, is it? What were you and Tom doing out there tonight?"

"Nothing," Spencer said, casually moving his hand to hide the mark. "I'm going to bed. Good night, Gracie."

"Spencer, wait. Come back."

He didn't.

She sat on the stairs for another ten minutes, listening to the sounds from the kitchen until she started to shiver. "Mum," she called in a soft voice. "Mum? Dad?"

Nothing. No one came. She waited there for five more minutes until the cold got too much and she had no choice but to put herself to bed, too.

HER PARENTS were already up when she came down for breakfast the next day. She knew as soon as she came into the kitchen that they'd been arguing. It was as if she could feel their fight still in the room. Her mother looked like she'd been crying, all red and swollen around her eyes, and she was making a lot of noise at the sink. It was her father who asked whether Gracie had slept well. Before she could answer, he said he hoped she hadn't been too upset by what had happened the night before.

"Now, you'll find out soon enough, Gracie," he continued, still using the cheery voice she usually heard him use only on the tours, "so you may as well know now. It seems both your aunt and your sister plan to stay in their rooms for the foreseeable future, so that's where they'll be if you need them. But don't go looking for them, as they've both made it clear they want nothing to do with any of us."

Gracie paused in the middle of pouring out her cornflakes. "They're not coming out? Either of them?"

"So they say," Henry said.

"Oh, well," Gracie said, trying to match his carefree tone. "Two less mouths for us to feed." She was joking, trying to cheer her parents up. She was pleased to see a glimmer of a smile cross her father's lips.

At the sink, however, her mother wasn't amused. "Actually, you're wrong, Gracie," Eleanor said, wiping the dishes in an angry way. "Because despite the fact they're both insisting they want to be left alone while also insisting that the rest of us are unfeeling, unsympathetic monsters, I do still have to feed them, don't I?"

Gracie was confused. Then she noticed the two trays on the wooden table, each set with breakfast dishes, a teapot, cup, and saucers. "You're giving them breakfast in bed? Mum, that's not fair. That's a treat, not a punishment."

"Thank you, Gracie," Henry said. "My own thoughts exactly."

"What am I supposed to do, Henry, leave them up there to starve?"

"You could try it. If they're really hungry, they'll come down. The exercise might do them good."

"You're right. Of course. Have it your way." With an angry gesture, Eleanor pushed the trays across the table. Gracie jumped as the teacups clattered. "Let the two of them wallow in self-pity, starving to death. Excellent idea. And meanwhile down here in the real world, you and I can try to salvage what's left of this once apparently brilliant business idea of yours."

"Oh, so now it was only my idea, was it?" Henry's voice was too calm, too mild. "How extraordinary. Because I can recall every detail of the many conversations you and I had about this in London, deciding that we'd make the best of this unexpected opportunity. 'A family business—what could be better?' you said."

"A family business that worked. Yes, Henry, nothing could have been better. But this? It's not a business. It's a never-ending struggle. We're not getting anywhere. Because any time we get the smallest way ahead, you blow it all again. It's not a game, Henry. This isn't a theme park for us as it is for our poor unfortunate visitors. This is our lives. And it's not working. You're not working and it's not working and we can't go on like this. I won't go on like this."

Gracie hated hearing her mother and her father speak like this to each other, act like this in front of her, talk about Templeton Hall like this. She looked back and forth between them, feeling those little warning prickles on the back of her neck again. Little flittering memories of similar words, of similar tones, before they'd moved house and cities other times. She had to do something now, say something, stop this before it happened again. She leapt out of her seat and stood between them.

"Not yet, Mum, Dad. Please, not yet."

Her mother turned away. Her father, however, gave her his whole attention. "What are you talking about, Gracie?"

"We're in financial trouble, aren't we? Again? Can't you sell some more antiques? Isn't that what you usually do? Please, Dad. Don't make us move yet."

"Gracie, we're not going anywhere. We're just having a rough patch."

Eleanor gave an odd laugh. "A rough patch. A rough patch someone in this room who isn't me and who isn't eleven years old promised to address more than a year ago and didn't, leaving us in an even more rough patch than before?"

"Eleanor, please—"

"No, Henry. No more pleading. No more excuses. Can't you see? Don't you realize? I have had *enough* of this. Of you, of everything. I've had enough of all of it."

Gracie and Henry could only watch as Eleanor left the kitchen, slamming the door behind her.

For a moment, the room was silent. Then Henry stood up, rubbed his hands together, and reached for the kettle. "A cup of tea, Gracie, don't you think? That will soothe our nerves and lift our spirits on this strangely agitated morning."

Gracie wasn't mollified or distracted by the talk of tea. She was still trying to take in the fact that her mother had just stormed out. That had never happened before. The flittering feelings of distress were now threatening to overwhelm her.

"What does Mum mean, she's had enough of everything? She's not going to leave like Charlotte, too, is she? Or lock herself in her room? Please, Dad, don't let her."

Henry sat down beside her and took her hands. "Gracie, please don't worry. Your mother didn't get much sleep last night so she's speaking in riddles a bit today. And she's upset with Hope and still excited after Tom's great victory yesterday. It was quite a day, wasn't it? Now, haven't you got something to do to get ready for the tours this weekend? Have you checked the bookings register?"

"Of course. We've only got two groups coming through so far. I'm doing the downstairs and Audrey's upstai—" She stopped. "She's supposed to be doing the upstairs. Will she be, Dad?"

"Will pigs fly?" Henry sighed. "No, Gracie, I think I'm correct in saying Audrey probably won't be up to much of anything tomorrow, and quite frankly at the moment I don't think I'd trust her to show three blind mice around the Hall, let alone any groups."

"Mice?"

He smiled. "No, Gracie, we don't have mice. There's absolutely nothing at all for you to be worried about in even the farthest corner of Templeton Hall, I promise you."

"You really promise? Everything will be all right again soon?"

"Everything not only will be all right, it *is* all right. Now, go and polish the silver, would you? Or dust the china? Or count the lamps?"

"I already did. There are still fifteen."

"Then go and play outside, would you? Or go and read? See if you can find your brother. You can do anything you like, but please, just give me enough time to go and find your mother and remind her how much I love her and let the two of us have a bit of a private talk, would you?"

Gracie was halfway down the drive when she heard Spencer's voice calling her. She waited as he caught up. He was obviously just out of bed, still wearing his pajama bottoms, his feet bare, a dirty T-shirt on top. His blond curls were tousled. "Are you going to see Nina?" he asked, slightly out of breath.

She nodded. "Mum and Dad are fighting. It's no fun in there at the moment."

"I'm coming with you. It has to be more fun at Nina's, even if Tom's at school. I went in to get breakfast and Dad told me to go and tidy my room first. And when I tried to ride my skateboard down the hall, Hope opened her door and started shouting at me. It's not fair. If she and Audrey want some peace and quiet, why don't they lock themselves out in the stables apartment and leave the house to us?"

"That's a great idea," Gracie said brightly. "I'll suggest it to Dad."

"If he likes it, it was my idea."

When they reached Nina and Tom's house five minutes later, Spencer became uncharacteristically shy, hesitating at the front door. Gracie savored the great feeling of being more at home here than Spencer.

"Oh, we don't knock, Spencer. We just go straight in." She gave her brother an encouraging smile and opened the door with a flourish. "Hi, Nina. It's us!"

Nina looked very happy, Gracie thought, though she barely had time to smile a welcome and say hello before her phone rang.

"Excuse me a moment," Nina said.

Spencer made a dive for the couch, disappearing in one smooth movement up and over the back. "If it's Mum and Dad, I'm not here," he said in a muffled voice.

It wasn't their mum and dad. Gracie watched as Nina answered in a cheery voice, which changed as quickly as her expression. She listened for what Gracie thought was a very long time, just murmuring, "Oh, Hilary. Oh, darling. Oh, Hilary," over and again. Then she started talking in a rush. "Of course I will. I'll get the first flight. Don't worry about that. Of course I can sort out something. I'll be there as soon as I can, I promise."

She hung up and Gracie was taken aback by her expression. This wasn't the smiling Nina anymore. Her face was tense and it was as if she'd forgotten they were there. She picked up the phone, rang another number, murmuring under her breath. "Come on, Jenny, answer." After a minute, she hung up, took out a phone book, checked it, then dialed another number. No answer again. "Come on, please," she said urgently. "Come *on*."

Gracie dared to speak. "Nina, is everything all right?" She saw Spencer pop up from behind the couch, too.

Nina seemed surprised to hear her voice, and turned, distracted. "Gracie, Spencer, I'm sorry. That was my sister in Queensland. Something's happened and her husband's away. I need to get to her as soon as I can."

"Is she hurt?" Gracie asked. "Was it an accident?"

"No. Yes. I can't really explain now. But I need to go to her and I need someone to pick up Tom and have him for a few days. I don't know how long I'll be away." She reached for the phone book again.

Gracie had the feeling Nina was thinking aloud rather than talking to them but she answered her anyway. "No, Nina, don't, please. What about us? We can take Tom."

Nina kept dialing. "No, Gracie. Thanks but no."

"Why not?"

"Why not?" Spencer asked from the couch.

Nina stopped mid-dial. "It's too much to ask. He needs to be taken to school, picked up again, driven to cricket practice. I'll ask one of the other school mums. They're used to—"

Gracie moved over to her. "But you can't get ahold of the other school mums. And we're here. Ask us." She noticed Nina hesitate. "Please, Nina, ask us. We'll say yes and you can go straight to the air-port."

Nina glanced up at the clock on the wall, back at Gracie, then ran her fingers through her hair. "Gracie, it's too much—"

"It's not, I promise. Mum and Dad are both home now. We can ring them this minute." Was this the time to tell Nina all about the fight they'd had that morning? About Hope and Audrey's in-room protests? No, perhaps not. Gracie moved swiftly, taking the phone from Nina and dialing the number of the Hall. After a long wait her mother answered.

Gracie spoke in a rush. "Mum, it's me. I'm at Nina's. She needs

our help. Urgently. And we have to give it to her, okay?" She handed
the phone to Nina.

FIVE HOURS LATER Gracie was happily sitting in the backseat of her
father's car as they drove into Castlemaine to collect Tom from
school. Spencer had insisted on coming along for the ride, too. Gracie would never admit it to Nina, but it had turned into such an exciting day. And all because of her! If she hadn't chosen that moment
to visit Nina, none of this would have happened.

"It's as if it was all meant to be, isn't it, Mum?" she'd said after
Nina called to the Hall to hurriedly confirm all the arrangements and
drop off a suitcase of Tom's clothes. Gracie had stayed close by,
standing very still as her mother and Nina spoke, telling herself it
wasn't eavesdropping. She was being the backup, taking in all the information so she could remind her parents later if need be. She'd
heard all sorts of words she'd never heard before, including "miscarriage," and seen the sad sight of Nina crying, as she'd told Gracie's
mother that she hadn't even known her sister was pregnant, her sister
hadn't even known she was pregnant, and it had been a shock to learn
about the baby and a heartbreak to lose it, all at once, and even worse
because Hilary's husband was away overseas and she was in the hospital on her own.

"Of course you have to go," Gracie's mother had kept saying.
"Don't worry about anything here. We'll take care of Tom for as long
as you need."

Gracie hadn't understood all of what Nina had said. She'd also
been a bit disappointed when Nina only gave her a distracted thank
you and a quick wave good-bye.

At the school, she leapt out of the car as soon as she saw Tom coming through the doors, reaching him before Spencer was even out of
the car. He'd had trouble undoing the faulty seat belt in the front seat,
which was one of the reasons she'd let him travel in the front, even
though it was actually her turn.

She ignored Tom's surprised expression as she ran up to him.
"Tom, you're coming to stay with us! Isn't that great! Your mum had
to go to Cairns for a few days urgently because her sister was going to

have a baby but then she didn't, and she's very, very upset and her husband is away and she needs your mother so your mother has just gone straight to the airport, but she wrote this note before she left, explaining everything." Gracie thrust an envelope at him. "So you're going to stay with us until she gets back. Isn't that brilliant?"

Chapter Fourteen

By FIVE O'CLOCK the next day, Gracie had changed her mind. It wasn't brilliant that Tom had come to stay. It was awful. She'd thought she, Tom, and Spencer would have great fun together, making up plays or playing cricket like that time at Nina's house—maybe even having midnight feasts together like the children in her favorite books. Spencer, however, had made it clear within moments of Tom arriving at the Hall the previous day that it was all about the two of them, not the three of them.

"He's staying here because he's my friend, not yours, Gracie, okay?" he'd hissed when she followed them out to the stables apartment.

"But it was my idea. I suggested it to Nina."

"So what? We want to do boy stuff."

"I can do boy stuff."

"You can't, Gracie. You're a girl." With that, Spencer shut the apartment door and she heard him turn the key. She could have knocked and knocked until he opened it again but she suddenly felt too sad. She'd pictured Tom all upset with his mother away, and her—her, not Spencer—making him feel at home, showing him his room, showing him the flowers she'd picked herself to put on his dressing table. But it had been Spencer who carried his case up for him, Spencer who threw it onto the bed, and—even worse—Spencer who mocked her flowers and insisted she take them out of Tom's room immediately. "Flowers are for *girls*, Gracie."

The two boys had then gone out into the garden, Tom showing Spencer over and over how to bowl a cricket ball as fast as he could, then they'd disappeared out to that dam they loved so much that she just found so boring, and they hadn't even come back for the sausages and mashed potato she'd cooked for dinner. She'd had to just serve it up and watch unhappily as they ate it an hour later, cold, when they finally came back in. They hadn't even sat down to eat it, just ate off their plates, standing up.

Her mother at least noticed she was unhappy. "Gracie, don't be hurt. Let Tom settle in. This has all been a bit sudden for him, and he might not be used to sitting down to eat dinner like we do."

"Of course he is. Nina's taught him lovely manners. It's Spencer leading him astray."

It was true. On his own, Tom was so lovely. Hadn't he spent that whole afternoon at Nina's playing cricket with her, and hadn't he even said that she was nearly as much fun as Spencer? Now, here she was, on her own, while the two of them were having all sorts of adventures without her.

Cross at the injustice of it, she contemplated for the moment the possibility of getting her own back on Spencer. She had the information to do it, after all, enough to get him into heaps of trouble, not just with their dad but with their mum, too. He'd get punished for it, for sure. Sent to his room, definitely. And then Tom would have to play with her.

It had happened earlier that week. Gracie had heard her father give Spencer a big talking-to, making him promise not to deliver any more bottles to Hope, no matter how much money she offered. Spencer nodded and looked serious and said of course he wouldn't, but Gracie didn't believe him. She knew he and Tom were planning something big, a motor-powered raft they would float on the dam as soon as it had enough water. Spencer would definitely need more than his pocket money to pay his share of it. So she hadn't been surprised to catch him in their father's study looking for the keys to the wine cellar.

"Spencer! What are you doing?"

"Nothing."

"Why are you in here, then?"

"Tidying up."

"No, you're not. You're looking for the keys."

"Stop being such a goodie-goodie, Gracie."

That hurt. She didn't try to be a goodie-goodie. She just thought it was better for everyone if they told the truth, if they were all nice to one another and everyone tried to be happy. The problem was she seemed to be the only happy one in the house these days.

She gave it some more thought now before deciding she couldn't tell on Spencer. He'd only get even more furious with her, and probably get Tom to call her a goodie-goodie, too. Instead, she took up position on one of her favorite spots of the staircase, five stairs from the bottom, ten from the top, rested her chin on her hands, and sighed.

Her quiet time didn't last very long. Within minutes she was conscious of voices coming from the kitchen. Raised voices. It sounded like her parents were fighting. Again. She carefully shifted down four stairs, pressing herself up against the wall, to the spot that she knew provided the best hiding and listening position.

They'd been cross with each other all morning. She'd noticed it when their father came in during their lessons and spoke to their mother in a strange polite voice, and they'd both used each other's names too much.

"I'm just going into town for an hour or so, Eleanor. Is there anything you need?"

"Thank you for letting me know, Henry. No, I'm fine, thank you."

Gracie usually only heard her mother use that voice when she was asking someone on their tours to please put the front door key back where they'd found it. People were always trying to steal that key, because it was so big and magical-looking, Gracie supposed. Her father had had several copies made, just in case.

She leaned forward as far as she could now, as a door opened and their voices suddenly became audible.

"You're pandering to their dramas," her father was saying. "Charlotte's right. Audrey's seen all the attention Hope gets when she locks herself away and she's trying to copy her."

There was the clatter of another dish being put down roughly.

"What do you care, anyway? It's not as if you're the one who's doing any of the work around here. What *is* it you're actually doing around here lately, Henry? Because it seems to involve nothing but reading your magazines and drinking as much whisky as you can, night after night, as far as I can see."

"I do apologize. I'd be happy to help out if I could fight my way through the Martyrs Anonymous camp that has taken root in the kitchen."

"Oh, fuck off, Henry."

On the stairs, Gracie gasped. She'd never heard her mother use that word before.

"That's helpful, Eleanor. Here I am trying to have some semblance of a discussion with you, and that's your contribution."

" 'Some semblance of a discussion'? I've been trying to talk to you for weeks, before everything crumbles to dust around us, but you've done everything you can to avoid talking to me, to avoid facing up to what's happening here, what's happened again and again, what somehow keeps happening no matter what bloody brainwave or new idea you come up with."

"Eleanor, you're sounding frighteningly close to fishwife-ish. You're overreacting. I told you. It's just a rough patch, businesses ebb and flow."

A shout from Eleanor. "Henry, stay here."

Gracie held her breath as she heard her mother go into her father's study, heard the rattle of the filing cabinet before she returned to the kitchen. There was the slam of something onto the table, a folder or a book, Gracie thought.

"What are these, Henry?" Her mother's voice was ice cold again. "These are what you call a 'rough patch'?"

Gracie held her breath, wishing she could see what her mother had just given her father, at the same time wishing she wasn't hearing this at all.

Her father didn't answer. It was her mother who broke the silence again. "Will I give you a hint, Henry? They are bills. Dozens of bills. Dating back from the renovations. Not just bills, but also solicitors' letters about the bills. And where did I find them? Down the back of your filing cabinet. Hidden"—she shouted the word—"hidden down the back of your filing cabinet. After you promised me you'd dealt with them. After you promised me we had paid them."

"Would you calm down, Eleanor, for heaven's sake. They must have slipped. Fallen somehow. I told you I thought I felt an earth tremor here the other night."

"No!" Another shout. "No, you won't do that to me this time, lie and joke your way out of this. Henry, even if these bills are just the half of it, and God knows what else you've hidden away somewhere, we owe nearly two hundred thousand dollars. On top of everything we still owe back home."

"I'm sure it's not that much. Anyway, it doesn't look like Audrey's in any hurry to go back to school, so we'll save on her fees at least."

"It's not funny, Henry. It's not funny. Why can't I get through to you?"

"Eleanor—"

"I mean it, Henry. I've had enough. If you don't sort this out, and I don't care what you have to do to fix it—go back to full-time work, sell everything we own, sell the Hall, to hell with the rules of the inheritance—but if you don't do something, I'm leaving you. And I mean it this time."

"Eleanor—"

"I mean it, Henry. I mean it."

As silently as she could, Gracie tiptoed up the stairs and into her room. She was finding it hard to breathe. Her chest felt all funny and tight and when she held out her hands she saw that they were trembling. For five minutes, she did nothing but sit on her bed, trying to forget everything she'd just heard, wishing she hadn't heard it, wishing she could tell someone but knowing there was no one to tell—not Charlotte, not Audrey, not Nina. She couldn't even tell her parents. They'd told her off often enough for listening when she shouldn't.

Hearing a car, she ran to the window in time to see her father drive away. Where was he going? Was he leaving them? She couldn't stay in her room any longer.

She ran down the stairs and into the kitchen. Her mother was there, calmly preparing two trays. "Hello, Gracie," she said.

Gracie blurted it out. "Is everything all right?"

"Everything really couldn't get any better, Gracie. Thank you for asking." She was speaking in that strange overly polite voice again.

"I'm sorry I'm not good enough at the cooking yet or I'd do all this for you. It's not fair that you do all the work around here."

Her mother's tight expression softened. "I know you would, Gracie. And I'm sorry if I snapped at you then and I'm sorry in advance if I snap at you tomorrow. Things around here are all a bit—"

"Atmospheric?" Gracie suggested.

To her relief, her mother briefly smiled. "Yes, Gracie. That's it exactly. It's a bit too atmospheric around here. Help me with one of these trays, would you, before I throw them both on the ground in a temper?"

UPSTAIRS, GRACIE carefully laid Audrey's tray at her door, then watched in amazement as her mother left a similar one outside Hope's room, stood midway between their two doors, and shouted.

"Audrey? Hope? Are you listening to me?"

Gracie had a strong feeling that both Audrey and Hope were up and listening at their doors. Her mother lowered her voice but not by much.

"Afternoon tea is served, but not for long. I'll do this for you both until the weekend and that's all. After that, you come down if you're hungry or you starve. It's your choice."

Another long pause, and then one voice.

"Fine," from Hope's room. Nothing from Audrey's.

"Good," Eleanor said.

After that, Gracie decided she didn't want to be inside any more. She'd go and find Spencer and Tom instead, even if they did tell her to go away again. She made her way to the dam. Only Tom was there, sitting on the bank, baiting up string. He looked up and smiled at her. "Hi, Gracie."

She settled herself beside him on the dirt bank. "Have you caught anything?"

"Not yet. Spencer thinks it's the bait we're using. He's gone to get something different."

She wasn't surprised they hadn't crossed paths. Spencer knew all the shortcuts between the dam and the Hall but refused to pass them on to her. "Can I watch?"

"Of course. Do you want to have a go?"

She shook her head. She still didn't understand the attraction of yabbies. They looked disgusting and apparently tasted like mud.

"It's good having you here with us, Tom."

"It's good being here, Gracie."

"Are you homesick yet? Do you need to ring Nina?"

He smiled. "I'm fine, but thank you." He held out the string. "You sure you don't want to have a go?"

"No, thanks. I might get pulled in and I'm not a good swimmer."

"They're about as strong as an ant, Gracie. I think you'll be fine. And I promise I'll grab hold of you if I see you heading for the water."

She was secretly enjoying the thought of Tom rescuing her when she heard a shout behind them.

"Tom, don't let her hold it!" It was Spencer, back again. "She'll let go if we get one."

"I wouldn't," Gracie said, indignant.

"Did you get the new bait?" Tom asked as Spencer reached them.

He shook his head. "Mum chased me out of the kitchen." He sat down with a thump beside Tom and started skimming stones across the surface of the dam. After a minute, Tom put down the string and started throwing stones, too. He offered Gracie a stone, and even showed her the best way to throw it to make it leap across the water. On her first try it skimmed the water three times.

Gracie couldn't believe it. She was here, playing with Spencer and Tom, and they hadn't told her to go away!

After a few minutes, though, she got a bit bored of skimming stones. "Does anyone want to play a word game?" she asked.

"No, Gracie. Word games are stupid," Spencer said, tossing his last stone away. "So is skimming stones. What about hide-and-seek, Gracie? Want to play that?"

"Out here? The three of us?" She was thrilled.

"Sure. You hide first, okay? We'll count to two hundred to give you time to find a really good spot and then we'll come looking for you."

She frowned, suspicious suddenly. "Isn't it one person seeks and the others hide?"

"Usually, but we've made up our own rules. It's more exciting this way."

Tom spoke then. "Spencer—"

Spencer ignored him. "Okay, Gracie? Off you go." He glanced down at his watch. "Now!"

As Gracie took off at a high speed toward the neighboring paddock and its clump of trees, Spencer made a show of loudly counting to a hundred before he turned to Tom and grinned. "That worked better than I thought. Come on. Let's go watch TV."

"What about Gracie?"

Spencer shrugged. "She'll give up after an hour or so. I'll tell her we couldn't find her."

"That's cruel."

"What's the alternative? She hangs around us for the rest of the day?"

Tom stood up. "You go and watch TV. I'll find her."

"You'll regret it. We'll never get rid of her now."

Tom just walked away.

IN HER HIDING PLACE three paddocks away, Gracie's heart was racing. She'd tried two other spots before this one, convinced each time she could hear Spencer or Tom coming toward her. She'd crouched low, darting from tree to tree, not daring to look back in case they caught sight of her. Finally, she'd found this spot, a large clump of rocks next to a small group of trees. She'd had to push past a spiderweb to tuck herself into a crevice and been alarmed to see a row of ants crawling over the nearest rock, too, but it was too late to move. Spencer and Tom would be seeking her any minute now.

Five minutes later, she was still there. Her heart rate had settled a little, but she was now transfixed by the ants. They were definitely getting closer. She also had a horrible feeling that the spiderweb wasn't empty.

She tried to shift a little to make herself more comfortable and discovered she couldn't move her left foot. It had got wedged between two rocks. She tried to pull it out and felt a sharp twist of pain. Oh, no! First ants, then spiders, and now she was stuck here, so well hidden they'd never be able to find her. She'd be out here all day. All night. She started calling their names, wanting to cry. But if they found her crying, they'd never let her play with them again. She blinked the tears away. "I'm here!" She tried again, more loudly. "I'm here. Spencer! Tom! I'm stuck!"

Five minutes passed before she got an answer. It felt like an hour.

"Gracie? Where are you?" It was Tom, not Spencer.

"I'm here!" She couldn't reach up enough to peer over the rock. "In the rocks!"

Several minutes later she heard the crunch of dry leaves, then a moment later Tom appeared. She'd never been so happy to see anyone. "Oh, Tom, thank God. I'm completely stuck." She knew it was okay to tell him. He'd always been kind to her. She spoke in a rush, explaining how she couldn't move. "I was getting a bit scared."

"That'll teach you to hide so well." He got down on his knees beside her hiding place and reached in, grasping her ankle. "Can you move now?"

She tried. It was still stuck. He pulled at the largest rock beside her and grasped her ankle again. "Now, Gracie?"

This time her foot moved, a rattle of stones falling as she pulled it out of the gap and wriggled her body sideways out of the hiding place. "Freedom at last!" she said, trying to joke, brushing away all the dust on the front of her dress.

"Well done," Tom said, smiling. "And you definitely win the game. I'd never have found you if you hadn't called out."

To her embarrassment, her eyes filled with tears. She quickly wiped them away. "I'm sorry to cry, but I'm just so relieved to see you. I kept imagining what it would be like if I wasn't found, if I was stuck here all night, in the dark and the cold. . . ."

"Oh, poor Gracie." He reached across and ruffled her hair. "You wouldn't have been here all night, I promise. I'd have found you eventually."

Gracie looked around. "What happened to Spencer?"

"He had to go home to get something."

"You won't tell him I cried, will you? It's just I gave myself a fright."

"I won't tell him, I promise," he said, as they started walking back to the Hall together.

They'd gone just a short way when he stopped and reached into his rucksack for something. "Here, Gracie, have this. Just in case you get another fright some time."

It was an old-fashioned silver whistle. She took it from him, turning it over in her hand.

"Mum gave it to me when I was a kid," Tom said. "In case I ever got lost or in trouble. I'm too old for it now but you can have it if you want."

"Really?"

"Really. And if you ever get lost again, just blow it and I'll come and find you, okay?"

Gracie felt the color rise in her cheeks. She held it in her hand for a few more seconds, feeling the smooth cool of the metal, before pushing it safely to the bottom of her pocket.

"Okay," she said.

She was still smiling when they reached the Hall.

AT BOARDING SCHOOL in Melbourne, Charlotte had just broken part one of her big news to Celia. She was now being subjected to a furious barrage of questioning.

"Ethan's *nanny?*" Celia said. "*You?* I don't believe it, Charlotte. How *dare* you!"

"What do you mean? I thought you'd be delighted for me."

"Delighted about what? That you've somehow pulled the wool over not just my cousin's son's eyes, but my elderly, rich, divorced cousin as well. Do you think it hasn't been obvious what you've been doing every weekend? What you've actually been up to? Weaseling your way into my family like this for your own ulterior motives?"

"Weaseling? Your very nice, not-so-elderly cousin kept inviting me to spend my weekends looking after his even nicer young son. I accepted his invitations. What's weaseling about that?"

"It was all because of this stupid family boycott of yours. How dare you use my family to get yourself out of your own mess. I won't have it, Charlotte."

"That's too bad, *Celia*. Because you have no say in it."

"Yes, I do. I'll ring my cousin and tell him you're not to be trusted. That if he wants anyone to look after his son, it should be me, his blood relative, not a complete stranger."

"You think he hadn't thought of that? You think he wasn't planning on offering you the job, until he saw how dismissive you were of Ethan that weekend we were there?"

"I was not dismissive. I was just busy, talking to—"

"The sheep farmer who is now your boyfriend who you have talked about incessantly since then? Just as well you weren't supposed to be minding Ethan, then, isn't it?"

"But if I'd known it was an informal job interview, of course I'd have paid more attention to him. It's not fair, Charlotte. What is it, a paid job for the rest of their time here?"

"Not exactly. A paid seven-days-a-week job. Well, not quite seven days. I get a day-and-a-half off each week."

"It's full-time? But how? What about school?"

"Have you forgotten we finish school at the end of the year? Or that those of us who have already decided not to bother sitting exams that we already know we're going to fail can finish up anytime we like, particularly once we turn eighteen and are officially adults?"

Celia blinked. "You're leaving school early?" At Charlotte's nod, Celia only looked more confused. "But what do your parents think about that? And how can it be full-time? My cousin and Ethan are only in Australia for another ten days. We're having a farewell party for them next week."

"I know. I'm helping organize it. It's a farewell-to-Australia party for them and for me."

Celia went still. "You're going back with them? Back to America? You?"

Charlotte made a mock bow. "You are looking at the newly appointed full-time Chicago-based rather-well-paid-if-you-don't-mind-me-saying nanny to one Master Ethan Giles."

"No way. Ethan's my relation. If anyone goes to America, it should be me."

"But you weren't offered the job, Celia. I was. You've barely ever spoken to Ethan."

"He's a kid, what could I possibly have to say to him?"

"It's your loss. Ethan's great. I really like him and he really likes me. We're friends."

"Friends? He's an eight-year-old boy. How can you be friends? What are you up to, Charlotte? You're going to go over there, have all your expenses paid, get your green card, and then just disappear? Leave them in the lurch? That's it, isn't it?"

"Why can't it be just what it seems?"

"Because it's you. Because this is all completely out of character and I don't trust your reasons. And I don't believe your parents have agreed to it, either. They're hardly going to let you go off across to the other side of the world with a pair of complete strangers to do a job you're not remotely qualified to do. Have they even met my cousin? How do they know he's not going to make a pass at you the moment you're on the plane?" She stared at Charlotte then. "Oh, my God. That's it, isn't it? He already has. You're having an affair with my cousin. Charlotte, you tramp."

Charlotte laughed. "Celia, for God's sake. No, I'm not having an affair with your cousin and nor is there a flame of desire flickering between us, waiting to combust as soon as we land on American soil. You're right. My parents probably won't agree to this. In fact, I'm sure they'll be horrified at the idea, but the fact is, the moment I turn eighteen"—she lifted her wrist and glanced at her watch—"which is in less than one week, four days, three hours, and whatever number of minutes, I am in charge of my own life, my own passport, and my own future, and there's nothing they can do about it."

"You bitch."

"Do you know, you're the second person lately to call me that? The first one was my sister and look what happened to her. Watch out, Celia. I seem to have supernatural powers of revenge that I barely know the extent of myself."

"You did this deliberately, didn't you? Made friends with me, talked me into inviting you away for weekends with me and my family, set your sights—"

"Oh, Celia, stop it, would you? How could I have engineered it?

Look at the facts. You took me to a boring party, I got talking to some kid who turns out to be great fun. He invites me to his birthday party, then to the zoo while his dad is working. I do it. More fun. And to the beach. And the museum. We have a good laugh and he entertains me more than any other male I've ever met. Then, out of the blue, his dad offers me a full-time job, all expenses paid, back home in Chicago. Now, I might be brilliant and I might be scheming, but even I couldn't have seen that point A would lead to point B."

"But I've always wanted to go to Chicago." Celia was now whining.

"And if you promise to be very nice to me, and stop this frankly slanderous carry-on, I'll let you come and visit me one day."

"You'll *let* me? They're my family, remember."

"Oh, yes. But remember, it's the hand that rocks the cradle—or in my case, the hand that holds the joystick—that rules the world."

Celia finally started to laugh, even as she picked up a pillow and threw it across the room at Charlotte. "You really *are* a bitch. You know that, don't you?"

Charlotte grinned. "Yes. But I'm a very nice soon-to-be-Chicago-based bitch."

Chapter Fifteen

AFTERWARD, GRACIE always thought of that day as Black Monday. She'd read the term during her history studies, something about a stock-market crash that had taken place in New York, one bad thing happening after another, bringing the whole world tumbling down. It had been like that in her house. A phone call from Charlotte had started it. Gracie answered it and had a quick chat with Charlotte before going to fetch her mother.

"I hope you've got good news for her," Gracie said before she put down the phone. "Everyone's so cranky around here lately. We need cheering up."

"Oh, it's great news, Gracie. I promise. For me, anyway."

Gracie crossed her fingers that it was something to do with Charlotte's standoff about Hope. A trial visit home, perhaps, on the condition that Hope stay locked up in her room, out of Charlotte's sight? Or an in-between plan, that they all meet up somewhere in neutral surroundings to break the ice? There were so many possibilities. It only seemed right and proper that she stay in earshot when her mother picked up the phone extension in the kitchen. There was a long silence as Charlotte explained her good news. Gracie could hardly believe her ears when her mother shouted down the phone in reply.

"Moving to *America*? Next month? You're doing no such thing."

Another silence, but this one was short-lived. Gracie was grateful that her mother's astonishment at Charlotte's news meant she kept repeating what Charlotte was telling her. "You? A nanny? You're just a child yourself. No, eighteen is not an adult in my eyes. Yes, we can stop you. What about a passport?" A long pause. "Don't you be sarcastic with me. Yes, I remember you on the plane from England. Charlotte, you can't. It's a ridiculous idea. Yes, I am forbidding you. I can. I want you to talk to your father first, before you do anything, agree to anything. No, don't hang up. Please, wait there."

Gracie heard the phone clunk onto the table as Eleanor ran out, calling for Henry. Gracie knew he was fixing a tap in the stables apartment. They'd be a few minutes at least. She crept into the kitchen and picked up the phone.

"Charlotte?" she whispered.

"Gracie?" Charlotte sounded relaxed and amused. "Are you eavesdropping again?"

"I'm trying to, but I only heard Mum's side of the story. What's going on?"

"I've been offered a job, Gracie. A great job, in Chicago."

"America Chicago?"

"Chicago, Illinois, America, to be exact. Starting the day I turn eighteen, as nanny to a fortunately adorable eight-year-old boy who has even more fortunately fallen in love with me and told his very rich father that I, Charlotte Templeton, and only I, can do the job."

"But you can't go! I was going to throw you a surprise eighteenth birthday party!"

"Gracie, I am going. I'm sorry. And I don't want a party, thanks anyway. I hate fusses."

"But we'll miss you so much! It's been bad enough you being in Melbourne."

"I had to spread my wings one day. I'm just going away for a few years, not dying, and we can ring or write in the meantime. Oh, Gracie, please don't cry."

Gracie couldn't help it. "But what about our family? Templeton Hall? We're in enough trouble as it is. We can't manage without you."

"What trouble?"

Quickly, with her eye on the door, Gracie told her about their parents' fights over bills, about the dropping visitor numbers, about Hope and Audrey still being locked in their rooms, and even Spencer losing complete interest in the guiding now that Tom was around.

"It's a mess, Charlotte. I'm the only one who even seems to care about the Hall anymore."

"Gracie, you were the only one who *ever* cared about it. It was never going to last. Dad's ideas never do. And don't worry about Hope or Audrey, either. Can't you see they're just looking for attention? Especially Audrey, with that ridiculous non-talking. The best thing you can do is ignore the pair of them. I know I would."

"But—"

"Gracie, give me the phone, please."

It was her serious-faced father, with her even more serious-faced mother standing behind him. Gracie handed over the phone and then went straight into the hall cupboard to hide.

FOR THE REST of the day, there was nothing but talk about Charlotte's news. Even Audrey emerged from her room long enough to join in. While she'd stopped wearing the sunglasses, she still wasn't speaking to anyone. She was asked again and again by her parents if she'd had any idea. She shook her head firmly, finally reaching for her notepad. She knew that Charlotte had been to some parties with Celia, she wrote, but the rest of it was news to her.

"She can't go, can she?" Gracie pleaded. "We don't know anything about these people."

"If she's telling us the truth, we can find out all we need to about this Mr. Giles by reading a few back issues of the *Wall Street Journal*," Henry said. "According to her, he's one of the most successful property developers in the U.S. Charlotte also informed me he's divorced from his son's mother, has full custody of his son, and is now involved with but not planning to marry a high-flying corporate lawyer in New York. And before any of you ask this as well, Charlotte assures me she isn't and has no intention of having an affair with him. And no, Gracie, I won't explain what I mean."

"But she's never been to America, let alone Chicago," Eleanor said, upset. "You have to stop her, Henry."

"I can't, Eleanor. She's eighteen, with a passport. She can fly to the moon if she wants."

Henry was right. It was soon clear that there was no stopping Charlotte. Despite a constant series of phone calls, threats, cajolings, standoffs, and even tears from Eleanor during one call, she refused to back down. She was going to Chicago with Ethan and his dad and that was that, and what's more, she wasn't coming back to Templeton Hall to say good-bye. If they wanted to see her, and more to the point, if they wanted to meet Ethan and Ethan's father in person, they'd have to come to Melbourne.

ONE WEEK LATER, Charlotte stood outside her boarding school waving good-bye to her family. Thank God that was over. She loved her family, she did, but she was now well and truly ready to put many thousands of kilometers between them.

At least the lunch meeting between her parents and her new employer had gone well, all things considered. Mr. Giles had been his usual businesslike self, Ethan adorable. Charlotte's parents had fired question after question at Mr. Giles at first, to Charlotte's embarrassment, but after the first tense twenty minutes, the conversation had settled and become quite jovial. Her father and Mr. Giles had discovered a mutual interest in eighteenth-century clocks, and it had been obvious that her mother had been quite charmed by Ethan's good manners and intelligence. Spencer hadn't seemed to care one way or the other, appearing far more interested in trying to impress that nice boy Tom, who'd come for the trip to Melbourne, too. Audrey and Hope hadn't come, to Charlotte's relief. The more Gracie had told her about their behavior recently, the more furious Charlotte had become. Her parents had to realize they were feeding off each other's dramas, surely?

"Don't indulge them, Gracie," she advised her little sister. "Neither of them will start behaving if everyone's always at their beck and call."

Gracie had been very cute all day, snuggling next to her at the restaurant table, whispering to Charlotte that she hoped she would be happy, that if she ever needed to confide in anyone about how things were going in Chicago, all she had to do was ring and Gracie would be all ears.

Gracie had even cried when Charlotte was hugging everyone good-bye. Charlotte saw tears in her mother's eyes, too, and maybe even a glimmer in her father's, but she'd pretended she hadn't, saying to them both, as she'd been saying all along, what a great adventure going to Chicago was, and how she'd phone home once a week. They weren't to worry about her. It was a fantastic opportunity and of course it was all going to work out. All true, too. She was just relieved there wouldn't be another family farewell at the airport in ten days' time. She'd insisted. This was the start of her independence, after all.

Returning to her dormitory with the suitcase of belongings that her mother had brought down from the Hall for her, Charlotte wished she was athletic enough to do a leap in the air and click her heels together like an old-fashioned movie star. No chance of that. As she walked briskly down the corridor to her room, she settled for singing a loud and enthusiastically off-key version of Frank Sinatra's "Chicago" instead.

BACK AT TEMPLETON HALL, Gracie spent the first few days after the Melbourne trip feeling sad and tidying up Charlotte's already tidied-up room. It looked so bare now that her clothes and knick-knacks were gone. It still felt strange to think her sister wouldn't be in the same country as her anymore. Gracie had already written Charlotte a long letter, and Charlotte hadn't even left yet. On the bright side, at least the trip to Melbourne had been good fun and Ethan seemed like a nice little boy. She hadn't had much of a chance to talk to his father, unfortunately. "Very businesslike and straightfor-ward," she'd heard her parents describe him. He was also very old and ugly, in Gracie's opinion.

Audrey had written her a note asking how the Melbourne trip had gone, but Gracie decided to follow Charlotte's advice and not tell her much. "I'll only answer your questions when you ask me, not when you put them in writing, Audrey, okay?" Audrey had just written two rude words in her notebook and gone back to her room again.

At least one good thing happened that week. On the fourth day after the Melbourne trip, Nina finally came back home from Cairns. Gracie let her and Tom have two hours back home alone together before she ran across the paddocks to their house. There was so much to tell her.

Tom was outside practicing his bowling against the tank. Gracie gave him a big wave and told him she'd be back in a minute, then went straight inside. To her dismay, Nina was on the phone, looking very serious, holding a letter in her hand. She gave Gracie only the briefest of nice-to-see-you-again smiles before she kept talking. Gracie got a bad feeling in her stomach. Nina was frowning and asking lots of questions. "But doesn't he have to give me more notice than that?" More listening, more questions, and finally good-bye.

"Is everything okay?" Gracie asked, hoping it wasn't more sad news about her sister.

Nina looked unhappy. "I'm afraid not, Gracie. It's about this house." She explained that the owner had decided to sell. "So they're ending our lease. Asking us to move out, in other words."

This was almost as bad as Charlotte leaving. Gracie stood up. "But, Nina, you can't move out! You can't leave us! Can't you buy it?"

"No, Gracie. I can't afford it."

"But what about Tom and his cricket practice? Where will he do it if he hasn't got lots of space and a tank to throw against? And what about Tom and Spencer's agreement? And our friendship? Nina, please, you can't move away."

"I don't think we have any choice, Gracie. I'm sorry."

Gracie didn't stay long after that. She was too unhappy.

That night, back at Templeton Hall, Gracie asked her father if he could loan Nina the money she needed to buy the house.

"If I could, I would, Gracie. But I'm afraid we don't have that kind of money either."

"But what will they do?"

"They'll find another house to rent," Eleanor said. "They'll be fine, Gracie. Wait and see."

Gracie knew her mother wasn't just being nice. She'd heard her ring Nina after Gracie came home and told them the news. Gracie was pleased they were friendly but she also hoped her mother understood that Nina was *her* special friend.

"But if she moves closer into town, I won't be able to visit her every day."

"Worry about that when you have to, Gracie. All sorts of things might happen yet."

THE NEXT MORNING over breakfast, Gracie couldn't believe her ears when she heard her parents' idea. Her mother told her first and then her father repeated it.

"Don't get too excited yet though, Gracie," he said. "It might not suit Nina. She might prefer to be in town."

"But of course it will suit her! It's a perfect idea!" She wished she'd thought of it herself.

She heard her mother phone Nina, but to her torment, her mother would only tell her that Nina was "considering it." Gracie lasted an hour, before slipping outside and running over to Nina's house. She started talking as soon as she saw her.

"Have you decided, Nina? Please say yes. Don't you think it's the perfect solution?"

"Gracie, it's taken me by surprise. I haven't had a chance yet to—"

"Oh, *please*, Nina. You have to say yes. The stables apartment is so lovely. You could even have your studio in the stables themselves. I'd help you sweep it out. We wouldn't charge much rent, no more than you pay here, and you would help us out of our financial difficulties and you would have a nice place to live."

"Gracie, it's such a kind offer, really, but I have to think about it some more."

"But you'll say yes then, won't you? Tom would love it, and I'd love it; you'd be our real neighbor then. And it would be so handy when you help us with the weekend tours."

"When I what?"

Gracie blushed. "It's just we're down a guide now that Audrey's decided never to speak again. Well, down two guides really, counting Charlotte. I was wondering whether you'd like to dress up and show people around with me? Tom too, if he wanted, but it mightn't be a good idea to put him and Spencer together. They bring out the worst in each other."

"They do? What have they been doing?"

"Nothing," Gracie said quickly. If Nina hadn't heard about Tom and Spencer spending all their time on the Hall roof smoking cigarettes, it wasn't for Gracie to tell. "Please, Nina, come and live in the apartment and be a guide. You'd enjoy it. I know you would."

Nina started to laugh then. "Gracie, I'll think about it. About renting the apartment, that is. Not the tour guiding. I can tell you now I definitely won't be doing that."

FOUR DAYS LATER, Nina stood at the foot of the stairs at Templeton Hall as Gracie fixed her bonnet under her chin and pulled at her long skirt until it draped nicely around her ankles.

"It really suits you, Nina," Gracie said, stepping back and admiring her work. "And if you forget any of your lines, just call out for me and I'll come and help."

"We really do owe you, Nina. Thank you so much," Henry said with a warm smile, sweeping past them in the entrance hall and opening the front door.

Nina saw there was already a small group of visitors waiting outside in the morning sunshine. Her stomach flipped. She suddenly wished she'd also got the flu bug that had confined not just Audrey and Hope to their bedrooms, but Eleanor and Spencer as well. Nina hadn't been able to say no when Gracie had turned up at her house and pleaded again, on her knees this time, for Nina to help them out.

So much for keeping her life separate from the Templetons. Since she'd made the decision to try and keep her distance, she'd never had more to do with them. She'd also wanted to dismiss the idea of renting their stables apartment out of hand, but Eleanor, and then Henry, had been very persuasive.

"Come and at least see it first," they'd said. "Think of it as a short-term solution. You've been so good to us. Let us help you for once."

Even Hilary thought Nina should at least see the apartment before making up her mind.

It was farther away from the Hall than Nina expected, reached by a separate entrance, at the end of a large section of the garden, the stone stables building hidden from sight of the Hall by a small orchard of apple and plum trees. The apartment was completely self-contained and very attractive, with open brick walls and wooden floors, a living room, a small kitchen, and two small bedrooms in a kind of mezzanine area. The people who'd leased the Hall before Henry inherited it had done all the renovations, Eleanor believed, as an extra space for guests. "Gracie's right. You could even use the stables as your studio. Please, Nina, think about it. You'd be quite independent from us, I promise you."

The property was certainly big enough for two families, Nina thought. The rent they were asking was also very low, much less than she'd been paying for the farmhouse. Even if she only did it short-term until something else came up in the area, it could be a great help financially. And it would cost next to nothing to move. . . .

Nina rang her sister with the news the moment the agreement was reached. If Hilary was pleased about the apartment, she was even more amused to hear that Nina had also agreed to step in as an emergency guide.

"You'll send me photos, won't you?" Hilary said. "Not of the apartment. It's you dressed in colonial costume I want to see."

"As soon as I've come out of hiding, sure." Nina was so glad to hear her sister sounding brighter again, she exaggerated the guiding role even more.

The past month had been a difficult time for Hilary, the sadness of her miscarriage made worse by the fact her husband had been away in South America on a longed-for work-exchange trip. In the days that followed Nina's sudden flight to Cairns, she had barely left Hilary's side, reassuring her many times that she would get pregnant again, she just needed to give herself time. She'd spoken to Hilary's husband every day, too. He'd been as upset to be away, insisting he would fly back, only for Hilary to be equally insistent he finish his project. Nina hadn't left Hilary until Alex returned home.

"You're sure you're feeling better?" she asked Hilary now. "I'll come back up again if you want me to."

"We'll be fine. And it will happen again for us, I know it. In the meantime, go and hop into your Templeton Hall time machine and save up every ludicrous thing you have to do or say. And ring me as soon as you get back."

"You think this is funny, don't you?"

"Funny?" Nina could hear the smile in Hilary's voice. "No, I think it's hilarious."

BY ELEVEN O'CLOCK on Saturday morning, Nina wished she were already home ringing Hilary. It wasn't funny anymore. She'd never felt so ridiculous in her life. Her bonnet kept slipping. She kept tripping over her dress. She couldn't remember any of the facts about the paintings or the furniture or even the goldrush itself. The people in her groups weren't listening to her anyway. They all seemed much more interested in talking about their next meal stop or leaving greasy finger marks on the priceless vases and lamps.

Six long hours later, only seconds after the final visitor had left the Hall, Nina sank down onto the staircase and pulled off her bonnet, wincing as she pulled at a lock of hair.

Gracie was there immediately. "You were fantastic, Nina! Like a duck to water."

"A lame duck, you mean. Sorry, Gracie. Never again."

"Never again?" It was Henry, loosening his cravat and coming to sit two stairs down from her. He smiled up at her, his real smile. "But Gracie is right, Nina. You were a natural. So easy with our visitors, so knowledgeable. A little creative with the facts, certainly, but you managed beautifully."

Nina started to laugh. "Are you often asked about pig-breeding practices in the 1860s?"

"Oh, yes, believe me," Henry said, laughing, too. "We get asked about everything from pig breeding to cooking with pomegranates to Hawthorn's chances in the Premiership."

Gracie nodded eagerly. "Next time just do what we do, Nina. Smile, be polite, and move swiftly on. Isn't that right, Dad?"

Next time? Nina chose to ignore that. She'd take the rest of Gracie's advice, though. She stood up, smiled politely, and moved as fast as her pinched feet would let her to the guests' bathroom, where her own clothes were waiting.

She'd told Henry and Eleanor she would give them her decision about the apartment today. As she changed back into her own clothes, she knew what her answer would be. No. The day as a guide had helped her decide. She and Tom were far too mixed up in the Templetons' lives as it was. It wasn't good for any of them. They'd be completely on top of one another, in more ways than one, if she and Tom moved in. She'd just have to hope another more suitable house would come up for rent in the area as soon as possible.

She rehearsed her answer as she gathered her belongings. When she came back to the foyer, Henry and Gracie were waiting for her. Nina tried to ignore Gracie's happy, expectant expression, or Henry's warm gaze.

"So then, Nina," Henry said, smiling at her. "Have you decided about the apartment?"

"I have, Henry," Nina said firmly.

An hour later she was back home and on the phone to her sister in Cairns.

"So let me get this straight." Hilary laughed. "You're doing the guide thing again tomorrow and you and Tom are moving into their apartment next week? Nina Donovan, you just can't say no to that family, can you?"

Chapter Sixteen

I⊤ WAS QUICK and easy to move their furniture and belongings from the farmhouse to the apartment. Nina's bright curtains, painted furniture, and colorful rugs looked even cheerier in their new home. It also seemed like a good omen when she got a commission to paint a series of designs for greeting cards the day before they moved.

She started work in her new studio the next afternoon and yes, the light there was good, and there was something very inspiring about painting with the door wide open, looking out across the paddocks and gum trees, without the tank and shed that had blocked her view back in the farmhouse.

Her main worry, that she'd be under the Templetons' feet and scrutiny, proved unfounded. The design of the apartment and its position at the eastern back corner of the Hall meant they actually had great privacy. As well as that, the gate that joined their gardens creaked, and the gravel on the path crunched loudly, so she had plenty of warning that Gracie—and it usually was Gracie—was on her way for a visit.

"Mum said I have to limit myself to one visit a day, but I could come in the morning and stay all day, Nina, couldn't I? And technically that would only be one visit."

"Technically, yes, but, Gracie, I really do need to get some work done."

"I'll be quiet as a mouse. You won't even notice I'm here."

As kindly and firmly as possible, Nina asked Gracie to please leave her alone to work until three each day. "After that, I'd be delighted to see you."

"But not until three? What if something major happens and I'm bursting to tell you?"

"If it's really major, that will count as special circumstances, but otherwise, please, Gracie, I need to settle in, establish some kind of working routine."

"I'll try," Gracie said solemnly.

OVER THE NEXT FORTNIGHT, life was almost idyllic for Nina. Gracie kept to her rules, mostly. Nina worked steadily on her paintings. Thankfully, Eleanor and Spencer recovered from their flu and Nina's services as a guide hadn't been required again. Audrey still wasn't speaking and had refused to go back to boarding school, but Gracie happily shared the news that her sister was joining her and Spencer for homeschool classes. "I heard Mum ring the school principal about her, too," Gracie told her. "This nonspeaking is a rebellious adolescent phase, apparently. We're not to worry too much. She'll talk when she's good and ready." As for Hope, Nina hadn't seen or heard anything of her since she'd moved to the Hall. "She's busy drinking again," Gracie had informed her, matter-of-factly. "None of us see much of her when that's happening."

Tom had settled into his new surroundings very well, Nina was glad to see. His cricket practice had also increased from three nights a week to five, as the state competition neared. Spencer wasn't pleased about it.

"You have to go to practice again?" he'd whined, when he called over one night just as Nina and Tom were about to drive away. "I never see you anymore."

Tom told her every day how much he liked their new apartment. "It's the perfect arrangement, isn't it? For everyone, us and the Templetons."

Outwardly, Nina agreed. Inside, she hoped he was right.

IN THE HALL, Gracie's worries were beginning to build again. It was wonderful to have Nina and Tom so close by, but in her own family things weren't good at all. It had nothing to do with Audrey and Hope this time, either. It was her parents again. They were fighting nonstop, either shouting or giving each other the silent treatment.

Gracie wondered if she was the only one noticing all the tension. Spencer seemed oblivious. He was too busy on the project he and Tom were working on, whenever Tom wasn't busy playing cricket, at least. She'd been to the dam and seen it under construction—the raft they'd been talking about for months. It was huge, three times the size of her parents' bed. She'd dared to suggest that perhaps it was just a little bit too big for such a small dam, but Spencer had just said, "What would you know? You're only a girl." Tom hadn't mocked her, though. He'd been lovely, explaining to her how they were building it. From what she could see, it involved strapping about two kilometers of rope around some rusty sheets of iron. He also promised to let her have a go on it once it was built. "Not until we've had the first shot," Spencer had shouted across. Tom just smiled at Gracie and sort of rolled his eyes in Spencer's direction and she'd gotten that warm feeling inside her again.

At least Audrey was coming out of her room more often, but she still wasn't talking to anyone. As for Hope, Gracie didn't really want to know how she was. The more her aunt stayed in her room, the happier Gracie was. She'd heard some clanking from Spencer on the stairs one afternoon, but decided to ignore it. Just because it sounded like he was smuggling bottles under his jacket didn't mean he was, did it?

At least Charlotte was happy in Chicago. Deliriously so, she told Gracie when they spoke each week. Mr. Giles's apartment—"It's called a condo here"—was enormous, apparently. It had a wonderful view of Lake Michigan. "It's more like the ocean than a lake, it's so huge." She'd been shopping for clothes and books on Magnificent Mile. "It's what they call a section of North Michigan Avenue, Gracie, and you should see the shops. I've never seen so many big names and I don't even care about fashion! Mr. Giles has even given me my own credit card!" Best of all, Charlotte told her, Ethan hadn't turned into an evil troll now that he was back on home turf. "It's the world's easiest job," she said. "I take him to school or baseball or to visit his friends, pick him up afterward, and then we spend the rest of the time playing computer games or watching movies on TV. It's like having a best friend sleeping over except he's eight and a boy. And I'm being paid. As Ethan would say, it's awesome."

The main person worrying Gracie at the moment was her father. When he wasn't fighting with her mother, he was spending nearly all his time in his office, opening and shutting his filing cabinet a lot, swearing under his breath, and talking on the phone at strange hours of the day. Her most recent overheard conversation bothered her the most.

"The timing couldn't be better. Three months' work at least, do you think, between the cataloging and the valuing? Perfect, perfect. Yes, I'll come first, and the rest of the family will follow. Or perhaps all of us together. I'll let you know once it's decided."

Once what was decided? And what did "all of us together" mean?

Gracie didn't have to wait long to find out. Two days later, she was summoned into the kitchen by her parents. Audrey, Spencer, and even Hope were already there waiting. Everyone looked very serious.

"Take a seat, Gracie, would you?" her mother said. "And please don't interrupt."

Her father did all the talking. He'd barely finished breaking the news before Gracie stood up, pushed back her chair, and started running down the hallway, out across the back garden, and through the gate. It wasn't three o'clock. It didn't matter.

"Nina, Nina!"

Nina's head emerged from her studio. "Gracie, what is it?"

Gracie burst into tears. "We're leaving, Nina. All of us. Leaving!"

JUST LIKE THAT?" On the phone that night, Hilary was as surprised as Nina.

"Just like that," Nina said. "Henry and Eleanor told the kids and Hope today. They fly out a week on Saturday, straight back to London."

"But what about the Hall? The groups? The tours?"

"They're putting a sign up at the gate. 'Closed for renovations until further notice,' or something like that. Henry's ringing the local paper, too."

"But why? What's happened? Why so suddenly?"

Nina had asked first Gracie and then Eleanor exactly the same questions herself. Gracie had been too tearful to tell her. When Eleanor had followed her daughter out to the stables, Nina hadn't been able to read the other woman's face. She had seemed calm, matter-of-fact about the sudden news, but surely it must have been a shock to her as well?

Nina told Hilary all she'd managed to find out. "They've been called back to England for family reasons, apparently."

"Apparently?"

"It doesn't make sense to me. Gracie told me they don't have any close family left in England. And it just seems so strange, to suddenly decide to go back for three months, to close the whole Hall up. And it seems even stranger that they'd invite me to rent the apartment and then announce only a fortnight later that they're moving."

"So where does it leave you?"

"I'll just have to start packing again, I guess. I'll ring the real estate people tomorrow, look for a house in town after all."

"There must be more to it. You can't even get the truth out of Gracie?"

"Not a word. The poor little thing hasn't stopped crying since she found out."

Over the next few days, Gracie was a constant visitor to the apartment, but anything Nina said to try to console her just sparked more sobbing.

"There's nothing good about any of this, Nina. It doesn't matter what you say. I won't be able to be your neighbor. We won't get to see Tom play cricket again. I won't get to pick the flowers I helped plant. It's a disaster."

"Do you have to go?"

A slow, unhappy nod. "We have to. We just have to. It's just the way it is."

"She's obviously been told not to tell you anything," Hilary suggested after Nina related that conversation. "And they're all going? Even the drunk one? The mute one?"

"Hilary!"

"I can't say I envy poor Eleanor. Presumably she's the one doing all the packing and organizing? If I was her, I'd want to just run away and leave them all to it, wouldn't you?"

SOMETIMES, NINA, I wish I could just run away and leave them all behind."

Nina had already been surprised when Eleanor appeared at her door again. She was even more thrown now. "You don't need to tell me anything, Eleanor. I don't want to pry—"

"I know you don't. I also know you don't go around telling everyone around here our business. That means a lot to me, Nina. Thank you."

Nina was struck again by Eleanor's dignity and grace. By something else, too. Her sadness. There was something very sad about the other woman.

"Is there anything I can do until you all get back?" Nina expected her to say no. She was surprised when Eleanor hesitated and said, as it happened, yes, there was something they hoped she could do for them. Nina listened as Eleanor explained.

"Be your caretaker? But how can I, when there's nothing to take care of? The Hall won't be open, will it?" She was puzzled. "I thought you were going to ask me to move out."

"Of course not. You've just moved in. This will only be a short trip away, while we, well, while Henry—I won't go into it. But we *will* be back. And it would give us great peace of mind to know you were keeping an eye on everything in the meantime. Airing it, arranging cleaners, that kind of thing. We'd pay you, too."

"Eleanor, no!"

"Nina, we would. It's a job, so we'd pay you for it."

"You're already giving me cheap rent."

"If you won't take payment, then we won't take your rent."

"But Gracie said you were in financial diffi—" She stopped, embarrassed.

Eleanor gave a brief smile. "Gracie says a lot of things that she doesn't quite understand. Please, Nina, think about it. A caretaker's role in return for rent-free accommodation."

It was so tempting. So incredibly tempting. Work had slowed down again. Money was as tight as ever. And as exciting as Tom's promising cricket career was, it was also expensive—the equipment, the uniforms, the travel. One day, years off perhaps, if he turned professional, all his costs would be covered, but for now, it was her responsibility. Three months of rent-free accommodation could be just what she needed to help get her through this tight patch. Give her some breathing space . . .

"You're definitely coming back?" she asked. "It won't be for long?"

"Of course we're coming back," Eleanor said. "We'll be away three months at the most. Please, Nina, would you just consider it?"

Nina knew she should think about it first. Talk it over with Hilary, with her parents, look at the whole situation with a careful eye. But Eleanor was standing there, waiting, that sad, secret look in her eyes. There seemed to be no way she could say no.

So she said yes.

TIME MOVED faster from that day. Nina agreed to the terms with Henry and Eleanor, even signing a contract to keep it formal. A sign announcing the Hall's temporary closure was erected at the front gate. A full-page article appeared in the local newspaper. Gracie finally stopped crying and spent her days choosing what to pack instead, running each item past Nina for her approval. "I'm not taking everything," she informed her during one of her many daily visits. "Just my favorites. We'll be back so soon there's no point taking masses of suitcases with us."

The day of the Templetons' departure felt like a strange dream to Nina, as they all gathered on the front steps of the Hall. She felt as if she was a head of state, moving from one to the other saying goodbye, Tom following behind her.

Audrey was first in line. She gave Nina a feeble hug. She still hadn't spoken a word.

"Good luck, Audrey," Nina said. "I hope things get better soon." There was no reply.

Hope was next. Nina hesitated before holding out her hand. "Good-bye for now, Hope."

Hope's voice was as sardonic as her smile, her handshake perfunctory. "It's been a pleasure, Nina."

Spencer shied away from her hug and shook hands instead. He did hug Tom, though. Very quickly.

Eleanor and Henry were next.

"Thank you again, Nina, for everything," Eleanor said, kissing her cheek.

Henry kissed both her cheeks and then hugged her. "We couldn't do this without you, Nina. Thank you."

Gracie was last. Nina held the little girl close, smoothing down a flyaway lock of her hair. "I'll miss you, Gracie." She meant it. "You'll write to me, won't you?"

A forlorn nod. "All the time. When I'm not writing to Charlotte, that is."

Their bags were in the car. There was nothing for the Templetons to do now but leave.

"See you in three months," Nina called, as their car turned in a slow circle and made its way down the tree-lined drive away from the Hall.

PART
TWO

Dear Nina

Hello from London!

I promised I'd send you a postcard as soon as we got here, and here it is! It was a very LONG flight and we are all tired. We are staying in a hotel at the moment until we find a house but Mum has told me not to worry about that. It is very cold, hardly daylight at all, but it feels SO Christmassy already and the shops look beautiful with all the lights.

I will write again soon once we have somewhere to live. Please say hello to Tom for me. I MISS you both already!

Love Gracie xxxxxxxxxxx

JANUARY 1994

Dear Nina

Thank you so much for your thorough detailing of the situation with the window shutters. Please do go ahead with the lowest quote regarding the repairs. I will arrange for funds to be deposited into the account this week.

This letter also comes with news that I hope won't prove difficult for you. We find ourselves in the situation where we need to extend our stay here in London. Is it a huge imposition to ask you to continue in your role as caretaker for another three months? Either myself or Eleanor will phone you shortly to discuss this further, but we do hope it might suit you too.

In haste, but with gratitude, as ever,

Henry

MARCH 1994

Hello Nina!

THANK YOU for your wonderful letter. Yes, I was SO sad at first to hear the news we're staying here for another three months. I haven't told Mum and Dad but I'd already packed, so I had to spend another whole day unpacking again.

That is wonderful news about Tom being picked for the state junior team!!!! (Please excuse all the exclamation marks.) You must be SO proud of him. I wish we could all have been there to cheer him on again. Does this mean he is now famous??? Can you please send photos of him and of you next time? I want to stick them on my bedroom wall.

Apart from the fact we're not coming back to Australia yet, my other bad news is I have to go to a local school. Mum has decided to go back to teaching full-time, rather than just teach Spencer and me. She said it was because she wants to stretch her learning muscles again, but I also heard her fighting with Dad about money they owe, so it may be because of that as well. Dad is working hard. I think so, anyway. He's not here much. The new job he has means he visits lots of big old houses full of antiques in the countryside. Audrey is <u>still</u> not talking (Charlotte is disgusted about it. She says it has nothing to do with the stage fright anymore, it's all about getting Mum's constant attention), but she has started going to school again, a different one than mine, luckily. Otherwise she'd be writing notes to me all day, like she does at home, and I wouldn't have time to try and make friends. Spencer says she's probably the ideal student, never answering her teachers back. Hope is still with us unfortunately (please don't tell Mum I said that) and still spending lots of time in her bedroom, though it's not as nice as her room at Templeton Hall. Our whole house is <u>NOWHERE</u> near as nice as Templeton Hall. But it's only for a few more months so I am trying not to get too sad about it.

I miss you Nina. Please write back soon.

Love from your friend,

Gracie xxxxxx

AUGUST 1994

Dear Nina

I know Henry has written formally to ask you to continue to take care of the Hall for us until the end of the year, but I just wanted to add my thanks. As you know, we'd hoped to be returning by now, but life is always unpredictable, isn't it? Fortunately, things appear to be settling down a little now. I have taken a short-term teaching contract at a local school and am enjoying it more than I expected. The children are as stimulating as always, in their different ways, although I'm sorry to say Audrey still hasn't recovered her speech. I had hoped a change in scenery would help her, but sadly not as yet. Gracie misses Australia very much, but is slowly settling into London life, I think. Spencer at least seems happy to be here. Henry's work is going well. Hope also seems to be in much better health. I'm glad to say Charlotte is having the time of her life in Chicago.

Thank you again, Nina. I hope you know how much we appreciate your understanding.

This comes with all best wishes to you and Tom from all of us,

Eleanor

NOVEMBER 1994

Dear Nina

I'm sorry not to have written for so many weeks. We've had to move again. We're in a new part of London and I don't like it. Spencer has started misbehaving <u>all</u> the time and this week he broke Mum's favorite cup and he said it was an accident but I was there, and it looked to me like he pushed it off the table.

Audrey still isn't speaking and hardly ever leaves the house except to go to school. She still writes a lot of notes though. Mum has tried to get her to see a doctor but I said to her what's the point? If she doesn't talk to us, her own family, she's hardly going to talk to a doctor, is she? Charlotte rang to talk to her last week (to tell her off, from what I could gather—she still thinks Audrey is making the whole thing up) but Audrey just listened for a few minutes and then hung up on her. Charlotte was furious about that, as I'm sure you can imagine!

Dad is so busy all the time, we barely see him anymore. He is now working with another friend of his, cataloging the contents of three stately homes. Right up his street as he said, but they are all a long way from London so he doesn't stay here at night much, once a week at the most. I asked Mum if she missed him and she just laughed, which I didn't think was very nice of her.

At least it's the Christmas holidays soon so I'll have a break from trying to understand algebra and physics. But I wish I was back at Templeton Hall with you.

Love Gracie xxx

MARCH 1995

Dear Nina

I feel like we covered so much when we spoke on the phone yesterday but I wanted to put it in writing once again how much we appreciate your flexibility and good humor regarding our ever-changing situation. I know you went to pains to tell me that continuing our arrangement for another year suits you and Tom as well, and I hope you are being truthful.

Would you please reconsider our offer to move into the Hall itself though? It seems very unfair to ask you to extend your caretaking for a second year and yet still be crammed into the small apartment when the whole Hall is there at your disposal. Please take your pick of any of the bedrooms and treat the whole Hall as your own home. But if you truly do prefer to stay in the apartment, we will of course understand your decision.

You did make me laugh with your stories of the more persistent visitors. Yes, I'm sure you did get as big a surprise as they did to find you in your pajamas feeding the chickens! Please do feel free to put up another sign at the front gate, and as usual, charge it to our account. I do apologize again for that difficulty with the last check we sent you. Please rest assured Henry has rectified that and there should now be sufficient funds in the account to cover all your expenses.

I hope you're enjoying that lovely late-summer weather. It's very cold here at present.

With warm wishes to you and Tom,
Eleanor

December 1995

Happy Christmas Nina and Tom!

With love from all the Templetons in England.

Henry, Eleanor, Audrey, Gracie, Spencer (and Charlotte in Chicago) xxxxx

January 1996

Happy New Year Nina and Tom

We will see you this year, we promise! It doesn't feel like more than two years since we saw each other but then sometimes it feels like it's five years, if that makes sense??

That is <u>wonderful</u> and <u>amazing</u> news about Tom getting the scholarship to that school in Melbourne!! He must have written an incredible essay. As Spencer said when Mum told him, "That's not fair. How come he got brains as well as the cricket stuff?" You will miss him during the week, won't you, but I'm sure he'll come home most weekends. I asked Audrey if she had ever known anyone who went to that school and she wrote me a note to say it was <u>the</u> private boys' school in Melbourne, and that it shows Tom is super smart if he got an academic scholarship there. But you must know that already. I hope he knows we are all very proud of him. I'm going to send him a congratulations card today. Charlotte's just been home for a visit—her first since she went to Chicago, can you believe it? (Between you and me, she's got a bit fat but she said she doesn't care, the food in America is so great it's worth it.) The good news is Audrey has actually started talking a little bit again, but only to us, her family, so far. She doesn't say much, hello and good morning and please and thank you, and when Charlotte was here she went completely quiet again, but I think she did it deliberately to upset Charlotte, and let me tell you, it worked! I am fine at my school. Not deliriously happy, but fine.

The other big news is that Hope has a boyfriend! I don't know where she met him—a drinking den, Spencer said, but I think he was joking. If anything, I think it was in one of those AA meetings. (That is short for Alcoholics Anonymous, in case you didn't know.) I heard Mum telling Dad about it. (It was nice to hear them talking for once. Lately they only seem to fight on the phone to each other.) Mum said she doesn't believe in miracles anymore, but if she did, this would be one. She'd been about to kick Hope out again, had even packed up all of her things. Hope went off, in tears and still a bit drunk and was gone for hours and Mum had started phoning the police and the hospitals, when Hope turned up again. I couldn't hear a lot of what she said to Mum, but she seemed to be making a lot of promises and saying that this time something felt different to her too, she really was going to try, that something had "shifted in her thinking." She'd seen a sign outside a church hall or something and gone in and started talking to this man and he's become her mentor, if that is the right word. I saw him drop her off here the other night (his name is Victor) and he seemed very old to me, but she is definitely much happier and seems to have stopped drinking again and the best thing of all is she spends a lot of her time at his house rather than with us.

Sorry this has mostly been about Hope. She's been all we've talked about here lately. I'll write again with more news about the rest of us soon.

Love Gracie

xxx

FAX TO: Nina Donovan
FROM: Henry Templeton
DATE: August 1996

Dear Nina,

This fax idea is a marvelous one, thank you for thinking of it. And may I say again in writing how grateful Eleanor and I are that you have agreed to stay on for a third year. Life has taken some unexpected twists and turns since we arrived back, but please let me assure you that we have absolutely no intention of leaving you in the lurch, responsible for the Hall and its grounds for the term of your natural life, if you'll pardon my colonial pun. I have all sorts of positive leads or irons in the fire or whatever the terms are these days, so Eleanor and I are both still optimistic that we shall be Australia-bound again very soon. We are all missing our Australian life very much, as I'm sure you would imagine, Gracie in particular, of course.

Please don't hesitate to write to me—sorry, fax me—at this number should any problems, no matter how small, arise and we will be back to you as swiftly as possible.

Yours gratefully, as ever,

Henry

FAX TO: Nina Donovan

FROM: Eleanor Templeton

DATE: October 1996

Dear Nina

Thank you for your most recent fax to Henry. I'm sorry if I appear over-controlling, but from now on could you please write directly to me at this fax address as well as Henry on any matters to do with the Hall?

I also apologize again on behalf of us both for not warning you prior to the arrival of the valuation expert. I can understand that you might have thought he was pretending. I wasn't aware Henry had been in touch with a local firm, or indeed that he had considered selling the contents of the Hall. You were well within your rights not to let them in. Henry has telephoned the head office in Melbourne and they now assure us we won't be charged for what they called a wasted journey.

I'll also arrange separately for a shipping company to pack the ornaments, vases, crockery, and smaller items of furniture as outlined on the fax attached.

I will call you soon to answer the many questions I'm sure you have. Thank you again, as ever, for all you do for us.

Eleanor

LONDON, FEBRUARY 1997

Dear Nina

I wish you were here. I know I probably write to you too much but you feel like a Dear Diary except unlike a Diary you write back to me. Nina, it's been so horrible here lately. Mum said I had to learn to keep family talk to myself, to stop broadcasting it to everyone, but how am I supposed to keep news like this to myself? Mum and Dad have split up. I don't know yet if they are going to get divorced.

He's going away for good and he won't say where, and Mum won't tell me where either, but he's my father and I should know, shouldn't I? Hope and her boyfriend have moved into a new house a few streets away and Spencer has started spending all his time there. He says it is much more fun, but I'm worried. He's only thirteen and I'm sure he's smoking or drinking or both (even though Hope and her boyfriend don't do either of those things anymore). Mum's teaching full-time in a different local school and we have to go to the same one now, and I keep being teased and Spencer won't stick up for me, not when he's got a whole cool gang that he hangs out with. All the girls my age knew each other for years before I arrived and no one talks to me. Except for one girl, but she is so weird I can see for myself why no one talks to her either. I asked Mum if she would <u>please</u> be able to teach me at home again, but she got upset and told me to stop wishing all the time that things were different and that it's time I accepted that life isn't always sunny and carefree. I know that, but I just wish it was more cheerful.

Audrey is still not talking to anyone but us. She's mostly fine at home but as soon as she goes outside, nothing. Mum's still taking her to hundreds of psychologists (or maybe the other one that is harder to spell) to try and get to the bottom of her problem. It's called "selective mutism," apparently. Charlotte rang from Chicago to say she'd read a newspaper article about something called Munchausen syndrome, which is when someone pretends to be sick to get attention. Mum just got mad at her and told her to start showing some compassion, so this time Charlotte hung up on Mum.

I am too unhappy to write any more. I keep thinking there's something I could have done to keep Mum and Dad together and to help

Audrey talk again. Everything in my family seems like a big mess at the moment. I miss you, Nina. I wish you lived nearer to us.

Love Gracie xxx

LONDON, APRIL 1997

Dear Nina

Thank you *so* much for your letter. I know you also faxed something to my mum about me being unhappy because she came and had a talk to me even before your letter arrived in the post and she let it slip that you'd mentioned something to her about me wishing I could fix things between her and Dad. She told me that there was nothing I could have done and also that I must never think their splitting-up was my fault. They split up because they couldn't stop fighting over lots of different things, all the overdue bills especially, and Mum thought it might do them some good to spend some time apart while Dad went off to try and sell as many antiques as he can (including all the ones you shipped over from Templeton Hall for us, thank you). We need a lot of money by the sound of things. Mum told me everything. Well, not everything, but a lot of it. I suppose she has no one else to talk to at the moment. If you ever had a spare minute, would you be able to ring Mum now and again? I'm not always sure I am giving her the best advice. And I'm biased, of course, because all I want is for Dad to come back, Audrey to talk again, Spencer to come home and stop smoking, Charlotte to decide she hates Chicago and wants to be with us again, and then for all of us to come back to Templeton Hall and run the tours and be happy again. Is that too much to ask, do you think?

Love from your friend,

Gracie xxx

LONDON, NOVEMBER 1997

Dear Nina

Thank you for your latest letter. You helped me so much. You're right. Life is like the sea sometimes, big waves and then calm days, but I am sick of the waves. I want some calm days. Thank you also for agreeing to look after the Hall for us for yet another year. It feels like a dream sometimes, doesn't it? All of us there, and Tom and Spencer and the dam and that raft they never finished making. I wish we could have seen Tom being interviewed on the television after that cricket competition. You made it sound so exciting and you must be so proud of him.

School is okay, thank you for asking. I still don't have any close friends. I don't know what's wrong with me, but I seem to get to a certain point in conversations with most girls my age and then I run out of things to say. I'm not very good at talking about clothes or makeup or boys and that seems to be all most of them want to talk about. But I'm not lonely, I promise, or feeling sorry for myself. I read a lot and spend my breaks in the library and I like it there.

I've started doing babysitting on the weekends to try and save up some money for when I go to university. I'm also doing voluntary work after school. It was quite funny how it happened, actually. I saw a poster in our corner shop asking for people to visit the local old folks' home for a Share-a-Skill Hour. I was curious what it meant, so I went along—I'm glad I did. I was the only person who turned up. There was a group of about ten old men and women there wanting to pass on a skill each of them had, and only me to pass it on to. So I stayed for the whole afternoon, not just an hour, and came back the next two nights, too, listening and talking to as many of them as I could, and it was so much fun I'm going back next week too. So far they've taught me how to play whist, juggle three lemons, say hello in ten different languages, play the spoons, and sing "Jingle Bells" backward! They're all so lovely and such good company, I think I'll keep going to visit them even after I've learnt all their skills.

Dad is abroad traveling a lot but he sends me postcards all the time. (He sends all four of us postcards all the time, actually. It's become a bit of a joke among us.) But on the positive side he does include an interesting fact about each city or country, so it's been helpful with my geography studies. He makes it sound exciting, that he's learning all the time about whole new areas of antiques and getting to use his French (which he says is already good) and Spanish (not so good). He said there's a possibility that he might also get to travel through the USA and that his first stop will be Chicago to visit Charlotte. I don't know whether to tell him that Charlotte is still furious with him for the mess he got us all into and has declared she won't talk to him again until he has paid off all our debts, with interest. Charlotte loves making these pronouncements, but she does actually stick to them. She still hasn't spoken to Hope in all these years. So perhaps I'd better tell Dad and save him a wasted journey.

I'll write again soon. Lots of love to you and to Tom, and please thank him again for the beautiful photograph he took of the sunrise over the paddocks behind the Hall. I felt so homesick to see it. I've stuck it above my desk and I'm looking at it now. I miss you both very much.

Love Gracie xxxxxx

LONDON, AUGUST 1998

Dear Nina

Thank you for the beautiful card and scarf. I know, sixteen, imagine! I don't feel any older yet. Or wiser. Though I'm pleased to tell you I've discovered the secret to managing my hair. It's grown long enough that I can now just tie it back into a plait. Spencer of course says I still look like a deranged kewpie doll but I like it.

Thank you for your congratulations card too. Yes, I was so happy with my GCSE results too. I was worried beforehand that I wouldn't get all nine, so it's been a huge relief. Now all I have to do is pass my A Levels and then after that decide whether I want to study history or classics at university. Perhaps both. There's the next five years of my life mapped out. . . .

Yes, Dad is now based full-time in America, in San Francisco at the moment. He rang last week to talk to Mum (not that she always takes his calls—I have to act as their go-between most of the time) but she was out so I got the news from the horse's mouth, so to speak. He's moved on from buying and selling antique furniture to vintage cars. There's a fad for expensive English cars in America apparently and he's at the front of the pack, he tells me. As Charlotte would say, if I was to tell her, which I won't, "Here we go again."

Can you please thank Tom for his latest photograph? No, don't. I will write and thank him myself. If he ever decides to stop being a cricket champion or an academic genius, he could be a champion photographer, don't you think? The latest photos of the Hall and the trees in that misty autumn light were so beautiful. If/when the Hall ever opens to the public again, I am going to ask Tom to be our official photographer and make souvenir postcards of all his beautiful photographs.

More soon and love till then.

Gracie

PS Spencer's got a girlfriend. It's quite funny. She pretends to be a punk, swearing all the time, but I heard her on the phone talking to her mother and she was very upper-class. Audrey's still not completely cured yet, though Mum must have taken her to every clinic and psychologist in London so far, but nothing has worked. She's now decided to go down the alternative therapy route, so perhaps there'll be a change there one day soon. I'd never tell Mum but I'd quite miss Audrey's note-writing if she started talking full-time again. As for Charlotte, she's still trying to take over the world, starting with Chicago. We spoke last week and she started dropping hints about the next stage of what she is calling her "ground-breaking career in childcare"—I'll let you know what she's talking about as soon as I find out myself. . . .

FAX TO: Nina Donovan
FROM: Eleanor Templeton
DATE: October 1998

Dear Nina

This is a brief note just to confirm our phone conversation that yes, we are happy to agree to lease the bottom rooms of the Hall for the purposes of a meditation retreat. We can't thank you enough again for your part in this, not just in minding the Hall for us (can you believe it is now nearly five years since we left?) but for somehow engineering this excellent solution to our current situation and ongoing financial difficulties. I promise I will fill you in on everything, one day, when we are face to face, but it's not something I feel comfortable writing about.

On the plus side, yes, Gracie is doing wonderfully at school. I am so proud of how hard she works at her studies, and she deserves every one of her good marks. She also seems to have taken over the old folks' home up the road as well. I don't know if she told you, but for the past year she's spent nearly every afternoon up there, reading to them or chatting away or organizing book discussion groups and concerts apparently! I was talking to the matron last week, who said all the residents love her and think she's a breath of fresh air. Hopefully it's a breath, and not a hurricane. . . .

Not so brief after all! I will try to call soon. Thank you again, for everything.

Eleanor

FAX TO: Nina Donovan
FROM: Gracie Templeton
DATE: July 1999

Dear Nina

I'm so sorry it didn't work out with the host family the cricket association arranged, but <u>of course</u> Tom can stay with us instead. We'd love to have him! Please excuse me using the fax instead of our usual letters, but Mum thought you'd both like to know straight away. We're all just sorry you can't come with him. But that is so exciting that you have started teaching too. You don't need any advice from Mum. I bet your students are already in love with you. I always thought you were the most fantastic artist and now all those lucky children will get to learn to paint like you too.

Mum is working two jobs at the moment, teaching in the day and tutoring at night, but she's also happy that Tom is coming over. Thanks too for sending over the newspaper cutting of Tom with the rest of his team. He's got so tall, hasn't he? Please tell him not to expect another Templeton Hall when he comes to stay, but I'll make sure our spare room is really comfortable and I'll be sure to meet him at the airport or the Tube station too, whatever is easiest for him.

Spencer has moved back home again. (I never did find out exactly why he left in the first place, but I heard Mum and Hope have a rather tempestuous conversation about it the evening before he turned up. Hope is still sober, but there's still quite a lot of tension between her and Mum at times.) As for Spencer, he's got very good at blaming everyone else for anything that goes wrong for him. His latest excuse is that his misbehavior and bad marks at school are all due to Dad's absence, that he missed the steadying influence of a father figure, or some nonsense like that. As I pointed out to him, he managed to ignore Dad's steady hand for the first ten years of his life, so why he would have started paying him any more attention now, I don't know. He's smoking all the time, in his room too, unfortunately. It stinks but he doesn't care, he says.

Audrey is doing so much better since Mum found the new therapist for her, and between you and me, I think he is becoming more than her therapist. His name is Greg and he's from New Zealand and he's started taking Audrey out on what she calls "excursions" and I would call "dates" most weekends. He's shorter than Audrey but has a nice kind face and he really does seem to know what he's doing. It's amazing to see (or should I say hear?) Audrey talking to people besides us. Charlotte (of course!) is still skeptical. She thinks that Audrey has just switched her attention-seeking behavior from Mum to this Greg but I don't know if she's right. Mostly I think it's good for Mum to have one less of us to worry about.

Speaking of Charlotte, she's decided to go into business with Ethan's dad, setting up a nanny-training business of all things. I'm glad for her but sad for us. I really thought now that Ethan was getting too old to need a nanny she'd come back to London permanently, but not yet it seems.

Congratulations again on Hilary's news. You must be so excited to be about to become an aunty. (No chance of that for me yet— Charlotte says she's a career woman, not mother material, though I'm getting hopeful it might be serious between Audrey and Greg. . . .) I told some of my friends at the old folks' home and they've started knitting furiously so I will have quite a parcel of matinee jackets to send Hilary by the time the baby arrives!

We'll ring you closer to the date to make the arrangements about meeting Tom but for now, please tell him we can't wait to see him again. I wish you were coming too. I miss you very much.

Lots of love

Gracie xx

FAX TO: Nina Donovan

FROM: Eleanor Templeton

DATE: August 1999

Dear Nina

This fax is just to confirm that we will ALL be at Heathrow on Tuesday next to meet Tom. No banners, though, we promise. I only wish he could stay with us for longer than five nights.

Congratulations again on the wonderful news of your sister's baby daughter. It has obviously been a long, difficult road for her and her husband (it hardly seems possible that it is six years since we had Tom to stay at the Hall when you went to Cairns to be with her) but I can imagine the joy they are now feeling. Please give her our warmest congratulations (and I will also pop something in the post to her, care of you).

All our best wishes for now.

Eleanor

TO: Nina <Donovan.Nina@victoria.edu.au>

FROM: Eleanor Templeton <etempleton@londoneducation.co.uk>

DATE: September 1999

Dear Nina

Thank heavens for school computers and my apologies if this seems brief. I am always terrified I am going to press the wrong button and the whole email message will be erased before I've sent it.

We'll talk soon I hope, but I just wanted to let you know that Tom has arrived safe and sound. What a fine young man he's become, and he is so tall for an eighteen-year-old (or perhaps it is that Spencer is so small for a sixteen-year-old??). And I still can't believe all that is happening to him with his cricket—to think we were there the day it all began!

I'll get him to call or email you as soon as he is settled in. (I do like that he calls you Nina now. How grown-up of him! Spencer announced this morning that he now wants to call me Eleanor. I wonder where he got that idea from?)

Love from all of us until next time,

Eleanor

TO: Nina <Donovan.Nina@victoria.edu.au>
FROM: Tom <tom.donovan@hotmail.com>
DATE: September 1999

Dear Nina

Hello from London!

Everything's going well. We've already done a tour of the Lord's Cricket Ground and met Test umpires and coaches and even some of the Australian players based here in England.

Things are great with the Templetons too, but very different. I thought Gracie was joking at first when she brought me to the house. I suppose I expected it would be another big mansion, even bigger than Templeton Hall, but it's an ordinary London terrace house. Spencer hasn't been around much. Eleanor (yes, she asked me to call her Eleanor) told me he lives with Hope (yes, she is still sober) and her boyfriend most of the time. It's strange Henry not being around either. He's in France or America working, Gracie said. She also told me I had to tell you her hair isn't like a dandelion anymore. It's not. She looks great.

It's cold here, though. Not what I'd call summer!

See you soon.

Love Tom

LONDON, OCTOBER 1999

Dear Nina

I'm <u>so</u> glad we decided to keep writing to each other the old-fashioned way, rather than faxing or emailing, aren't you? I love hearing the post land on the mat and wondering if there will be one there from you.

Now I not only miss you but I miss Tom as well. I loved having him here to stay. I don't know if he told you anything, but Spencer went off the rails again while he was here and went back to live with Hope again, so poor Tom had only me for company most of the nights. He was so nice about it and it was great to be able to show him a little bit of London. I'll write and tell him myself, but I wanted you to know as well that he's welcome to come and stay with us anytime he feels like visiting England again, cricket trip or no cricket trip.

Apart from missing Tom and missing you still, of course, all is well here. I spend all day and what feels like all night studying. (Everyone tells me that A Levels are harder than university, but surely that can't be true?) If you need to know anything about Greek mythology, ancient Rome, the division of plant cells, or the irony to be found in Shakespeare's subplots, please just ask!

Lots of love

Gracie xxxx

NOVEMBER 1999

Dear Nina

Hi from Charlotte-in-Chicago!! Thank you SO much for sending all the Australian bits and pieces over. My now not-so-little charge Ethan's presentation at his high school was fantastic. He went straight to the top of the class. Yes, I can hardly believe I'm still here myself. When I took the job I thought it would be for a couple of years before I got sick of him and he got sick of me, but we're great friends still. Not that he needs me looking after him as much these days. He's growing up so fast. (He's fourteen now, a teenager. I can hardly believe it.) I don't know if Mum told you, but I've branched out a bit in the past year. I had lots of spare time when Ethan was at school and so I started to think what would be the best way to fill it. Nothing like having an internationally successful businessman as your boss! The long and the short of it is, Mr. Giles and I have gone into business together. Well, I'm doing the work and he's funding it, but it's still a partnership. I told Mum it's all her and Dad's fault. They're the ones who gave me this English accent and it turns out an English-accented nanny is quite the thing here in Chicago. Very posh and lah-di-dah, it seems. I'm no expert, I made it up as I went along with Ethan but we spent so much time with other nannies I found out all the horror stories as well as all the best things. So I've started training nannies myself! I'm going to take it slowly, just do it via word-of-mouth to begin with, but then that seems to be the way the nanny network operates.

You'll have heard all the rest of the Templeton news from Gracie, I'm sure. You do realize you are her surrogate mother and big sister and best friend rolled into one?? I should be grateful to you, and I am. Sorry if this sounds sour. I always felt a bit guilty leaving Gracie back then, especially after they went back to London and things, well, fell apart with Mum and Dad. But she sounds so happy at the moment. Her school results have been so brilliant and she can't wait to go to university next year. She hasn't stopped talking about your Tom either, by the way. The local London boys don't stand a chance with her compared to him. (I keep asking her about her love life and she tells me all the boys she meets seem too immature and anyway, there'll be plenty of time for that when she's finished her studies! Gracie really does amuse me sometimes.) She sent me over a bunch of photographs she took when Tom was staying with them—you've produced quite a hunk, haven't you, if you'll excuse my American slang! The female attendances at cricket matches will skyrocket the second they put him on the national team.

Mum tells me you still refuse to move into the Hall. Unbelievable. If it was me, I'd have been in there like a shot. But she also told me you've managed to rent some of the rooms out. That will help matters, I'm sure. Every little bit helps.

I'm getting worse than Gracie now, divulging family secrets. Better shut up while the going is good!

Thanks again for all the koala and kangaroo toys, and especially the didgeridoo. You should have seen the postman's face when he delivered that!

Love from Chicago

Charlotte xx

TO: Nina <Donovan.Nina@victoria.edu.au>
FROM: Eleanor Templeton <etempleton@londoneducation.co.uk>
DATE: February 2000

Dear Nina

I could feel your pride bursting off the computer screen! What incredible news for Tom, and for you, too, for him to be offered a placement at the national cricket academy—many, many congratulations from us all! And I think it is a fantastic idea of his to do some traveling at the end of his eight months there, and how wonderful that he plans to head in our direction again. I do hope he makes it to London and please tell him there is always a bed here with us. Lots of the sons and daughters of my fellow teachers at school have done the solo-backpacking-around-the-world thing, and survived to tell amazing tales, so please don't worry too much.

We spoke about it on the phone, I know, but I also wanted to say again how grateful I am for the way you handled the situation with the meditation clinic people. How ironic that people concerned with peace and clarity in modern life should turn out to be sneaky businesspeople. Henry assured me via his lawyer (sadly that is the only way we communicate at present) that he has deposited another sum of money in the Hall account this week, so please be sure to use that to pay for any cleaning or maintenance work you feel needs doing to set the ground-floor rooms to rights again.

We are all fine, I'm glad to say. Audrey continues to make wonderful progress. Her therapist (a very nice young man from New Zealand) coaxed her into a new form of treatment based on dramatic and artis-

tic crafts such as puppetry, pottery, etc. As I'm sure you can understand, we were concerned and skeptical at first, in light of the fact it
was her unfortunate experience with stage fright that triggered her
speech problems. However, it has had a very positive impact. She's
like a different young woman, not only talking easily outside the
home now, but eager to head out and about with him every weekend.
Gracie is convinced there's more than therapy going on between
them, but she always did have a romantic heart.

I'm sure you feel we are just sounding like broken records by this
time, but yes, I assure you that from my point of view at least, the plan
still IS to come back one day, to get Templeton Hall up and running
again, even to prove something to myself. I can't speak for Henry. I
don't want to and I wouldn't dare and he has obviously moved on
with his interests in any case (a combined vintage car and limousine-
hire business in San Francisco is his latest venture, if you can believe
it) but I am determined to see the Hall's beauty open to the general
public again one day. I know the mind plays tricks and memories can
seem rose-colored but our time there does seem bathed in a warm
glow to me sometimes. Then again, that could be because the sky is
gray outside, the neighbors behind us have been doing renovations
for the past four months and all we hear are the squeals of drills and
circular saws, and it feels like years since I felt a warm breeze on my
face rather than biting icy wind.

Enough of my complaining! Congratulations again, Nina, to Tom
and to you. We feel as proud as if we had coached him ourselves.

Love
Eleanor

TO: Nina <Donovan.Nina@victoria.edu.au>
FROM: Eleanor Templeton <etempleton@londoneducation.co.uk>
DATE: April 2001

Dear Nina,

We have a card and a present on the way to Tom for his birthday
but Gracie is worried they'll arrive late—could you please pass on

this email to Tom so he definitely gets something from us all on the day!

All good wishes to you both,
Eleanor

Happy 20th birthday Tom from all the Templetons!
Henry, Eleanor, Charlotte, Audrey, Gracie, Spencer, and Hope
xxxxxxxxxxxxxxxxxxxxx

MAY 2001

Dear Nina,

I've written to Tom already (he and I have also decided to ignore modern technology—real letters are so much better than emails) but I just wanted to tell you as well that it's brilliant news he's definitely coming to London as part of his big trip. It will be fantastic to see him. We've moved house (again) since he stayed with us last. That one turned out to be too big and this one is possibly too small, but it's close to a great park so if he needs to go jogging or anything else to keep fit, then it will be handy. We all wish you were coming, too—though you wouldn't have to do all the backpacking through Asia first, of course.

Mum told me she's told you the incredible news about Audrey announcing her engagement to her therapist—Charlotte has had plenty to say about it, as I'm sure you can imagine. Audrey is so happy now though, talking normally again, and he seems very nice. I really like his New Zealand accent, too (though not as much as I like your Australian accent, of course). Audrey's second piece of bombshell news was that she and Greg are moving to Manchester. He's apparently been headhunted by a clinic there. Audrey is quite funny now. After not talking for so long she now talks nonstop, mostly about Greg and how wonderful he is. . . .

I'm sorry this is briefer than usual. I have three essays to finish before Monday. And I thought the life of a university student was supposed to be all sleeping-in and doing nothing??

I hope all is well with you and that you are just as busy. I feel like we haven't been writing to each other as much as usual—that's my own guilt there, I'm sure. I promise I'll write much more as soon as I get all my studies out of the way.

Lots of love,
Gracie xxxx

JUNE 2001

Dear Nina

Please excuse this brief postcard but I just had to give you the latest in the Audrey & Greg Romance Saga—they've eloped! Well, to be precise, they secretly got married in a registry office in Manchester. Audrey said neither she nor Greg wanted the fuss of a wedding, and she especially didn't want the tension of Mum and Dad under the same roof. Charlotte thinks Audrey just did it to try and seem all bohemian and interesting. I'm staying neutral!

Love for now, and don't worry, we're all counting down the days until Tom arrives in London. I hope all is well there. Please do write when you get a chance. I feel like I haven't heard from you in ages.

Gracie xx

TO: Nina <Donovan.Nina@victoria.edu.au>
FROM: Eleanor Templeton <etempleton@londoneducation.co.uk>
DATE: August 2001

Dear Nina

The quickest of emails to let you know that Tom rang last night to say he's arriving in London on Wednesday. I'm unfortunately away at a work conference that day, but Gracie's now on holiday from university and will meet him at Paddington station. He'll be in touch with you himself soon, I'm sure, but in the meantime, we'll take the very best care of him.

Love from us all
Eleanor

Chapter Seventeen

GRACIE KNEW as soon as she saw Tom step out of the train carriage at Paddington that this visit would be different. As she stood on the platform in her favorite red coat and green silk scarf, her hair tied back in its usual long plait, she spotted him immediately. Taller than the people around him, his figure lean, his hair a mass of dark curls. He was wearing jeans, a dark reefer jacket, and had a battered rucksack on his back.

He put down the rucksack and they hugged as two old friends meeting, but even that moment, that touch, felt different. An electrical charge, that's how she described it to him later. He'd felt the same thing, he told her.

During his visit two years previously they'd spent their time together sightseeing and teasing, nothing so much as a kiss between them. All the letters they'd sent to each other since had been between two good friends, too, nothing more. Yet this time, from the first minute, every cell of her nineteen-year-old self was physically aware of him. They couldn't seem to stop touching each other, accidentally at first, she reaching for his rucksack at the same time as he did, briefly taking his arm to direct him to the right Tube entrance, before seeing the message that there were delays on the track. It was an unseasonably cold August day. She suggested a hot port while they waited, at the same time he suggested a hot whisky.

In a dark, smoky pub around the corner from the station, they had one of each. She was worried there wouldn't be anything to talk about, that she should have tried harder to track Spencer down to get him to meet Tom as well. But their sentences tumbled over and into each other's.

She told him about life at university, how much she'd enjoyed her first year, the joy of studying for study's sake. About her plans to move into a flat of her own as soon as she could afford it, how she was still babysitting and now waitressing, too, to try and save as much as possible. He asked about her family, and she talked about her parents' separation, her mother's teaching career, her father's constant travels, Charlotte's nanny business, Audrey's marriage to her New Zealand–born therapist, Spencer's ongoing wild streak and ever-growing bond with his aunt Hope, who was, yes, still sober and now running her own rehabilitation clinics with Victor, her wealthy, elderly boyfriend.

Tom listened intently, asking questions, laughing at times, shaking his head when she finished, telling her he felt like he'd just watched an omnibus edition of a family soap opera.

"That's us in a nutshell," Gracie said, laughing too.

In turn, he told her about his eight months at the cricket academy, about the second placement he was due to start after his holiday. He talked about Nina's new life as a teacher. He spoke about his travels through Laos, Cambodia, Thailand, Vietnam; the scenery he'd seen, the life of a solo backpacker, apologizing several times, midstory. "I haven't been talking to many people lately, sorry, Gracie."

"No, please, go on."

Two hours into their reunion, they stopped talking and there was a moment when all they seemed to do was smile at each other.

"You look great, Gracie," he said. "London suits you."

"You look beautiful yourself." She meant it, even as she laughed and said he was beautiful in a manly way, of course. He looked so strong and handsome and fit, she thought, like someone in an adventure story. She almost told him as much, before searching for more normal conversation. "In years to come you won't be able to sit here undisturbed, will you?" she said. "Cricket fans will be mobbing you."

He shook his head and smiled that shy smile she'd already committed to memory. "You're confusing cricketers with pop stars. See that man over there?" She turned and looked at an old man in the corner he'd indicated. "He might have been the greatest bowler in English history, for all we know, but people don't remember faces. Not when we're all dressed in white and look the same."

"They'll remember you," she said loyally. "Especially after you've bowled out the entire English team in every Ashes series."

"I need to make the team first," he said. "Minor detail."

"You will, Tom. I know it."

She took him back to her mother's house after a third drink. There was no sign of Eleanor, just the note she'd left on the table that morning welcoming Tom, saying to make himself at home, that she'd be back from her conference as soon as she could. There was no message from Spencer. Gracie apologized on his behalf. "I think he might be away with Hope again. She travels a lot and Spencer seems to go with her as her bag-carrier or PA or something. We're not too sure what exactly."

Tom smiled. "Don't worry. It'll be great to see him whenever he turns up."

Was Tom getting tired of her company already? "I can try a few different numbers for him, if you like? He might be back or he might be staying with other friends of his. He moves around a fair bit."

"Can we go and have something to eat first? You and me? We've hardly caught up yet."

The attraction between them intensified during dinner. He seemed to find every excuse to touch her, as she found to touch him. They ordered a bottle of wine, pasta, dessert, the conversation flowing easily, the two of them laughing together, swapping tales. Coming out of the restaurant, it was the most natural thing in the world to hold hands as they dodged the traffic, ran from a sudden rain shower, to keep holding hands even when they didn't need to, until they got home again.

Eleanor still wasn't back. There was a message on the answering machine. The conference had run late, she was staying with one of her colleagues, she'd see them tomorrow instead. They had the house to themselves.

They decided to pretend it wasn't summer and light the fire in the living room. He helped her bring in wood from the small garden shed, set the fire, choose music. There was more talking, more laughing.

Gracie offered another glass of wine and was embarrassed to discover there was none in the house.

"I'll go and get some. There's a wine shop just down the road," she said.

"I'll come with you. It's getting dark out there."

"I'll be fine on my own, I promise." She needed to slow this down, catch her breath, even for a few minutes. "Would you like to take a shower while I'm gone?"

"Is that a not-very-subtle hint?"

Another smile. "You don't need one, no, but would you like one?"

"I'd love one, actually. You're sure you'll be okay on your own?"

"I'm sure," she said, about to jokingly ask if he was sure he'd be okay in the shower on his own. Fighting a sudden blush, she showed him where the towels were, told him to help himself to Spencer's shampoo, now even more physically aware of him than before.

Outside, the cool night air helped calm her down. She walked to the store, chose a bottle of very good wine, and then sat on the graffitied bench down the road to do some thinking.

What was going on? Was she imagining this? Or was there definitely something happening between the two of them?

She tried to look at it rationally. It was Tom. Tom, Nina's son. Tom from the farmhouse. Tom who played cricket. Tom who had visited two years earlier, without anything like this happening between them. Tom whom she'd known since she was eleven years old. Tom, whom she'd had—yes, whom she'd had a small, secret crush on since she was eleven.

But she was nineteen years old now. He was nearly twenty-one. And yes, something *had* changed. All she wanted to do now was kiss him. She wanted to do more than kiss him.

She'd never felt like this before, so intensely physically aware of someone, so attracted. More than attracted. It felt like some kind of magnetic pull, almost out of her control. It had never felt like this with Owen, the closest she'd had to a boyfriend before. He'd been another volunteer at the old folks' home, a nice, friendly Scottish boy her age. They'd gone to the cinema several times, eaten pizza and watched DVDs at home together, had a day trip to Brighton. They'd kissed and done a little more than kissing, but Gracie hadn't wanted to go any further. Barely a month into their dating, she'd re-alized they'd run out of things to say to each other. She'd put off breaking up with him, not wanting to hurt his feelings, and then felt only relief when he broke up with her first.

But everything that had been missing when she was with Owen—real attraction, curiosity, constant conversation, physical longing, yes, *longing*—was all she was feeling with Tom. She'd felt it from their first minutes together that afternoon.

She stood up abruptly. She'd been gone long enough already. Per-haps she was imagining this. Perhaps she was a little bit drunk. Per-haps it was just that it was Tom, Tom Donovan, whom she'd known for so long. He was just an old family friend come to stay. She was confusing familiarity with something else. That was it.

She knew she was fooling herself from the moment she saw him again. As she walked into the living room with the wine, he turned from where he'd been putting some more wood on the open fire. She was instantly aware of every detail of him. His dark hair was damp. He was barefoot. He'd changed into faded jeans, a blue T-shirt, his arms bare, tanned, muscled. He smiled at her and her breath caught. She wasn't imagining it. She wasn't imagining any of it. Something was happening to her, with him, between them. Something *amazing*.

"Gracie? Are you okay?"

"I'm fine." She smiled at him. "Really, really fine."

He smiled back. "That's good. Really, really good."

From that second, she knew what was going to happen. She longed for it to happen. It was as if all the conversations they'd had as children, the games they'd played, the kindness he had shown her, the letters they'd written in the years since, the photographs he'd taken especially for her, everything, all of it, had been leading to this mo-ment when the two of them were there alone in the room, illuminated only by the firelight.

Did she sit down on the sofa first, or did he? Did he open his arms or did she? Afterward, she couldn't remember the detail of that exact moment, though she remembered every second of what followed. The first beautiful slow, soft kiss, every touch, every caress that fol-lowed, the unhurried, gentle slipping off of clothes, her top, his shirt, her skirt, his jeans. . . .

She gasped when he first kissed her bare skin.

"Will I stop?" he whispered.

"No, don't. Don't stop." She'd already decided. She wanted this to happen tonight, to make love with him now, tonight, his first night, their first night. It was soon, but it wasn't too soon, not for them. More touching, more kissing, more sensation. Waves of it, building inside her. She tried to find words, could only tell him again, "You're so beautiful."

She felt the smile on his lips as he kissed her neck, her breasts, lower. "Handsome and rugged, Gracie, not beautiful. You're the beautiful one."

If she'd imagined the way she'd feel the first time she made love, it had never been as good as this. If she had ever dared to imagine some-thing happening with Tom, she'd never pictured it being like this, like a slow dance, gentle movements, then the tempo increasing, each ca-ress becoming more urgent, more important, a sound track of their soft voices underneath. They moved from the sofa on to the floor, on to the soft cotton rug, warmed by the fire. "Is this okay?" "Does this feel all right?" "Are you okay?" Step by step, touch by touch, as if they were leading each other toward that final moment together, an explosion of feeling, of warmth, closeness, something wonderful. It hurt her only a little. He noticed, asked her was she okay, then asked her something else. "Gracie, was that your first time?"

She nodded, shyly. She had to ask. "Was it yours?"

He hesitated for a moment and then shook his head. "But it was the best."

The second time that night it didn't hurt. The third time the next morning there was only pleasure, ripples, then waves of it. By the time Eleanor arrived home in the early afternoon, his bed looked as if he'd slept in it, though he hadn't. Her bed looked slept in, too, though they hadn't slept there either. There seemed to be no time or no need for sleep. All she'd wanted to do all night was talk to him, touch, kiss, and hold him.

It was like a hunger, Gracie discovered over the next few days. A longing. A secret. Their secret, their special knowledge. Just a touch of his skin, the sound of his voice, the feel of him close by sent a kind of shimmer through her. As though there was a kind of current linking them, humming between them.

Eleanor noticed.

"It's that obvious?" Gracie said, mortified and delighted at the same time.

"Two's company, three's a crowd. Are you being safe?"

"Mum!"

"Are you?"

Gracie nodded. They were now. They hadn't been that first time, there in front of the fire when it had only been about making love then, there, quickly, now. Neither of them had wanted to stop, or been able to stop. She'd done some calculations since and knew that, fingers crossed, all was fine.

"It's taken me a bit by surprise," Gracie said to Eleanor, glancing at the door. Tom had gone out to get ingredients for the dinner he was cooking for the three of them. Eleanor was impressed when he offered. He'd smiled shyly at her praise. "Nina said I wasn't leaving home until I knew how to cook ten proper meals," he explained.

"Enjoy every minute," Eleanor said to Gracie. "You're a lucky girl."

Gracie had to ask something else, before he came back. "Is it okay with you?" She meant so much with that one simple question. Did Eleanor mind it had happened so quickly? Was it okay with her if Tom slept in her room . . . ?

"Gracie, you're nineteen years old. An adult. I think you can decide that for yourself."

She was still blushing when Tom came back from the shop.

Gracie discovered over the next week that Tom could do more than kiss her and touch her so gently, so beautifully that every part of her, her whole body, her skin, her bones felt like they were melting. He could do more than cook well. He could do more than make her laugh. She felt like he *got* her. He wasn't just her sudden, beautiful unexpected lover. He was the friend she hadn't been able to make until now. She'd often seen girls of her age walking with their boyfriends, talking and laughing, so happy and comfortable with each other, and she'd wondered how that would feel, how they knew what to say to each other. Now she knew. She didn't even have to think about it. It just came spilling out. It was the most natural thing in the world to want to hold hands, to want to share what was on her mind, to know how he was feeling, to want to be physically close to—revel in the closeness of—each other. She'd never felt a connection like this with another person. It made what was already special even more special.

On holiday from university, she was free to spend each day with him. They explored different parts of London, taking bus trips, Tube trips, walking across bridges, visiting galleries and museums, sitting hand in hand in Trafalgar Square, taking a picnic to Hyde Park, strolling beside the river. He listened, he asked her questions, he challenged her. He liked reading as much as she did. They discovered a mutual love of crosswords and spent a whole day doing one after the other together.

One afternoon in her room, she was at her dressing table, tying her hair back into its plait, while he lay on the bed reading through the pile of postcards from her father that she'd given him, wanting him to see them. There were more than fifty, sent from the dozens of cities and countries Henry had visited in recent years through his work. Each of them began with the same line: *Having a wonderful time, dearest Gracie, wish you were here*, before listing a quick geographical fact about each place and then an extravagant sign-off in his large, looping handwriting, *With love as always from your Dad xxx*.

Tom had asked her a lot about Henry, about his antique-selling, the vintage car business, all the different fields he was now—by all accounts, very successfully—involved in. He asked her whether she missed him, if it had been upsetting for her when her parents separated. It had been, at first, she told him. Especially when it became obvious her parents couldn't bear to be in the same room together. "I don't see him often, but I love his postcards. They're almost the next best thing. We all get them, dozens of them. Charlotte says he sends them out of guilt, of course, and that Dad's problem is he can't handle any of us now that we're adults, and Spencer says he doesn't even bother reading them anymore, but I love them. I know it means he's thinking of us. Audrey says it's not enough, that he should make more of an effort to visit us, but he does his best, and it's not like he's just disappeared into thin air or he's died—oh, Tom, I'm sorry."

"It's okay, Gracie."

It was a moment she'd been waiting for. The opportunity to apologize for something that had been on her conscience, ever since she'd realized the mistake she'd made, all those years before.

She came across to him now, took his hands in hers, her face serious. "I should never have been the one who told you about your father dying, Tom. I'm sorry."

She knew from his reaction that he'd always remembered it was her. He squeezed her hand. "It would have hurt no matter how I found out."

"I'm still sorry."

He reached up and touched her cheek. Even then, his touch sent an immediate ripple of desire through her. He smiled. "It's okay, Gracie."

It was as he was putting the postcards back on her bookshelf that he noticed it. The silver whistle he'd given her as a child, lying on one of the shelves. He recognized it immediately. "You've still got it? After all these years?"

She nodded, embarrassed. "It's my good luck charm."

He picked it up, held it in his hand, smiling at her. "Has it worked?"

"Better than I expected," she said, blushing more. From that afternoon, she started carrying it with her all the time, tucked carefully away in her handbag.

Eight days after Tom arrived in London, Eleanor casually announced to Gracie over breakfast that she needed to go up to York on a work trip. "Will the two of you be okay here on your own?"

"Of course," Gracie said, too quickly. "We'll be fine, Mum."

"Spencer might turn up yet, too. I've left another message at Hope's house to remind him Tom is in London."

"It's fine if he doesn't." She blushed. "I mean, Tom wants to see him, of course, but—"

Eleanor smiled. "First love is a wonderful thing, Gracie. I'm envious."

She hurried to try to make her mother feel better, said how sorry she was again about all that happened between her and Henry, until Eleanor held up her hand.

"Gracie, it's your turn, not mine. Enjoy yourself."

"You like Tom, don't you?"

"I like him very much. I always have. Do you like him?"

"I love him," she said.

She told Tom that night. She'd read in magazines that the last thing a woman should do is be the first to say she was in love, that she should play it cool, be assured and aloof, keep the man guessing. She didn't want to keep him guessing. She didn't want to keep anyone guessing. She wanted to shout it from the rooftops. She was in love with Tom Donovan, kind, gentle, funny, clever Tom Donovan.

She'd pictured telling him in a romantic, dramatic way. She never thought she'd just blurt it out. They were in Camden, at a comedy venue. He'd gone to the bar and was coming back toward her, a pint in one hand, a glass of wine for her in the other. Someone turned and bumped into him and he just smiled and told them not to worry. That was all it took for Gracie to be sure.

"I love you," she said, as he came closer.

"What?"

"I love you," she repeated.

"Why?"

"Because of the way you are. Because of the way you were with the spilt drink and that person just now."

"You love me because I'm clumsy?"

"You're not clumsy."

"Because I can carry two drinks at once?"

"Yes, but that's not why I love you. I just do."

He sat down beside her, passed her the wine, then leaned down and kissed her on the lips. "That's a happy coincidence," he said, matter-of-factly. "Because I love you, too."

The next day, Spencer turned up.

It was early afternoon. Gracie and Tom were in bed together when she heard the front door open. She stopped Tom from kissing her neck, went still, lay there, and listened. There was a kind of dragging sound, a door slamming, and then a loud "Fuck!" as something fell from the hall table and landed with a crash onto the floor.

"It's Spencer," she said, leaping up. "Quick, Tom."

He didn't move, just watched her with an amused expression. "Quick, what? Finish what I started?"

"No. Yes." She stopped. "Why am I panicking?"

"You tell me."

Gracie knew why. Because Tom was Spencer's friend. Because she was naked in bed with Tom. Because any minute now Spencer would come charging up here and she didn't want him to know about this yet. She didn't know why not. She just knew she didn't.

She heard his steps on the stairs, heard him shout, "Mum? Gracie? Where is everybody?"

"I'm in here," she shouted back. "Stay where you are. Don't move."

"Why? Is this a stick-up?" Spencer called back.

She pulled on a T-shirt and jeans and slipped out the door. Spencer was standing there with his hands in mock hold-up style. He was dressed in a grubby T-shirt, faded jeans, his unruly curls almost dreadlocks these days. He grinned. "Not very terrifying, Gracie."

She reached for the doorknob behind her and pulled it shut.

"Sleeping in?" he said.

She nodded.

"Cat got your tongue?"

"Of course not."

"Where's Tom?"

"Asleep. Out."

Spencer looked at her. She looked back.

"He's asleep *and* he's out?" Spencer said. "Or he's asleep outside? Or you don't know where he is and you're pretending you do? Or you're feeling guilty about not telling me that you and Tom have got it on and he's probably in there, in your room, right now?" He leaned past her and called through the closed door. "Hey, Tom. Welcome to London. Get up, you lazy bugger. We're going on a pub crawl."

Gracie hit him. "You know? How do you know?"

"That lady who lives here, too. What's her name? Oh, yes. Mum. She rang me last night."

"*Mum* told you?"

"Why? Was it a state secret? She asked me to show some sensitivity, not to come charging in on you both."

"Like you just have?"

"I'm being sensitive now, aren't I?" He pulled an exaggerated sensitive expression. "I'm so pleased for you, Gracie. He's a lovely, lovely man. I hope you'll both be so happy together." He changed his voice back to normal and shouted through the door again. "Get up, Donovan. We're wasting valuable drinking time. I'm practically eighteen now. I'm practically legal. Let's celebrate."

"He can't," Gracie said. "We've got plans for this afternoon. A film—"

Behind her, the bedroom door opened. Tom appeared, in jeans, barefoot, a blue linen shirt not quite buttoned. "Spencer."

Spencer grinned. "Mate! Welcome, welcome. Come on, let's go. You might want to put some shoes on, though. It's raining again."

Gracie frowned. "Spencer, I told you—"

Tom unself-consciously put his arm around her. "Maybe we've time to go for one, Gracie."

"One?" Spencer said. "Better than nothing, I guess. It'll have to be your round, though. I'm skint."

TWO HOURS LATER, she, Spencer, and Tom were still in the pub two streets away. Spencer was in high-octane form. He'd been away with Hope and Victor, he explained. Touring Wales with them, as they searched for a possible location for another of their rehabilitation clinics.

"I'm kind of Hope's pet, Gracie, aren't I?" Spencer said.

"That's one word for it. Charlotte's word is 'parasite.'"

"Gracie! Don't listen to a word Charlotte says." He turned to Tom. "Hope had an epiphany, Tom. Did Gracie tell you? A true miracle. The skies opened above her one day, a large hand appeared, a finger pointed, and a deep voice said, 'Never drink again, fall in love with a very rich, very old ex-alcoholic called Victor, and spend the rest of your days spoiling your favorite and only nephew Spencer.' And like magic, that's exactly what happened. Neither of us have looked back since."

"Congratulations to you both," Tom said.

Gracie just rolled her eyes.

Spencer laughed. "Gracie, just because Hope appointed me the Chosen One, there's no need to be so scornful."

"The Chosen One? Spencer, you bleed her dry and I'm amazed you get away with it."

"Bleed her dry? I'll have you know I work hard for every penny she gives me. I'm her Voice of Youth. I keep her in touch with what the young people of today are thinking, what drugs they're taking, what they like to drink too much of. You think those clinics of hers are so successful without that kind of insider knowledge? She needs me as much as I need her. It's the perfect relationship." He lifted his pint, took a big swallow, then grinned again. "Enough about Hope and me. Let's just talk about me."

At first Gracie laughed alongside Tom at all the stories Spencer told of misadventures in his social life, calamities in his occasional work life. Officially he was taking a gap year before doing his A Levels and going to university. Unofficially he had no intention of doing either. He told Tom—Gracie already knew—that all he really wanted was to be rich, as quickly and easily as possible. So far, though, it had been all pain and no gain. His attempts to get work in share trading had failed. The music business was his next goal, he'd decided. Not as a performer but as a manager, where the real money was. Unfortunately the closest he'd got to any musicians was picking up glasses in a nearby venue, and he was already on a warning there for sneaking drinks from the bar. He somehow made it funny.

"I'm starting to think it might have something to do with me," he said. "It's all right for you, Tom, basking in the love of a grateful sporting nation, your talent molded and coaxed and cherished, a place in the cricket academy set aside for you, like a seat at the throne of some royal sporting kingdom. What about serfs like me? The talentless scum of the earth? Do you need someone to bleach your whites? Polish your bat? Carry your ball—"

Gracie decided she'd had enough of feeling stuck in a locker room with a thirteen-year-old. "Okay, Spencer, thanks. We get the idea."

He turned his attention to her. "We? 'We get the idea.' The royal we? The royal couple?" He laughed. It wasn't a nice laugh. "How long has this been going on between you? A week? Ten days at the most? No need to carry on as if you're about to celebrate your fiftieth wedding anniversary, up there on your fluffy white lovey-dovey cloud, Gracie." He took a big sip of his drink. His fifth pint. He was drinking two rounds for every one of theirs. So far, Tom had bought every round. "Excuse me for putting a dampener on love's young dream and all of that, but a little look at the facts of the situation here mightn't do you any harm. In the real world, Gracie, there are things called holiday romances. Have had one or two of them myself, as it happens. Nothing like being a glass collector to be able to scope out a room for visiting international beauties. They come, I see, I conquer. Now, young Tom here, sure, he looks like a gentleman on the outside, beautiful manners, as my mother didn't stop banging on about on the phone last night—'And he cooks, too. No wonder Gracie is smitten.' " He did an uncomfortably good imitation of Eleanor's voice. "But my role in this family is to keep us all real, Gracie, and I don't want you thinking more of this than there is, okay? Tom's here on a holiday. He'll be gone without a backward glance one day soon and it's up to me to keep your feet on the ground and stop you from getting too attached or too hurt, or thinking—"

Gracie didn't wait to hear any more. She stood, picked up her red coat, and was outside seconds later, hands shaking from anger or the cold wind, she wasn't sure which. In less than a minute she'd gone back in time, back to being the little girl standing on the sidelines as Tom and Spencer hatched plans and had fun without her. How dare Spencer come crashing in like this, reclaim Tom as if they were back playing at the Templeton Hall dam again. And why hadn't Tom said something, stood up for her, stood up for what was happening between them? Because what Spencer had said was true? Of course. That was it. How could she have been so stupid? It *was* just a holiday romance for Tom, a little interlude overseas before he went back home and his life was taken over by cricket once and for all. . . .

She heard the door open behind her, then a voice.

"If we hurry, we'll be able to get to the five o'clock session."

She spun around. Tom was there, buttoning his coat, carrying her scarf. She'd left it on the back of her chair.

She said nothing, just stared at him.

"Unless you don't want to go to the cinema anymore? Pity. I liked the sound of that film."

"What about Spencer?"

"I don't think Spencer would like the sound of that film. In fact, Spencer isn't invited to see that film."

"You don't want to stay in there? Stay with him?"

Tom pretended to give the idea some consideration. "Let me think. Choice one. Stay in a pub and watch an old childhood friend get progressively more drunk and insulting. Choice two, go to see a film with my beautiful, non–holiday romance girlfriend, just the two of us. Or maybe not go and see a film. Go for a walk. Go and count bridges. Do anything that keeps me close to her for as long as possible. I really can't decide."

"But he's your friend. I thought you were enjoying it."

"He's your brother. I thought you were enjoying it. Sorry, Gracie. I'm not a big drinker. A few pints do me."

"So why did you stay as long as you did?"

"Because he's your brother. Because he was—is—my friend. I liked him. I still like him. I just didn't like the rubbish he started to spout at the end. When he sobers up, I'll tell him. Rule number one for dealing with intoxicated patrons, Gracie." He smiled. "Spencer's not the only one who's worked in bars. You can't talk sense to anyone when they're drunk."

Gracie relaxed.

He gently draped the scarf around her neck, once, twice, then leaned down and kissed her forehead. "So, the film? Or the walk? Or the bridges?"

"Can we just go home?"

"Option four, you mean?"

"Yes, please."

"Can we run rather than walk? Hail a taxi, even?"

She smiled. "There's the minor problem of Spencer having a key. I suppose I could always get the locks changed."

"Poor Spencer. Do you want to check he's okay before we leave?"

She hesitated. Right now, she'd be happy if she never saw Spencer again. She always forgot what a troublemaker he could be. But he *was* her little brother. Her too-often insulting, annoying, misbehaving little brother . . . She should say good-bye at least. She put her head back in through the pub door. Spencer was up on a table brandishing a pool cue like a guitar, miming to a Bon Jovi song on the jukebox. A pair of pretty young women were cheering him on. She called his name several times. He didn't hear her.

"Bye, Spencer," she said. Then, linking arms with Tom, she turned and walked down the street toward home.

OVER THE NEXT WEEK, Gracie kept waiting for something to change between them, for the gloss to fade. It didn't happen. It got brighter. London became an enchanted city, filled with beautiful buildings that she and Tom wanted to see, plays and films and comedy they wanted to watch, parks and gardens they wanted to visit together. The sun shone five days in a row. They even managed another night out with Spencer, a good night this time, a pizza together, and then a band in a local pub. Spencer spent most of the evening pointing out how well behaved he was being.

One afternoon, Gracie was surprised to get a phone call from Hope. Her aunt got straight to the point.

"Gracie, I hear things have become quite serious between you and this Tom Donovan. I think I should meet him again, don't you? Cast my approval. No arguments, please."

The next day she and Tom were standing outside the Dorchester Hotel in Mayfair, as ordered. Tom had been happy to agree, curious to see the "new Hope" in action.

"Don't be nervous of her, will you?" Gracie said to him as they walked in through the grand entrance. "She's really quite different these days."

"I'm not nervous," Tom said.

"She's sober, but she's still herself, if you know what I mean. Quite sharp tongued, but there's nothing to be afraid of."

He laughed. "I'm not afraid, Gracie. I think you're the one who is."

She stopped. "You're right. I am. I'm terrified."

Hope was sitting in one of the prime positions in the elegant lounge area of the hotel. She stood up, looking every inch the rich, successful woman, dressed in a beautifully tailored crimson suit, very high shoes, her face perfectly made up, her dark-brown hair cut in an expensive and flattering style. Gracie thought of her mother, too busy with her two teaching jobs to spend time on fashion and makeup. She preferred her mother's looks.

Hope gave her a dramatic kiss on each cheek, told her in an off-hand way that she was looking lovely, and then turned her full attention to Tom, gazing from top to bottom.

"Well, well. Look at you," she said in her mannered voice. "Didn't you get tall, dark, and handsome while none of us were looking? Come and sit here next to me, Tom Donovan. Tell me everything you've been up to since I last saw you. What has it been, five years?"

"Closer to eight, I think."

"Time does fly when one is having fun and sobering up. You're a cricketer, is that right? I do like an athletic man. You work out a lot, do you, from what I can see?"

An excruciating half hour later, Gracie stood up. She couldn't take much more of Hope's far-too-flirtatious behavior, she decided. And as amusing as it was, she wasn't sure Tom could cope with having his hand held by Hope much longer either.

Hope didn't try to stop them, checking the elegant gold watch on her wrist and saying she had an appointment to go to herself. "Another client, as it happens. My darling Victor and I are fighting them off these days. Society's mess is fortunately our gain." She kissed her niece on both cheeks again, kissed Tom far too close to his mouth, and then stood back and looked at them both, nodding thoughtfully.

"Yes, Gracie, I approve. He's handsome, he's smart, he's got beautiful manners and, quite frankly, a gorgeous body. A shame he's Australian rather than English, but I suppose you can't have everything. Off you both go now. And I know you'll talk about me once you're out of earshot, so do make sure it's complimentary, won't you?"

They barely made it out onto the street again before they both started laughing.

TWO DAYS LATER, Tom suggested to Gracie they go traveling together. She'd been dreading him telling her he'd decided to move on from London. She'd heard all about his trip so far, how much it had meant to him to feel so free, to decide on the spur of the moment where to go next. She wanted to travel, too, but there hadn't been the opportunity or the funds yet. She'd thought she'd finish university first. But now she wasn't so sure about that. Perhaps she could take a year off. After Tom had gone back, for example. Go back to Australia, perhaps, to see Templeton Hall again. See Nina. See Tom.

"Have you ever been to Scotland, Gracie?" he asked, as they lay on her bed together, legs entwined. They were both reading, fully dressed, but Tom's caresses on her bare arm were making her feel it was time they took their clothes off again.

She looked up from her book, already feeling her eyelids go heavy, the gentle molten sensation in her body, wondering again how it was possible to just want to have sex with him all the time, as though she were some kind of addict. "Did I want to make love, did you say?"

"That was my next question." His hand moved farther down. "But can you answer the Scotland one first? Before I get too distracted?"

"No, I haven't been to Scotland."

"Would you like to?"

She closed her eyes in pleasure as his hand slipped under her T-shirt.

"Gracie, are you ignoring me?"

"Mmm."

"Scotland? Yes or no?"

"Yes. Someday, definitely." She kept her eyes closed.

"On Friday? With me? And then Ireland maybe? Wales? Europe? The world?"

Her eyes snapped open. "Go traveling together? You and me? Together?"

"Don't you want to?"

She sat up. "I'd love to. I'd *love* to. But I thought this was your big trip, your chance to run free."

"I've done that. I ran free as a bird in Asia. Now I'm here. Now I'm with you. I want you to come with me. I'm begging you to come with me." He rolled off the bed in a graceful movement, landing on his knees on the side of the bed. "I beg you, Gracie Templeton. Come traveling with me."

"But I can't. I have to be back at university in three weeks' time."

"I'll have you back in time, I promise. I'll walk you to the university grounds myself. Sharpen your pencils. Carry your books. Shine a crate full of apples for your lecturers. But come traveling with me first."

She laughed. "I don't have a rucksack."

"I'll carry your clothes in mine."

"I think my passport is out of date."

"We'll renew it."

"I haven't got much money."

"Nor have I. We'll stay in hostels. Juggle for money. Eat scraps together." He hesitated. "So you'll come?"

She scrambled across the bed, down onto the floor, too, beside him. "I'd love to," she said.

THEY STARTED WITH ten days in Scotland, taking buses, trains, even hitchhiking one day. They fell for the grandeur and graciousness of Edinburgh and stayed there for four nights, talking so casually about returning for the Festival one year, perhaps even living there one day. That's how far it had gone between them, Gracie realized. They'd somehow skipped over the angst-ridden "Does he/she love me?" questions Gracie always assumed would happen in a relationship. It felt so comfortable being with him but also so . . . thrilling, was the only word she could use. Tom thrilled her. She loved talking to him, laughing with him, sleeping with him, making love with him, being with him. It was all so good she started to worry about it. Surely love wasn't supposed to be this easy?

She raised it with him one evening, as they sat in a bar in a village on the west coast of Scotland. They'd planned to stay there one night. The wild beauty of the area and the promise of a boat trip to the Isle of Skye had turned it into a three-night stay.

Tom listened as she explained her concerns, then nodded, very seriously. "You're right. It's going too well. Let's break up. I'm too happy. You're too happy. It will never last."

She frowned. "Shouldn't it be harder, though? Shouldn't we be fighting?"

"Of course. What's your stand on the nature v nurture debate? Roe v Wade? Should Churchill have moved against Hitler sooner?"

"I don't mean fight like that, about issues, about politics."

"We can fight about sport, then. Did Maradona touch the ball or was it the Hand of God?"

"You're not taking me seriously."

"No, I'm not. Let's fight about that instead. Should I or should I not take you more seriously?"

She started to laugh. "You should. You should take me seriously. You should also adore me, listen in amazement to everything I say, and think I am the most beautiful girl in the world despite my unfortunate hair."

He reached across and tweaked a lock of her still-flyaway white-blond hair. "I do adore you, you do amaze me, and your hair is what I love most about you."

The uncertain feeling wouldn't go away, though. That this was temporary. That it was somehow too good to last.

After Scotland, she and Tom traveled to Ireland by ferry, catching buses and spending a week touring the country. Two nights in Dublin, a day in Cork, two nights in Galway, a boat trip to the Aran Islands, across to Dublin again, then back to London. Tom's ticket back to Australia was already booked. They were just coming into Euston station after the overnight journey when Tom spoke.

"Have you ever been to France, Gracie? To Italy?"

"No." She was getting embarrassed about how little she'd traveled. "One day, I hope."

"Let's go next week. For a few weeks. A month, even. We could hire a car, take the ferry from Dover to Calais, just drive when and wherever we felt like."

"But we can't. You have to be back at the academy next week."

He shook his head. "I rang them last night."

"You did?" She remembered him saying he needed to make a couple of phone calls, that he'd promised to call home at least once a month. When he came back she asked if everything was okay and he just nodded and said that Nina sent her love.

"I've asked my coach for extended leave."

"But how? Why?"

He looked a little sheepish. "I said I was having a few personal issues, that I needed a few more weeks away—"

"Personal issues?"

"I was going to tell them I'd fallen in love and that being with you over here was more fun than playing cricket, but I decided that was too much information."

"But you love playing cricket."

"And I love traveling with you as well. So I was telling the truth. I am having a crisis. You or cricket? Cricket or you?"

"You don't have to decide between us, Tom. I know what cricket means to you."

They'd talked about it as they traveled. He'd spoken of the discipline of being a sportsman, the physical pleasure of being so fit, so focused, knowing that he was special—one in a thousand, he finally, shyly admitted to her. In the fifteen key matches he'd played so far, each of them leading toward a possible place one day on the national team, he'd taken a record number of wickets. He told her he didn't just love the matches, either. He loved the training, too. The camaraderie with his teammates. Gracie had heard talk of wild team antics, heavy drinking, and misbehavior. Tom shrugged. Yes, it happened, but it wasn't compulsory. He kept himself to himself, pretty much. And there were other people around, too, experienced people to talk to and work with, mentors really. He had two: his coach, and another man called Stuart Phillips, a well-known cricket journalist who'd swapped sides to work as an advisor at the cricket academy. In his mid-fifties, Stuart had three daughters, none of them sporty. He saw Tom as the son he didn't have, he'd told him.

"And you?" Gracie asked.

"The father I never had. Pretty obvious, isn't it?"

He shared the details of his conversation with Stuart and his coach with her now. He'd told them that he knew once he returned home, cricket would take over his life for the next few years, beyond that if he made the national team. He wanted these final, extra weeks of freedom and then his life was theirs again.

"Stuart gave me the third degree, checked I wasn't going off on wild drink or drug benders. When I just happened to mention you, he made me assure him you were of sound mind and flawless beauty. I told him you were both and then he gave me his blessing." Tom smiled. "He told me he was jealous, actually. He loves France and Italy. He also told me if I wasn't back at the academy in a month's time exactly, he'd, well, I don't need to tell you his threat." His expression changed. "Gracie, I'm sorry. I should have asked first, been sure you wanted to come with me."

"Go to France and Italy with you for a month? It sounds horrible. Hateful. The very last thing I want to do."

"So you'll come with me?"

Her smile was her answer.

IF ELEANOR WAS SURPRISED with this latest development, she didn't tell Gracie. As far as Gracie knew, Nina hadn't said anything to Tom either. Gracie hadn't written to Nina since Tom's arrival, but she was sure Nina would be as happy for them as Eleanor had been. There was the minor matter of Gracie having to borrow some money from her mother to supplement her savings—she'd insisted to Tom that she'd pay her share of the car hire and trip costs. After a short lecture, Eleanor gave Gracie not just the money, not just her blessing, but the loan of her own small Volkswagen for the month, too. She rarely used it, she told them. Two days later, there was another welcome surprise. A motorcycle courier arrived at their front door bearing a large envelope from Hope. Inside the expensive-looking bon voyage card was a check for two thousand pounds. The note was brief and to the point. *This is a gift, not a loan. Spend it unwisely. Love, Hope xx.*

The only hitch was Spencer. He surprised them both with his insistence on joining them.

"I need a break. I've collected more than three thousand glasses in the past month. My hands are like claws. They'll never open properly again. When I'm not battling drunks and glasses, I'm hammering against every bloody door in any strand of media I can and all I've got in return are bleeding knuckles. It's not me that needs a holiday in la belle France and bella Italia, it's my poor tendons. I need it, I deserve it. Anyway, if it wasn't for me, you'd never have got together. I'm the one who found Tom for you, Gracie. I'll leave you alone to live love's young French and Italian dream for three weeks and then join you for the last one. So where will we meet? Rome? All roads lead there, don't they?"

From the moment she and Tom arrived on the ferry in Calais it was a special trip. Gracie had schoolgirl French and Tom had learnt it for two years at school in Melbourne. Between them they managed to get directions from one village to another, to negotiate nights in small hotels or *pensions*, order cheap and beautiful meals in little cafés and restaurants. They spent two days in Paris, and did everything tourists should: going to the top of the Eiffel Tower, cruising along the Seine, taking a walk up the Champs-Élysées, sipping champagne in the Latin Quarter. The rest of their time in France they stayed in rural villages, sitting in sunny squares, living on cheap wine, crusty bread, cheese, fruit. Two days in the glamorous south of France were enough for them both, the excess too much after their gentle meanderings. In Italy they were both without the language, but it didn't matter. They pointed, tried in English or even French, so relaxed and at ease now that language seemed secondary to their needs. The weather was perfect, warm days, balmy nights. The Italian scenery bewitched them both. Golden yellow fields dotted with straight green cypress trees. Hilltop villages. Bustling cities. Sunlit piazzas. Noisy bars, enthusiastic conversations, friendly people. The sight of clothes drying on lines strung from balcony to balcony across cobblestoned alleys. Red geraniums on sunny stone steps. Gracie had never imagined a country could be so beautiful.

As they sat outside a café in Florence one afternoon drinking coffee in the sunshine, Tom surprised her by asking if she was still carrying the silver whistle he'd given her. Of course, she said. She took it from her handbag.

"I'll be right back," he said. She watched as he traced their steps back to a small side street lined with jewelry shops. He returned fifteen minutes later, with the whistle now nestling in a small velvet box. She took it out. He'd had it engraved: *For Gracie with love from Tom.* She'd already treasured it. Now it was even more perfect.

They talked constantly, about all they saw, where they were going, and increasingly about their future together. Could she come to Australia again soon? Tom asked. She could get work there, study, do whatever she wanted, he was sure of it.

Gracie had thought about it already. Thought a lot. It was the next big step in their relationship. Yet she hesitated before answering.

He noticed. "You don't want to go to Australia again? You don't like our animals? Our insects? I'll kill them all. Just let me know which species to start with."

She laughed. "I love your wildlife. I was thinking about visas, grown-up things like that."

"You won't need a visa."

"Why not?"

"Because I'll marry you."

He was joking, she knew, but she went along with it. "Why, thank you, how kind. But I'm much too young to get married."

"We'll just get engaged to begin with, then. We can get married on your fiftieth birthday."

"*That* was your proposal?"

"Wasn't it romantic enough?" He smiled. "Sorry, Gracie. I'll make up for it next time."

From that day, whenever they found themselves in front of a land-mark sight or looking at a beautiful view in any of the Italian towns or cities they visited, he asked her the same question. "Gracie Templeton, will you marry me?"

"Of course, Tom," she said each time.

By the tenth proposal, she barely acknowledged it. "Sure. Do you feel like a coffee?"

As they'd arranged three weeks earlier in London, she checked her emails the day before Spencer was due to arrive. Sitting in a small Internet café off the Piazza Navona in Rome, waiting for a computer to become free, she looked out at Tom, sitting on a stone bench, his face tilted up to the sun, his long legs stretched out in front of him. She smiled. She seemed to smile constantly these days. Tom had pro-posed to her again that morning, as they stood in front of the Trevi Fountain. She'd accepted with great enthusiasm for once, throwing her arms around him as though it was the first time, not the eleventh. A group of people behind them overheard and applauded.

Sitting down on some sunny steps a few streets down, he'd taken her hand, leaned back, and said in a casual way, "I mean it, you know. I do want to marry you."

About to joke back, she saw the expression on his face. He was serious. She bit her lip, her heart suddenly racing.

His expression changed. "But if you don't want to, that's fine. Honestly. Forget I even mentioned it."

She laughed, unable to help herself. "Forget which proposal? All of them or just that last one?"

"All of them. Forget I said anything." He smiled then. "No, don't forget the third one, the one in the square in Siena. That was really something special. I want you to remember that one when you are old and gray in your nursing home, looking back on your youth and wondering whatever happened to that nice young cricketer you knew once."

"That nice young cricketer I hope will be sitting beside me in my nursing home."

"I'll be there beside you? So you will have married me?"

"No. I'm hoping you'll have retrained as a nurse and be looking after me."

He'd kissed her hand, then stood up in the graceful, easy motion he had, pulling her up beside him. "You will marry me one day, Gracie Templeton. You wait and see. Protest as much as you like, but it's written in the stars."

Looking out at him now from the Internet café, she smiled at the memory. Once Spencer had gone, when they were on their own again, she would talk about it with him, seriously. Talk about the two of them, seriously. Because she realized something that made her feel strange and excited and scared, all at once. The next time he proposed to her, she would say yes and she would mean it. She did want to marry him. She would move to Australia to be with him. Have children with him. All of it.

As her turn at the computer came up, she crossed her fingers, hoping Spencer had changed his mind, that his email would say he couldn't make it after all. Her heart gave a lift when she read his subject line—Bad news—and then fell as she read on.

Don't collapse with disappointment but can only join you for four nights not seven. I HAVE GOT A JOB IN THE MEDIA. An honest-to-God, no-nonsense paying job that doesn't involve late nights or intoxicated wankers (myself excluded). Job is courier driver for a film production company. I know, it doesn't sound like much, but it's a start, the first of my stepping stones to media mogul-ness. My own van—all right, their own van—and all. It's small, it's white, it's beautiful. I am in love with my van. Anyway, will fill you and Tom in over a Campari or twenty. Arriving Roma Termini 2 pm Saturday. Be there or else. My last days of freedom. Will be in celebratory mood!

GRACIE AND TOM were waiting at the end of the platform when Spencer's train came in. The sun was shining, the two of them hand in hand, as Spencer stepped out of his carriage and came striding and smiling toward them, oblivious that he was about to ruin both their lives.

Chapter Eighteen

On the other side of the world, Nina was sitting opposite Hilary at the kitchen table of the Templeton Hall apartment. Hilary had arrived that day for a brief holiday while her husband took their two-year-old daughter, Lucy, to stay with his parents. The table was covered with lunch leftovers as well as a pile of the postcards sent by Gracie and Tom over the previous six weeks: brightly colored images of London landmarks, Scottish mountains, Irish pubs, and sunlit French and Italian villages.

Putting down the last of them, a card from Florence that had arrived the previous day, Hilary sighed. "Well, I think it's absolutely gorgeous. Gracie and Tom a couple, imagine." She noticed her sister's expression. "Why are you looking so unhappy?"

"I'm not."

"Nina, I know you. What's wrong? Aren't you happy for them?"

"It's not about me being happy. It's none of my business. It's his life. He's an adult. It's up to him who he goes out with, what he does."

Hilary laughed. "I'm sure that's how you think you *should* feel, but I can also see that's not how you really feel. Nina, it's Tom and Gracie. Your Gracie. Don't you think there's something, I don't know, perfect, about the two of them getting together? Fated?" She picked up the postcards again. "She sounds over the moon, he's so carefree, the two of them zipping around Europe together. I'm sick with jealousy. I know you must miss him, but—"

"I miss him when he's in Adelaide, let alone the other side of the world."

"He's coming back, Nina. He won't travel the globe for the rest of his life."

"No? What if he decides he wants to live in England with Gracie? You know he asked for an extra month's leave from the academy? What if he gives up playing cricket permanently?"

"Then I guess that's what he'll do. Or maybe she'll come out here instead and they'll spend the rest of their lives fruit-picking." Hilary laughed again. "Nina, he's nearly twenty-one years old. A grown man. You can't expect him never to have a girlfriend. And at least you know Gracie. It's not like he's met some complete stranger over there. Gracie's one of the Templetons. Your Templetons."

Nina abruptly stood up and started clearing the table. "They're not my Templetons."

"Well, pardon me for stating the obvious, but short of being adopted by them yourself, you couldn't get any closer, could you? You live in their apartment, you caretake their Hall, you and Eleanor are practically pen pals—"

"Hilary, I had an affair with Henry Templeton."

Hilary's mouth fell open. "I beg your pardon?"

Nina repeated it.

"But how? When? Where?"

"Here."

"Here? *Here*?"

Nina nodded.

Hilary was shocked. "But how could you do that to Eleanor?"

"I didn't do anything to Eleanor. They'd separated by then."

"Hold on a minute. This wasn't when they were living in Templeton Hall?"

Nina shook her head. "It was last year. When he came back to—"

"He came back *last year*?" Hilary looked around as if she expected him to appear again. "And you didn't tell me?"

"I couldn't at the time. I'm sorry, Hilary, but I just couldn't."

"Tell me now," Hilary said.

IT HAD BEEN a warm Thursday afternoon. Nina was in her studio, tidying up, not painting, feeling restless and unsettled. Her contract teaching position at one of the local schools had finished for the year. What was left of her freelance work had slowed again, too. She'd delivered her latest commission three days before deadline and waited to hear about her next project. And waited. Eventually, she'd rung the company's office. It took three tries before her call was returned. *We'll keep you in mind if anything else comes up. It's just . . . economic realities . . . computer technology . . . changing markets . . .*

She got the message. Since then, the days had stretched out long and lonely. The nights felt even lonelier. It wasn't that she was unused to being on her own. It had been that way since Tom had won his scholarship to his Melbourne school, coming home only some weekends and during the holidays. His visits had been even less frequent since he'd moved to the cricket academy in Adelaide. Lately she'd begun to wonder if it was good for her to be on her own this much. Would she be better living in town with neighbors to smile at, the main street a five-minute walk rather than a twenty-minute drive away?

There were still the advantages of her rent-free accommodation. She also still loved her surroundings: the gentle hills, the wide paddocks, that big sky, the Hall like a natural structure itself, the sandstone shifting between colors depending on the time of the day. But there was no mistaking the change in her thinking. A negative change. She wasn't just physically lonely these days. It was an emotional loneliness. A deep, hidden, sad feeling that life had passed her by. That there was no longer the chance of something good, exciting, or surprising happening to her.

She hadn't talked about it with Hilary, or even with Jenny, her closest friend in Castlemaine. She didn't have the right words for it yet. It had been creeping up on her since her fortieth birthday three years before, so slowly, so determinedly that she was reluctant to bring it out in the open in case it overwhelmed her completely. But it was there every day, when she looked at herself in the mirror and saw lines where there had been none, a softening of her jaw line, less sparkle in her eyes. She felt it when she got dressed each day and reached for clothes that she knew didn't flatter her, but were comfortable. It was beyond the physical, too. It was as if her spirit had left her. As if she could no longer see the point of anything—of her work, of herself, of her life. She wasn't suicidal, she knew that. She was . . . bored. Bored with herself, of what her life had become.

If her mother were there, or if more to the point Hilary were there, Nina knew what both of them would say. "It's just a phase, a reaction to Tom growing up. Empty-nest syndrome. You just need to change your attitude, not your life. Come on. Spruce yourself up before you've nothing left to spruce."

For the past week, she'd been trying that approach, starting from the outside, making herself wear makeup even if there was no one to see it but her. She put her sagging skirt and the old T-shirt with the tear under the left arm into the bin and started to wear the bright summer dresses, the expensive jeans, the silk tops she'd bought on a shopping trip to Melbourne with Hilary several years earlier. She even shaved her legs, gave herself face masks, plucked her eyebrows, did her nails. She felt ridiculous at first, like a teenager playing with her mother's makeup, all dressed up with nowhere to go. What was the point? Who was looking at her? It wasn't working, anyway, was it? That sad abandoned feeling was still there, under the bright clothes, beneath the makeup, as if that feeling of loneliness, that weariness, was part of her body now, had seeped into her skin. But she wouldn't give in to it. She couldn't let herself give in to it. Not yet.

When she heard the sound of a car that Thursday afternoon she wasn't surprised. Despite the *Closed* sign at the main highway turn-off, despite a second sign halfway up the driveway and a third sign where the car park used to be, determined visitors still sometimes made their way to Templeton Hall, lured by long-out-of-date entries in guidebooks. "When will it be open to the public again?" she'd been asked countless times. "We heard it was hilarious back then. Whatever happened to that family anyway?"

She had a stock answer. "The Templetons had to go back to the UK for family reasons but they're still hopeful to return one day." She'd said it so many times she didn't know whether or not she believed it herself anymore.

As she heard a car door closing, Nina hurriedly checked her reflection in the mirror, wiped off a smudge of dust from her forehead, and made her way down the side path.

A man was standing, eyes shaded, staring up at the Hall.

"Good afternoon," Nina called in a friendly tone. "Sorry, but we're closed to the public."

He turned, smiled, and spoke. "I know. Hello, Nina."

It took a second for her brain to take in his appearance, his use of her name. "Henry? *Henry Templeton?*" She knew her mouth was open. "What on earth —" She stopped and laughed. "I'm sorry. Did I miss a message? Did you tell me you were coming back?"

He came across to her, all smiles, kissing her on both cheeks, his manner as relaxed as if they'd seen each other a month before, not seven years before. He barely looked any older, though she knew he must now be in his mid-fifties at least. Tall, still lean, his face and figure as elegant as it had been the first time she saw him. His hair was grayer, perhaps, but his eyes were still as blue, his expression as intelligent and alive. "I'm afraid not. I didn't know myself that I'd be coming back. A trip to Melbourne came up out of the blue, I had a spare afternoon, and it seemed the car had a mind of its own and brought me here before I quite knew what was happening."

"You're back for good? I mean, it's great. It's great to see you. It's just a surprise." Nina switched into hostess mode. Awkward, surprised hostess, but a hostess nevertheless. "Come in. Come and have a drink, a tea, a coffee. But you'd want to look inside the Hall before anything else, wouldn't you? If I'd known you were coming—"

"You'd have baked a cake? Nina, relax, please. I'm not here to check up on you. Did you say would I like a drink? Do you know what I'd love? A dry, sharp, citrusy glass of local Riesling, if you by any chance happened to have one on hand."

"It's my own favorite wine. Of course I do."

Ten minutes later she and Henry were sitting at the small table she'd set up underneath an apple tree on the edge of the apartment's garden. The harsh afternoon sun had given way to a balmy, soft evening. The birds filled the trees with their calls.

Henry raised his glass. "Cheers, Nina. To you, to Templeton Hall, to weather like this for the rest of my life."

"How are you? How are things?" She laughed self-consciously as they clinked their glasses. "I'm sorry. I still can't quite believe you're here."

"You thought you'd really never see us again? Nina, so little faith. It's only been five years, hasn't it?"

"Closer to eight," she said.

"Good heavens." He laughed. "We didn't leave you too much in the lurch, though? Please tell me that and assuage my guilt."

"If anything, I got the better end of the deal. To have lived rent-free all these years. It doesn't seem quite right."

"Nina, it's not rent-free. You're our caretaker. Eleanor and I are the ones in your debt."

"Does Eleanor know you're here?"

"She doesn't, no." His expression was neutral. "I'm afraid Eleanor and I haven't spoken in nearly four years."

"I'm sorry to hear that."

"It's been a difficult time, for us all." He suddenly changed the subject. "And how is your wonderful son, Nina? Is he still playing cricket?"

She told him about Tom, living in Adelaide now, attending the national cricket academy, planning an overseas backpacking trip.

"I won't meet him this time, then?" Henry said. "Shame. I'd like to have taken the opportunity to nobble him somehow, for the sake of England's future Ashes campaigns."

"You might be sorry you didn't. His coach thinks he'll definitely make the national team one day." It sounded like she was boasting. She *was* boasting.

"Well, I'll be," Henry said. "I still think of him as that small boy."

"Not so small. He's six-foot-three now."

"Skill and height. We don't stand a chance."

As they both took a sip of their wine, there was a moment's silence. Nina hurried to fill it. "And you, Henry? What brought you to Australia?"

"The sunshine? The fresh fruit?" He smiled. "Work, I'm afraid. All I do now is travel for work."

"Antiques, still?"

"Sometimes, yes, but I've branched out in recent years."

"Vintage cars?"

"You know?"

"I think it was Charlotte who mentioned it. Or maybe Gracie."

"You've quite a Templeton information network going. Yes, it started with buying and selling vintage cars, and has moved on since then, into luxury cars, chauffeur-hire businesses, that type of thing. Nina, I don't think we were ever completely candid with you when we left, but there were financial reasons. You're nodding. You knew?"

"I didn't know for sure. I guessed, I suppose."

"We were in a huge mess, to put it bluntly. My fault. My guilt. And therefore, it was up to me to fix it. I hoped it would be something we would face together, as a family. Unfortunately, Eleanor felt differently. She saw it as my mess entirely and my responsibility entirely to turn the situation around."

"Money matters are always difficult," she said, feeling uncomfortable, remembering faxes from Eleanor. She hadn't gone into detail, but Nina had been under the impression that Eleanor had been very involved in everything. His next question surprised her.

"Nina, do you ever wonder what your marriage would have been like, what your life would have been like, if your husband hadn't died so young?"

Nina didn't have to think about it. "Everything would have been different. The person I am. Where I lived. My work."

He poured more wine into her glass, then into his. "Tell me what you'd have loved to be doing. If life could have worked out perfectly to plan."

Nina smiled. She'd played this imaginary-life game on her own many times over the years, sometimes to console herself on lonely nights, other times to prove to herself that she'd still managed to make a good life for herself and Tom. She felt flattered, charmed even, to be asked the question now. Everything about this whole situation felt charmed, she realized. As if she'd found herself playing a role in a film, the Hall the perfect backdrop. She took a sip from her wine and started to talk.

By seven o'clock that night, they were still outside, still deep in conversation, still slowly drinking the wine, savoring each mouthful. By nine o'clock, they were in her kitchen, eating a pasta dish she'd prepared. They'd opened a second bottle of wine to drink with it. That bottle was nearly empty.

Standing up to clear the table, Nina realized she was light-headed, not just from the wine but from something else, too. She was having fun. She was happy. She also didn't want it to end. "You'll stay the night, won't you? You can't drive back now. Wine or no wine, it's far too late. There's plenty of room here. Eighteen of them, in fact." She laughed then. "I can't believe it. I haven't even shown you the Hall yet."

"Good God, the Hall. I'd forgotten about it, too." He smiled back. "I expected to call in, say hello, have a quick look around, and be back in Melbourne by dinner time. What a surprising change of plan." He moved forward then, and touched her cheek. "What a surprising, interesting woman you are."

OH, NINA, NO!" Hilary's disgust showed on her face. "You fell for a line like that?"

"Please, just listen."

SOMETHING HAPPENED TO Nina when Henry touched her. She found a relaxed smile, though, kept her voice light, even as she tried to ignore the sudden intense feeling of attraction rushing through her body. It was the wine, she told herself. The fact she'd spent so much time alone recently. The fact that it was five years—five—since she'd been alone with a man like this. The last time had been a short-lived relationship with Jenny's newly divorced cousin. She'd gone out to dinner with him four times, slept with him once awkwardly, the second time a little less awkwardly. Two days later he'd called her and said he felt it was too soon, that he was still in love with his wife. "If I wasn't, I'd give it a go with you, though," he'd said as some kind of consolation.

Tonight's experience couldn't have been more different. She'd never talked to a man the way she felt able to talk to Henry. Not just about the Hall, or their families. They'd covered politics, theater, books. He made her laugh at stories about different clients in the antique business, and surprisingly, about the month he'd spent working as a chauffeur in Los Angeles. She'd been astonished to hear that. "It was necessary," he explained. "How best to learn a business than from the bottom up? I did it for a month and I was very, very bad at it. The ideal chauffeur is the quiet type. I couldn't keep my mouth shut."

Now, as she went through to her bedroom to get the key to the Hall, she found herself checking her appearance in the large mirror that hung opposite the front door. Her cheeks were flushed. Her eyes were bright.

"You look lovely."

She spun around.

"You do." He smiled. "Now, will you give me the formal tour, or will I do it?"

"I'm not sure I remember it."

"Oh, Nina. How could you forget? Come, let me show you." She let him take her by the hand around to the front of the Hall. As they reached the three steps leading up to the front door, he released her hand and threw out an arm as if addressing a waiting crowd on the empty forecourt. "Welcome! Welcome, all of you, to Templeton Hall, one of the country's finest examples of colonial architecture. Step inside and step back in time, as you spend a day at home with the Templetons. Well, one Templeton and one—" He stopped. "Nina, I'm so sorry. Remind me of your surname?"

"Donovan."

"Of course it is. As you spend a day, no, an evening, at home with a Templeton and a Donovan. This way, please."

Once they were inside the darkened Hall, Nina made her way to the fuse box. She kept the power turned off as a precaution against shortages rather than as a cost-saving measure. He was waiting by the front door when she switched on the main hall light. The small chandelier above their heads slowly began to glow, its brightness increasing until a warm golden light filled the entrance hall.

Henry gazed around, smiling. "I'd forgotten quite how glorious it is."

She let him lead the way as he moved from room to room, watching as he occasionally pulled back the dustsheets to touch the pieces of furniture that remained. All the smaller items had been shipped back to the UK years before. He stopped when they reached the drawing room. "What a beautiful place. What a shame we had to leave. It's as though we simply fled in the middle of the night, isn't it? As if we were abducted by aliens. Here one day, gone the next."

"The aliens theory did come up locally a few times."

He laughed. He had an attractive laugh. She was noticing many attractive things about him.

They moved upstairs to the bedrooms, bare of all ornaments now, furnished only with unmade beds and empty wardrobes, also covered with dustsheets. She pointed out the window shutter she'd had replaced, a floorboard that had needed repairing, the antique dressing table and wardrobe in the master bedroom that she'd recently had polished.

Henry shook his head. "The more I see, the more I realize how much you've done for us over the years. I'm ashamed, to be honest." He came across to her and once again touched her cheek, gently. "Thank you again, Nina. For everything."

FOR GOD'S SAKE," Hilary said. "Couldn't he keep his hands to himself?"

"Don't interrupt."

NINA KNEW THEN what was going to happen between them. All she wanted to do was reach up and touch her lips to his cheek. To touch his skin the way he'd touched hers.

For the rest of the tour she was conscious of everything about him—his voice, his body, the way he moved. It was as if her ordinary, black-and-white life had suddenly turned Technicolor. As if the arrival of Henry that afternoon, out of the blue, being so interested, so charming, so attentive, had changed her and her life in some way. As if she could do anything, *anything* she liked today.

When they found themselves at the doorway of the final bedroom, when she saw him looking at her, his expression one of interest, of admiration, when he said, "Nina, am I imagining it, or are we—," she was the one who interrupted, who said no, he wasn't imagining it. She was the one who reached up and kissed him first.

It didn't matter that he'd arrived only hours earlier, that he was virtually a stranger, that he was Eleanor's estranged husband, Gracie's father. None of that mattered. All she wanted to do was kiss him. Slip off his jacket. Touch his skin. Feel, in turn, the delight of his lips on hers, his fingers on her skin, on her back, slipping her shirt open, gently pushing her lace bra off her shoulder, kissing her neck, lower . . .

She was the one who said "Don't stop, please," when he hesitated. She silenced him with her lips. She wanted this to happen. It was going to happen. The bed creaked when they first lay on it, the noise soon covered with the sound of her gentle moans as his hands removed her clothing, his own soft sighs as she in turn took off his clothes, until they were both naked.

His voice soft against her skin, his lips warm. "It should be silk sheets, Nina, not dustsheets."

She kissed him into silence again.

THEN WHAT?" Hilary said. "You can't stop there."

"Use your imagination."

"I don't want to. Was it good, bad, indifferent?"

Nina hesitated for just a moment. "It was wonderful."

SHE WAS LYING. It hadn't been wonderful. Not the first time. It had been exciting, though. Sexy and fast and urgent and clumsy and over too quickly. Afterward they had talked, kissed, talked more. Then they had made love again, more slowly, more in tune with each other. He was a good lover. Very good. Gentle, skilled, experienced. She was self-conscious the second time, fighting against the feelings rising inside her, until she just gave in to it, to his touch, his fingers, his lips, his body. She cried afterward.

"Nina, what is it?" he said. "Is something wrong?"

She smiled, laughed even. It wasn't pain. It was relief. It felt so good to do this again.

They slept after that second time. She woke up first, the room dark, the dustsheet scratchy beneath her. For a moment, she had no idea where she was. She was naked, there was a man beside her, she wasn't in her bedroom, her mouth was dry, she'd been drinking. Where *was* she? She sat up as it all became clear. She was in bed with Henry Templeton. She had just had sex with Henry Templeton. Lots of very good sex. Oh, *God*. She carefully, quietly put a leg out, onto the floor, moving slowly, wondering where her clothes were, wondering—

His voice made her jump. "You're not running away, are you? Haven't we just got started?"

The warmth in his voice stilled her. "Have we just made a terrible mistake?" It felt easier to say it in the darkness.

She felt his fingers on her bare back, felt them stroke her spine, slowly downward, felt the stirrings of desire again. "I thought we made quite a wonderful job of it myself. But if there were areas you felt we could improve, then I'm certainly happy to try again. And again." His voice slowed in time to his caressing fingers, which were now tracing patterns on her waist, moving higher, as she felt him sit up, come closer, felt his hands cup her breasts, his lips touch her shoulder, her neck.

She turned back into his arms.

They stayed in Templeton Hall for the next two days. They made love, talked, laughed, made love again. Nina was aware her real life was only meters away. Henry had work waiting for him in Melbourne. He'd explained it to her. A contact in L.A. had told him about a chauffeur business up for a quiet sale there. He'd been planning a visit to Singapore for the antiques side of his work and decided to make a detour en route. The chauffeur business could wait for the time being, he'd decided. It would work in his favor if he didn't appear too eager. He would also postpone his meeting in Singapore. She heard him make calls to both parties, heard him sound charming, persuasive.

Henry brought his suitcase into the Hall. She went back to her apartment for as short a time as possible, for clothing, coffee, bread, cheese, wine. All they needed to live on.

She decided it was like being marooned on a very luxurious sandstone island. She couldn't believe what was happening. She felt like a different person. Not just physically, though her body felt changed into something sensual, something beautiful. She'd always watched her weight and stayed fit and now she reveled in the lines of her body, reveled in the feel of Henry's fingers tracing her curves, kissing her skin, touching every inch of her. In turn, she gloried in the feel of a male body again. How had she lived this long without it, without this touch, this pleasure?

On the third morning, she was in bed when she heard Henry's mobile phone ringing downstairs. She heard him answer, heard low murmurs, and she knew even before he came back into the bedroom, carrying tea on a tray, that things were about to change.

"Nina, I'm so sorry. I've been called back to real life. It's the deal in Singapore. I can't put it off any longer."

She didn't get upset. How could she? "Of course. When do you have to go?"

He had to be on a flight that night, he said. "But we still have today."

He brought her breakfast in bed. He found a bottle of champagne long hidden in the cellar downstairs. They made love again. She watched, the sheets around her naked body, as he packed.

Their farewell that afternoon was brief, but perfect. Standing on the front steps of the Hall, he held her close, smiling down at her. "Nina, this was wonderful. You are wonderful. I didn't expect this to happen but I am very, very glad it did."

"Will I see you again?" She didn't feel desperate or needy asking the question. She knew this wasn't the end. She knew something special had happened between them.

He touched her cheek. "Of course. I'll be back as soon as I can."

There was one more kiss, one more "Thank you, Nina, for everything," before he drove away. She stood, waving, until his car was out of sight. Afterward, she went back into the Hall, turning on the lights in each room, not because it was dark, but because she wanted to celebrate somehow, to be in bright light. She went to the room they'd made love in, tidied it, moved to the kitchen and washed the glasses they'd left, all in a kind of daze. When she went to bed that night, back in her own room again, she was still smiling.

AND THEN?" Hilary said.

Nina just looked at her.

"Nothing?" Hilary said. "Not even a phone call? A note?"

"I never heard from him again."

"But all the things he said to you—"

"Yes," Nina answered.

SHE WAITED a week without worrying. Wishing, but not worrying. She replayed every conversation they'd had. They became more witty, more sparkling. She remembered each time they'd made love. Her skin felt more sensitive, her body more sensual. She had new and sudden energy. She painted more pieces in the week after he left than she'd painted in the month before. She used brighter colors, her work more confident.

People in Castlemaine commented on how well she was looking. "I think I'm in love," she wanted to say. That was the surprising, the amazing, the wonderful truth. She had fallen in love. With Henry Templeton, of all people.

As she painted, as she gardened, as she cleaned her house, did her washing, lived her ordinary life on the outside, inside everything felt different. She imagined whole scenes starring herself and Henry. Trips away. Dinners out. Theater evenings. Long afternoons in bed together. Her conversation was always clever and witty, Henry's replies full of charm and intelligence. She made him laugh. She proudly introduced him to her friends. To Hilary. "I've heard so much about you," Hilary would say. Afterward, she'd confess to Nina, "He's fantastic. And he's mad about you, I could see it. It was obviously meant to be."

That's how it felt. Fated. As if this new bright, happy feeling was a reward for her long years of loneliness. She was glad now it had been that way. There wouldn't have been room for Henry in her life otherwise. He had shown her a new way of living her life. A better way. With him she'd become the best version of herself—relaxed, sexy. Loved.

Another week went by. No word. By the third week, she was still able to tell herself that the deal in Singapore must be complicated. By the fourth week, she knew but refused to admit it.

The fifth week, she couldn't stop herself. She emailed Eleanor, ending her carefully, casually written email with an even more carefully, casually written question. Had she heard from Henry lately?

It was two days before she received a reply. There was news about the children, the London weather. Nina skipped over that until she found what she was looking for:

> I understand from Gracie that Henry is in America again. Was there anything important you needed to talk to him about?

Nina let a day lapse before she wrote back. No, she said. There was nothing she needed to say to Henry.

AND THAT WAS IT?" Hilary asked. "You never heard from him again?"

Nina stood up and shook her head. "So maybe now you'll see why I'm not wild about the idea of Gracie and Tom being a couple."

"But you can't tar her with his brush. You always said Henry had charm to burn, that he could coax the birds from the trees. He's obviously just one of those kinds of men."

"But I'm not one of those kinds of women." Her raised tone surprised them both. "How *dare* he, Hilary? How dare he come crashing into my life, say all those things to me, and then just leave, never get in touch with me again?"

"Nina, I'm sorry, but men have been doing that to women for years."

"Not to me, Hilary. Not to me."

"Look, I'm so sorry you still feel hurt about it—"

"I'm not hurt anymore. I'm angry about it. I'm furious about it."

"I understand that, but you can't let it influence how you feel about Gracie and Tom."

"Why can't I? Why would I want my son to get mixed up with that family again? They can't be trusted, any of them. They said they were leaving here for three months. How long has it been? Eight years? Leaving me in the lurch, cleaning up their messes—"

"You've never been in the lurch. You've often said yourself how well it worked out—"

"Not anymore. It's time I started thinking about leaving. Time the Templetons faced up to a few realities about the way they treat people."

"Nina, just because Henry—"

"Because Henry what? Screwed me, literally and metaphorically? Took me for a complete fool? I told you the first time I met them that they were bad news. I should have trusted my judgment then, Hilary. Had nothing to do with them."

"Nina, you're overreacting—"

"I'm not. They're bad news, Hilary. The whole family. All of them, selfish, self-centered. I should have seen it long before now. And I swear to God, Hilary, if anything bad happens between Gracie and Tom, if she breaks his heart, if she hurts him in any way, I'll—"

"You'll what?"

Nina was silent for a moment. "I'll never forgive her."

Chapter Nineteen

Gracie could tell Spencer was in one of his reckless moods from the moment she and Tom met him at the railway station in Rome. She wasn't surprised when he produced a bag of dope out of his pocket and rolled it into a joint as they drove through the labyrinthine Rome streets, making their way out to the small villa apartment in the hills north of the city that she and Tom had rented cheaply.

"Gracie? Tom?" he'd offered. They both said no. "Great. More for me."

It was fun at first. They went sightseeing, sunbathed, listened to music, had long lunches, spent hours deciding where to eat each night. On the fourth evening, Spencer's final night with them, it was Gracie who chose the restaurant. She'd read about it in a guidebook. It was outside Rome, along a stretch of twisting country roads, apparently one of the region's best-kept secrets.

"A best-kept secret printed in a guidebook?" Tom said. "Wow, that is secretive."

The evening started well, the three of them having fun, laughing, being entertained once again by Spencer's stories. Until he started ordering shots of different liqueurs: grappa, limoncello, sambuca. Gracie bowed out, having volunteered to be the driver. She was surprised when Tom kept going, meeting Spencer drink for drink for the next two rounds.

"Good for you, Tom," Spencer said, raising his glass. "To the final days of our carefree youth."

"He's a bad influence on you," she tried to joke, when Spencer left to go to the bar again.

"These are my last days of freedom, Gracie. Spencer's right."

Her feeling of unease grew from that moment. The night took on a different mood. She felt one step behind them both. They seemed to be talking too loudly, laughing too much, while she grew quieter. She wanted Tom to notice, wanted him to do what he'd done that time in London, take her away so it was just the two of them, not the three of them, her on the sidelines.

She was the one who called a halt, as Spencer stood to buy another round, the fourth, or was it their fifth? "No, Spencer. We have to go. Now." She went to the bathroom to escape the taunting that she knew would come, Spencer calling her a spoilsport, a killjoy.

When she came back, he was gone. Tom was standing by the front door, looking out over the dark hills and valleys, the lights of Rome visible as a distant haze.

"Where is he?"

"Waiting in the car in a sulk."

"You're not mad at me, too, are you?"

Tom leaned down, kissed the top of her head. "Mad at you? At my Gracie? Never."

Spencer was in the driver's seat when she and Tom got there. The door was open, the engine revving. "Sporty little number," he called across.

She stood by the door. "Get out, Spencer. You're too drunk to drive."

"I'm not. I'm sober as a judge."

"Get out."

Spencer held up his hands in surrender. "Jesus, Gracie. What's happened to you? Tom, how do you stand it? It must be like dating a fishwife. God help you if this lasts between you. You're young, Tom. You should be carefree like me, not having someone nipping at your heels every minute like her."

That stung Gracie. That was too close to the bone, too close to how she'd been feeling all night. "Fine," she said, too loudly. "You drive, Spencer. You get us home."

"Gracie, relax," Tom said. "Don't listen to him. He's drunk."

"I am drunk," Spencer said. "You are drunk. We are all drunk. Do you think I could teach English?"

"Get out, Spencer," Gracie snapped. "Give me the keys and get out."

There was a dance between Spencer and Tom then, exaggerated politeness, each opening a car door for each other. Gracie sat upright in the driver's seat, furious, wanting to ignore them, wanting her brother to go away. Eventually they took their seats, Tom in the front beside her, her brother in the back.

As she slowly drove the car down the restaurant's driveway, then indicated left, Spencer started singing "That's Amore" in an exaggerated comic opera voice.

Tom joined in. She stayed silent, concentrating on driving on the right-hand side. Their apartment was only a few kilometers away. The road ahead was dark. That was one good thing about staying this far out in the countryside. They had the road to themselves.

Tom and Spencer kept singing, each of them trying to make the other laugh with exaggerated operatic flourishes, building up to a crescendo. *That's amore . . ."*

As Spencer sang too loudly right behind her, he started tugging at her plait, deliberately trying to annoy her. She ignored it the first time, just reached back and swatted his hand away. Moments later he did it again. She tried to swat him away again. "Stop it, Spencer. It's not funny." The third time he did it, still singing, pulling even harder on her plait, her anger was like a hot rush inside. She spun around to shout at him. "I told you, Spencer. Stop it!"

Their song was still in her head when she woke up the next morning in the hospital. She remembered a shout from Tom, or was it Spencer? "Gracie, look out!" The lights of a truck appearing over the hill, headed right toward them. The sound of a horn. Screeching. Their brakes, the truck's brakes. Then feeling took over from sound. The moment of impact, slow, slow at first, and then everything turned into fast motion, as she jerked forward, the seat belt like a whip across her chest, holding her, her neck twisting, her chest hitting against the wheel, falling back, the car all motion, wrong motion, filled with sound, more screeches and bangs and shouting, her shouting, Spencer's shouting. Tom's silence.

For just a few seconds, everything was quiet, deathly quiet, but there was still movement, their car still seemed to be moving, and she was dizzy with it. What had happened? She sat up, somehow, touched her head, felt liquid. Blood. Everything was dark. She heard whimpering. Was it her? Tom? Spencer?

She said their names over and again. She was sure she said their names, but there was no sound in return. Was she dead? Had she died? Were they all dead?

"Gracie, are you all right?"

The voice came from behind her. Spencer.

Still no sound from Tom.

"We've had a crash," Spencer said. The stupidest, most obvious thing in the world to say.

"We need to get out," she said. She could smell petrol. The car was going to explode.

Tom's body was slumped away from her, against his door. She had to get him out now. Quickly. She somehow got her door open, feeling a sharp pain in her chest as she leaned forward, a worse, tearing pain in her ankle as she got out. She kept moving. She had to get Tom out. She fell, got up again, another blast of pain. She heard crying, panting, and realized it was coming from her.

The truck driver was getting out of his cabin. He was walking. His head was bleeding, but he was moving. He was shouting at them, shouting at them in Italian they couldn't understand. As Gracie reached Tom's side of the car, she heard another car stop, a person get out, more Italian being spoken, heard the truck driver speak into his phone, shout into his phone, heard *polizia* and *ambulanza*. She was beside Tom now, trying to open his door, but the handle wouldn't work. She could see him in the flickering light from the truck's indicators. She said his name over and again. "Tom? Tom?" The glass of the window was cracked but not smashed. He was lying at a bad angle, she could see that. His eyes were shut. He wasn't moving. He was there. He was dead. She'd killed him.

Spencer was beside her. "Gracie? Is he all right?" He sounded like a child.

She grabbed her brother's hand so tightly she felt a jolt of pain up her arm. She was crying, the tears were flooding down her face but she couldn't wipe them away. "I think he's dead, Spencer. He's—"

"He's not. Gracie, he's not. Look, he's moving."

She could only stare through the glass, put her free hand to the glass. Spencer was right. Tom was moving. His eyes were still shut but she saw him move his arm. She called his name, again and again, still pulling at the door, as if she could open it with her bare hands, pushing at the window as if she could get to him through the glass. She pushed again and heard the glass crack, like gunshot in the silent night air.

"Leave it. Don't touch him. Leave him." An American accent. A man, mid-fifties, bearded. In charge. "Step back. You need to step back. Don't push the glass on him. Don't try and move him. If his spine is injured, you could cripple him for life. Leave him."

"He's my boyfriend. I need him to know I'm here." She said his name again. There was blood on his forehead. "Tom, can you hear me?" She couldn't stop saying his name.

Sirens. Lights. More noise. The American voice again. "Miss, step back. Let the ambulance people through."

They made her stand far back, too far back. She could do nothing but watch as the huddle of men and women spoke, as they decided the door was too damaged, they'd have to cut him out. Her ankle pain was almost unbearable but she wouldn't move. Spencer was in the ambulance. She saw him talking to the nurse, smiling even. He was smiling. They called for her. She shook her head, shook their hands off her. She had to be there with Tom, had to let him know she was there, saying his name, trying to make herself heard over the terrible, ear-splitting sound of the cutting equipment.

With Spencer beside her again, she watched as the ambulance crew freed the still-unconscious Tom, as they gently, carefully placed a collar around his neck, eased him onto a hard stretcher. Her hands shook, her body shook, tears ran down her face. She saw the ambulance door shut, watched a second ambulance arrive for her and Spencer. Two policemen coming toward them, asking in accented English, "Who was the driver?"

She must have fainted then. Shock and loss of blood. When she woke up the first time, she was in the ambulance. The second time, she woke in the hospital, with her forehead bandaged, her ankle in plaster. It took an hour to find someone who spoke enough English to answer the question she couldn't stop asking. "Is he all right?"

"Your brother? He is fine."

"Not my brother. The other man. Tom. Is Tom all right? The man in the crash with me."

"More serious. Surgery. Your mother is on the way."

Spencer had phoned Eleanor, she learnt later. While she was taken into the emergency ward, given brain scans and X-rays, he had telephoned Eleanor in London. "We'd been out to dinner, having a few drinks. Gracie was driving and she ran into a truck."

They took blood samples while she was unconscious to check her alcohol levels. She was under the limit. But it was too late to change the story that Spencer had unwittingly spread. They'd been out eating, drinking, and then she had driven. She was a drunk driver.

It took Eleanor eight hours to get to them from London. Gracie cried as soon as she saw her mother's anxious face. Eleanor was crying, too.

"Mum, I'm so sorry." Gracie couldn't stop apologizing. "I'm so sorry."

"Gracie, it was an accident. An accident. We all know that. Nina will understand."

Her mother thought she was apologizing for what had happened to Tom. "Is Nina here already?"

"She's on her way."

"I have to see him," she said, trying to get out of the bed, pushing against her mother's hands as she gently, firmly moved her back.

"Gracie, your ankle's badly broken in two places, you've got bruised ribs, a bad cut on your head. You have to stay still. And he's in intensive care, darling. You can't see him yet. Not yet."

"But I have to see him. He has to know I'm here."

"They're only letting family see him, Gracie. I'm so sorry."

It was thirty-six hours before Nina arrived in Rome. Gracie heard her voice late on the second afternoon, outside in the corridor. Confined to her bed, she could only sit up and wait for her to come in. But

Nina didn't come in. She stayed outside, talking, shouting at someone. At Eleanor, Gracie soon realized.

Nina's voice was more like a cry, her words tumbling over one another in her panic and shock. Gracie heard Nina shout Tom's name, say something about Tom, then say her name, heard her shout "drunk driving." But she hadn't been drunk driving. She'd been under the limit. Who'd told Nina she'd been drunk? She waited for her mother to tell Nina it wasn't true, but there was only silence. They had moved out of the corridor, out of earshot.

Gracie could only wait, her hands clenched, praying for Nina to come in, come straight to her bedside, to hug her, to let her say sorry, to say it was an accident, to understand, the two of them feeling this together, loving Tom, helping each other, helping him, whatever the future was going to bring. . . .

When Eleanor came in ten minutes later, she was on her own. Gracie tried to sit up. "I need to see them, Mum. I have to see Tom and Nina now. I wasn't drunk. I promise I wasn't. It was an accident. I have to tell Nina the truth."

"She's too upset to see you yet, Gracie. And they're still not letting anyone but her see Tom."

"Is he all right?"

"They don't know yet."

"Is he going to die?" Her voice rose. "Is that what you mean? Mum, no. He can't—"

"Gracie, no, not that. It's his spine. There's serious damage. They think—"

She couldn't hear it yet. "Please, Mum, please. Ask Nina if I can see Tom. If I can see her. I need to talk to her, too." She saw something in her mother's face. "What is it? What's happened?"

"Gracie, we're getting you and Spencer flown back to London tomorrow."

"But I need to talk to Nina first. I need to see Tom."

"No, Gracie. I'm sorry, but it's not possible."

"I have to."

"She won't let you."

"But he'll want to see me."

"Gracie, he's still unconscious."

She sat up then, chilled by the tone in her mother's voice, by the expression on her face. "You have to let me see him. Please, let me talk to Nina."

"Gracie, I'm sorry, but you can't. He's being moved to another hospital this afternoon. One with a spinal unit. She has to make all the arrangements."

"But I need to see her. To see him."

"Gracie, I'm sorry, but you can't."

She cried until her chest hurt even more, until there were no more tears, but it made no difference. Eleanor just said the same thing over and over again.

The return to London was a nightmare, slow, painful, difficult. The days that followed were worse. Confined to the house, unable to put any weight on her ankle, she waited for a phone call from Nina, from Tom. All she could do was ask her mother again and again to please make contact, please help. She had to know he was all right. She had to talk to him. She didn't understand. Why wasn't her mother calling Nina? Why wasn't Nina calling Eleanor? Gracie needed to tell her the truth. She hadn't been drunk. It was an accident, a terrible accident.

Spencer came to her room a week later, the day he started work with the film company. His scratches were already healed. It was the first time they'd been alone together since the accident. He'd never acknowledged his part in it, the fact he'd been so drunk, his pulling at her hair. That didn't matter to her. All that mattered now was Tom.

"Have you heard anything, Spencer? Anything at all?"

He shook his head, not quite meeting her eyes.

"What is it? What do you know?"

"No more than you do. Just what Mum told you. Nina doesn't want to talk to any of us."

"For now? Just for now, do you mean? Or ever? Spencer, what do you know?"

But Spencer was gone.

A week later there was still no word. She made herself get out of her bed, ignoring the pain in her ankle, made her way downstairs to the kitchen, where her mother was standing, staring out the window.

"Is he dead, Mum? Is Tom dead and you're just not telling me?"

She began to cry again. She couldn't stop crying. She had to know something. She begged her mother to help her. To find out something. Anything.

It took another week of pleading before Eleanor asked an Italian-speaking teacher at her school to help. With Gracie beside her, the teacher rang all the major hospitals in and around Rome, pleading for information, asking for names of specialist clinics, spinal wards. On the seventh call to a clinic south of Rome, they found him. Yes, there was a Tom Donovan there. A young Australian man. Eleanor's colleague asked as many questions as she could before the hospital clerk hung up. "He's alive, Gracie. No brain damage. He's conscious, talking. He's got movement from the waist up, but there's serious lower spinal damage. They've operated, but it's too early to know the exact situation."

Three days later, a letter arrived from Nina, addressed to Eleanor, not Gracie. No greeting, no signature. Just hard, black letters in the center of a page.

My son will never walk again. We are in the process of arranging to bring him back to Australia. Tom and I want nothing more to do with your family. I will leave Templeton Hall immediately.

Gracie read the letter a dozen times, searching for something she knew wasn't there. A message to her from Tom. He would want to talk to her, she knew he would. She had to talk to him. She needed to talk to him. She had to say sorry. Why wouldn't Nina let her? Why wouldn't her mother understand? Help her? She pleaded with her again, to travel to Rome with her, to see Nina and Tom before they left for Australia.

"Gracie, it's very difficult, I know, but we have to accept what she says. She's his mother."

"But he was my—" Her what? Her boyfriend? Her almost-fiancé? She could see it in everyone's eyes, not just her mother's. *You and Tom were just kids. It wasn't serious. Put it behind you. It's just one of those tragic things.*

Eleanor was deaf to her pleading. "Gracie, there's nothing more I can do. Nina couldn't be any clearer. I'm sorry."

But Gracie couldn't understand Nina's actions. She couldn't understand her mother's behavior, either. She needed Eleanor to be on her side, to say, "I'll keep phoning Nina, Gracie. Don't worry, she'll understand, once the shock passes." But her mother wouldn't.

"What did Nina say to you at the hospital?" She remembered her mother's expression, after the two of them had been talking, after Nina had been crying outside Gracie's room that day. "Did you have a fight with Nina?"

Her mother's face gave something away. Gracie saw it, a sudden emotion.

"What did she say to you? Was it about me and Tom? Was she unhappy about us?"

"She didn't say anything."

"She said something."

"Gracie, you saw her letter. Nina doesn't want anything to do with us again. We have to respect that."

How *could* she respect that? How could she even understand that? Nina had been her friend. That had been one of the extra, wonderful things about what had happened with Tom, knowing that Nina, her friend Nina, would be happy for them both. Hadn't they been friends for so many years? How could she just cut them out of her life like this?

"I'm going to go to Australia," she said, a week later. "I have to find him."

"Don't, Gracie. Don't make it any harder on yourself than it already is."

"I have to see him. I have to say sorry to him. Can't I at least write to him?"

"I don't know where they are. All I know from our solicitor is she's already moved out of the Hall."

Someone had to know where they were. One day, when her mother was out, Gracie rang the Castlemaine police station. She asked for the inspector who'd been there when she was a child. He'd long ago retired, she was told. She didn't know anyone else's name. "I need to speak to someone who knows Nina Donovan. Nina and Tom Donovan."

"I'm sorry. I'm new to the area myself." He sounded young. "Who is this?"

She couldn't give her name. She hung up then.

She thought of Nina's sister in Cairns, then realized she didn't know her surname or where she worked. There was no way of tracking her down. She tried hospitals in Victoria, in New South Wales, in South Australia. If Tom wasn't at home yet, he might still be in a ward somewhere. No one would give out any information.

She tried the cricket academy in Adelaide. She'd decided to ask to speak to Tom's friend Stuart Phillips. He would know, surely. A cheery female voice answered. Gracie's heart started to thump. The lie came easily. "I'm calling from London, from the *London Cricketer* magazine. Could I please speak to Stuart Phillips?"

"I'm sorry. Mr. Phillips is on long-service leave. Can anyone else help you?"

She made herself ask. "I was hoping to get an update on Tom Donovan's condition."

"Tom Donovan? Is he a coach here or a player?"

"A player. A bowler."

"I don't know the name, sorry. Let me ask someone else." She heard the receptionist ask a person beside her. "Do you know anyone called Tom Donovan? Some magazine in London wants an update on him."

"Tom Donovan? Is he that guy crippled in the car accident overseas?"

Gracie hung up.

Her father came home to London to see her and Spencer. It didn't help. Her mother greeted her father with such loathing that Gracie wanted to scream at them both. "Forget about your problems for a minute, would you? Can't you think about us, about me for once?" From their shocked expressions she realized she'd said it aloud.

"I'll come back tomorrow, Gracie," Henry said. He let himself out.

He returned the next day when her mother was out, the timing deliberate, Gracie knew. He brought her a jigsaw, grapes, a bag of sweets, as if she were eight, in the hospital having her tonsils out.

But if her mother couldn't help her, perhaps her father could. He and Nina had always gotten on well. "I need to talk to Tom, Dad. Talk to Nina. Can't you help me find her? Find him? Ring the solicitor in Castlemaine? He'll tell you where they are, surely."

"Gracie, I'm so sorry. No, I can't. I've seen the letter. Nina's made it clear how she feels."

"Please, Dad. I have to talk to her. I have to say sorry."

"We're all sorry, Gracie."

But there was no one more sorry than Gracie herself. Tom would never walk again and it was her fault. She started writing to them, to Tom, to Nina, to both of them, many letters each week, sent to every address she could think of in the hope that even one would find its way to them. Heartfelt letters, filled with remorse, anguish, sorrow. She begged her mother to post them for her. She saw the worry in her mother's eyes. Two days later, she asked her aunt Hope as well. Hope had been a regular visitor since the accident. She'd even sat with Gracie sometimes, brought her lunch, magazines, books. Gracie grasped at any kindness on offer. To her relief, Hope agreed to post her letters, too.

A month passed, then another. She should have been back at university but she couldn't face it. She used her still-painful ankle as her excuse. The truth was the outside world seemed too frightening. She kept writing her letters, but there was still no word at all from Australia. Once her ankle finally healed and she could walk without crutches, she forced herself to go to the British Library to read the Australian newspapers, desperate to find some mention of him, of an accident in Italy involving a promising cricketer. If it had made the news, she couldn't find it.

Eleanor made her stop. "You're tormenting yourself, Gracie."

"It can't end like this."

"It has to, Gracie. You have to accept it."

She tried one more time. "Please, Mum. Can't you try and find Nina? She was your friend. She'd talk to you. Please help her to understand. Please, Mum."

"I can't, Gracie. I'm sorry, but I can't."

All Gracie could do was keep writing to him. If Nina wouldn't answer her, perhaps Tom would, eventually. For the next two months, she sent two or three letters a week. She told him how much she cared about him. How much she loved him. How she was thinking of him every day. How sorry she was. At night, every night, she kept trying to imagine him now, unable to walk, unable to run. The images tormented her. She tried to keep other pictures in her head. Tom on the boat to the Isle of Skye, pulling her up the stairs onto the top deck, the light of the water silver and magical. Him in that Italian piazza, face to the sun, his long legs stretched out. The feel of his skin, his body, against her in bed. Then those images made her feel even more distraught. There was no peaceful place in her mind anymore.

A fifth month passed. She felt like her own life had stalled. She hadn't gone back to university. She was still living at home. Everyone else seemed to be getting on with their lives. Spencer never mentioned the accident. All he talked about was his courier job and the film world. Her sisters' lives were busy and productive, too. Charlotte's nanny-training business was going from strength to strength. Audrey had surprised the whole family with her news—she and her husband, Greg, had decided to move to New Zealand. She visited Gracie the day before their flight, so happy, so excited, talking nonstop. "I really hope you get back to university soon, Gracie," she'd said. "Have you thought about doing some voluntary work in the meantime? It might help take your mind off things."

But Gracie couldn't think of anything but the accident. What else was there to think about?

She knew her parents were especially worried about her. Her father rang once a fortnight, sent her even more postcards, as well as books and magazines from the countries and cities he was working in. They didn't help. She found it impossible to read. She found everything difficult. She barely managed to speak to Charlotte or Audrey whenever they rang. What was the point? She could never make them understand. Her mother tried to help her see reason. "Gracie, it was a terrible accident, but accidents happen. You have to try to move on." But she couldn't move on. How could she? There was nowhere for her to go.

She kept writing to Tom. A letter a week. Sometimes a page, sometimes more, pouring her heart out to him, telling him everything she could, even trying to cheer him up sometimes, with little stories, memories of their traveling together, anything to try to keep a connection between them. It became her job. She structured her day around it. She could spend hours on each letter, choosing the best words, redrafting each one until it was perfect. Every morning she checked the mat for the post, her fingers crossed, endlessly hopeful that today would be the day she would hear something, anything, back from him or from Nina. Anything. It was the silence that was killing her.

Six months after the accident, a letter arrived from Australia in the morning post. It was addressed to her. Nina's handwriting.

Eleanor had gone to the supermarket. Gracie was home alone. She was usually home. She'd formally withdrawn from university. She rarely ventured far from her neighborhood. She found it too difficult traveling around London now. There were too many places that reminded her of Tom. She picked up the letter from the mat and held it in her hands. Her heart started thumping and her hands shook as she carefully, slowly opened it. She wanted it to be from Tom but Nina was the next best thing.

It was two sentences, no greeting, no signature.

Stop writing to us. We've nothing to say to you and we can never forgive you.

Gracie was still by the front door, crying and holding the letter, when her mother arrived home an hour later.

PART
THREE

Chapter Twenty

Whitby, Yorkshire, England
2009

GRACIE SAT on the edge of the bed in her cheap B&B, her laptop on the bed beside her as she practiced her presentation for the fifth time that morning. She glanced at the bedside clock. Nine-twenty-five a.m. Thirty-five minutes until her interview.

She'd been up since five, finally giving up on sleep after her nerves and the scratchy sheets made anything other than a few hours' rest impossible. Once dawn arrived she dressed in jeans and a sweatshirt and went for a fast, bracing walk along the cliff path, detouring back deliberately to stand underneath the Captain Cook statue that looked over the harbor to the stark ruins of Whitby Abbey. "Please help me get this job," she said quietly and self-consciously, surreptitiously touching the base of the statue for luck. Doing that didn't seem like enough of a ritual, so she circled the statue three times, then touched it again. "Please, please, please help me get this job," she repeated.

A month earlier, she'd come home late one evening, physically exhausted from working a double waitressing shift at the busy Greek restaurant near her flat in Kensal Green. She'd supported herself with her waitressing for the past two years, in between trying for other "proper" jobs, as her sister Charlotte liked to call them. Tired but too mentally alert to sleep yet, she'd logged on to a job website. Less than a minute later, she'd seen the ad for an assistant curator position at the award-winning Captain Cook Memorial Museum in Whitby, Yorkshire. She read it twice, hardly believing how perfect it was—not just a perfect job but the job for which she was the perfect candidate, surely. The right age, too, at twenty-seven, neither too young nor too old. Her fervent application letter had led to today's panel interview in the town of Whitby itself. She'd been asked to make a ten-minute presentation on all she knew about Captain Cook and what skills she would bring to the position.

She had to get it. She wouldn't get it. She might get it. Her thoughts went round and round, canceling one another out. She practiced her presentation again. She'd begin with a brief history of Cook to display her knowledge and passion, move on to ideas for future exhibits, and end on what she hoped would be a deciding factor—the fact that one of her own ancestors had learnt to sail with Cook. Should she mention the fact that James Cook's mother had also been called Grace? It had to be a good luck omen.

The digital clock clicked over to nine thirty a.m. Time to leave. One last check in the mirror. She hoped she'd chosen the right outfit: a crisp white shirt, a knee-length blue linen skirt, vintage shoes with a small heel. Her still almost white-blond hair was cut into a short crop. Hoping she looked the perfect combination of studious and modern, she took a breath, picked up her belongings, and pulled the door shut behind her.

She'd walked down Whitby's steep paths and across the harbor to the museum the evening before to get her bearings. All the guides to successful job-hunting recommended a reconnaissance trip before-hand. She'd been disconcerted by the sight of Goths everywhere—in the street, in coffee shops, walking into pubs and restaurants—until her landlady informed her that Whitby wasn't just the birthplace of Captain Cook but also the Goth center of the UK, home to a twice-yearly Goth festival, on account of its *Dracula* connections. Bram Stoker had written some of the novel while staying there, featuring the Whitby beach in the opening chapters. Another time Gracie would have asked a dozen questions. Not this time. She was too con-cerned that details of *Dracula* would mix up with facts about Captain Cook in her head, making a muddle of her presentation the next day. She'd excused herself and gone to her room as early as possible in-stead.

Her mobile rang just as she was in sight of the museum, ten

minutes before her interview was due to begin. Her oldest sister's name appeared on the caller ID. Gracie hesitated for just a moment before answering. As usual, Charlotte launched straight into the purpose of her call.

"What on earth does she want this time, Gracie? Have you rung her back yet? I honestly think I preferred it when she was a lunatic drunk, not this new-and-improved-let's-make-amends-over-and-over-again version. I'm going to say no, whatever it is, and you have to as well, okay?"

"Charlotte—"

"No, Gracie. It's the Easter Bunny. Where are you? I thought you unemployed people lay around in your pajamas all day long. Why didn't you answer your home phone?"

"I'm not unemployed. I'm a waitress. And I'm not home. I'm in Whitby."

"Where?"

"Yorkshire. I've got a job interview in"—she checked her watch—"seven minutes."

"Another job interview? Another job? Gracie, are you going for some sort of record?"

"I can't talk now. I'm trying to compose myself."

"Forget that job. Come and work for me. God knows I've asked you often enough."

"I don't *want* to work for you or be a nanny. I want to work in the Captain Cook Museum here in Whitby."

Two passersby looked surprised by her fervor.

Charlotte ignored it. "So you haven't heard Hope's voicemail yet? She said on her message to me that she was ringing everyone today. I haven't tried Audrey or Spencer yet, mind you. Spencer's probably propping up the bar in some Irish pub and I can never work out what time it is for Audrey in New Zealand. You're sure Hope hasn't left a message on your phone?"

"I'm not home, I told you, and she hasn't got my new mobile number yet. Charlotte, I have to go. Wish me luck, would you?"

"With what? Oh, that job. No, I don't want you to get some stupid job with Captain Cook. I want to you to come and work for me. I hope you make a mess of the interview." At Gracie's anguished wail, she laughed. "Of course I wish you luck. You'll be brilliant. And ring me back as soon as you get out. We have to get to the bottom of this Hope business. United we stand, divided we fall, remember."

Gracie pushed the mobile into the bottom of her bag. It was three minutes to ten. She hesitated, then reached into her bag again, searching for the silver whistle, holding it for just a few seconds, trying to calm her nerves. It worked. It always did. Straightening her shoulders, she walked across to the museum.

Fifteen minutes later, in front of a panel of three, she knew the interview wasn't going well. She hadn't even got to her presentation yet.

"You don't seem to stay long in any job, Ms. Templeton, do you?" one of the interviewers asked, glancing down at her résumé. "You've had what, twelve jobs in the past eight years? Stayed at each of them for an average of six months? How can we be sure this position would be any different?"

"Because I really want this job," she said passionately.

"So you didn't really want the job as"—the man looked at her résumé again—"a theater administrator in Brighton? Community festival organizer in Stoke Newington? Nursing assistant in Reading?"

It was an awful kind of *This Is Your Life*, hearing him list her failures like that. She made a last-ditch effort, racing through her laptop presentation about Captain Cook's life, ending on the highlight that her great-great-great-uncle on her grandmother's side had actually sailed with Cook.

"Really?" one of the interviewers said, looking interested for the first time. "What was his name?"

Gracie's mind went blank. Had she ever known his name? Had her father ever known his name? She felt the color rising in her cheeks. "I'm sorry, but I can't remember."

"We've got records of the names of Cook's fellow sailors on those early ships if you'd like to look through them?"

Gracie suddenly had a horrible feeling her father had made that story up. She started to talk, to try to cover her embarrassment. "I might have it wrong. It might have been on my grandfather's side. My great-great-grandfather. He was from Yorkshire, I think. Or Scotland, perhaps. I haven't really studied my family tree lately. It was my father's great interest. He told me all the stories when I was a child. We used to live in Australia, you see, which was founded by Captain Cook—"

"Oh, really?" one of the interviewers said drily.

She couldn't seem to stop talking now. "My father inherited a beautiful colonial house. We lived there for three years, running it as a kind of museum. That's when I first got interested in history, and so I thought this job could be perfect. History and Cook together." Her voice trailed off. She knew from their expressions that they either didn't believe her or weren't really listening anymore.

The woman who showed her out from the museum ten minutes later was kind. "I'm sorry you weren't successful today, Gracie," she said. "It's just that we've had a few too many people coming and going lately and we need to be sure the new person stays for a few years. And I'm afraid your track record just doesn't give us that confidence."

"But I would have stayed, I'm sure of it."

The woman didn't seem convinced. "Have you ever thought about counseling?"

Gracie nodded. "I tried it for five months, but that didn't work out either."

"I'm not suggesting you *be* a counselor, Gracie. I think it might help you to see one."

On the train back to London, Gracie thought about the woman's words. It wasn't the first time counseling had been mentioned to her. Her mother, her sisters, even her short-lived work colleagues had made everything from gentle to blunt suggestions that she could benefit from what her mother called "professional help."

"The accident was a traumatic experience, Gracie," Eleanor said. "There's no reason why you should bounce back from it or be ashamed that it is still impacting on you. Look what a difference it made to Audrey to get professional advice."

Gracie tried to make light of it. "You're trying to marry me off as well?"

Her mother smiled. "No, darling, I'm not. I'm trying to make life better for you."

"My problems finding a job aren't connected with the accident."

They both knew she wasn't telling the truth. In the eight years since that night in Italy, she'd found it hard to settle on anything for very long. She hadn't just tried many different jobs, she'd moved from flat to flat in different parts of London, living on her own, living in share houses, moving back home, out again. She'd even tried to return to university again, without success. No matter how hard she tried, each new venture didn't last long. Something had changed inside her. Everything had changed.

If she'd ever been stopped in the street and asked why, she knew the accident was the answer. Everything before then had seemed lighthearted, fun, promising, optimistic. Not bathed in a constant happy glow, of course. She'd been a witness to the slow disintegration of her parents' marriage, after all. But before Italy, she'd felt optimistic about so many things. She'd believed that the world was a good, fair place, full of possibilities and adventure.

Most of all, she'd known that what she felt for Tom, and he felt for her, wasn't just the flush of first love. It mattered. It was serious. The fact their relationship had developed so quickly, so naturally, was fate, not luck, wasn't it?

Yet that was where her thinking came unstuck each time. If she believed fate had brought them together, she also had to believe fate had torn them apart. Or could she have somehow avoided it happening? What if she and Tom had picked a different place in Europe to meet Spencer, if she had chosen a different restaurant that night, somehow changed all the steps it took for the three of them to be exactly where they were that night, in that exact spot when Spencer pulled at her plait, at the exact moment that the truck appeared over the hill? Would everything be different now? Or had fate decided from the moment she and Tom met as children at Templeton Hall that it would end in disaster, physically for him, emotionally for her?

Gracie bit down on her lip to try to stop her thoughts from going any further. She'd learnt by experience that the only way to do that was by distracting herself. She tried now, turning up her iPod, taking out a magazine, staring out the train window at the passing scenery when the magazine didn't help. None of it worked. Too many memories of that night, of the days afterward, the years afterward, were now in the carriage with her. They were always with her.

"You need to work through it," people kept telling her. "Talk about it."

She knew she did. But there were only two people in the world who could understand how she was feeling. Tom, most of all. Yet despite every possible approach, every wish and hope, he had never contacted her again. That's what hurt so much, as much as the guilt she still felt about the accident, every single day. His silence.

As for Spencer . . . Since that night in Italy, she and Spencer had spoken about the accident only once, two years afterward. They'd fought, not talked.

They'd been at their mother's for dinner. Spencer had just returned from his latest jaunt, once again funded by Hope. After Victor had died suddenly six months previously, Spencer had moved back in with his aunt. "She needs my company and support," he'd said in one of his rare emails to his sisters. "You need a free place to live now you've lost that courier job, more like it," Charlotte had emailed back. Charlotte also had plenty to say when Spencer emailed to gloat about the big backpacking trip through South America he was about to take, again at Hope's expense. "It's a thank-you gift," he'd said. "Hope said she couldn't have coped with her grief for Victor if I hadn't been around." "She's had enough and is paying to get you out of her sight for a few months, you mean," Charlotte replied.

Spencer had seemed so carefree, Gracie recalled, his blond curls long and tousled, his skin tanned. He looked sixteen, not nearly twenty. He greeted her cheerily, asked only in passing if she was working yet—she wasn't—before going to the fridge, helping himself to a beer, flicking through the latest batch of postcards that had arrived from his father, and then taking a seat at the dining table, sure of his place again, sure of his charm.

Reluctantly, wanting to keep her distance, Gracie had sat back a little. Before long, though, she'd found herself smiling as story after story spilled from him. Calamity-filled trips on decrepit public transport. Nights spent sleeping on beaches, being woken by urinating dogs. Surfing lessons in Mexico, where two weeks later he'd ended up running the classes.

"You can't surf, can you?" Eleanor asked. "You can barely swim."

"Neither could the students. That's why we got on so well."

As Eleanor laughed, a jealous feeling flashed through Gracie. Her mother had been so low lately, after more fights with Henry over outstanding bills via their lawyers. Gracie knew she hadn't been any fun to have around either. Yet here was Spencer, waltzing in, throwing his charm around, clearly telling lie after lie, not only managing to make their mother smile again, but to laugh—laugh so much, in fact, she was actually crying.

"It's as well I don't know half of what you get up to, Spencer," Eleanor said, wiping the tears from her eyes. "I'd never sleep at night."

"I actually decided it was time you knew exactly what I got up to while I was away." He grinned. "So I've brought back documentary proof."

He rummaged in the battered backpack on the floor beside him, finally taking out a large envelope which he passed to his mother.

As Gracie saw her mother's eyes grow wide as she read whatever was inside it, she couldn't resist going across, too. It was a newspaper article, with a large headline: SHARK BOY! Underneath was a photo of Spencer grinning into the camera, giving a thumbs up and holding up his shirt to show a large white bandage on the left side of his chest. A large, dead shark lay on the sand beside him. It was a short article.

Lucky to be alive: Pictured on Saturday, Spencer Templeton, 19, originally from the UK, beside the shark that nearly took his life. "If I'd known it was as big as this, I'd have swum twice as fast," the lucky youngster said. Templeton, in the middle of a backpacking trip through the region, was attacked by the shark on Thursday while surfing with friends. He says he still doesn't know how he managed to fight the shark off, attributing it to a combination of "blind fear and adrenaline—and a strong desire not to end up as shark food."

"It's fake, isn't it?" Gracie said. "One of those dummy newspapers."

Spencer lifted his shirt. There was a long scar down the left side of his chest.

"Spencer!" Eleanor gasped. "Why didn't you tell me?"

"One mercy mission in a lifetime is enough, don't you think?"

"What on earth happened?"

He shrugged. "Just as it said in the paper. I was surfing with some mates and my board suddenly tilted up. I thought it was one of them messing around, then it happened again. Next thing I knew I felt this God-almighty pain in my chest and I don't know what happened next, whether it was instinct or blind fear, but I used the board and pushed it away and then it came at me again. I pushed again, and then a wave took me, just swept me up and away from it. I landed on the beach, blood everywhere, people screaming, me screaming. Everyone saw it happen."

Eleanor's hand was at her mouth. "You swam away from a *shark*?"

He nodded proudly.

"You're like a cat with nine lives, Spencer," Gracie said.

"Cheers, Gracie." He laughed then. Sniggered, she'd thought afterward. Like a schoolboy in a comic. "Except it's not true, of course."

"The photo's a fake?" Eleanor asked.

"Oh, no, that's real. And there was a shark. It's the story that's made up. It was a local English-language paper. No one reads it but a few tourists. They needed a story to go with the pic, so my mate and I hatched it up between us."

"But what about your scar?" Gracie asked.

A grin. "Dad's number-one rule. Base a lie on the truth. I'd ripped my chest open a couple of days before when I was trying to surf. Some bastard ship-owner had thrown a box out. I fell off my board onto it, bled like mad. It looked like a shark bite, it bled like a shark bite, so the next day when someone caught an actual shark . . ." He shrugged. "The paper took loads of photos of people beside the shark. How was I to know they'd use mine?"

"Let me see the scar again, Spencer," Eleanor said, worried now. She frowned as he lifted his shirt. "I want you to go and see the doctor here, in case it's infected."

"Too late for that. It's long-healed," he said, kissing his mother. "Eleanor, stop worrying that pretty little head of yours. I'm fine. It's the poor shark you should feel sorry for."

Later, Gracie was in the kitchen washing up when he came in, whistling.

"So, what have you been up to here, Gracie, while I've been

channeling Jules Verne or whoever it is that did battles with scary creatures of the deep?"

"Scary creatures? Boxes, you mean?"

"It could have been a shark."

"It wasn't a shark."

"It might have been."

"It *wasn't*, Spencer. It wasn't a shark."

"Jesus, Gracie, calm down. What's your problem?"

You, Spencer, she thought. *You're my problem.* "Nothing," she said aloud. Then she changed her mind. She turned, crossed her arms, leaned against the sink, trying to choose her words carefully. "Do you know what annoys me the most?"

"About me?" He grinned. "I can't possibly imagine but I really can't wait to hear."

"Everything is so easy for you, isn't it? Nothing bad ever happens to you. You never worry about anything. You lose your job—too bad, Hope bails you out again—off you go traveling, doing what you like, conning people—"

"Conning who?"

"That newspaper, for starters."

"It was a crappy tourist rag, Gracie, for God's sake. Chill out, would you?"

"Like you? Like you do constantly? One day, Spencer, you'll have to face up to real life. Stop living life as if it is one big joke, as if everyone and everything is here just for your amusement, while the rest of us try our best, try to get over things, get work. . . ." She was starting to cry. Damn it. She was starting to cry.

He didn't go across to her. He stayed where he was, his arms crossed now, too. "This is about Italy still, isn't it? Not about me." He sighed. "Gracie, you have to move on. It was an accident, a lapse of judgment on your part. You got distracted—"

"By you pulling my plait, Spencer. By *you*! Don't you feel any guilt at all?"

"Look, I'm as sorry about Tom as you are. But it could have been worse."

"Worse? How could it have been worse than it was?"

Spencer shrugged. "Tom could have died, I guess. Or you could have lost your license."

Her tears disappeared. Anger returned. "Tom nearly did die, Spencer. And who cares about my stupid license?"

"So what's the problem?"

It was all she could do not to scream at her brother, shout at him, throw something at him, make him admit he was as much to blame as she was. Only the thought of upsetting her mother in the next room stopped her. She kept her voice calm with great difficulty. "*Everything* is the problem, Spencer. Have you blocked it *all* out? Don't you ever even *think* about Tom?"

"See what I mean? That's what this is all about, isn't it? You and Tom. It's nothing to do with me."

"Tom can't walk anymore, Spencer. Because of what we did to him, you and me, *both* of us. Don't you feel even the slightest bit guilty about it? Feel any responsibility at all?"

He shifted position then, the first sign of awkwardness she'd seen from him. "Of course I wish it hadn't happened. And I feel sorry for Tom, sure. But it was an accident, Gracie. Accidents happen. Don't turn your guilt on to me, just because Tom and Nina wanted nothing to do with you, with any of us, after it happened."

In the train seat now, Gracie realized her breathing had quickened again, her fists were clenched, at the memory alone. Six years after that conversation, eight years after the accident itself, and it was as if she'd made no progress at all. Spencer had completely moved on, living in Ireland with his latest girlfriend, running his own business—under completely false pretenses but so far he'd gotten away with that, too, hadn't he? Her two sisters had made something of their lives as well. Charlotte was a high-flying businesswoman in Chicago. Audrey was not only deliriously happy in New Zealand with Greg, but even had a successful performing career these days. Gracie was the only one who hadn't found her way.

She'd tried, again and again. She'd done everything she could think of in the years since the accident to make up for it in some kind of karmic way. She'd volunteered for charities. Applied for jobs that meant something to people, that weren't only about earning money.

It didn't seem to matter. The jobs didn't last. Her fault each time. She didn't seem to have a proper attention span anymore. The longest she'd stayed in any of them was six months. If it hadn't been for her waitressing skills, she'd have been in serious trouble financially. She tried going back to study—not at the university, but at a local college—but dropped out after the first semester. She tried traveling again, with two classmates from college. She spent the whole time wishing she were with Tom, wishing she were somewhere else, and she knew the two girls wished she were as well.

She'd tried dating again, hoping that might help. The first man had been a waiter in the restaurant she worked in. He'd been very keen, inviting her out time and again until she'd said yes. They'd gone to see films together, bands, comedy, and at first she'd thought that perhaps it might work between them. Until she realized two things in the same night, six weeks after they started seeing each other: he never asked her any questions and she hated the way it felt when he kissed her. Six months later, she tried again with a different man, a fellow volunteer at a community festival she was working on. That lasted two months, progressing from casual dating to being lovers, until the night he accused her of being constantly distracted, even when they were in bed together. "There's someone else, isn't there?" he'd said. He was right.

Tom. She now knew with certainty it had been something special with him. Regardless of their age, regardless of the length of their relationship. Would it have been different if they'd been together longer, if imperfection and impatience had crept in? If she had unhappy memories to dwell on? If he hadn't stayed frozen in her mind, in her heart? If she knew something, anything, about the man he had become?

She still missed him, every single day. She missed him so much it hurt, long after any pain from the accident had gone, long after she'd given up hope that the postman would bring a letter, even a postcard, from him. She knew he blamed her for what had happened. Nina blamed her. They had every right. It was her fault. Nothing could change that. Nothing could ever get it completely out of her mind. No music, no magazine, no view from a train window. She lived with it always.

It was after six by the time she got back to the small flat she rented on the top floor of a terrace house in Kensal Green. She didn't make herself dinner, change out of her interview clothes, or ring her mother to let her know how she'd got on. She needed to do something else first. She'd made a decision on the train. If she couldn't get rid of her memories, she could get rid of other physical reminders.

She went to her wardrobe and reached up to the highest shelf. The box was nestled behind her winter jumpers. She lifted it down, opened the lid, and moved aside the bundle of theater tickets, newspaper clippings, and postcards from her father that had served as a kind of weight on it for years, keeping it pushed down and out of sight. It was still in its envelope with the Australian stamp and Melbourne Mail Centre postmark.

She didn't need to read it one last time. She knew every curve of Nina's handwriting, every word of those two stark sentences off by heart. She took the letter out of the envelope and crumpled it into a ball. Placing it on a saucer on her windowsill, she struck a match and held it against the paper, watching the flame slowly lick across the letter, blazing for a second before turning to ash. Then she opened her window wide and watched the wind take the fragments and blow them out across the garden.

Her only other reminder of him was in her bag. The antique whistle. She traced the lettering again now. *For Gracie with love from Tom.* She always carried it with her. In the days after the accident, back in London, she'd even slept with it clutched in her hand. It had gone from being a good luck charm to a talisman to something more. She'd held it as she made her way to the first day of every new job, called on it for luck every time she sent off an application, held it in her hand whenever the sadness threatened to overwhelm her again. She'd needed it as recently as that morning, before her interview.

It hadn't brought her luck today, though, had it? Perhaps that was the sign she'd been waiting for. The proof it wasn't good for her to have kept it for this long. But what could she do with it? Put it into one of the bins outside on the street? If she did, this time tomorrow it would be collected, gone from her life.

She held it in one hand, then the other, tracing the engraving one last time.

She couldn't do it. It was all she had. She put it back in her bag, pushing it right down to the bottom, out of sight.

Chapter Twenty-one

Sligo, Ireland

Spencer, wake up."

"I am awake."

"Wake up, get dressed, and get in the van, I mean. You're late."

"I'm not late. I'm hungover and I need more sleep."

"Spencer, come on. Donal just rang. He hasn't got the key, the morning class is there, and that guy from the newspaper is due in half an hour."

"Tell Donal the key's on the key ring. You talk to the newspaper guy. You're much nicer than I am."

"He doesn't want to talk to me. He wants to talk to you. Come on, Shark Boy. It took weeks to set this up. Don't blow it on me now."

Spencer sat up, pushed his curls off his face, and stretched noisily. The white scar on the left side of his chest stood out against his brown skin. He patted the bed beside him, leering in cartoon fashion at the pretty, dark-haired woman glaring at him. "Come back here first, my little Ciara. I'm awake. I'm in bed. We may as well make use of it."

Ciara threw the pillow at him. "Spencer, get up and get ready. I'm leaving in ten minutes. You come with me or you can walk."

He stretched again. "You're turning into a nag, did you know that?"

"And you're turning into your father."

The phone on the bedside table rang. Ciara stepped in front of it. "Leave it, Spencer. Let it go to voicemail." Seconds later, the mobile on the floor beside the bed rang. Ciara reached down and snatched that up, pushing it into her pocket. "If it's urgent, they'll ring back. Hurry up, Spencer. Get up and into the shower before I drag you in there myself."

"You'll get into the shower with me? Now you're talking."

"Spencer, *move*."

Ten minutes later they were in their small blue van, pulling out from the driveway of the old farm cottage they rented on the out-skirts of Sligo town. Ciara was driving. Spencer fiddled with the radio controls before deciding against any of the talk programs and switching it off. He reached across and put his right hand on Ciara's left thigh. She shook it away. He did it again, tiptoeing his fingers across, touching her leg, retreating, then moving close again. She pushed it away again. A few minutes later, he made a third attempt, exaggerating the slow movements of his fingers across the seat, mak-ing a whining noise like a forlorn puppy, until his hand reached her jean-clad leg again. That time she let it stay there, shaking her head, but unable to stop a small smile.

"You're incorrigible, Spencer Templeton. You know that?"

"I know. I can't spell it, but I agree." He smiled, squeezed her leg once more, and then reached into the glove box and took out a pack of tobacco and some papers. After rolling a thin cigarette, he wound down the window, lit it, took a deep drag, sighed in satisfaction, and then turned toward Ciara again.

"That wasn't very nice earlier, you know. Comparing me to my fa-ther."

"I didn't mean to be nice."

"You've only met him once, haven't you? That time he was in Gal-way for that antiques fair?"

"Yes, but I've talked to him on the phone several times, and seen photos, and read those postcards he sends you. Spencer, any fool, and especially any fool like me who happens to stupidly find herself in love with and living in sin with you, couldn't help but notice the sim-ilarities between you and your father."

"Thrill me."

"Good-looking. Articulate. Charismatic . . ."

Spencer pretended to preen.

"Conceited. Unreliable. How many times has he said he'll come and visit and canceled at the last minute?"

"He's a busy man."

"Yes, Spencer. He's also far too charming. Only a fool would believe a word either of you had to say."

"Ciara! Ciara, my one and only love! You mean this loving, passionate two-year-old relationship of ours—"

"It's fourteen months."

"—isn't based on a bedrock of trust? Of mutual respect? It's only about lust and convenience? A marriage of business minds rather than one of bodies, hearts, and souls?"

"Shut up, Spencer. Save the smooth talking for the journalist, would you?"

Five minutes later they were driving through the village of Strand-hill, past the Strand Bar and turning left onto the esplanade. It was a crisp, cool morning, the huge sky a light blue, only a bank of clouds to the east. The sea flickered with silver and blue flashes of sunlight, the long rows of foaming waves already dotted with early-morning surf-ing students. Two more groups of learners were on the beach itself, dressed in wetsuits, standing beside their boards. Ciara pulled into the closest parking space, just a meter from the sign she'd only fin-ished painting a week previously: *Shark Boy Surfing School this way*, the jaunty arrow in the shape of a shark fin. She was glad to see the front door of the brightly colored building open. Donal had obvi-ously found a spare key somewhere. Their morning group of students was gathering in front of the storage shed, pulling on wetsuits, taking out the boards.

Before she and Spencer had time to get out of the van, another car pulled in beside them. A young man climbed out from the driver's seat, a middle-aged man holding a camera bag from the passenger's seat.

"Damn it. They're early," Ciara said. She hastily reached for some peppermints in her bag and thrust them at Spencer. "Eat those and make it snappy, Shark Boy. A surf hero stinking of smoke is not the right image."

An hour later, Spencer had finished being interviewed and was posing for photographs, first standing in front of the Shark Boy premises with a surfboard under one arm, then leaning against the landmark cannon on the Strandhill esplanade. Ciara watched from a short distance, hoping Spencer would manage to stay serious. The last photo session she'd organized had to be scrapped when she discovered Spencer had pulled faces in nearly every shot. So far, so good today. He definitely looked the part of a surfing instructor, his blond hair a tangle in the buffeting wind coming off the water, his bright-blue wetsuit a contrast to the white of the board.

Spencer had just laid the board on the ground and was doing some mock surfing positions on top of it when his mobile phone, still in Ciara's pocket, started to ring. She took a step back out of hearing range, saw the name, and answered it. "Hi, Charlotte. You're up late."

"Ciara? Are you Spencer's secretary now? The sooner you and I meet in person and I put you straight about my brother, the better. Or have you stolen his phone? Good for you. And no, I'm not up late. I'm up early, trying to round up my siblings before Hope attempts a takeover. Has she cornered Spencer yet? Don't tell me he said yes."

"Charlotte, I'm sorry, but I've got no idea what you're talking about."

"Aunt Hope. Our Blessed Aunt Hope who's now more trouble than she ever was when her only friends were a bottle of wine and her own evil mind. She hasn't rung Spencer yet? That's either a good sign or a bad sign."

"She might have. We got in late last night and we haven't checked our messages yet."

"Good. If she's called, tell him not to ring her back until he's spoken to me. She's up to something and I don't want anyone to agree to it until I've got the whole story. Actually, Ciara, there's an idea. Can you ring Hope back and tell her—"

"No way. I have enough trouble with one Templeton without starting on a rogue aunt."

"But she'd love you. That accent of yours, the beautiful way with words you Irish have—"

"Stop your patronizing right there." Ciara laughed. "I'll get Spencer to phone you back. He's just getting his photo taken."

"For a police lineup?"

"A national newspaper, actually."

"Oh, for God's sake. Not more Shark Boy nonsense. He still hasn't been found out?"

"What do you mean, 'found out'?"

"I haven't time to even *begin* to tell you. And tell him not to phone me back after all. I've got a graduation ceremony today and I haven't signed the certificates yet. I'll call him back later. Thanks, Ciara." She hung up before Ciara had a chance to say good-bye.

Back in the office after the journalist and photographer had driven away, she and Spencer had a postmortem on the interview.

"I was stupendous, if I say so myself," Spencer said. "Witty, self-deprecating. If I didn't already own the business, I'd sign up as a student myself."

"*We* own the business, not you. You told them about the increase in our student numbers? How we get students from all over the world?"

He hit his hand against his forehead. "Oh, no. I forgot. I spoke about the price of gold and England's World Cup hopes instead." He rolled his eyes. "Yes, Ciara, I did mention the subject of the interview a couple of times. You would have been proud of me."

"And they got all they needed, photo-wise?"

"They asked for one of me surfing but I explained about my pulled muscle, to their great sorrow. So they asked if we could send them a scan of the Shark Boy article instead. They wanted to take it with them but I said it was too precious to leave our sight. That was the right answer, dearest Ciara, wasn't it? Or should I have checked with you first?"

Ciara ignored his sarcasm, reached up, and took the framed article in question off the wall. The photograph of Spencer at nineteen was a great one, she knew. It was the headline above the photograph that also gave the surf school its name: SHARK BOY! Now nearly twenty-six, he hadn't changed that much, Ciara thought—he still had the tousled curls, boyish face, and cheeky grin. Her mother had dubbed him the Artful Dodger, straight out of *Oliver!* when Ciara first brought him home to Sligo to meet her family, just a month after their meeting in an Irish pub in London.

Spencer had responded in kind, amused. "Artful Dodger? Very

nice, thank you. The sweet and mischievous film version or the cunning baby-faced criminal from the book?"

"I'll reserve my judgment," Ciara's mother had said.

Ciara passed on the news of Charlotte's call as he sat behind the desk, opening their mail. He just shrugged. "Charlotte's always had a problem with Hope. She probably just wants to meet up for a drink or elderberry cordial or whatever's taking her fancy these days."

"I'd like to meet Hope."

"No, you wouldn't," Spencer said.

"I'd like to meet all of your family, actually."

"Believe me, you wouldn't."

It wasn't until Ciara had finished scanning and emailing the Shark Boy photo to the newspaper that she brought up the rest of Charlotte's conversation. "You get on okay with Charlotte, don't you?"

He laughed. "No one 'gets on' with Charlotte. We do what Charlotte tells us or feel the whip of her steely tongue. Or the steel of her whippy tongue. Why?"

"She said something to me on the phone about this 'Shark Boy nonsense.' "

"Ignore her." Spencer shrugged, midway through rolling another cigarette, even though he was sitting directly beneath a *No Smoking* sign. "She just thinks I've milked it too much."

"She didn't say it like that. She said, 'He still hasn't been found out?' " She did a very good impression of Charlotte's clipped British accent. "What is there to find out? That it wasn't you who had the run-in with that shark?"

"Charlotte's just a troublemaker, Ciara. She always has been. Can I go home and back to bed now? Haven't I been a good boy? Shown my face, charmed the press—"

"You don't want to have a surf first? You're dressed for it, for once."

"In this weather?" He did a mock shiver. "You've got to be joking. Now, if I had my surf school in Hawaii, maybe, under a blazing sun and swaying palm trees—"

"You know, Spencer, I had the funniest thought last night in bed."

"Did it involve a French maid's costume?"

She ignored that. "I realized I've known you for over a year, lived with you for eight months, started up a surf school with you, done all I can to help promote it, and yet the strangest thing of all is I've never actually seen you surf."

"You must have."

"Not once. When we met in London you had bruised ribs. When we moved back here you had that calf trouble. And since then you've either had more injuries or said you're too unfit and it wouldn't be good for any prospective students to see you in the water until you're back at your peak."

"See how diligent I am about my students' welfare?"

"Seriously, Spencer. Don't you think it's funny that I help you run a surf school yet I haven't seen you surf?"

"Your uncle's a surgeon but have you ever seen him operate?"

"Well, no, but—"

"Your mother's a florist. Have you ever seen her plant any flowers?"

"Spencer—"

"Sometimes, darling Ciara, you think and worry too much. Can't you just relax? Could our lives together get any more perfect? Who needs me in the water when we have assembled a team of the finest Australian and Kiwi instructors to do the work on our behalf? We're already making a profit, after just six months in business. Due to your sterling efforts, we're about to get more publicity and make even more profit. We have ourselves a USP—that's Unique Selling Point, my dearest love—with me at the helm, Shark Boy himself, setting us apart from any other surf school on this majestic island of Ireland. What more could we possibly ask for?"

"Are you talking to me or practicing a courtroom soliloquy?"

He grinned. "You did ask."

She carefully returned the article back into the frame, her face thoughtful. "It would be funny, though, wouldn't it? If it turned out you didn't actually know how to surf at all."

"It wouldn't just be funny. It would be hysterical." He threw away the half-smoked cigarette, pulled Ciara close, and kissed the top of her head. "Now, come on, my beautiful, overworked, overthinking, sexy, sweet girlfriend. If you won't let me go back to bed, then I'm taking you out to breakfast."

Chapter Twenty-two

Auckland, New Zealand

AUDREY TEMPLETON LEANED down to the sock puppet on her left hand, pretended to listen closely to something it was saying, and then turned and smiled broadly at the two hundred wriggling children sitting cross-legged on the floor in front of her. She'd been in the shopping center since four p.m., three hours and five performances ago now, and was nearly fainting with hunger and exhaustion. She still managed to summon up the bright cheery voice the children expected as she continued her conversation with the puppet.

"That's right, Bobbie! We've got time for just one more song, haven't we? Will you sing this one with me, children? It's Bobbie's favorite, my favorite, and I bet you all know the words, too! Ready?"

Behind her, a large screen flickered through a range of colors and the words *If you're happy and you know it, clap your hands* appeared, with a bouncing ball guiding the squirming children through the song.

"Another day, another dollar, another two thousand hysterical six-year-olds," her production manager, James, said ten minutes later, as he escorted her into what her contract dictated should be "a comfortable dressing-room area." In this case it was a storage room with a tiny mirror, lit by what was also clearly a borrowed bedside lamp.

She really did wish James wouldn't be so cynical all the time. "They seemed to enjoy it, that's the main thing."

"Audrey, kids have no taste. They'd enjoy it if you rolled Bobbie into a ball and kicked him around for two hours."

She pretended to cover Bobbie's nonexistent ears with her hand. "Don't listen to the nasty man, Bobbie. Those children love you. Their parents love you. Greg and I love you."

"I love you, too, Bobbie," James said with a sigh. "Blame it on my hangover. I dreamed of Hollywood once, you know. The West End. Even Bollywood. And where am I? Trapped in overheated shopping centers week after week after week."

Audrey decided she'd had enough of James for one day. She checked her watch. Just past seven p.m. "Have you seen Greg? He thought he'd be here by now."

James shook his head. "Your phone rang a couple of times during the show, though. Maybe he's caught in traffic. In that fifteen-minute rush hour we get here if we're lucky."

Audrey ignored that as well and fished for her phone. There were two missed calls. She frowned as she saw the name of the caller. Not her husband, Greg, but her sister Charlotte. Charlotte never rang just for a chat. Audrey's immediate thought was a bad one. Her parents. Something had happened to one of her parents. "Excuse me," she said to James, moving outside the door again. A sudden squeal from the remaining children brought her hurriedly back.

"You might find it's quieter out that other door," James said. "Here, give me Bobbie."

She held out her arm obediently as James peeled off the now sweaty puppet.

"Air him a little before you pack him away, would you? It was like a sauna out there today," she said, before going out through the back door and pressing the redial button. As she waited for it to connect, she tried to calculate the time in Chicago. If Charlotte was in Chicago, of course. She might already be in London, if the news was truly bad.

The call went straight to voicemail. "This is Charlotte Templeton, CEO of Templeton Nanny Services, the award-winning nanny training and placement agency and number-one provider of childcare and governess education in the Midwest. For a full service tailored to the needs of your family, or to receive details of our award-winning training courses, just call our toll-free line. Alternatively, leave me a message and I'll return your call as soon as humanly possible."

Humanly possible? Audrey thought. As apart from what? She sighed as she waited for the extended commercial to come to an end. Finally, the beep sounded. "Charlotte, it's me, Audrey. Is everything all right? I'm offstage now. Call when you can, okay?"

Once the thought of something having happened to Henry or Eleanor was there, though, she couldn't wait until she heard back. She did a quick calculation of the time difference. Early morning in England. She rang Gracie's mobile number. Also a voicemail. A normal one at least: "This is Gracie. Please leave a message."

"Gracie, it's Audrey. Is everything all right with everyone? I missed two calls from Charlotte. Can you ring me back?"

She scrolled down to Spencer's number, pressed the call button, then canceled it. She wasn't in the mood to talk to Spencer. She rarely was.

She jumped then as the phone rang. Not Charlotte or Gracie, but her husband. She smiled. "Hi, darling."

"How did you go? They screamed themselves hoarse looking for encores? I'm about ten minutes away. I've picked up dinner. And don't tell me you have to pack up first. That's what we pay lazy James to do. And I'll ring him and tell him that myself. See you soon, darling."

"You too, sweetheart." She was still smiling as she started taking off her makeup. Her dearest, darling Greg. What would she do without him?

She'd been asking herself the same question for years. What would her life have been like if her mother hadn't taken her to Greg's consulting room that day? Would she be in some kind of institution by now? Locked behind walls of silence? "Out of darkness comes light," one of her favorite quotes said, and it was so true in her case. What were those terrible silent years she'd endured if not a kind of darkness of the soul—and she *had* endured them, she hadn't been making it all up, no matter what Charlotte said.

It was like thinking of another person, not herself, looking back to that time of her life. She could still recall the terrible night of the stage fright, the humiliation, the terror, that awful blankness, like nothing she had ever experienced before or again. What choice had she had, but to retreat into herself, to try to block out the world in whatever way possible?

"Selective mutism" it was called, she now knew that much. There had been nothing selective about it in her case, though.

Even now, so many years later, she could summon up the feeling of safety and yes, even peace that choosing to be silent had given her. It had taken so much pressure off. Everyone's expectations had suddenly been lowered. And all right, if she was to admit it only to herself, she'd quite enjoyed all the attention it brought her, too. Attention without any response needed on her part. She never meant to worry her family, her mother especially. Of course she hadn't. If she'd truly been able to speak normally, she would have, and saved her mother all those years of concern and research into treatments. But the mind was a puzzling thing, as Audrey herself had been told many times by different specialists and doctors.

And it could have been so much worse, couldn't it? She might have turned to drink or drugs like Hope. She might have started self-harming. Developed an eating disorder. In the scheme of things, her subconscious decision to simply stop talking, to block out the world through silence, was in many ways the kindest thing she could have done to her family. Even Gracie had told her once how much she loved the notes Audrey used to write, hadn't she? And her father had often told her how peaceful it was to have her around. She had been in pain, yet she had managed to keep the pain to herself, unselfishly. Not that Charlotte had given her any credit. Or Spencer. They'd both been so impatient with her, even after she'd made the decision, and yes, the incredible effort, to communicate with her family at home. "If you can talk to us, then why can't you talk to everyone else?" It wasn't as simple as that. They just didn't understand. Nobody did.

Until Greg came into her life. She could still remember her first appointment with him, at an alternative therapy center in Shepherd's Bush. She was twenty-two. Greg was on the floor, surrounded by pieces of Lego, when she entered his room. She was surprised at how young he was, late twenties or early thirties, his round face making him look even more youthful. All the other specialists she had seen had been in their fifties and sixties, in suits and ties, not in T-shirts and jeans like this man. He smiled at her first, then at her mother, and then very nicely, in his soft New Zealand accent, told her mother that he and Audrey would get on just fine together if she wanted to wait outside.

"I've read your file, Audrey," Greg said, still on his hands and knees on the floor. "You haven't spoken to anyone except your family for over six years now, is that right?" He didn't wait for her to nod or to suddenly start speaking, like some of the other specialists had done. "I'm sure you've got your reasons and maybe one day you'll tell me about them, but for now, can you help me fix this mess up? I had a little boy in here and I had the bright idea to build a castle while we had a chat, except it didn't go so well. More of a ruined castle than an actual castle. Unless that was what he had in mind in the first place."

She got down on to the floor with him, and he chatted away to her, asking her questions requiring only a nod or a shake of her head, until they had tidied up all the bricks. He paused then, and that's when she'd waited for the usual questions: *So, tell me, Audrey, what is it? What happened? Why won't you speak? Shall I get you some paper and you can write it down for me?*

Instead, he upended the tub of bricks again, smiled at her, and said, "You and I are much more mature. Shall we try and build a proper castle together instead?"

Forty minutes later, her appointment was over and the castle only half built. She looked at it, looked at him, said nothing, but he seemed to read her mind. "It's a shame not to finish it, isn't it? Will you come back tomorrow? Around eleven?"

They finished the castle the next day. The following week, she had another two appointments with him. They painted landscapes together. The following week, it was puppetry. Another week, pottery. "I never actually did any medical training," he said, in the gentle constant chatter that formed the soundtrack of the hour they spent together. "I actually wanted to be an art teacher, then I got interested in people's minds as well as their eyes and hands. And I realized that everything in this world comes down to creativity in some way, doesn't it? Bridges wouldn't be built if someone didn't first imagine them. Or roads. Or skyscrapers. Books, plays, films, poems. Even wars and coups and crimes, none of it would happen if people hadn't first imagined life a different way. That's what you can do, too, you know. Imagine a different life for yourself."

At their session in the twelfth week, she spoke. He asked her how she was. She said, "Fine, thank you." He didn't react, didn't send up a flare. He simply nodded, said he was glad to hear that and then they started on that week's art project—a colorful collage of paper and paint. Her mother was so happy when Greg told her. The following week she spoke three sentences as they prepared a spring window box together, pushing tulip and snowdrop bulbs into the brown soil.

The following week, in addition to her regular weekday appointments, Greg suggested a Saturday outing as well. Only if her mother approved, he said. Her mother did. Over the next three months they went somewhere together every Saturday: to Hyde Park one week, Covent Garden another, to Oxford for a day trip, a cruise on the Thames, to the Tate Gallery. They rode on the Tube, took taxis, walked, and caught buses and trains. It was Audrey who thanked drivers, asked for tickets or directions, and suggested where they went next.

Four months after she'd spoken to him for the first time, he told her that he was sorry but he needed to hand her therapy over to another of his colleagues.

"But why?" she'd answered in the soft voice she was still learning to use. "Don't you like me anymore?"

"That's the problem, Audrey. I more than like you. Actually, I think I'm in love with you. So ethically I can't treat you anymore."

Charlotte was Outraged of Chicago as soon as she heard. "He should be struck off the medical register," she'd said to their mother. "He's obviously taken advantage of her. Sue him. Or I will if you won't." She was only mildly appeased when she learnt Greg actually wasn't on any medical register. "*What?* Alternative clinics can just spring up like mushrooms in Britain these days? What's happening over there?"

So many good things, one after the other. Their engagement. Their move to Manchester when Greg was offered a position in a clinic there. Their wedding day, their own special day, the two of them together, their only witnesses two people from the registry office, both of whom had no difficulty hearing her clear, happy tones repeating the vows. It was the closest they could get to eloping. There'd been no question of a church wedding. Greg was not only far from home and family, but had been brought up without any religion. As for herself, she didn't want the drama of trying to get her parents into a church together. It was her day. She didn't want it hijacked in any way.

After the expected rumblings about denying the family a big day out, Charlotte gave her blessing, though Audrey was forced to endure her questionable humor at first. "Married? How on earth did you say 'I do' when you needed to?" Now Audrey was speaking again, Charlotte found it endlessly hilarious to make jokes about her silent days.

Gracie was nothing but welcoming and friendly to Greg, of course. Audrey couldn't remember if Spencer had been friendly to Greg or not. He hadn't been around a lot then, or if he was, he was usually too out of it to say much.

Once Eleanor had gotten over the fact that it was ethically all right for Audrey not just to have fallen in love with her therapist, but also to have married him, she seemed only happy for her. As for her father . . . "Shouldn't I meet him before we get married?" Greg had asked once. "Not to get his permission, but to at least introduce myself?"

That had been easier said than done. None of them was ever sure where their father actually was. "He's traveling for work," was the catchall phrase they used. In the UK, in America, Asia, wherever the work was. Their mother never referred to him, though as far as Audrey knew, he was still sending her regular checks. She'd opened one of his letters by accident and had been taken aback by the amount. She'd dared to mention it to her mother, daring also to wonder why she was still living in an ordinary part of London if Henry was sending this kind of money as maintenance. Her mother's angry reaction had startled her.

"I'm supporting myself, Audrey. The money your father is sending has nothing to do with maintenance. And believe me, those checks are just a drop in the ocean."

Greg had asked her once if her parents would get divorced and she'd been a bit embarrassed to admit she didn't know. She also couldn't really remember if she'd been that upset when they announced they were formally separating. She'd had so much going on herself at the time, after all, so many different sorts of treatment. All of it leading up to meeting Greg. Her darling Greg.

Their adventures hadn't stopped with their surprise wedding. They'd been married for just a few months when she noticed Greg getting so homesick, talking wistfully about the scenery and freedom of his childhood, about how he was getting more bothered by the crowds everywhere, long traveling times, the constant gray skies. He also made New Zealand sound so beautiful, so unspoiled. So very, very alluring . . .

She brought it up one morning as they were having breakfast. While he was working, she was volunteering in the art therapy room of a local hospital. It was his suggestion that she not go back to study or try full-time work yet. There was plenty of time for that down the track, he'd told her.

She saw the immediate positive reaction in his eyes, and also noticed how quickly he tried to hide it. "But what about your family?" he asked her. "How could you leave them?"

Easily, she realized. She was much happier with Greg than she'd ever been with her family. She thought it best to put it a little differently, however. "I'll be happy wherever you are, and if you'd be happier in New Zealand, I would be, too."

Their flight to Auckland was just a few months off when Gracie, Spencer, and Tom had the accident in Italy. It had been so sad. Poor Tom. Poor Gracie, too, of course. Audrey could only imagine how guilty she must feel.

At Greg's urging, Audrey offered to delay the trip to New Zealand, but her mother thankfully insisted she and Greg shouldn't change their plans. Spencer was already on the mend, Gracie would only recover in her own time and in her own way, her mother told her. There was nothing anyone could do but let time do its work. "Go, Audrey. It's time you lived your own life."

And so she had. The following month would mark their eighth year here in Auckland. Eight happy years. They had a beautiful house in Ponsonby, all light and glass and close to so many excellent restaurants and art galleries, and an even more beautiful weekend house on Waiheke Island, with its wonderful scenery and boutique vineyards, just a short ferry ride away. They'd talked about having a baby but decided the parenting life really wasn't for them. They had so much to do with children in their work life, after all. Their wonderful, successful work life. She still sometimes needed to pinch herself about how that had all turned out so wonderfully for her as well. All due to Greg, too, of course.

He'd seen the ad in the paper about auditions for a local theater group six weeks after they arrived. "Just try it. If you don't like it, you don't have to go again." The group was casting for its annual children's pantomime, that year a mixture of actors and puppets. The catch was the actors had to supply their own puppets and write their own material.

"What do I know about puppets?" she wailed that night at home.

"You just keep it simple and colorful," Greg said. "Like this, watch." There and then, he pulled out a long orange football sock from his chest of drawers, dragged it over his hand, and started a funny, playful conversation with it.

"A sock puppet?" Audrey said. "Are you mad?"

Greg called in their neighbor's two children as guinea-pig audience members. Audrey, self-conscious and giggly in turn, tried her puppetry skills and different voices out on them. The children were unimpressed. It was only when she pretended the puppet was whispering to her, that only she could hear what it had to say, that she caught their attention.

"He's funny," one of the kids said. "What's his name?"

"The same as yours, actually," she said. "Bobbie."

Three weeks after Audrey's well-received role in the pantomime came to an end, Greg saw an ad for open auditions for a new TV-NZ children's program. Magicians, performers, puppeteers welcome, it read. They both agreed that football-sock-Bobbie may have been enough for a pantomime, but wouldn't be enough for a TV show. They had a new puppet made, socklike in appearance, of better-quality materials but with the same bright-orange body, black button eyes, and shock of blue hair. When Audrey was offered a regular presenting spot by the TV producers, as the link person between imported cartoons and advertiser-sponsored competitions, Greg urged her to accept it.

"It's not the West End, no, but it's paid work, it's fun, and you're great at it. Why don't you at least give it a try?"

Now, more than six years later, *It's Bobbie Time!* was one of New Zealand's most popular children's TV shows, had won a series of educational awards, and had also been sold to cable TV networks in Australia, Singapore, Denmark, and parts of Latin America. The show had not just made her mildly famous in New Zealand. It had made her and Greg wealthy. While Audrey's personal contract was with the TV station, she had, by luck rather than design, retained the copyright to any merchandise relating to the Bobbie puppet. In the previous three years, the range had expanded to include Bobbie toys, lunchboxes, raincoats, jigsaw puzzles, board games, drink bottles, and even Bobbie toothbrushes. Greg had given up his therapy work and was now the full-time manager of Bobbie Enterprises.

"St. Greg," Charlotte called him, though she and Spencer found it more pathetically amusing to call him Saint Grig, in exaggerated New Zealand accents. If they weren't laughing at Greg's accent, they laughed at Audrey's job.

"Has Peter Jackson rung about the next *Lord of the Rings* film yet?" Spencer had said the last time she was home on a brief visit. "I can just see it, *The Bobbit.*"

"The stage is Bobbie's first love, surely?" Charlotte said. "I can just imagine him playing Hamlet. 'To Bobbie or not to Bobbie, that is the question.' "

The pair of them had practically screamed laughing.

Audrey was on the phone to Greg in tears for a long time that night. She'd been so excited about sharing all the details of her life in New Zealand. She'd even bought DVDs of *It's Bobbie Time!* to show them. They'd barely watched ten minutes of it.

"Ignore them," he'd said. "They're just jealous."

"They're not jealous. They're mean."

Eleanor had seemed the most interested in her stories, but she was distracted, Audrey could tell. Hope wasn't to blame for once, either. Her aunt had been sober for years by that time. The more Audrey thought about it, the more she realized her mother had *always* been distracted. One of the therapists she'd gone to during her "bad time," as she referred to her period of nontalking, had tried to press her on her relationship with her mother. Audrey had thought it was all right between them, but maybe it hadn't been?

At least Gracie had seemed to care. "My sister the television star!" she said when she met her at Heathrow on one of her visits home. She told Audrey she thought Bobbie was lovely, that it was fantastic that she had found her niche, that children's television was a really valuable form of entertainment, helping form young minds, stimulate their imaginations. If anything, Audrey thought Gracie had laid it all on a bit thick. As if she was playing a part of the interested sister, but not really meaning it.

Gracie had been between jobs at that time, Audrey remembered now. Greg wondered whether Gracie's employment record had something to do with the accident, whether it had perhaps caused a kind of guilt-induced trauma, making it difficult for her to settle on any one job or interest. Audrey had explained to him that Gracie had been like that since she was a child, racing from idea to idea, activity to activity, endlessly enthusiastic. But the accident *had* changed her, Audrey thought. Made her more serious. Sadder. Not that Audrey had ever dared to bring up the subject of Tom with Gracie. At first, because her mother had warned her that it was too distressing for Gracie; that she was already tormenting herself with guilt. Audrey had then decided that if Gracie wanted to talk about Tom, she would raise the subject herself. So far, to her relief, Gracie hadn't.

Audrey would never have said it aloud, even to Greg, but she was glad to have thousands of kilometers between her family and her new life. Perhaps they felt the same way about her. None of them had bothered to make the trip out to New Zealand, after all. There was still the often repeated charade by her father that they would all go back to Templeton Hall one day and he and the others would stop over in New Zealand on the way, but Audrey had no faith in that day ever coming. It had always looked unlikely enough as it was, even more so once their parents separated. But after the accident with Tom, when Nina had moved out so abruptly, well, who knew what kind of condition it might be in these days?

Audrey often dreaded getting one of the kinds of calls Nina must have had, news that something had happened to someone in her family and they needed her to return to England immediately. Especially at a time like now, when she was so busy with Bobbie. That was one positive thing about Charlotte's message at least, she thought. If it *had* been bad news about her parents, surely Charlotte would have told her, not just left a missed call message? She tried the number again now. Straight to voicemail. With a sigh, Audrey left another message.

"Charlotte, it's me. Can you try me again? But not too late. I need an early night." She thought that might not sound very nice. "I hope everything's all right," she added. Then she went outside to happily wait for Greg.

Chapter Twenty-three

Chicago, Illinois, USA

THE TALL, SLENDER, immaculately groomed young woman stood with perfect posture in front of the microphone, speaking slowly and clearly to the 150 people gathered before her in the sophisticated lakeside hotel's main conference room.

"Thank you all so much, once again, for choosing Templeton Nanny Services for your training, for putting your future in our hands, and, more important, the future of your charges in our hands, the children who will shape our future. It is now my great honor to call upon our founder, Charlotte Templeton, to present your graduation certificates."

Charlotte rose from her seat in the center of the podium, smoothed the too-tight skirt of her extra large navy-blue suit over her unfortunately ever-expanding thighs, waited a moment for the applause to die down, and then made her way to the microphone. She turned to her assistant, Dana, nodded her thanks, wished silently to herself that her assistant didn't look so much like an after-Weight-Watchers ad compared to her own in-dire-need-of-Weight-Watchers figure, and then turned toward the audience. She waited one second, two, three, all the way to ten before she spoke again. It was a trick she'd learnt years before at a public-speaking course and had used to great effect ever since.

"Thank you, Dana," she said, in her deliberately maintained English accent, "for that gracious introduction, but the truth of today's ceremony is that the honor is all mine. To be here today, to see my latest graduates as they prepare to step out into the world, is not just a moving experience for me. It is a moment of fulfillment. Today marks the culmination of months of hard work and dedication, the coming together of ambition, intelligence, compassion, and just as importantly, a sense of fun—all the ingredients that make up the finest nannies in America, the Templeton Nannies. Today, my dear graduates, as I stand here looking out proudly at you . . ."

As she continued her speech, Charlotte's mind drifted toward thoughts of that night's dinner, about phone calls she needed to make, and a forthcoming interview she was doing with a leading parenting magazine. She'd given speeches like this four times a year for the past eight years, adding just a few new sentences each time to keep herself entertained. Apart from that, it was an autopilot performance. Oh, she meant it all, of course she did. She didn't have to feign sincerity. When she talked about Templeton Nannies being the number-one nanny agency in the Midwest, she was telling the truth. She'd worked hard to claim that position. But these days she was just the figurehead. As her dear friend and mentor Mr. Giles had told her many times over the years, the higher you rose in your business, the less you had to do. "If you do it right, if you surround yourself with the right people, they do all your work for you."

She tuned back in completely again as she reached the final, inspirational lines of her speech ("You leave me today in body, but I will always be with you in spirit") and turned once more toward her assistant as she stepped forward with a tray of graduation certificates. Charlotte was happy to stay fully in the moment, as the saying had it, during this part. She always found it somewhat miraculous that the fifteen or twenty—or in today's case, twenty-five—graduates now stepping one by one up onto the stage could have changed so much from the sloppy, laid-back students who had signed with her four months earlier.

"You're more like a finishing school than a nanny agency," one of the parents had said to her once. "I hardly recognize my daughter. You've worked miracles."

"And in turn your daughter will work miracles on the children in her care," Charlotte said. Sometimes she nearly made herself sick with her saccharine statements but it was what people wanted to hear. When it came to other people's children, either the trainee nannies or the children of her clients, she could never be too sincere, too concerned. And she did mean what she said. Most of the time.

"Don't get too cynical," Mr. Giles had warned her during one of their monthly catch-ups. She'd been telling him about one of her clients, the airhead mother of a frankly dense four-year-old. Charlotte had turned their first encounter into what she felt was a very amusing anecdote. "Don't get too big for your boots, Charlotte," Mr. Giles said. "Yes, you probably are smarter and funnier than many people you'll meet in life, but it doesn't mean you have to laugh at them. Show them respect and they will show you respect."

If anyone else said that to her, there would have been war. No one spoke to Charlotte Templeton like that. No one but Mr. Giles, that was. They'd had an honest, straightforward relationship from the start. He'd recognized something in her that he needed for his son. She'd seen in him a chance to escape, and to learn. It was a gamble but it had worked for them both. She still called him Mr. Giles, too, even all these years later. It was almost a pet name now. His son, Ethan, her first charge and in many ways the person who had changed her life, was now twenty-four and if she did say so herself, a model citizen. He'd moved smoothly from private school to Ivy League university to postgraduate study and was now working as an architect in New York. They were still great friends, the age difference scarcely a factor. She'd had dinner and gone to a Broadway show with Ethan and his girlfriend only two weeks earlier and it had been a wonderful night. She'd never have thought it possible, but he'd turned from her little fun client into a good teenage boy, and now an even nicer adult. It could have been so different. He could have been a spoiled brat, someone she went running from, shrieking in horror, only weeks after arriving in Chicago. Mr. Giles could have turned into a lecherous old man. It was what everyone had expected, she knew that, but it hadn't happened.

Soon after arriving in Chicago all those years ago she'd started to keep a diary. Not filled with her thoughts or first impressions, she didn't have the time for that, but with goals, ideas, hopes. She'd reread it recently. It entertained and amused her to see how much of it had come true. "Be my own boss." "Be independent and independently wealthy." Had she predicted her own future somehow? If she had written "Be happily married," "Be in love," would her dating life have been different? It was the only area of her life that hadn't worked out so well.

At first there hadn't been time. Her nanny duties included minding Ethan most evenings and on her one night off she preferred to laze in front of the television eating delicious American cookies rather than head out to Chicago's bars and clubs with other nannies she'd met. She'd gone on a few blind dates in those early years but they'd been as unsuccessful as the ones she'd tried with her friend Celia in Melbourne. She just didn't seem to like men her own age. One night, one of her nanny friends had gotten drunk and announced she had a crush on Charlotte. For a moment Charlotte had wondered whether that was where she'd been going wrong, whether it was women she should be dating, not men. But unfortunately that hadn't turned out to be the case, either. The more she thought about it, the less interested she was in dating either sex. There was too much going on in her life career-wise. It also didn't help that she'd seen so many failed relationships. Her own parents', for starters.

In her admittedly limited experience, marriages foundered for one of five reasons—basic incompatibility, money problems, infidelity, boredom, or all of the above. Her parents clearly came under the money problems banner. Severe money problems, from what Gracie had told her. Charlotte knew they had arrived in Australia with debts and it seemed they had left Australia the same way. All her father's fault, too, by the sounds of it. One far-fetched plan after the other, Templeton Hall the straw that broke the camel's—or the accountant's—back. None of it surprised Charlotte. As the oldest, she had heard plenty of their fights, even managed to see some of the crisply worded letters from various solicitors during some of her regular secret forays into her father's office.

At least Henry hadn't asked her to talk to Mr. Giles about a possible bailout. That would have been too much. Instead, he had seemingly embarked on an international tour of antique hotspots, dealing in everything from clocks to china to furniture in an attempt to raise as much cash as quickly as possible, assuaging his guilt about never seeing his children with a constant onslaught of postcards. Gracie had only ever seen the bright side of their father's actions, of course. "He's working so hard to try and fix everything, Charlotte," she'd written once. "He's been traveling all over England and America. I don't think there's an antiques store or an old manor house in the northern hemisphere that he hasn't visited in the past few years. Poor Dad."

Poor Dad indeed, Charlotte thought. He'd telephoned her once when he was in Connecticut on a buying trip. "You could always visit instead of telephone, Dad. I'm just an airfare away. Your poor abandoned eldest daughter, so far away from home and hearth."

"I'd love to, Charlotte, but my time is just not my own this trip. I'll be back, though."

If he had come to the Midwest, he hadn't visited her. Did she care? Sometimes. She had mixed feelings about her father. Perhaps she had done all her emotional stepping back from him and her mother when she first went to boarding school all those years ago in Melbourne. Certainly, the news that they had separated didn't cause her world to tumble down or her heart to break. If anything, she was amazed they had stayed together for so long. They were so obviously ill-suited. Her father was charming, but so unreliable, so easily distracted, chasing one money-making venture after another. Her mother, by contrast, was so serious. Intellectual rather than emotional. The "adult" in the relationship. On the bright side, from the little that Charlotte had been able to pry out of her mother over the years, all the debts had now been cleared. Not that it meant her parents were back talking again.

Poor Gracie had been so upset about it all. Charlotte had tried to console her over the phone, trying to explain that it wasn't Gracie's fault, that their parents had a relationship quite separate to their roles as parents. She'd tried every approach she could, but all Gracie had ever wanted was for everyone she knew to be happy and live happily ever after. She had always been so sweet. Too sweet for her own good, possibly.

Perhaps it was no wonder that the accident with Tom and Spencer had upset her so much. Time would heal things for her eventually, Charlotte felt sure. She was only twenty-seven. Plenty of time yet.

Charlotte's thoughts turned to Spencer. Her brother at least seemed to be making up for everyone else when it came to accumulating notches on his bedpost or however people counted relationships these days. In her opinion he was too much of a chip off their father's block, all charm and not to be trusted, but there was no denying he was great amusement value, and those hippyish, boyish looks of his certainly seemed to attract girls in droves. The latest, Irish Ciara, sounded very nice on the phone. Nicer than Spencer's Swedish Anna or Polish Katerina had ever sounded. Ciara also sounded smart. Organized. Charlotte would bet a thousand dollars it was Ciara's brains that were behind this ridiculous but bafflingly successful Irish surf school, too. Shark Boy, indeed. P. T. Barnum had it right. There was a sucker born every minute, and anyone who fell for Spencer's tale deserved to be taken for all they had.

And to continue her audit of her family—what about Audrey? Charlotte thought about her sister for a moment, then decided there was nothing worth mulling over. It was a little embarrassing to admit it, but Audrey bored Charlotte. Her complete self-obsession. The whole "Greg saved my life" carry-on. The "None of you see me for the artist I am" business. Yawnsville, Arizona, as one of her nanny students was too fond of saying. The sooner Audrey faced up to the fact that she made her living by sticking her hand up a sock's kabootie, the better. Enough of the artistic temperament. Save it for the real artists. Not that she would ever say that to Audrey, of course. Knowing her, there'd be every chance she'd lapse back into nonspeaking and Charlotte would have to put up with hours of earnest phone conversations with Grig, who seemed perfectly nice, but God, could he get any more boring either? And to think Audrey and Grig between them were in charge of the televisual stimulation of thousands of children around the world. What were they creating, a generation of sock puppet–obsessed zombies? Charlotte had sat through half of one episode of *It's Bobbie Time!* during one of her rare visits to London and been appalled at how backward it was, all patronizing talk into the camera and ancient songs. Thank God they hadn't managed to sell Bobbie to any of the U.S. cable networks. That would *really* have damaged Charlotte's credibility with her client base.

Families, families, Charlotte thought. What was the saying? Can't live with them, can't live without them? She had her own version. Can't live with them, don't want to live with them. In the time since she had left Melbourne to come to Chicago she'd seen her family only once a year, sometimes even less than that. Never for Christmas. Not while Hope was still coming to the Templetons for Christmas each year, even when her boyfriend was still alive. Boyfriend? It had always sounded such a juvenile word when the pair of them were so old. Meal-ticket friend might have been a better description, from what Spencer had told Charlotte about Hope's live-in lover. Rich, dim-witted, new agey, and inexplicably devoted to Hope until the day he suddenly dropped dead.

Hope or no Hope, the main reason Charlotte hadn't returned home for turkey and tree-trimming was that Christmas time in Chicago was nanny bonus time. Mr. Giles and Ethan always went away for Christmas. Charlotte spread the word around the nanny circles of Chicago that she was available for short-term work over the holiday season. She'd been inundated with high-paying offers. Those fraught Christmases hadn't done anything to convince her of the positive aspects of marriage and love. She saw more examples of bad marriages in those years than she ever wanted to see again. Couples worse than strangers. Fathers who barely knew their children. Mothers who clearly favored one child over another, or didn't seem to like any of their children. Why would her luck be any different? Charlotte asked herself. If she did happen to meet a man, fall in love with him, have children, what was to stop it all from falling apart within a few years? In the end, it had been an easy decision. She'd become a businesswoman instead, fulfilled every one of her goals. Not just fulfilled them, she'd surpassed them. Today's graduation ceremony was just the latest example.

It was almost two p.m. by the time she shook the final father's hand, kissed the last mother's cheek, and hugged the final graduate. All twenty-five of them had placements throughout the Midwest. Another successful term under her belt, and a waiting list one-hundred strong—not just for students but potential clients as well. The knowledge gave her satisfaction every day.

She turned on her phone again as she climbed into the backseat of her car, a black Mercedes-Benz S-Class. This car, and her driver,

Dennis, were her one luxury in her business and personal life. It had been Mr. Giles's idea. "Think about all the time you spend commuting, all the work you could be doing instead of cursing the traffic and getting stuck in snarls. Your driver equals at least four extra working hours a day." He'd been right, of course. She sometimes managed to do more work in the car than she did in two or three days in the office, especially now that she had her BlackBerry.

It had been an easy decision to move out of Chicago to the small, historic town of Woodstock, just over an hour away. She actually liked the life of a commuter. Now and then she took the train from Woodstock to Chicago and back, especially in the warmer months when she didn't mind the walk to the station, but she usually started work so early and stayed in her office so late that getting stuck in rush-hour traffic wasn't a factor for her—or for Dennis, at least. She occasionally stayed in one of Mr. Giles's investment apartments in Chicago—he always made sure one was available for her use, for the nights she worked especially late—but she preferred the small-town life of Woodstock on weekends. She liked the feeling she got as she passed the *Welcome to Woodstock: A distinctive destination* sign each evening. She liked the fact that the town had an unusual claim to fame, having been used as a location for the film *Groundhog Day*. She loved her house, especially. It had taken her only two weekends of touring available properties with a local realtor to find it: a two-story, two-bedroom wooden stand-alone on the main road into the historic square, with a porch, stained-glass windows, and a garden filled with flowers and fruit trees. It was warm in winter, cool in summer, light-filled all year around, and just the right size, enough space but easy to keep tidy. It also, very importantly, had a large, modern kitchen. She loved to cook. She loved to eat, too, far too much, unfortunately. On the bright side, her excess weight was surprisingly good for business. People liked fat nannies and fat nanny trainers, she'd discovered. Fat nanny trainers with English accents even more. Her voice gave her authority, her width gave her the cuddle factor.

She mostly kept to herself in Woodstock, venturing into the bookshop or one of the cafés or restaurants on the square on weekends if she was in the mood, occasionally attending a concert or play in the old Opera House, talking to her neighbors enough to be polite, but beyond that, happy to keep her own company. She did enough talking at work. She had the best of both worlds this way, she decided. A successful career, a peaceful home life.

In the back of the car now, she took a sip from the bottle of chilled water Dennis had thoughtfully placed in the leather holder and checked her BlackBerry. Fifteen work calls to return and six personal messages waiting for her, as expected—two each from Audrey, Spencer, and Gracie. She did like it when they jumped to her bidding like that. Sending quick text messages back to each of them, she arranged a conference call for noon the next day, then turned her attention back to her working life.

Chapter Twenty-four

I SUPPOSE WE SHOULD begin this with a catch-up," Charlotte said at the agreed time the next day, putting herself in charge, because, well, she was in charge, wasn't she? "Audrey, how's Grig? Bibbie?"

"It's Greg and Bobbie, Charlotte."

"Sorry. I just can't seem to master that New Zealand accent."

"They're both fine, thank you." Audrey's voice was frosty.

"Spencer? Sorry, Shark Boy, I mean," Charlotte said. "How's the surf? And those scars? Shark's teeth are so full of venom, I suppose."

"You're thinking of snakes, Charlotte," Spencer said in an unruffled voice. "And we don't have those in Ireland. Couldn't be happier, thank you for asking."

"All that sea air and Irish mist, I suppose. Gracie, are you still there? And don't just nod. We can't see you, remember."

"I'm here."

"Gracie was in Yorkshire this week for a job interview with the Captain Cook Museum, weren't you, Gracie?" Charlotte said.

"There's a Captain Cook Museum?" Spencer said. "Are we in it?"

"What was the job, Gracie?" Audrey asked.

"I don't know if we're in it and it doesn't matter what the job was. I didn't get it," Gracie said.

"Good," Charlotte said cheerily. "Now you have to come and work for me instead. My evil plan worked. I rang deliberately to distract you, you know."

"I actually wanted that job, Charlotte."

"No you didn't."

"What happened, Gracie?" Audrey asked.

"They were worried about my work record," Gracie said briefly.

"You deserve an award for your work record, in my opinion," Charlotte said breezily. "So young, so many jobs."

"Stuff them," Spencer said. "If they didn't have the brains to hire you, I hope they all get attacked by islanders and die. That was an excellent allusion to the real Captain Cook story, by the way, in case none of you got it."

"Got it, Spencer, thanks," Gracie said.

"Look, we're all sorry you didn't get that job, Gracie," Charlotte said, pulling rank again, "but there are plenty more jobs in the sea and we better get to the point of this call, fun and all as this telephonic family reunion is. So have you all heard Hope's message now? No nods, remember. You need to speak."

"Yes."

"Yes."

"Yes."

"Anyone have any idea what she's actually up to?"

"Couldn't she be genuine?" Audrey said. "Maybe it's exactly as she said. She wants to go back to Templeton Hall to lay some ghosts to rest, to make amends for her behavior back then, and she's inviting as many of us as possible to join her. Greg thinks it's very generous of her. The airfares alone would cost a fortune."

"Generous of her?" Charlotte scoffed. "Generous of her wealthy dead boyfriend's last will and testament, more like it."

"I think it's a waste of time and money," Spencer said. "Why doesn't she dig out one of the old brochures and meditate in front of a photo of Templeton Hall for an hour instead? Save all of us the bother."

"All of us? So you're going to accept, Spencer?"

"Are you joking? Go back to Templeton Hall for a week?" He started laughing. "Why on earth would I want to do that?"

"As a thank you to Hope for all the money she's given you over the years?" Gracie's voice was cold.

"Hope and I have a very good relationship about money, Gracie. She gives it to me, I take it. Simple."

"All right, both of you." Charlotte took over again. "Has she asked Mum to go, does anyone know?"

Gracie answered, "Yes, she did. Mum said no."

"Because she can't stand being in the same room as Hope at the moment either, or did she lie and say she's too busy at work?"

"She lied," Gracie said.

"Okay, that's two down, three to go. I can't go, of course. I'm surprised Hope even asked me. She loathes me, I loathe her. If I wasn't so busy at work, I'd go for the sport of it, though. Audrey, what about you? It's just a hop across the sea for you, isn't it? The rest of us would have to fly halfway across the world. That's an idea! You can go and represent all of us, without getting any jetlag in the process. Thanks, Audrey, that's—"

"No!" Audrey's shout reverberated down all their phone lines. "I've decided not to go either. I discussed it with Greg—"

Charlotte sighed. "Well, there's a surprise."

Spencer snickered.

"And quite apart from the fact I'm taping the new series of the program over the next two months, Greg feels it wouldn't be a good idea psychologically for me to go back there."

"I disagree," Spencer said. "You spent the last months of your time there locked in your room, didn't you? It might be helpful psychologically for you to see what the place actually looked like."

Charlotte laughed. Gracie stayed quiet.

Audrey reacted immediately. "Oh, you think you're so funny, Spencer, don't you? And you, too, Charlotte, but you know what? You're not. And I don't even know why I'm wasting my time discussing this anymore. I've already told Hope I can't go with her. I rang her last night."

"My, you *have* been proactive, Audrey," Charlotte said, ignoring her outburst. "Thank you for gracing us with your audio presence today all the same. Poor Hope. At this rate she's down to a party of one, her lovely sweet self."

"What about Gracie?" Spencer said. "You're not working at the moment, Gracie, are you? You always thought Templeton Hall was a piece of heaven. Why don't you go back and help Hope unload her psychic burden of guilt? It might help you, too. Who knows?"

"Spencer!" Charlotte warned.

"That's a horrible thing to say, Spencer!" Audrey added. "Gracie, ignore him."

There was no answer from Gracie.

"Gracie?" Charlotte said, concerned now. "Are you still there? Spencer, you unfeeling little idiot, apologize to your sister."

"Sorry, Gracie."

"In an adult voice, Spencer," Charlotte said.

"Jesus, no wonder you're a nanny high priestess, if that's how you talk to your charges."

"It's how I talk to everyone." Charlotte's tone softened. "Gracie, are you still there?"

There was a pause, then Gracie's voice. "Yes."

"Pet, of course we don't expect you to go back with Hope on your own. I'll ring her tonight and tell her that we're all very sorry, that much as we'd love to go on this emotional decluttering journey with her, we're far too busy but we hope she'll give the dear old Hall a pat from us and would she please turn off the lights on the way—"

"I will do it. I'll go with her."

"What?" Charlotte laughed. "Gracie, you have to be joking."

"I mean it. It's only for a week and it's important to her."

"It's not a holiday to the Bahamas, Gracie." Charlotte wasn't laughing now. "It's a week with Horrible Hope at Templeton Hall. With *Hope*. Remember her? That mad, slurring, swaying aunt of ours?"

"She's different these days, Charlotte." Gracie's voice was calm.

"Not that you'd know, Charlotte," Spencer said. "How long since you've seen her? Decades?"

"Sixteen years to be exact, and don't try to be smart, Spencer. You're one to talk. From what I hear all you do is treat her like a human ATM. Anyway, of course she and I have spoken. When she had that epiphany or whatever it was she kept ringing me until I had no choice but to talk to her. It was that or put up with another five hours of her breast-beating on my voicemail. Gracie, we'll come back to you in a second, I promise. I'm still trying to come to terms with what you just said. I've just thought of something. Does anyone know if she's invited Dad?"

There was silence.

Charlotte again. "Has anyone spoken to Dad recently?"

More silence.

"Anyone know where Dad is?"

Silence.

"Fine. We'll assume she hasn't invited him. He'd surely have picked up a phone and called one of us if she had."

"Called you, perhaps." Audrey's tone was petulant. "I kept a note last year and apart from those postcards and, all right, a birthday present, in the entire twelve months he rang me only once. Once. And that was to ask me to keep an eye out for paintings by some long-dead New Zealand–born painter he'd heard was increasing in value. It was nothing to do with me. He didn't even ask about Greg or Bobbie, or—"

"Poor Audrey," Charlotte said. "You're right. I hear from Dad all the time. He never stops visiting me or ringing me—"

"And if he's not ringing you, he's ringing me," Spencer said. "I've had to put a block on the phone I was hearing from him so often. It was bordering on harassment."

"Are you serious? He rings you both that often?"

"No, Audrey. That was a joke," Charlotte said. "Do you have jokes in New Zealand?"

"Could we please talk about Hope's invitation?" It was Gracie. "Charlotte, do you have to be the one to ring and tell Hope I'll go, or am I allowed to do it myself?"

"You're scaring me, Gracie. Are you seriously serious about this? Do you actually realize what you're getting yourself into?"

"She's right, Gracie," Audrey said. "I think you should give it some more thought."

"So do I," Spencer said. "Surely you've got better things to do with your time than fly across the world to spend a week with Hope."

"Actually, no, I don't," Gracie said. "I'll ring Hope tonight."

Gracie hung up then. If her brother and sisters had anything more to say to her, she didn't want to hear it.

The next day, she emailed all three of them.

FROM: Gracie <gracietempleton@yahoo.co.uk>
TO: Charlotte; Audrey; Spencer

Dear Everyone

I spoke to Hope last night and told her I'd go back to Templeton Hall with her. She was very nice and very grateful. She asked why the rest of you weren't coming too, so I explained you were all too busy at work. She may be ringing each of you, so please back me up. It was hard enough having to lie to her. She's been in touch with the solicitors in Castlemaine and their services apparently don't extend to opening up the Hall and getting it ready for habitation again, so Hope has asked if I will go back a day or two before her to get it all organized, beds made, food in etc. Before you get outraged on my behalf, Charlotte, Hope has made it clear that she considers this a work trip, not a holiday, and is paying me for my time. I protested but she wouldn't take no for an answer.

I leave in three weeks' time. She's following two days after that. Talk to you again before I go.

Love Gracie

FROM: info@sharkboysurfschool.ie
TO: gracietempleton@yahoo.co.uk

She's PAYING you to go with her?? Why didn't she say that in the first place?? I'd definitely have come. DAMN. How much?? And don't start getting any ideas about Templeton Hall. That belongs to ALL of us.

Gracie didn't reply.

AUDREY RANG Gracie the next morning.

"Gracie, I've been thinking about this overnight. Are you sure you can actually cope with this? Not just Hope. The whole going-back-there thing. I know that Templeton Hall meant more to you than any of us, even before all of that happened with Nina and Tom."

Gracie was glad Audrey had brought it up. Apart from Spencer's one unkind reference, Nina and Tom had been the elephants in the room during their conference call. It had been the same when Gracie phoned Hope the previous night, too. Hope had made lots of allusions to the Donovans, talking about difficult memories and a miasma of past guilt, but she hadn't directly mentioned Nina or Tom's name like Audrey just had. Gracie felt suddenly fond toward her sister. Audrey wasn't usually so thoughtful.

"Maybe it'll be for the best," she said. "I don't think I'd have gone back voluntarily."

"I can see why," Audrey said. "You must feel guilty every day about Tom's injuries, do you? Gracie, you have to stop thinking like that. Number one, it was eight years ago. Number two, it was an accident. A terrible accident. You have nothing to be guilty about, even if you were the driver."

Audrey didn't give Gracie a chance to reply.

"Gracie, I can't tell you how to feel, though God knows I know what it's like to pull yourself out of the darkness, but have you thought this through? Quite apart from being with Hope, will you even be okay on your own in the Hall those first few days? I always hated being there alone—all those rooms, no one for miles around if something awful happened. You won't be too scared? Too nervous? There'll be a lot of memories waiting there for you, remember."

Gracie decided to change the subject. "It's the spiders I'm worrying about, not the memories. Remember those big ones, the huntsmen?"

Audrey's tone softened. "You don't have to pretend with me. You must be so nervous, I know. You were closer to Nina and Tom than any of us, after all. I think it's important before you go to maybe think about them a bit, just prepare yourself for how you might feel if you were to meet them, how you might feel to see Tom in a wheelchair, for example. There might even still be some anger from them toward you, and the more prepared you are for it, the better. I know Greg would be more than happy to have a chat with you if you think it would help. He's really great at role plays. Though, of course, Nina and Tom might not even be living near Castlemaine anymore. We never did hear from them again afterward, did we?"

There was a pause. "No, Audrey, we didn't."

"I'd have thought Nina might have kept in touch with Mum, at least. I mean, I know it was a difficult time, but it *was* just an accident. Once everyone came to terms with the fact Tom wouldn't walk again, wouldn't it have been better for everyone to move on together?"

"Audrey, could we please stop talking about—"

"Of course, Gracie! I'm sorry." There was a male voice in the background. "Thanks, darling. I'll be right there. Gracie, I have to go. I'm doing a big shopping center event today, but I'll talk to you again soon. Let me know if you want to have a chat with Greg, won't you? And don't even think about Tom and Nina. Just try and put them out of your mind, okay?"

As Gracie put down the phone, she didn't know whether to laugh or cry.

Chapter Twenty-five

AFTER PLAYING phone tag for nearly four days with her aunt, Charlotte finally managed to get her on the other end of a line by calling one of the three counseling centers Hope and Victor had funded.

Charlotte never wasted time on pleasantries. "I'll get straight to the point, Hope."

"I've always liked that about you, Charlotte."

"No, you haven't. You've never liked anything about me and I've never liked anything about you. You suffered me because I'm Eleanor's daughter and I suffered you because you're Mum's sister. So let's cut out the garbage—"

"Garbage? You are American these days. Or do you mean trash?"

"What exactly are you up to with this whole back-to-Templeton-Hall trip? And don't give me the new-age nonsense you gave Gracie because I don't believe it."

"Were you always this cynical, Charlotte? Or has dealing day-in day-out with harassed mothers using their husbands' money to assuage their guilt about leaving their allegedly loved and wanted children in the hands of another woman turned you this way?"

"You're a professional counselor and *this* is how you speak to people?" Charlotte gave a short laugh. "Such a brief speech, yet so many insults, not just to me but to all my clients. Modern mothers have a choice these days, Hope. They're allowed to have children *and* a career. But it's so good to see you haven't lost your touch in all these years of sobriety. Unless that's a front as well, is it?"

"I haven't had a drink in twelve years, Charlotte."

"That rules out alcohol. Shall we discuss chemicals? Tablets?"

"Mind your own business."

"How did you fool that poor, sorry, rich boyfriend of yours?"

"There was no fooling going on. We loved each other."

"I'm sure he did love you. And I'm sure you found his massive fortune extremely loveable in return."

"It was immaterial to me whether he was a wealthy man or as poor as a church mouse. We were soul mates from the first moment we met."

"Eyes meeting across a crowded AA meeting. Yes, Spencer told me all about it. Rising out of your evil ways together to create an empire of healing centers. Blah, blah, blah."

"Have you ever been in love, Charlotte? In fact, have you ever had a relationship with anyone, man or woman, apart from your own monstrously ill-informed ego? I had hoped you'd changed, that America would have matured you in some way. Knocked some of that arrogant stuffing out of you. It appears I was wrong."

"As you would not have the slightest idea what I am like or what I was like, seeing as you haven't laid eyes on me in sixteen years, and before that you were permanently pissed or off your brain on God-knows-what, I don't really think you're in any position to make judgments, positive or negative, about my character, thank you, Hope."

"Not in any position and not interested, in fact. And if you don't intend to get to the point of this otherwise riveting conversation in the next two minutes, Charlotte, it is only fair I tell you that I plan to hang up. I have better things to do with my time than listen to the opinionated, self-important ranting of a long-lost niece."

"You know why I'm ringing. I want to know what you're up to at Templeton Hall."

"I'm not up to anything. All is as it seems. I am fortunate enough to be in the financial position where I am able to travel at will. A central part of my journey to sobriety has involved taking an inventory of my life and facing up to the wrongs I've done wherever possible."

Charlotte sighed.

"I'm so sorry to bore you, Charlotte. Or perhaps this is beyond your comprehension, as it involves thinking of people other than yourself. In a nutshell, I wanted to bring you all back to Templeton

Hall to apologize. However, it seems that all of you apart from Gracie are too busy to hear that, so I will apologize to Gracie alone. I have reflected on the situation further, though, and I now feel this is all meant to be. I believe Gracie may also find solace in returning. The past eight years have been extremely difficult for her and she still requires a great deal of care and concern. I certainly haven't seen you rushing back to offer that support, either eight years ago or more recently."

"Don't you try and make trouble between Gracie and me. I've only ever been a flight away. Gracie's always known that. And we've all been there for her."

"Really? Sometimes only an outsider can see the truth, Charlotte. Surely you know that after all your years in business? As for the rest of you caring about her—you know as well as I do that the only person Spencer cares about is himself. And yes, Audrey has come back occasionally but only when it suits her and she spends most of the time sulking that she isn't getting enough attention about that ridiculous creature on the end of her hand. And certainly you *have* only ever been a flight away but it's not a flight you've taken very often. The fact is you've all let your mother carry the burden of helping Gracie through her difficult years. That's what this phone call is about. I've made you confront a few cold truths about yourself and so you've resorted to the age-old tactic of attack being the best form of defense."

"Save your mumbo-jumbo for your counseling sessions, would you? This has nothing to do with Gracie. And I've always done what I can for her. We were talking only this week."

"This week? Did you come back after the accident? Do you have any idea what that accident did to her? The guilt she felt every single day about Tom? About Nina? The guilt she still feels, years later?"

"Of course I do."

"You knew she cried herself to sleep every night for months, possibly years afterward? That she wrote letter after letter to Nina and Tom, begging their forgiveness? Dozens of them? That she used to sit and watch for the postman, like a poor abandoned animal, day after day, hoping for word back?"

"She did not."

"She did, Charlotte. I suppose you were too busy living the high life, building up your own empire, thanking your lucky stars every day that you'd escaped from your family. You would have left Templeton Hall, left Australia, whether I was there or not. I was just a handy excuse. You're good at that, aren't you? Good at finding other people to blame for your own shortcomings, or at producing what look like valid reasons that pave the way for you to do exactly what you want to do. I know people like you, Charlotte. I see people like you in my sessions every single day. We call them Pretenders. They have the intelligence, they have the vocabulary, they are better at self-deception than most other addicts. Because they can always justify their actions as being the fault of someone else. And that wasn't a slip of the tongue. I do see you as an addict. A power addict. A self-righteousness addict."

Charlotte didn't speak.

"So shall we start this conversation again?" Hope said. "You rang to ask me what I was up to taking Gracie back to Templeton Hall? I believe I've now explained. If you require further clarification, then I—"

"Gracie really wrote so many letters to Nina and Tom?"

"For nearly six months, Charlotte. Eleanor would post them for her. I posted some for her, too. Yet there was only ever total silence in return. That's what hurt her the most, I believe. The fact that she never heard anything from either of them, ever again."

"Nothing? Not even a note, a postcard?"

"Not a thing. Can you imagine how that made her feel? Have you ever felt guilt, Charlotte? True, festering guilt, guilt so strong, so all-encompassing that it is all you think about, from the moment you wake to the moment you try to get to sleep? It's the closest thing to madness. All you can do is go over and over every second of every hour of every day that led you to the moment the terrible event happened. You try and change it, you try and rewrite history, you try and convince yourself that it was out of your hands, but that's impossible, because the more you think about it, the more you replay it in your head, the more are forced to see the same conclusion. It *is* your fault. You *are* to blame. And nothing, nothing will ever change that. That's what Gracie lived with. That's what Gracie is still living with. And it is worse for her, because there was love involved. Not just for

Tom, but for Nina, too. Your sister's life was destroyed that night in Italy, Charlotte, and you never had the decency to recognize it."

"I have to go, Hope." Charlotte hung up without saying good-bye.

Hope just smiled into the phone. "Really? What a shame. Thank you so much for calling."

CHARLOTTE SPENT fifteen minutes pacing around her living room. Outside, the large cherry tree was a flurry of feeding birds, the leaves quivering. Her neighbor was disgusted that she hadn't set up nets to keep the birds away, that she let the fruit just rot like that. They'd had a sharp conversation about it, ending only when Charlotte produced her haughtiest tone of voice and stood erect, reminding him that it was her tree, her property, her business. They hadn't spoken since. The birds had been noisier than ever, though. Normally the sound soothed her, the sight of them amused her. Now, she wanted to go outside with a pellet gun and shoot the lot of them.

She'd expected the conversation with Hope to be entertaining. She hadn't expected to feel like this. Angry. Guilty. Confused. Her nerves were actually jangling. She wanted to rewind every moment of her call with Hope, inspect everything she had said, work out what was truth, what were mischievous lies. That wasn't possible. She had to do something, though. She couldn't leave it like this. There was only one person to talk to. She picked up the phone and dialed the number.

"Gracie, it's me," she said as soon as her sister answered. "I've been talking to Hope."

"Did you terrify her on my behalf? Warn her that if she tries to upse—"

"Gracie, she told me about the letters you wrote."

"Sorry?"

"She told me about the letters you wrote to Tom and Nina. The dozens of letters, after the accident. Is she telling the truth?"

There was silence for a moment. "What did she say?"

Charlotte told her exactly what Hope had said. More silence and then Gracie spoke again.

"It's true."

"Why didn't I know any of this?"

"You weren't here."

"Gracie, I still should have known. You should have told me, not just about the letters, but about all of it. I didn't even realize it was that serious between you and Tom."

"I loved him, Charlotte."

"But you were only kids."

"I loved him, Charlotte."

"But surely if it had been that serious—"

"He'd have written back to me? That's what I hoped. But I was wrong."

"You just never heard back?"

A pause. "Not from him. Nina wrote to me once."

"But Hope said you never heard anything."

"I didn't tell Hope. I only told Mum and she promised not to tell anyone."

"What did Nina say?"

"I'd rather not repeat it. But I'm sure you can guess."

"Gracie, I wish you'd told me. Why am I only hearing this now, all these years later?"

"Because it's only now you're asking me about it."

"I'm so sorry. I was so busy back then, setting up the business and—"

"I know that, Charlotte. I'm not angry with you. I'm just telling you how it was."

"I would have come back if you'd wanted me to. But Mum said you'd get better in your own time, in your own way."

"She was right."

"I feel terrible."

"Don't. I *am* better."

"What did Nina say to you? It wasn't good, was it?"

"No, but if I tell you, if I say it all out loud again, it sticks in my head and I—"

"I understand. I'm sorry, Gracie. I'm sorry I wasn't there when you needed me."

"You were, in your own way. Charlotte, please, don't worry. Ignore Hope. You know she's always liked making trouble between us. I like her much more now, but just because she's sober doesn't mean that aspect of her personality is any different."

"If anything like this ever happens to you again, please, would you tell me—"

"If I ever have another car accident and cripple one of my passengers, you mean?"

"I'm not joking, Gracie."

"Neither am I."

FOR HALF AN HOUR after she'd finished the call with Charlotte, Gracie tried to finish what she'd been doing, packing for the trip. She'd be there for a week: she'd need four dresses, three skirts, T-shirts—

It was no good. Charlotte's call had stirred her up too much. She'd been trying her best to concentrate only on her happy memories of Templeton Hall, to try and make herself look forward to the trip with Hope. Those memories had disappeared again. Now only thoughts of Tom were back in her mind, in full color, as if she had seen him the day before, not eight years before.

She went across to her computer, even though she knew what she was about to do was a mistake. She'd forced herself to stop doing it years before, hours of endless searching the Internet hoping for some, any, mention of him. She told herself now these were unusual circumstances. She was going back to Australia in just a few weeks. Back to Templeton Hall. As Audrey had said, she needed to be prepared in case she . . .

She just needed to be prepared.

She opened an Internet search engine and typed in his name. Tom Donovan. After hesitating for just a second, she pressed Search.

Entry after entry appeared. She'd long ago discovered there were hundreds of Tom Donovans in the world. Thousands. The screen in front of her was full of mentions of them. A Tom Donovan, skiing in New Zealand, part of an Australian team. Twenty-three, five years too young. Tom Donovan, running for office in local elections in Ireland, aged forty-two. A Tom Donovan on Facebook, aged eighteen. A priest called Tom Donovan. Baseball players, musicians, plumbers, political commentators. A sports commentator called Tom Donovan in Melbourne. When she'd first found a mention of him, six years earlier, her heart had immediately begun to beat faster. She'd clicked on entry after entry, finding articles he'd written about cricket, about the Australian team's performance, about other sports as well, football, rugby. She'd read every word, even found transcripts of a regular radio slot he did on Melbourne radio. She'd been shocked at first at how right-wing he'd become, how deliberately provocative, even racist, he was at times. She'd clicked on more links until a photograph of him appeared and she'd realized, with some relief, that it wasn't her Tom Donovan but another much older one, a former cricket player in his mid-fifties who'd reinvented himself as a controversial pundit. His name appeared again now, as she scrolled through the dozens of pages. She didn't read his articles this time. She kept looking, hoping for something new, anything, the tiniest fact about her Tom Donovan, where he lived now, what he was doing. She found an architect in Sydney called Tom Donovan, a Thomas Donovan house painter in Perth, a Tommy Donovan disc jockey for hire in Brisbane. After a moment's hesitation, she started again, putting more detail into the search line. Tom Donovan wheelchair. *Stop,* the voice in her head said. *Whatever you find won't make you feel better.* She ignored it.

She found a wheelchair-bound Tom Donovan blogging from his new home in America. Her heart began to beat faster again, until she clicked on the biography section and found a photograph. He was fifty, with red hair. A Thomas Donovan, working in a Sydney university as a lecturer in the medical school. Sixty-two years old and bald. Another in England . . .

She reentered Tom Donovan. Added cricket Australia. She finally found him on the sixth page of entries, a passing mention in the biographies section of an out-of-date online cricket magazine. This was him. This was definitely him. She recognized his birth date, his education record. Knowing it was going to hurt, but now unable to stop, she clicked on the link and held her breath. The first thing she saw was a photo, bad quality and nine years old, but it was him, his dark eyes, dark hair, smiling at the camera. She read the first two lines of the paragraph of text beside it, then turned quickly away, shutting the laptop, breaking the connection. She wasn't quick enough. She'd seen it. There had been a mention of his place in the cricket academy and then the sentence: *A promising career cut short*—

She didn't need to read on. A promising career cut short by an accident. A promising career cut short by Gracie Templeton. A promising life destroyed because of her.

What did you expect? the voice told her. What had she expected? What did she think she'd find? His own website? Photos of him playing basketball, skiing, competing in international wheelchair games, rising above his injuries, successful and happy again?

One thing was now clear. There was no way she could try to find him while she was back at Templeton Hall, back in Australia. What was there left to say that she hadn't said in each one of those letters he'd ignored? "I'm sorry—again—for ruining your life?" She had no right to expect anything from him, be it anger, understanding, or forgiveness. She'd relinquished any claim on him the moment she'd driven into that truck.

She now regretted telling Hope she'd go with her. Was it too late to change her mind? She considered it, then decided she had to go through with it, for Hope's sake as much as her own. She had never forgotten the unexpected kindness Hope had shown her in the months after the accident. Somehow looking up the Internet entries made it simpler, though. She would now just fly in, stay with Hope for the week, then fly out again. And this time, perhaps she could leave the past behind.

Chapter Twenty-six

Melbourne, Victoria, Australia

Nina! quick, come here!"

Nina ran into the living room of her inner-city Melbourne home, expecting to find Hilary in danger, or more worryingly, her niece in danger. Instead, both Hilary and her ten-year-old daughter, Lucy, were sitting in front of the television set. "What is it? What's wrong?"

Hilary pointed at the TV set. "Quick. Look. That woman there."

Nina looked. It was a children's TV program, all Technicolor and cheery voices, with the presenter, a thin, smiling, red-haired woman in her early thirties, dividing her time between speaking directly to the camera or to a blue-haired sock puppet on her right hand.

"That's right, Bobbie!" she was saying in a chirpy English accent. "Today is orange day! So let's think of all the orange things we can. What's that, Bobbie?" She leaned down and pressed her ear close to the sock puppet's sewn-on mouth. "That's right! Oranges are orange! And we know a song about that, don't we?"

"Thanks, Hilary," Nina said. "I'd completely forgotten today was orange day."

"You don't recognize her?"

"The woman or the puppet?"

"The woman. The puppet's a boy. Hold on, I'll turn down the sound, that music's distracting." The woman on screen looked even stranger without sound, swaying from side to side and smiling in an overanimated way at a sock.

"Give up?" Hilary asked.

Nina nodded.

"It's Audrey Templeton."

Nina went still. "How can it be?"

"I don't know, but it is. Her name was in the opening credits."

"We were looking for *SpongeBob SquarePants* on the cable channels and this Bobbie show came on instead," Lucy said.

Nina couldn't take her eyes off the screen now. "Is it an English show?"

"I don't know," Hilary said, as two possum puppets appeared beside the sock. "Would an English show have animals like that? Does it look like her? Your Audrey?"

"She's not 'my Audrey.' I haven't seen her in sixteen years. And I've no idea what she'd look like now."

Hilary picked up something in Nina's tone. "Sorry. Do you want me to turn it off?"

"No!" Lucy said, moving closer to the screen. "That puppet's funny."

Hilary left her daughter with the remote control and followed Nina into the kitchen. "Can I help with dinner?"

Nina shook her head as she moved the salad bowl into the fridge. "I'm nearly ready."

"Sorry, Nina."

"For what?"

"For calling you in just now. I should have just switched off the TV and not mentioned it. It's probably not even her."

Nina was now busy at the stove, checking saucepans. "It might be. She always wanted to be a performer."

"She's the one who stopped speaking, isn't she? Good to see she got her voice back. Shame about the mute sock, though." Hilary grinned at her sister. "Nearly made you smile. Come on. It won't crack your face."

"That is so childish."

"Don't get uppity. What is it, Nina?"

"Nothing."

"Come on. Tell me. You've been jumpy as a cat since we got here."

Nina took a seat, glancing toward the living room. Lucy was now standing in front of the TV, dancing and singing along.

"It's just strange for that to happen today. To see a Templeton on TV like that."

"Strange because?"

Nina hesitated. "I had a letter this week—"

"From one of the Templetons? After all these years?"

She nodded. "From Hope."

"*Hope* wrote to you? Evil drunken Hope? Why? To order some Australian wine?"

"To invite me to spend a week at Templeton Hall, actually. Next month. All expenses paid."

Hilary started to laugh. "You're joking, aren't you?" She looked closely at her sister. "You're not joking. Why on earth didn't you tell me?"

"I didn't know what to say about it."

"I'd have thought that was fairly obvious. 'Hilary, out of the blue I've heard from a family I never want to see again and I've been invited to have a holiday in the one place on earth I never want to go again.'"

"Remind me to hire you as a speechwriter some time, would you?"

"Why on earth would she invite you there? For a week of solitude?"

"No. I'd have company."

"She's going, too?" Hilary laughed. "This gets even better. Just what you'd enjoy. A cozy reunion with Hope—"

"Hope and Gracie."

"*Gracie?*" At Nina's nod, Hilary gave a slow whistle. "Oh, my God. I have to see this letter."

Nina went to her room and returned with an official-looking envelope. Hilary opened it. There was a typed note on letterhead from a solicitor in Castlemaine. Attached to it was a long handwritten note on lilac paper. The handwriting was large, the letters looped and flamboyant. Hilary had trouble reading it.

"Let me help," Nina said. She took the note from her sister and began to read aloud.

"*Dear Nina, this letter will come as a surprise, I know, and possibly an unwelcome one, but I do hope you will read through to the end and consider what I have to say. I am writing to invite you to join me—at my expense—for a week at Templeton Hall. I have also invited my sister and her entire family, but to date it is only Gracie who is able to join me.*

"*Over the past twelve years, since I was given the grace of sobriety, I have had the cause and opportunity to reflect on many aspects of my life, and in particular, reflect on times where I caused pain to others through my own selfish behavior. I have made it my mission to make amends wherever possible. It has been a difficult and lonely road at times, but a journey I am honored and humbled to take. Many times my approaches have been rebuffed and I accept that. Every day I give thanks that I have had the opportunity to not just change my own behavior, but to change my life, and I cannot expect others who remain damaged or hurt by or suspicious of me and my motives to join me openheartedly on my journey.*"

"Good God. What new-age dictionary has she swallowed?"

Nina kept reading.

"*I have many people to thank for giving me the support I need to be emotionally brave and mentally fearless, and still more to whom I feel an apology is necessary. I have taken what I think of as an inventory of my life, and the period at Templeton Hall still remains a time of sorrow and shame on my part. Tragic circumstances—the death of an adored life partner—have left me with the silver lining of unexpected wealth and I see this as a sign that more action is needed: strong, firm, generous action on my part. Sometimes the only way to heal is to return, and this is what I hope to do now. The time at the Hall so many years ago was, I believe, life changing for each of us in different ways, as events occurred, rifts formed, and, in regard to my dear niece Gracie and your beloved son Thomas, relationships were established that led, sadly, to traumatic outcomes.*"

Nina broke off from reading then. "He's never been Thomas."

"Don't worry. Go on," Hilary said.

"*This is not the time or place to expand on my beliefs, but I truly feel there are deep wounds from that time that need to be healed. I take full responsibility for my own role in that damage, I wish to assure you. I have attempted to make amends with each member of the family before now, but geography and circumstance have worked against me and continue to do*

so. Nevertheless, I look forward to my time there with Gracie in those familiar and pleasant surroundings, and pray that we will both find some
peace and healing.

"I have instructed my solicitor in Castlemaine to liaise with you should
you accept my invitation too—as I dearly hope you will. I will of course
cover—in advance—any travel costs you may incur should you decide to
make this journey with me."

Nina looked up. "Then there are names and phone numbers of
those whom I should ring if I accept her offer."

"If you *accept* her offer? You're actually considering it? Have you
lost your mind?" Hilary took the letter and scanned the contents once
more as Nina silently watched her. "As I said, she's either swallowed
more than her fair share of self-help books or she's started her own
religious cult. And why on earth would you ever want to see Gracie
again, after the way she abandoned Tom?" Hilary folded the pages
with firm movements. "Put it in the bin, Nina. It's a letter from a
ranting, raving mess and the solicitor had no right to send it to you.
How did he know where you were anyway?"

"Jenny told him."

"Jenny in Castlemaine?" Hilary frowned. "How do you know?"

"The solicitor told me when I rang him about the letter."

"You've already rung him? You really *are* considering this? Nina,
what could you possibly have to say to any of the Templetons? It'll
just bring everything back, open it all up again. Don't you remember,
you made me swear that I would never let you have anything to do
with any of them again. *Any* of them, Nina. Don't fall for Hope's
games. For heaven's sake, it's not as if you have anything to feel guilty
about, is it?"

Nina hesitated for just a second. "No, it's not."

"Then ignore her and her crazy letter," Hilary said firmly. "Matter closed."

ACROSS THE OTHER SIDE of Melbourne, in a tall glass building
overlooking the Docklands, the newspaper editorial department was
a bustle of sound, flickering computer screens, wall-mounted TV
sets, and phone conversations. Glass-walled cubicles lined the walls

and a cluster of open-plan desks took up the center space. At a desk in a corner of the sports department, a dark-haired man sat in front of his screen, phone tucked in under his chin as he typed. His desk was a clutter of printed emails, lists of team names, playing schedules, and old coffee cups.

"Welcome back, stranger," a young smiling woman said as she walked past his desk. "All right for some, sunning themselves in the West Indies for a week." She deposited a pile of mail in front of him. "Shred these or open them; all old news by now."

He smiled his thanks, and began to open them, still talking into the phone. The envelope with the Castlemaine postmark was third in the pile. He pulled out a lilac-colored letter with a compliments slip attached, glanced at it, then looked more closely. Moments later, he hung up and kept reading. The phone beside him rang once, twice, three times. He ignored it until, eventually, it stopped.

After reading through the handwritten letter a second time, he slowly folded it, pushed it back into the envelope and then into his pocket. He sat for a moment, his hand resting in his dark curls, staring at the computer screen in silence.

The phone began to ring again. He ignored it once more. Instead, he stood up, reached for the stick leaning against the side of his desk, and walked out of the office.

Chapter Twenty-seven

Hope leaned back in her chair, took a sip of her mineral water, and watched as Eleanor read through the itineraries she'd brought over. "We're both flying business class, of course. Gracie seemed quite pleased about that."

"I'm sure she'll enjoy it. That's very generous of you," Eleanor said.

"You don't need to completely overwhelm me with gratitude, Eleanor. Just a speck would be nice. A glimmer, even."

Eleanor put the itinerary down. "Why are you doing this, Hope?"

Hope sighed extravagantly. "First Charlotte, now you. What is it with this family? Can't someone try to repay the many kindnesses shown to her over the years without being submitted to the third degree?"

Eleanor held up her hand. "I do appreciate what you're doing for Gracie, Hope. What I don't understand is why you're still going back when only Gracie is able to come with you. If it's about making amends with us, why don't you just change the location?"

"Eleanor, I can't move on or forgive myself completely without first going back. You of all people must remember my behavior. I treated you appallingly when we were there. I had no self-control, no self-respect. I paid your son to supply me with alcohol—"

"You *what*?"

"Eleanor, all of that behavior is behind me now. But I wanted to prove to you all that I meant it. Bring us back together under one roof again."

"Oh, come on, Hope. You truly thought everyone could just drop everything like that? When it's the middle of the school term for me, a busy time for Charlotte, not to mention Audrey with her TV show, and Spencer—"

"Yes, yes. I've already heard everyone's excuses. If it wasn't for Gracie's selflessness I'd cut quite a sad figure strolling the Hall grounds on my own, wouldn't I? Did I tell you she's going out two days before me to get everything ready? She insisted on it."

"She told me it was your idea."

"Perhaps it was. I can't remember. It's fate, in any case. There are a lot of hurts in need of healing in this family, Eleanor. Gracie needs to follow where her soul is leading her."

"Why can't I believe I'm hearing these words from you, Hope?"

"I thought you agreed that becoming sober was the best thing I ever did."

"I do agree. I'm just not sure about what you did next."

"If I hadn't gone to those AA meetings, I'd never have met Victor. If I hadn't met Victor, I wouldn't have become a counselor myself, been in the position of being able to open our clinics, and help so many other lost souls."

"And if Victor hadn't been so rich or died so suddenly, you wouldn't be as footloose and wealthy as you are now."

"Life is there in its mysteries for us, Eleanor. Our paths are preordained. We just have to have our hearts open and be ready to see the journeys unfolding in front of us." Hope glanced at the expensive watch on her wrist. "I'd better go. I'm seeing a client this evening. A well-known actress, as it happens. Not that I can tell you her name."

She was almost out the door when Eleanor spoke. "Hope, wait."

Hope stopped in the doorway. "I know what you're going to ask me. Did I invite Henry?"

Eleanor nodded.

"If he was going to be there, would you have changed your mind about going?"

"Yes or no, Hope? Is Henry going to be there as well?"

"If it's what fate has planned for us, yes. Beyond that, I can't say. Good-bye for now."

As Eleanor stood at the front window and watched Hope drive

away in her quiet, gleaming car, it was all she could do not to pick up a vase and throw it across the room.

How in God's name had it come to this? How had the tables been so completely turned? If she could time-travel backward to when Hope was at her worst, drinking a bottle of wine or more a day, swallowing tablets by the handful, could there have been a moment she could imagine her sister's transformation into this . . . this what? This smug, self-satisfied, preaching, infuriating . . .

It didn't even help that Eleanor had seen this new version of her sister evolve, from the time Hope finally dragged herself to an AA meeting, then to a Narcotics Anonymous meeting. ("Is there a Pain-in-the-Arse Anonymous group she can join as well?" Charlotte had wanted to know.) She'd seen Hope miraculously become sober, move in with Victor, watched in further amazement as they opened a trio of very successful, equally expensive treatment clinics around London. She'd been by Hope's side at Victor's funeral, seen her play the role of the bereft widow so convincingly. But not once had Eleanor trusted her sister. She'd never been able to, not as children, not as young women, and not now. The current Hope may have changed her behavior, but she hadn't changed her personality.

"She's just melodramatic," Henry had said once.

"She's malicious," Eleanor said. "Dangerous." She truly believed it. After all her years as a teacher, she'd realized dangerous people did exist. It was obvious even in the classroom. It sometimes started with casual, physical cruelty: a little boy killing a frog or burning ants with a magnifying glass, a group of children ganging up on the class weakling. But Eleanor had seen other methods of cruelty, too. Belittling. Mocking. Finding pleasure in manipulating other people. That's where Hope's skill and interest lay.

Eleanor had grown up believing that if she was kind and truthful, good things would happen to her and the people she loved. When she was nineteen, twenty-nine-year-old Henry's arrival in her life had been unexpected but in perfect symmetry with her thinking. She'd been the one to volunteer to undertake the painstaking, time-consuming work of finalizing her grandparents' estate. As a reward Henry had come into her life.

She'd once made the mistake of expressing her beliefs to Hope.

Her sister had laughed loudly. "If it hadn't been Henry who pinpointed you as a little rich heiress worth chasing, it would have been some other vulture of an antiques expert, Eleanor. Don't be so naïve."

All their lives, Hope had been ready with the putdowns and the insults. Yet Eleanor had never been able to cut herself off from her only sister. The family bonds, the sisterly bonds, were too deep. Especially once their parents had died, within two years of her marriage to Henry. The best of times, the worst of times. Never had a quotation been so apt.

A part of Eleanor wished she felt able to accept Hope's offer, as much to protect Gracie as witness Hope's alleged cleansing ritual. But she'd realized eight years ago she could never go back there again. Any good times she'd remembered had been wiped away in an instant by Nina that day in the hospital in Rome.

No, she wouldn't think about that day, about Nina, about Henry. She wouldn't.

It was too late. Thoughts of him, of the two of them, were already spilling into her mind, sparked by Hope's casual mention of Henry, her refusal to confirm or deny if she'd invited him. It was at moments like those that Eleanor knew the malicious Hope was still there, under all the compassionate talk. Hope had always known Eleanor's weak spots. She'd always known Henry was Eleanor's weakest spot of all.

Eleanor had always strived to be a woman of intelligence, education, discernment. But if that was so, how could she still love Henry after all he'd done over the years? Still want to know where he was, what he was doing. Who he was sleeping with. Why hadn't she ended it between them years ago, when she first realized he wasn't faithful to her?

It had been just a few years into their marriage. Charlotte and Audrey were small. Her growing suspicions about Henry's interest in a work colleague had been confirmed by something as clichéd as a receipt in his suit pocket for a necklace she hadn't been given. Had that been her first, her biggest, mistake? Should she have confronted Henry that night? Told him what she'd guessed, told him it was unacceptable, rather than just push the receipt back in his jacket pocket and run to her sister?

On the surface, Hope had been so supportive, so outraged on her behalf. "I don't want to say I told you so, but I told you so."

"I loved him, Hope. I still love him."

"You want to stay with him?"

Eleanor had nodded, miserable. She did. It didn't make sense, but she did.

Hope was there for her again, two years later, when Eleanor suspected a second affair. There were phone calls late at night, hang-ups if Eleanor answered. Henry suddenly had a lot of dinner engagements. A year later, a third affair that lasted only a few weeks. Eleanor knew all the signs by then. Henry's distracted air, overly busy workload . . .

"Leave him," Hope urged each time. "How can you put up with this?"

"I love him. I can't help it. And I can't leave. I couldn't do it to the girls."

"Then confront him."

Eleanor couldn't. She was too scared of what she might hear. She waited, instead. And soon enough, each time, something told her that Henry was all hers again.

It became the pattern of their lives. When Henry wasn't occupied elsewhere, she couldn't have been happier. She learned to compartmentalize her life. Whenever he became distracted, she forced herself to blame his work. And perhaps it was his work sometimes. By the time Charlotte was five and Audrey four, he was becoming one of the best-known antiques experts in the country, his client list long and prestigious.

At the same time, Hope's own career as a garden designer was taking off. She'd started calling around several nights a week. Her drinking was heavy but controlled. In front of Eleanor one evening, Henry and Hope discussed one of his clients, owners of a large estate in Kent needing a garden redesign. Perhaps Hope could travel with him, meet them, see what might come of it?

When they came back, something was different between them. Eleanor accused them both, one night after dinner. She'd just put the girls to bed, was tired. She was always tired. In the dining room Henry and Hope were laughing, telling stories, smoking, drinking, while she fetched drinks, made dinner, cleaned up. Hope's latest boy-friend was supposed to have been there, but she'd arrived on her own. "He's a fool," was all Hope would say, not apologizing for not letting her know, or for the waste of food.

A loud burst of laughter from Hope while Eleanor was in the kitchen at the sink was the last straw. She came in and threw the glass she'd been washing onto the floor. It shattered noisily. "What happened? What happened when you were away together?"

Henry just raised an eyebrow. "Good Lord, darling. That glass was valuable."

Hope laughed. They both laughed again, looking at each other, not at her.

Eleanor knew in that moment that something *had* happened. "I want to know or I'll break every glass, every plate, and every piece of furniture in this house."

Henry stood up. "Eleanor, nothing happened! Darling, what's got into you?"

Hope slowly stood up then, too, confidently, elegantly. Eleanor was reminded of a cobra.

"Henry, tell her. Or if you won't, I will." At Henry's hesitation, Hope continued. "Eleanor, you're right. Something did happen. But it wasn't important. Just something silly. One drunken kiss. That's all, I promise."

Eleanor saw from the look on Henry's face that it was true. She turned to her sister. "Get out of my house."

"Henry started it. Don't blame me."

"Get out. Henry is my business."

"You might want to remind him of that."

Hope took a long time to gather her coat, pick up her bag, walk out to the hall. They waited for the sound of the front door closing. It slammed.

Only then did Eleanor turn to her husband. "I won't put up with this, Henry. I turned a blind eye to all the others, but not this time. Not Hope. I want you to leave."

His reaction shocked her. He started to cry. Not just tears. Sobs. He started talking, the words pouring out of him, explanations, apologies. "Please, Eleanor, don't do this to us. We need each other.

I love you so much. I love the girls. It was madness. I was worried about the business, about money. They were just distractions."

"It was Hope, Henry. My sister."

"She was playing with me. It was a game. It was one kiss, Eleanor, one kiss and she only did it to try and make trouble between us. She's always been jealous of you, of you and me. Can't you see that? Eleanor, don't let her win. Don't let this be the finish of everything between us. I'm begging you."

Back and forth their conversation went. He was so passionate, so persuasive. And she still loved him.

It was past midnight before she started to waver. "I have to be able to trust you."

"How can I help you?"

"I don't know, Henry. But you have to try."

For the next few years, they were the perfect couple. She saw Hope only rarely, and always separately from Henry, deliberately. If her sister asked, she told her everything was fine. She hinted that it was better than fine, smiled secretly, knowing it would infuriate Hope. She noticed, with a kind of pleasure, that Hope was drinking more, taking something else, too, tablets of some kind, drugs of some description. There were times when Eleanor could have stepped in, tried to stop her, but each time she didn't. It was a deliberate decision. Let her drown in her own sorrows, she thought.

She and Henry began trying for another baby. And tried. Nothing happened. There was sex, regularly, at the right times, at more than the right times. Still nothing. Was it that she didn't completely trust him yet? Their regular moves began around the same time, to Brighton, to Yorkshire, back to London, back to Brighton. She blamed her problems getting pregnant on that instead. On her study load, too, her decision to gain a teaching degree, to specialize in home education. The stress of two young children. Charlotte was a stubborn child even then; Audrey needy, often tearful. Until finally, she became pregnant with Gracie. Less than a year later, Spencer was conceived.

She was soon so busy with the four children and her own studies that her relationship with Henry was the least of her worries. He was traveling for work more than ever. She asked him once, "Can I still trust you?" He'd kissed her, smiled the smile—his real one, which made her feel so good—and told her, his gaze direct, that he loved her, he loved his family, that yes, she could trust him. But did she? She was honestly too tired to care some nights.

At the same time, Hope was spiraling rapidly downward. Eleanor would hear the front doorbell at two a.m., even later sometimes, and go downstairs to find her sister slumped on the front step. Never a sign of how she had got there—no taxi idling, no car driving away. Eleanor would bite back the anger, help her in, put her to bed in the spare room, and let her sleep it off. Sometimes it took a day, sometimes more. At first she helped her, tried to shield the children from what was happening, made excuse after excuse. Hope was unwell, was under stress at work. The truth was Hope hadn't worked in months. She'd been living off what was left of their parents' inheritance. After getting advice from a local doctor, Eleanor tried what was called "tough love." Not answering Hope's calls. Not letting her stay if she arrived drunk. Ignoring her rambling messages on the answering machine. Until the day some sixth sense made Eleanor call to Hope's apartment, hammer repeatedly on the door, finally obtain a key from the landlord and get inside to find her sister unconscious on the floor, an empty wine bottle and scattered pills beside her. An hour later and Hope would have been dead, the ambulance man told her. Everything changed from that day on. Hope became Eleanor's main responsibility.

They were back living in London, Gracie was eight, Spencer seven and the two older girls in their early teens, when Henry arrived home one afternoon from his latest buying trip. She knew immediately that something big had happened. There was an air of excitement about him.

His expression, however, was calm. "Eleanor, I had a phone call while I was in Yorkshire from a solicitor in London, working on behalf of a legal firm in Melbourne. They've been trying to track me down for some time. I've been at their offices in Chelsea today."

She tensed, expecting it to be bad news. The reality was more unexpected.

He handed her a photograph. It was of a two-story mansion, a beautiful, classic design. The setting was unusual: dry-looking grounds, a vivid blue sky. Perhaps it was in Spain or France.

"What do you think?" Henry asked.

"It's beautiful. The blue sky as much as the house. Is it a new job?"

"In a manner of speaking." He paused. "Eleanor, it's mine. Ours."

"How lovely." She thought he was joking. She was used to him returning from jobs with gifts for her: a small piece of jewelry, an unusual vase, a delicate cup that he thought she'd like. But a house? She went along with it for the moment. "And where is it, Henry?"

"Australia."

"Australia?"

He explained, then repeated it. She couldn't take it all in. "You've *inherited* this house? Is that what you mean? But how? From who? And why only now?"

He told her again all the solicitor had explained to him. The house had been built during the Victorian goldrush, by a long-distant relative, a businessman called Leonard Templeton, the youngest son of a family of London merchants. A cousin in England inherited it, but didn't live in it. The land surrounding it was sold for grazing. A complicated lease arrangement was set up, managed by a local firm of solicitors, but the ownership had always remained with descendants of that original Leonard Templeton.

"It was my father's great-uncle who owned it last. I never met him. I don't even think my father met him. It's taken this long for the solicitors to untangle the lease arrangements, but what it comes down to is this, Eleanor. I'm next in line. It's mine. Ours."

It was incredible. Incredible. She looked at the photo, turned it over as if hoping to find more detail there. "But if no one's been living in it for years, it must be in ruins inside."

No, Henry assured her. It had always been well maintained. It had been leased to an Australian pastoral farmer and his family until recently.

"But what will we do with it?"

He paused. "I thought we could live in it."

More laughter until she realized he was serious.

"Eleanor, I'm in something of a predicament."

That night he talked more than he ever had to her about his work. It was an unusual trade, the antiques business, he explained. So much of it was on supply and demand. It depended on so many factors—

who wanted an item badly enough, perception, rarity. Who was to say that one piece of silverware was worth ten thousand pounds when another was worth less? From his point of view, there was also often a fine line of honesty to cross. If an elderly woman was showing him one item, and he knew it was worth nothing compared to the small brooch she was wearing, was it criminal to casually make an offer for that as well? If he was asked to sell on consignment, was it immoral or simply good business to buy the entire lot himself, pay the seller what he or she believed was a good price, and not divulge that four of the pieces in the two-hundred-item lot would fetch many more thousands? Hundreds of thousands, even? As for another hypothetical situation—what if the seller of some rare jewelry preferred not to disclose the items' origin? Was it Henry's role to push for details, or simply to find a buyer?

"You've been dealing in stolen property? Is that what you're saying?"

"I have to make moral calls every hour of every day, Eleanor. I've realized there are degrees of deception."

How that sentence would come to haunt her.

She picked up the photograph of the sun-soaked mansion. "So we'd be running away?"

"We'd be withdrawing discreetly for the time being."

"To do what? Lie low in the Australian outback?"

"Not just lie low, no. I need to do some more family research, but I've had an idea, Eleanor. A crazy idea, but we might even be able to make a business of it. All I'd need is the start-up capital. A lump sum to get us on our feet."

She knew what he was talking about. The rest of her inheritance. By the time they went to bed that night, she'd agreed.

HENRY FLEW OUT to Australia first, to inspect the property and set his plans in motion. When Eleanor, Hope, and the children arrived two weeks later, a full-scale renovation was already under way.

"Can we afford this?" she asked as he showed her sketches, fabric, and wallpaper samples.

"Of course."

Of course they couldn't, is what he should have said.

Hope had come with them, ostensibly to assist Henry with the garden design, in truth because she had no one left in England to take care of her. She was completely in the grip of her addictions by then. Secret drinking. The tablets. The erratic behavior. But always the tears afterward, the heartfelt gratitude. "Eleanor, what would I do without you? I'd be dead if it wasn't for you."

For all the heartbreak that followed, Eleanor had to acknowledge that there had been good times at the Hall. Henry had been the very best version of himself at first: busy, motivated, charming. She'd watched in amazement as his business idea became a thriving tourist attraction. It had felt good to work together, as a couple, a family. . . .

Until the cracks began to appear again. The mail started to go missing. The bills, more specifically. After that, it was like dominoes falling, one event setting off another. She and Henry fighting all the time. Spencer's wayward behavior. Charlotte's refusal to come home, her announcement about her job in Chicago. Audrey's school play disaster. And Gracie, Eleanor's little Gracie, falling in love with and practically moving in with Nina . . .

Nina.

Had it been happening between Nina and Henry even then? Under Eleanor's nose? No, she refused to let it be true. She would have known, wouldn't she? And Nina had been a friend then, to all of them, hadn't she? They couldn't have done without her in the first years after they left, either, calmly accepting every explanation they offered about why they weren't coming back, even going to the trouble of packing and shipping all the belongings and paperwork they'd left behind in that first hasty departure.

Too busy working full-time, arguing with Henry about the outstanding debts, it had taken Eleanor years to find the energy to go through even a few of the boxes. It wasn't until she had the house to herself, after Gracie had gone to France and Italy with Tom, that she'd made a proper start on them. Within minutes she'd been cursing Henry's filing methods. His lack of filing methods, more accurately. There were folders filled with more bills and more lawyer demands bundled in with old brochures, magazine cuttings, school reports. But in one box she'd found folders filled with paperwork she'd never seen before.

Henry had been doing more than reading his antique magazines night after night in his office, it seemed. She found pages and pages of notes about his family's history, early research into his family tree, sketches. Not just the details of the stories they liked to tell during the tours. This was different, more private, as if he was truly trying to find his place in the world. She was surprised how much it moved her.

She and Hope had always known exactly where they came from, who their parents, grandparents, great-grandparents were. Henry hadn't had that. He hadn't known his mother, who'd died when he was only two. His father had died when he was in his teens. The fact that he'd virtually raised himself had made him an even more romantic figure to her.

Something changed inside her as she read his notes that night. The fury she'd felt toward him started to dissolve. For the next two days, alone in the house, she found herself remembering only good things about him. How he could make her laugh. His stories. The way he made love to her. He had always been a wonderful lover, skilled, attentive. . . .

She left the boxes from Templeton Hall alone and found herself drawn toward the family photo albums. She was in tears by the time she finished looking through them: their wedding, the arrival of the children, Christmas parties, summer holidays, Henry at the center of each image. How had she forgotten those times? How had she let money come between them? Yes, he'd made mistakes. Yes, he'd lied to her about the bills, but hadn't she vowed to stay with him through good times and bad? Was it too late to try again as a couple, as husband and wife?

She was walking toward the phone that evening to call him, to ask him to come back to her, when it rang. For a joyful moment she thought it was Henry, ringing to ask her for a second chance. It was Spencer, barely coherent, calling from Italy, the words tumbling from him—an accident, hospital, Gracie, drinking, Tom badly hurt. . . .

It took Eleanor more than eight hours to get to them, between flight delays and overbooked airplanes, her fear rising as each hour passed, worrying for her children, for Tom, for Nina. It was Eleanor who'd broken the news to her. Spencer had begged her to make the call. Nina's voice had been almost unrecognizable. "Is he going to die, Eleanor? Will he die?" All she could tell was all she knew, that Tom had been in surgery for almost three hours, that he was in intensive care, that she should get there as quickly as she could.

Eleanor was waiting in the hospital foyer when Nina arrived. She ran in, they hugged, two mothers. "He's this way." She took her by the hand. They barely spoke. What was there to say? Nina had to be with Tom.

It was two hours later, after Tom was recovering from more surgery, that Nina came to her again. She had stopped crying. She was now angry. She met Eleanor outside the ward Gracie was in, in the corridor, her voice too loud. She didn't ask about Gracie or Spencer. She stood in front of Eleanor and delivered a statement, almost shouting. "Tom won't ever walk again. It's Gracie's fault. Gracie was drunk driving."

"Nina, she wasn't." They'd done blood tests. She was under the limit. She tried to tell Nina.

Nina shook her head. "I've read the police report. The truck driver said she was driving all over the road."

"Nina—"

"Your daughter has destroyed my son's life, Eleanor."

"It was an accident."

"She was drunk."

"She wasn't. It was an accident."

Nina's voice was getting louder. "It's my fault. I should have told him to come home. I should never have let him stay with you. I should never have had anything to do with any of you. I should have trusted my instincts years ago."

"Nina, please, don't—"

"It's the truth. It's the truth, Eleanor." Her voice rose again. "My son is in pieces. His whole body, everything's broken. His face is . . ." Her tears started then, her body heaving with them. Eleanor's compassion returned. She led Nina into an empty room nearby, held her, let Nina cry, tried to think of soothing words but could find none.

There was only bad news, and the bad news was all Nina's. It was only luck, some kink of fortune, that had it this way around, Tom with the terrible injuries, Gracie and Spencer almost unhurt. Like a terrible lottery, Eleanor the only winner. She would be as angry at Nina if the positions were reversed, she knew. As shocked, hurt, scared, crying as hard . . .

She tuned back in then to what Nina was saying. Nina was talking about Henry. Why was she talking about Henry?

"It's a game to you, to Henry, isn't it? Just a stupid game, to lure people in and then laugh in their faces, turn them into fools. Your family is dangerous, all of you. You seduce people and then you destroy them. Henry did it to me, and now Gracie has done it to Tom. You've destroyed us both, all of you. I want you to leave me alone. You, Gracie, Henry, Spencer, all of you. Leave us alone. Do you hear me?" Nina was now shouting and crying at the same time.

Eleanor took a small step back, unable to believe what she was hearing. "Nina, what are you talking about? What do you—"

"I'm talking about your husband, Eleanor. Your lying bastard of a husband."

"Henry? You've seen Henry recently?"

"Yes, I've seen Henry, Eleanor. I recently spent the weekend in bed with Henry."

Eleanor wasn't hearing this. Nina was upset, angry. She was raving. It was jetlag, shock. . . . "Nina, what are you saying?"

"I'm talking about your husband screwing me, Eleanor. In every meaning of the word."

Eleanor went still. Their children were hurt, lying in hospital beds only meters away, but this was her focus now. Sharp, cold, clear. "When, Nina? Where? Tell me."

Nina's chin lifted, her eyes hard, glittering. "At Templeton Hall, of course. Where else?"

The words tore into Eleanor. It didn't matter that she and Henry had been separated for years. It didn't matter when it had happened between Nina and Henry. The pain of it felt like a knife in her heart. She tried to find words, any words. . . . "But he's my husband. You're my friend. I trusted you."

"Trust? Will I tell you what he said, Eleanor? What your liar of a husband said to me?"

Eleanor held up her hand, stopping Nina. She couldn't hear it, whatever it was, whether it had been happening when they all lived there, whether it had just started recently. She had to stop her saying anything else. Hurt her, too.

She forced her voice to stay calm, her expression composed. "I don't want to hear, Nina. Not any of it. You think I haven't heard it before? You think he hasn't been having flings on the side for years? That you were unique? That you were special to him? He says what people want to hear, Nina. He always has done, he always will do. You weren't the first and you won't be the last. Let me tell you that."

"Eleanor—"

Eleanor silenced her again. All hope of a reconciliation with Henry had just died. Her husband had not just had affairs with colleagues, possibly with Hope; he had slept with her friend Nina. Had sex with Nina. Their friend Nina. She felt grief and anger rise inside her, fire and ice in her veins, masking her pain, overshadowing concern for Tom, changing everything. Her voice was as cold as her expression when she spoke again.

"And you dare to tell *me* to leave you alone, Nina? To tell me to keep my family away from *you*? You get out of our lives. You and your son, get out and stay out of *our* lives."

"Eleanor—"

"I don't want to hear it, Nina. I don't want to hear anything you have to say. Leave me, my children, and my husband alone, do you hear me?" She walked out of the room first.

Facing Gracie afterward was one of the hardest things she had done. Hearing her youngest daughter crying, begging to talk to Tom and to Nina, knowing it was impossible for more reasons now than she would ever be able to share.

Back in London, it got worse. Henry arrived to see Gracie and Spencer. All concern and love, making Spencer laugh and even Gracie smile within minutes. Eleanor had to leave, barely able to look at him, let alone be in the same house as him.

One afternoon, she nearly told Gracie, needing to somehow put a halt to Gracie's hope and despair about Tom, to stop her writing letter after letter to them both. At first, despite everything she'd said to Nina that day in the hospital, Eleanor had posted them for her. Eventually, Eleanor broke all her own parenting rules and stopped at a café down the road and read two of the letters. Her heart nearly broke to see Gracie's guilt and grief laid bare, pages of heartfelt lines begging Tom to write back, telling him how much she loved him, how she would do anything to turn back time. She told him that if she could swap places, if she was the one unable to walk, she would do it. Her letter to Nina was as sad, so confused, so guilty, pleading with Nina, telling her how much Nina meant to her, how she loved her, too. It was that letter that stopped Eleanor from telling Gracie about Henry and Nina. Her daughter was already devastated, already so fragile. What would news like that do to her?

It barely seemed possible eight years had passed. Eleanor knew that something had stalled for her and for Gracie since then. Not for Spencer. He'd somehow emerged untouched. He had the same charm as Henry, Eleanor knew, the expectation and knowledge that people liked him, were drawn to him, that things would turn out well. It was helped by his looks, his sparkle—Henry's traits, replicated in the next generation.

But Gracie's spirit had dimmed since the accident. Her joy, her enthusiasm to experience life had turned to a low flame rather than the blaze it once was. Eleanor saw it in herself, too. She'd felt her own interest in so many things dwindle. Was it simply part of the aging process? She was in her mid-fifties, after all. It felt more like disappointment. Sadness. Loneliness. Months had turned to years without any contact between her and Henry. There were no longer outstanding bills to be paid. All he sent now was the figure they'd agreed when they first separated, which he'd somehow honored, month after month, on top of the other debts she'd made him repay. Eleanor had barely touched it, living off her own earnings. She'd divide Henry's money between her children one day.

She knew all four of them had relationships with Henry independent of her, but if they did meet up with him, they'd obviously decided not to tell her. They'd all seemed to come to terms with the separation. It was she who still hadn't, who still found herself burning with slow outrage toward him, and even more infuriatingly, feelings of love, despite everything. What would it take to sever any feeling for him?

Perhaps if she knew where he was, where he lived, who he lived with, it would be easier. That's what made it so difficult, not knowing anything. She understood Gracie's anguish about Tom more than her daughter knew, the longing for some small detail, the silence harder than any facts would be. Was Henry living with another woman? Did he even have more children? It was possible. He had no reason to tell her if that had happened.

It was late, after eleven, but Eleanor was now too restless to sleep. An urge came over her to see photos of the Hall again. All the boxes of paperwork were still in the attic. There'd been no desire and no need on Eleanor's part to go through the rest since that time eight years previously, when her heart had softened at the sight of Henry's attempt to trace his family tree, when she'd wanted to invite him back home, until all her hopes were destroyed by everything that happened in Italy. She'd finish the job now.

Two hours later she was on her knees in the attic, surrounded by the final piles of papers, the remaining contents of the filing cabinets from Henry's office at the Hall: old business plans, accounts, tourism newsletters, brochures, pages written in Henry's strong handwriting, tales of the different rooms, the scripts for the tours of the Hall. Nearly three years of their life now tidied neatly into folders. It read like family history, not just paperwork. Perhaps Gracie might like to see it before she flew back, Eleanor thought. It might help remind her of happier times.

As Eleanor reached the bottom of the final crate and took out one last folder, she yawned, tired now. She expected it to be more brochures, more scripts, possibly even more of Henry's hidden invoices. It took only a quick glance at the first page for her to realize it was none of those things.

Ten minutes later she was still there on the floor, reading through the sheaf of stapled, photocopied papers for a second time. She'd thought she could no longer be shocked by Henry; that there were no more deceptions for her to uncover. It seemed she was wrong.

Chapter Twenty-eight

IT WAS THE LIGHT in Australia that was so different, Gracie realized, as she drove beyond the airport, heading north toward the goldfields for the first time in sixteen years. On either side of the freeway, the scenery was changing from scattered suburbia to sunburnt rolling hills, clumps of gum trees, that big, big sky all around. She fiddled with the car radio, finally settling on a station playing classical music, in need of the soothing tones.

She'd promised to call Charlotte and her mother on her arrival, to phone Hope, too, but she hadn't yet. She'd ring once she got to Templeton Hall, she decided, once she was inside and had real news to impart, something beyond the obvious—that the flight had been long, the sky was blue.

Charlotte had been all concern in their final conversation. "You're still absolutely sure you're okay to go back? You won't be too nervous there in the Hall on your own?" A pause then. "You won't do anything silly, will you?"

"Like what?"

"Go looking for Tom and Nina. I can understand you might want to find them, Gracie, I do, but I don't think you should do something like that on your own."

Sometimes Charlotte knew her too well, despite the years and distance between them. Because it *had* crossed her mind again as her departure date neared—more than crossed her mind. Perhaps if she saw them face to face, even for a minute, even if it ended badly, it would be better than the picture she'd imagined for so many years.

Being there, in Australia, would surely make it easier to track them both down. She could go into Castlemaine, ask around. Someone there would know what had happened to Nina, and once she knew where Nina was, Tom would surely be nearby. It was at that point that her imagination kept failing her. She couldn't picture him anymore.

She'd once seen a documentary about young people with spinal injuries and her heart had filled with sadness. She'd seen so many bright minds in broken bodies, reliant on round-the-clock carers, their days punctuated by feeding, washing, their hopes and plans changed in a split-second. Many still had remarkable spirits, great senses of humor, changing their goals and ambitions to small, attainable things—lifting a finger, breathing on their own for a few hours a day. Some had married. "My body was damaged, not my brain. I can still communicate, still fall in love," one said. The interviews with the carers—almost invariably the mothers—were as heartbreaking. Footage of elderly women gently washing their grown children. "I did it when he was a baby. I'm happy to do it now." But what happened after the mother died? Hospitals? Nursing homes? Is that where Tom was now, confined to a bed, a wheelchair? And if she did find him, would he even allow her to see him, give her the opportunity to say to his face how sorry she was, how sorry she would always be? Or would he send her away before she had a chance to speak?

Just over an hour later, something about the landscape made her slow down. A sign came into view: CASTLEMAINE 25 KM. She wasn't far away now. She hadn't been sure she would find her way so easily. There were no longer any roadside signs pointing to the Hall, after all. But it felt so familiar. The broad paddocks, gentle tree-covered hills, the big sky, the space. So much light and space. She stopped briefly to double-check her map, and the smell when she opened the car door almost overwhelmed her: warm soil, gum leaves, the scents of her childhood.

Five kilometers later she was at the turn-off. The huge gum tree at the junction of the highway and the dirt driveway had always been their landmark. She indicated left and drove slowly, jolting over potholes and loose stones. As she tried to negotiate her way around the worst of them, she saw broken tree branches, crooked posts, gaps in the fencing. Her father would never have let the approach road look this uncared for. "First impressions are everything, my darlings," she could almost hear him saying.

The closer she came, the more neglect she saw: uneven patches of grass where there had once been smooth green lawn, bare brown earth where she'd once picked flowers, rows of fruit trees now left to grow wild, their branches heavy with unpicked, rotting fruit.

One final bend of the driveway and there it was in front of her. Templeton Hall.

She slowly brought the car to a halt, feeling as though her heart was trying to beat its way out of her chest. She'd expected the building to look smaller, but it seemed bigger. Two stories high, large shuttered windows, an imposing front door reached by a flight of wide steps made from the same golden sandstone as the house itself. It needed painting, several roof tiles were broken, and one of the window shutters was missing a slat, but it was still standing, almost glowing in the bright sunshine, as beautiful as she remembered.

As she walked toward it, the sound of the gravel crunching beneath her shoes mingled with unfamiliar bird calls from the trees all around. She automatically reached for the antique silver whistle, holding it tight in her hand.

She climbed the first step, the second, the third, wishing, too late, that she hadn't offered to arrive early, hadn't volunteered to be the first to step back inside the Hall again.

The front door opened before she had a chance to put the key in the lock.

In the seconds before her eyes adjusted completely from the bright sunlight, she registered only that a man was standing there. A tall man with dark, curly hair, holding something in his right hand. As she saw his face, she felt a rushing sensation from her head to her feet. She heard herself say his name as if from a long distance away.

"*Tom?*" She tried again. "Tom?"

"Hello, Gracie."

He took a step forward into the light.

"I've been waiting for you," he said.

She was imagining this. She had to be. She was still on the plane, daydreaming, picturing what she would most love to happen, the person she would most like to be there waiting for her. Tom, standing in front of her, tall, strong, looking down at her, his face as familiar as if she had kissed it only the day before, not eight years previously. His hair as dark and curly, his eyes as dark brown, his gaze as direct.

"I was going to invite you to come in, but it probably should be the other way around."

If he wasn't real, if she was imagining this, how was he talking, stepping back into the doorway of the Hall, calmly waiting for her to come inside? If she was truly in charge of this, this *apparition*, he wouldn't be saying that. He wouldn't be keeping his distance. He would be smiling at her, throwing his arms around her, kissing her, telling her he had missed her so much, how hard it had been for them both. Of course he understood the guilt she felt, but at last, here she was. Here they both were—

"Gracie?"

She wasn't imagining this. It *was* Tom, waiting for her to answer him. An unsmiling Tom. After years of imagining this moment, of rehearsing every line, every plea, every apology, she couldn't think of a single word to say to him.

For a long moment they stood, staring at each other. Then they both spoke at once.

"I thought you were . . . I always imagined you . . . but you're walking. You're—"

"I'm sorry to surprise you, but Hope told me you were arriving today."

He smiled then, the briefest of smiles. "You first."

She ignored for now his mention of Hope, having to say what she'd started, needing to know now. "You're all right? You're walking? You're okay?"

"I'm okay." A shutter came down over his face then.

She couldn't stop her questions. "But Nina said you'd never walk again. She said—"

"It turned out she was wrong." Where there had been a wary expression on his face, there was now something different. A blaze of something in his eyes. Anger. At her?

"Tom, I—" She stopped there. Where did she start? How could she explain everything? How happy she was for him, how shocked, how amazed, how confused. She was now filled with words she wanted to say, but there seemed to be no way to begin. "Why . . . ?" Again, she stopped.

"Why am I here?" That brief half-smile again, too quick. "I wanted to see you."

That smile was enough. It would be all right between them. She knew in that instant. He was here, she was here, the two of them, alone, so much to talk about, so many questions. She smiled back, relief flooding through her, the shock of seeing him fading so fast, replaced with something else. Wonder, a kind of happiness. She felt tears come into her eyes and didn't try to wipe them away. "Tom, I can't tell you how long, how much . . ." She laughed, the words suddenly rushing from her. She couldn't tell him everything she needed to say quickly enough now. "I can't begin to tell you, how it feels to see you, to see you're all right. You must have been so tired of my—"

"Hello there." A voice interrupted her. A female voice.

Gracie turned. Nina? Nina was here, too?

It wasn't Nina. It was a young woman, about Gracie's age, maybe younger. A pretty woman with dark curls, as dark as Tom's, in a crimson summer dress and blue cardigan. Gracie noticed every detail, as she stood, midsentence, watching the woman walk gracefully across the foyer to where she and Tom were still standing in the doorway, walk as if she crossed that tiled floor every day, so confident, getting closer, relaxed, curious, bright eyed. Gracie could only keep watching as she came up close to Tom, looped her left hand through his arm, and smiled again.

"You must be Grace."

"Gracie." She sounded rude; she couldn't help it. "It's Gracie, not Grace."

Another smile, a dimple appearing in the other woman's cheek. "Sorry, Gracie. It's just it seemed like a pet name and a bit forward of me to call you that when we hadn't met yet."

"Who are you?" She wouldn't look at Tom. She could already sense what the answer would be and she wouldn't, she couldn't, look at him.

The woman held out her hand, keeping the other linked to Tom. "I'm Emily. Tom's fiancée."

The next ten minutes were the hardest of Gracie's life. She felt as though she were suddenly in a stage play: an awkward, stiffly written play, with fake lines, fake manners, fake exchanges. Inside she was reeling, unable to take any of this in. Being back in the Hall again was difficult enough, but to be greeted by Tom, to be greeted by Tom and his fiancée, was a nightmare. She was dreaming it. She would wake up and she would be there on her own, none of this happening.

But it was. Tom, with Emily beside him, standing calmly and casually as if something like this happened every day, his voice as controlled as her questions were breathless.

"How did you know I'd be here today?"

"Hope told me you were coming."

"*Hope* did? But how did she know where you were?"

"She got in touch with our solicitor in Castlemaine. He's always known where I was."

Was there something in his voice? An accusation? But she had written to that solicitor herself. Not just once, either. Surely he knew that? But he was still talking.

"She explained you were both coming back. Asked if Nina and I wanted to join you, be part of your reunion."

"She *what*?" It came out wrong. Gracie was astonished at Hope's duplicity, not at the invitation. She knew immediately that Tom had taken it the wrong way. That shutter again, the wariness and something else back in his expression. She wanted to go to him then, take him into the next room, tell him how much she had thought about him, how much she still thought about him, explain everything, open her heart to him. But that was impossible. There was Emily beside him, her hand on his arm, her ownership clearly obvious, the message she was sending even more so. *He's mine now*.

She had to talk to him. "Tom, can I, can you and I—?"

"I'm sorry, Gracie. I can't stay long. I've a flight to catch this afternoon, a work trip—"

"You work?" That came out wrong as well.

"Yes, Gracie, I work."

"Where? What do you do?"

Emily answered for him. "He's far too modest to tell you, but he's one of the best young sports journalists in Australia. He won a Walkley last year."

"A journalist? But how did you . . . ?" She stopped there. Where did she start? All the questions she wanted to ask, that she couldn't ask, not with his fiancée there beside him, not when she was still so completely and utterly bewildered.

"I'm a cricket writer, Gracie," he said. "I'm about to go on tour with the Test team. But when I got Hope's letter, I thought I should say hello at least."

"And I wanted to meet you," Emily said brightly. "I've heard so much about you all. The tours and all of that. It must have been great fun growing up here. Tom's told me so much about your whole family."

Was she really having this conversation? Standing here in the entrance hall, reminiscing, when Tom, her Tom, was there, meters away from her and all she wanted to do was run to him, to cry at the sight of him? She blinked hard once, twice, to stop the tears she could feel appearing.

Emily was still chattering away, sharing all she knew about Templeton Hall. Gracie turned away from her, looked at Tom, trying to plead with him with her eyes, to stay longer, to let her talk to him. There was a moment, a moment, when she saw something in his eyes, when it was like looking at the old Tom, her Tom. But then he looked away, smiled down at Emily, gently interrupted her chatter, and said he was sorry, but they really should get going. He moved then. She saw a limp, a careful movement. Then she saw, too, her heart almost stopping, that he was reaching for a walking stick, a half-crutch really, made of dark metal, black and stylish, but unmistakably a walking stick. She saw, too, that Emily got to it first and handed it to him unself-consciously. *Look how close we are*, she was saying to Gracie.

They were leaving. She couldn't let him leave. Not yet. Not now. She found a bright voice from somewhere, made herself smile at Emily, directed it all at Emily. Happy, smiling Emily. Hateful Emily.

"So you're engaged? When's the big day? There must be so much to organize." She had never used the words "big day" for a wedding before in her life. She'd never been to a bachelorette party, or been a bridesmaid, and yet here she was urging this stranger to confide in her, to be girlfriends with her. She felt sick inside.

It worked. Emily stopped moving toward the door, but continued to hold Tom's arm.

"We haven't quite set the date yet. It's hard to do it with Tom traveling so much, but we're keen to start a family, so the sooner the better, as far as I'm concerned." She gave a happy laugh.

Gracie did her best to laugh, too. "And where did you meet?"

Emily smiled up at Tom. "We were matchmade really, weren't we?"

Tom wasn't smiling. "Emily—"

"Oh, Tom. Don't be shy. Let me tell Gracie all about it. Women love these sorts of stories, don't we, Gracie? It was when he was in the hospital for all those months, after he got back from Italy."

She brought it up as casually as that. Gracie realized she was holding her breath.

"My father used to work at the cricket academy. He used to be a journalist but he'd crossed over to the dark side and was working with the young cricketers, as a mentor, media-training advisor, that kind of thing, and he and Tom were close—"

"Stuart? Stuart Phillips is your father?"

Tom's head jerked up.

"You met my father?" Emily's voice changed imperceptibly. "I hadn't realized that."

"No. No, I remember Tom talking about him." She wouldn't look at Tom. She couldn't.

Emily's voice brightened again. "I'd heard Dad talk about Tom all the time, how brave he was, all the operations, the different methods they were trying to get him walking again. It was practically experimental, wasn't it, Tom? You were their guinea pig, really? And of course after the operations there were all those months of physiotherapy and rehab. . . ."

Gracie didn't want to hear this from a stranger. She wanted to hear it from Tom. If there had been a miracle—there clearly *had* been some kind of a miracle—she wanted *him* to tell her. She wanted to be alone with him, holding his hands as he told her every single thing he'd been through in the past eight years. It wasn't possible, though. Emily was still talking, talking, talking, smiling up at Tom, smiling at Gracie, her hand holding Tom's arm so tightly Gracie could see the tension.

"Anyway," Emily said, "Dad kept going on about him, what a great guy he was, and so eventually I thought I'd better see him for myself, so I came in with Dad one day and it was love at first sight really, Tom, wasn't it?"

Tom didn't say anything. Gracie looked at him. He was looking back at her.

Another hand squeeze from Emily. Gracie saw it. "Well, love at first sight for me, anyway. It took Tom a few months to catch up." She laughed then, a pretty, musical laugh. "I'll stop there. He's getting embarrassed." She glanced at her watch. "Gosh, look at the time. Tom, we'd better get going if you're going to make your flight."

"Where are you going, Tom?" Gracie had to ask him something, had to prolong this meeting for as long as she could somehow, no matter how hard she was hurting inside.

"To Perth. It's a match between Australia and England."

"Who do you think will win?" A ridiculous question, but she wouldn't let him leave yet.

That half-smile again. Her old Tom was in there. He was in there somewhere. In that moment she was sure of it. "England doesn't stand a chance."

Gracie's heart lightened. He was referring to the old family joke. She opened her mouth, was just a moment from mentioning it when she realized how completely inappropriate it would be. She stopped, silent, and felt her face grow red.

Emily was looking back and forth between the two of them. "Well," she said brightly and too loudly, "it's been lovely to meet you, Gracie. I hope your visit goes well. Come on, Tom. We should get going."

Tom reached into his pocket. "I've got something for you, Gracie. I should have sent it back years ago, I'm sorry." It was a big brass key. A key to the Hall.

She held out her hand. He held out his. For a second the key was the link between them.

"I thought Nina . . ." She stopped there. What could she say? "I thought Nina had returned everything to us?" No, she didn't want to say that. "Thank you." She made herself ask the question. "How is Nina?"

"Fine. Good."

Where is she? Has she forgiven me yet? Would she see me even if you clearly never want to see me again, if you and Emily are too happy together, getting married and having children, to ever want to see me again? "Oh. Good." A long pause. Too long. "Please tell her I was asking after her."

A nod.

"Well, bye, Gracie." Emily, all smiles.

"Bye, Emily."

"Good-bye, Gracie."

"Good-bye, Tom."

There was no smiling between them.

Gracie stood at the door as they walked to the side of the Hall where their car was parked, out of sight. Tom's limp was now hardly noticeable. She watched and waited until they got in the car, until he started the engine, until the car was on the driveway. She waved when they did, waited until they were completely out of sight, before she went back inside the Hall, shut the front door, and burst into tears.

Chapter Twenty-nine

Tom WAITED until they were on the main road, until they had left Templeton Hall several kilometers behind them, before he turned to his passenger. "Thank you."

Emily bowed her head, smiled, and said, in a deep American accent, "'And the Academy Award for best actress goes to Emily Phillips.' I was good, wasn't I? Really, really good, if I do say so myself."

"You were. I just don't remember agreeing to say we were engaged. Or that I'd won a Walkley Award."

Another grin. "Sorry about that. You probably will one day. And I just thought 'fiancée' would make it that much more authentic."

"I hadn't realized it was love at first sight for you, either. Thanks."

"From the second I spied you across the crowded hospital ward, my heart skipped a beat and I thought, That's the man I'm going to marry. Well, I would have if I hadn't already been married. Or engaged at least, back then." She dropped the joking tone and laid her hand on his arm, briefly. "Are you okay?"

He hesitated, then shook his head.

"Harder than you expected?"

A nod.

"I thought so." Her tone became businesslike. "Tom, let's swap places. You can't talk about this while you're driving. Let me just ring home first." She took out her mobile phone, pressing a number on speed dial. "Darling, hi, it's me. Yes, on our way back. I don't know yet. We haven't had a postmortem. Is Sam okay?" She winced.

"You've tried that gel on his gums? Tried taking him out in the car, just driving around? That works sometimes. Oh, the poor little bloke. I'll be there as soon as I can. Tom's going to drop me off, then head straight to the airport. Okay, see you soon. Love you."

Tom glanced over as she put the phone away again. "Sam's sick?"

"Just teething again. Can you believe it? Your little godson on to his fourth tooth already? Tom, please, pull over. Let me drive."

"I'm fine, Emily."

"You're not fine. I can see it. I've known you a long time, remember. You're my husband's oldest friend, remember, my father's protégé, the brother I never had. Pull over or I'll lift up the handbrake and ruin your engine."

Tom pulled over.

Emily waited until the car had stopped completely, until Tom had unfastened his seat belt and turned to her before she spoke. "I'm going to be blunt with you."

"There's a change."

"I mean it this time. Tom Donovan, if I didn't have a husband trying to cope with a hysterical child home in Melbourne and you didn't have a flight to catch, I would make you turn this car around and go straight back there. I know women don't usually say this about other women who are allegedly rivals in love, but I liked Gracie, Tom. She was lovely. She was also very upset to see you."

Tom didn't answer.

Emily's tone softened. "Tom, I was happy to play the game today. I'd do it again if you asked me, but now I've met her, now I've seen her, seen the way she looked at you—" She paused then. "I don't understand why you needed to do this."

"Needed to do what? See her again?"

"Not that. I don't understand the pretense. The pretense that you had a fiancée."

"I asked you to be there as my girlfriend, not fiancée."

"Whatever. Tom, from the very little you said about Gracie, from the little we could ever wring out of you once you got back, I had the idea that she'd abandoned you. That she'd let you down. That she was some kind of, I don't know, hard-faced cow."

"I never called her that."

"Then what was today about? Why did you want me there with you, pretending to be your girlfriend? Who were you protecting, you or her?"

There was a short silence. When he spoke again, his voice was low. "Me. I didn't know what it would be like to see her." Another pause. "I didn't want her pity."

"Pity? Why would anyone in their right mind pity you? We all think you're incredible. Look what you've done, through sheer bloody-mindedness, determination, months—God, *years*—of pain, walking again when dozens of doctors said you never would. What is there to pity about that?"

"After the accident, she told my mother she never wanted to see me again."

"Why? Because she thought you'd never be able to walk again?"

"She told my mother it would be too difficult. That it was better for her, for us both apparently, if she stopped all communication between us."

"Even though the crash was her fault?"

"It wasn't her fault."

"Tom, your strangely misplaced loyalty is a lovely thing to see, but I know the whole story, remember. You'd been out to dinner, you'd all been drinking. Nina told me all about it. But, I don't know, I think your Gracie might have had a change of heart somewhere down the line. She didn't look like a person who never wanted to see you again. She looked like a person who wanted to cry she was so happy to see you."

"You don't know that."

"Tom, women know these things about other women. Gracie was overjoyed to see you and she wanted to kill me."

"You're wrong."

"I'm not."

He turned back to the wheel again, started tapping it with his fingertips. "We need to get going again. And before you ask, yes, I am all right to drive."

"If you ask me, you two have unfinished business."

"It finished a long time ago, Emily. Eight years ago in Italy. I've hardly thought about her since then. It was only when this letter from her aunt arrived that I got curious."

"Oh, really."

"Really."

Emily's husband, Simon, was waiting at the gate of their Hawthorn house when they drove up. He handed a red-faced, tear-streaked Sam straight to Emily, then came around to Tom's window. "So how was it?"

Emily spoke first. "She's beautiful, with short white-blond hair, big dark eyes, and Tom couldn't stop staring at her. If he really was my partner, I'd have a word or two to say to him. You try and talk some sense into him, Simon. God knows I've done all I can."

Simon leaned against the car. "What happened, Donovan?"

"Emily's exaggerating. It was fine. I'm fine. I needed to see her, now I have, so can we all just move on?"

"He's been lying to himself like that since we drove away," Emily said, jiggling Sam in her arms.

"Ignore her, Simon. Now that you've given up your law career, haven't you got some dishes to wash, Emily?"

She grinned. "Good try, Donovan. And hint taken. I'm going inside. But I think you should cancel that plane ticket to Perth and drive straight back there."

"That plane ticket is my work."

"Yes, exactly. It's work. This is your life." She leaned in, kissed him quickly on the cheek. "See you, Tom. Think about it."

Simon waited until she was inside. "So what happened?"

"I was there when she arrived, we said hello, we spoke for a few minutes, she met Emily, then we left."

"That was it? After eight years, that was it?"

Tom nodded.

"You didn't ask her why she never got in touch with you after the accident?"

Tom was tapping the steering wheel with his fingers again. "She did get in touch, with Nina. To say she never wanted to see me again."

"But did you ask her today why not? After everything that had happened between you?"

"It didn't seem like the right time. And not in front of Emily. For both our sakes."

"It was a mistake to bring Emily, then?"

"No, she was brilliant. A born actress. And I'm glad she was there." Tom ran his fingers through his hair. "It would have been hard whatever way I did it. But it's done now. Over."

"Really?"

"Really." His tone was firm but he didn't meet his friend's eyes. "I'd better go. See you when I get back."

"Sure." Simon thumped the roof of the car twice with his hand in farewell. "Take care, Donovan."

IT WASN'T UNTIL two hours later, as Tom took his seat on the plane, plugged in his iPod, shut his eyes, and leaned his head back that he allowed himself to think about her again.

He hadn't known what to expect. All he knew was that since the letter from Hope arrived at the newspaper office he'd been unable to think of anything or anyone else. She'd always been in his mind somewhere, despite his best efforts to block thoughts of her. But every memory came rushing back then, ending each time with the same stark truth. The fact she'd wanted nothing to do with him after she'd been told he wouldn't walk again.

He'd never been able to understand it. That had never seemed like the Gracie he'd known: the Gracie he'd met as a child, written to as a teenager, met again in London as an eighteen-year-old, and then fallen in love with two years later. He knew that his mother, his aunt, his friends all thought he'd made too much of the relationship. That they were just kids. Yet it hadn't been like that. There had been something special between them. He'd read about it once in a book, or heard it in a song, a poem, somewhere. Someone more lyrical than him had described meeting the person you loved as feeling like coming home. He'd felt it that first night when they met at the railway station in London. Once he saw her standing there, smiling at him, her dark eyes, that red coat, that big beautiful smile, he hadn't wanted to be alone again.

The Gracie he'd known and traveled with didn't match the Gracie who hadn't got in touch with him again after the accident. If he'd been able to, he would have phoned her from his hospital bed. If he'd had even half an hour without pain, without shock, once he'd regained consciousness, he would have used the time to talk to her. But no one would let him. When he was barely strong enough to realize where he was, let alone hear news like that, Nina had come to his room and told him about her conversation with Gracie. She'd been as upset by Gracie's decision as he was, he'd seen that. They'd been friends, too. Nina could hardly meet his eyes as she told him what Gracie had said as they stood on the steps of the Rome hospital, moments before she, Eleanor, and Spencer flew back home to London.

He'd been dazed with the pain, the drugs, still in shock. He'd asked for more detail.

"She feels it's for the best, Tom, for you and for her."

He'd accepted it at the time. What choice did he have? But when he was back home in the clinic in Australia, when he had the strength again, he'd written a letter to Gracie. It had taken him a long time, physically and to find the right words. He'd given it to his mother to post for him. When no reply came, he wrote again, telling himself the first letter had gone missing. For the next weeks, months, he'd waited for word back. Nothing.

He'd picked up the phone beside his bed many times, on the verge of calling her, needing to hear her voice. But then the reality of what he was now had rushed at him. Why would she want to be with him? Why would any woman want to?

His months of depression began around that time. He learned afterward that he'd followed the textbook cycle of a patient with sudden spinal injuries. Disbelief. Anger. Depression. Acceptance. Optimism. More disbelief. Then true acceptance. But he couldn't let it end like this for him. This wasn't what his life was going to be.

Everyone feels like that at some stage, a counselor told him. It's a natural reaction. But acceptance will come. You'll learn to make a different sort of life for yourself.

He didn't want a different sort of life. He wanted his old life back. He wanted to be able to play cricket again. He wanted to be with Gracie.

He'd been in the clinic in Melbourne for just two days when Stuart Phillips walked into his room. He didn't know it then, but Nina had been in touch with the academy from the earliest days after the accident. Stuart arrived without warning, calm, strong, tough. Tom cried to see him, cried in a way he hadn't done in front of Nina. She'd done enough crying for them both. Then he'd got angry, embarrassed, ashamed of himself, his body, as if what had happened had been deliberate, his fault.

"Why are you here, Stuart? I'm not a cricketer anymore, am I?"

"Not for the moment, no. But you're still my friend."

"You've got a job to do back at the academy. Why are you wasting time here?"

"I've taken leave. They owe me weeks of holiday. They begged me to come and see you, get me out from under their feet."

Tom found out only months afterward that Stuart had taken extended leave-without-pay. He'd brought get-well messages from everyone at the academy, from his wife, from his daughters, Tom's surrogate family in Adelaide.

"I've been reading up on your injuries," he said that day.

"Fairly short book, I'd say. *You're crippled. The end.*"

"What kind of attitude is that?"

"A realistic one."

"You know there's another clinic in Melbourne that's at the forefront in spinal research?"

"No, I didn't. Will I take a stroll over to them, if I ever learn to stand up on my own two feet again?"

"You could, if you were behaving like a petulant kid. Or you could get there sooner and in the comfort of an ambulance, like most of their patients. Or clients, as I think they call them these days."

"Sooner?"

"As in next week. I know someone there. He knows a few other people there. Between everyone we both know, we can get you admitted, get a program started before the month is out."

Tom laughed. Not a nice laugh. "Great. Terrific. And pay with what? My grateful smile?"

"I hope you will be grateful. I hope you will smile." He dropped the teasing then. "Tom, you had travel insurance. You were also insured by the academy. We'll get you into the clinic. That'll be the easy bit. It's once you're there that the hard work really starts."

The understatement of the century. Tom had once thought the hardest he'd ever physically worked was during his time at the academy. There had been constant gym work, beach runs at dawn, intense exercise programs, lifting weights, bench presses, sit-ups, repetitions. Those workouts were the equivalent of lifting a pencil compared to what he was now asking his body to do. He soon discovered more pain than he'd thought possible. There were exploratory operations, countless procedures, tests, scans, X-rays.

Until, nine months after he returned to Melbourne, he was given good news. The damage to his lower spinal cord wasn't as severe as first diagnosed. The effects of the initial spinal shock, combined with the extensive bruising, swelling, and tissue damage he'd suffered in the accident, had caused initial paralysis, but in the weeks and months since, there had been positive signs of nerve regeneration. With time, more treatment, painstaking rehabilitation, there was a strong possibility he would have a gradual return of feeling in his legs, followed by movement. How much movement remained to be seen.

He read every report, every diagnosis, every prognosis, until he realized he didn't want to know the facts. Instead, he started concentrating on his feelings, picturing his body healing, his muscles getting stronger, the swelling around his spine disappearing, imagining himself standing, moving, walking, fixing on a mental picture day after day until it was as if he was returning his body to working order by sheer force of will.

Did he think about Gracie much during those days? The truth was no. He blocked it if his mind ever drifted toward her. The only way he knew how to achieve anything, to get any movement back, was to remain focused, optimistic, think only positive thoughts, surround himself as much as possible with people who believed in him. She didn't. None of her family did either. They'd all been silent, through guilt, shame, discomfort, whatever their reasons were. He would do this without them. He would do it for himself.

While he was working physically, Stuart started work on him from another direction.

"So you can't go back on the cricket field yet. I won't say never. Never say never. But you can still watch the game. Watch hundreds of games. Study them. Analyze the play. Learn everything there is to know about the science and psychology of cricket."

"Why?"

"A sport doesn't just need players, Tom. It needs coaches, tacticians—"

"A coach in a wheelchair. That's inspiring."

"I didn't say 'coach.' What was I for thirty years before I got coaxed out of it?"

"A journalist."

"You're a smart kid, Tom. A smart man, not a kid. You're analytical. You're graceful with words." He noticed Tom's surprise. "I read the application letter you sent to the academy. I also saw your school results. High marks in English, History, Classical Studies. If you hadn't been a sportsman, you'd have gone to university, am I right? You're a listener, a watcher, a quick learner, you don't miss a trick. You were good on the field and I think you'd be just as good off the field. I want you to think about studying for a journalism degree."

It wasn't just Stuart who supported him through the months of study that followed, the months of constant pain, therapy, hospital visits, training, and more pain. Nina was always there. She had moved from Templeton Hall the weekend they returned from Italy, renting a house just three streets from the spinal clinic. She was beside him at every step of his treatment, and as enthusiastic about the journalism degree as Stuart was.

They didn't talk about the Templetons. Their silence must have been as hard for her, but she never raised the subject. That suited him. A conversation about the Templetons would lead to talk about Gracie and that would bring a different kind of pain.

Then one day, out of the blue, she mentioned them. Mentioned Gracie. It had been a difficult day, of setbacks, of fighting the depression that sometimes threatened to overwhelm him, of attempting to come to terms with what lay ahead for him.

She'd been in his room, tidying the pile of books beside his bed, when she spoke. "Tom, I need to ask you something. About Gracie."

He'd tensed.

She seemed to be having trouble finding the right words. "If you could get in touch with her again, would you?"

He shook his head, straight away. Why would he want to? Hadn't Gracie made her feelings clear? And what did he have to offer her now, in any case?

That was the last time they'd spoken about her.

It was Stuart who eventually forced him to confront his feelings, eight weeks after The Day. Two years after the accident. The day he'd taken his first step unaided, after months of forcing himself, inch by inch, to move with the help of frames, of supports, of a physiotherapist on either side. He'd expected it to be a day of celebration. It had been a letdown. Yes, he'd taken that step, but what next? He had to learn to take another step. Another. The pain and effort involved was all he could see, stretching out for months, years, ahead of him.

In his room in the independent living section of the clinic—he hated the term; there was nothing independent about him—he sat in the darkness of his living room. He heard a knock at the door, didn't answer, heard the door open, knew it was Stuart. He heard the fridge open. Nina had brought champagne the day he'd walked. He hadn't opened it yet.

"This stuff goes off if you don't drink it, you know."

"Is that right?"

"You're cheerful."

"Bursting with cheer, Stuart. I couldn't be happier. Life couldn't be better."

"Stop the bullshit, Donovan."

Tom pushed a book off the table and shouted then. "*You* stop the fucking bullshit. What is this, some kind of game for you? A project before retirement? Get the kid's hopes up and too bad when he crashes? It was fun to watch?"

"More bullshit. Start talking sense or I'm leaving."

"So leave."

"No. Not till you've apologized."

"That's not what you said."

"I'm right. You will make a good journalist. You listen." He sat down, opened the bottle, poured two glasses. "What's happened, Tom?"

"Nothing new."

"What's bugging you, then? If it's nothing new, it must be something old."

Tom shrugged. Out of nowhere, a memory came to him. Spencer shrugging as a kid. Spencer as an adult, with them in Italy. He thought of Gracie. Not just in Italy, but in London, Scotland, Ireland, France. Gracie in bed with him, laughing with him, talking to him. In the darkness of his flat, with Stuart sitting there, quietly waiting, Tom started to talk. He told him everything. About Europe, about Gracie, about the message passed to him through Nina that she never wanted to see him again. That she couldn't cope with him like this.

For a minute or two afterward, Stuart was quiet. When he did speak his words were measured. "Is it that she didn't tell you herself, or that she said it at all?"

"Both." It was a strange relief to be admitting this to someone. "I want to hate her and I can't. I just don't understand it. It doesn't make sense. It didn't make sense when Nina first told me and it still doesn't."

"That any woman could be immune to your charms?"

He smiled briefly. "That she would feel like that. That she wouldn't tell me herself."

"She'd been in the accident, too, Tom. Not only that, she was the driver. She must have been in terrible shock."

"At first, yes. But after? When she was back in London? Still nothing."

"You never heard anything from her?"

Tom shook his head.

"And it's still eating you up, two years later?"

A nod.

"So write to her yourself. Ask her."

"I did."

"And?

"I never heard back." He didn't admit to Stuart that he'd written not just one letter, but two, waiting and waiting and hearing nothing back. "It's pretty obvious, isn't it? If she'd cared, if any of them had cared enough to find out how I was—"

"And you're sure they haven't?"

"I'm sure."

"In that case, you have to forget about her, Tom. Accept that you made a mistake about her and get on with your life. You're not the first and you won't be the last. No one on earth gets through life without a broken heart."

"My heart had to be broken as well as everything else?"

"Looks like it."

"Drew the short straw with this lifetime, didn't I?"

"Too soon to tell, I'd say. You might feel better once you see your name in print."

"When I what?"

"When you see your name in print in the sports pages of *The Age*." It was the city's main broadsheet newspaper.

"*The Age* wants me to write for them?"

"A short column, once a month. Just for a trial period. They're trying for younger readers. They want observations from a young cricket fan. I suggested you."

"With a photo of me in the wheelchair, dressed in white, looking pathetic?"

"I hadn't suggested that. Great idea. Could you cry on command for the photographer?"

"Fuck off, Phillips." Tom was smiling.

"Donovan, a reader doesn't care if you're lying in the bath writing your column or sitting in a wheelchair, mate. Get over yourself. Write the best stuff you can. We'll take a look at it and see how it goes. And don't hand in any old rubbish. I've pulled a few strings for you in the paper and it's me who'll look stupid if it doesn't work out."

"You're serious, aren't you?"

"Couldn't be more serious." He paused. "There's just one problem."

Tom waited.

"Your name," Stuart said.

"My name? What's wrong with my name?"

"Nothing in itself. Tom Donovan is a fine name. It's just that as you might be aware, you're not the only man in town with that fine name." He threw a tabloid newspaper down on the table between them. It was turned to the sports pages, to a full-page comment piece by the city's best-known, most opinionated and controversial newspaper and radio sports commentator, a former player in his mid-fifties called Tom Donovan. His article that day called for not just the current captain of the Australian cricket team to be sacked, but the entire team and the board.

"But he's been around for years. Everyone knows that Tom Donovan."

"Exactly. Which is why a new cricket column written by another Tom Donovan might cause some confusion. *The Age*'s sports editor suggested you write under another name and I agree. Not for the rest of your life, just for these columns. It's no big deal. Anyway, how often do you get the chance to pick a new name for yourself?"

"Any name I like?"

Stuart nodded.

"Donald Duck? I could call the column 'Sitting Duck.'"

Stuart's lips twitched. "Very droll, Donovan. Maybe stay closer to home. What's your middle name?"

"My father's name. Nicholas."

"That could work. Tom Nicholas. What do you think?"

Tom thought about it. He liked it. He more than liked it.

"Tom Nicholas it is," he said.

Tom wrote his first column about his own experiences. Not about the accident. He wrote about his childhood memories, describing the process of learning to play cricket, the hours spent pitching the ball against the rainwater tank, the day he mastered one bowling technique, then another. The sheer pleasure of the game. There was a good response. He wrote a second column a month later. A third. He did an interview with a current Test bowler, over the phone, on the eve of a big match. It ran as a feature piece. The commissions kept coming. Sometimes finding the right words was as hard as the physical work he was still doing each day, but it was worth it, to see his name—his name and his father's name, together—in print.

His walking continued to improve. Two years and eight months after the accident, he moved from the clinic into his own flat, on the ground floor of a block in inner-city Richmond. Nina wanted to help him decorate it. He told her he'd do it himself and he did. He was determined to regain his independence in every way he could. He held

Christmas lunch there, with Nina, his aunt Hilary, uncle Alex, and cousin Lucy. He cooked. It was burnt but he still served it.

He started spending each New Year's Eve with the Phillips family: Stuart, his wife, their daughters, and their partners. Emily, the second daughter, had had a whirlwind romance with and then married another of the academy players, Simon, also one of her father's protégés. Tom had liked him very much in the academy days. In the years since, Simon had given up the game after one too many injuries and moved into sports marketing. He became, after Stuart, Tom's closest friend.

Another year passed. Another. He finished his journalism studies, graduating with high distinctions. He joined the full-time staff of the newspaper, still writing under Tom Nicholas. He liked the anonymity, he realized, even if all his friends and family knew it was him. Around the same time, Nina started working full-time as an art teacher in a small primary school in Brunswick, on the other side of the city to Richmond. She got him to come and talk to the kids occasionally, about writing, about cricket. They were always more interested in talking about the stick he still sometimes needed to use.

Four years after the accident, his friends started matchmaking him. Simon was blunt. "Everything's back in working order, isn't it?"

"No, Simon. They had to amputate it at the clinic. It was interfering with my balance."

Simon grinned. "Then it's time we got you out into the social whirl again."

In the past four years Tom had gone out with five women. He'd been relieved to confirm that everything was in working order. But something was missing each time. He didn't care enough about the women. Cared a little, almost a lot in one instance, but still not enough. He was the first to call a halt with two of them. The other three broke up with him, the most recent only six months ago. She'd been very angry. "You're all locked away, Tom. You won't let anyone near you, will you? You've got some ideal woman in your head, but you know what? She doesn't exist!"

Her accusation brought thoughts of Gracie rushing back again. He did his best to block them once more. She had been just a stage of his life. Even the accident was almost behind him. He barely limped anymore. He now owned his own house, a small terraced cottage in Carlton. He had a good job, covering a sport he still loved, traveling throughout Australia, with more and more trips abroad. He'd already been to the West Indies this year. His editor had mentioned more overseas trips in the future. India. Maybe even England for the next Ashes series. But England meant Gracie. Would he try to track her down while he was there, for old times' sake? To lay some ghosts to rest at last? She'd already been in his mind when the letter arrived from Hope. It seemed like fate. He didn't need to wait until he was in England. Gracie was coming back to Australia.

The biggest surprise after the letter arrived was his mother's reaction. He'd called around to her the same afternoon he'd received it, phoning her from his car on the way.

"Is everything all right?" she'd said immediately.

It was her default position since the accident, that something bad would happen to him again. "Everything's fine. I just have to talk to you about something."

Hilary had been there, too, on one of her regular visits to Melbourne. He kissed her hello, then waved in at ten-year-old Lucy, curled up on the sofa in the living room, watching TV. She gave him a sleepy wave back.

After a coffee together, Hilary announced she and Lucy were going to catch the tram into town. Tom waited until they'd left before he showed Nina the letter from Hope.

She read it, then folded it and put it on the bench, her hand on top of it. "I don't want you to go back there, Tom."

He smiled. He was twenty-eight years old. He could and would go if he decided it was what he needed to do. Still, his tone was gentle. "And you'll do what if I do go? Stop my pocket money? Ground me?"

She wasn't smiling. "Tom, please, don't write back. Don't accept the invitation. She's not right in the head. She never has been."

"Did you get a letter from her as well?"

A long hesitation, then she nodded.

"Can I see it?"

She shook her head. "It's the same kind of thing as yours. Ramblings. You don't need to see it."

"Would you have told me if I hadn't shown you this one?"

"I don't know. Tom, please, ignore it. She's trying to make trouble, I'm sure of it. She drank too much, took too many drugs. Her mind is damaged. God knows she's probably making the whole thing up. You could arrive there and the place will be empty. It'll just open up old wounds again. Tom, please. I'm begging you."

He told her he hadn't decided what to do about it yet. It was only in the car on the way home that he realized neither of them had mentioned Gracie.

At home the next night he had a phone call from his aunt Hilary.

"Nina's told me about the letter from the Templetons, Tom. From Hope."

Tom waited.

"Don't go, please. For Nina's sake. It'll bring back too many bad memories for her—all that happened with the Templetons, having to leave the Hall like that. It was a terrible time for her."

"For her?" He managed a laugh.

"All any mother wants to do is protect their child from pain and harm, and she felt like she failed you in some way."

"Hilary, what happened in Italy had nothing to do with Nina. She wasn't driving the car. Or the truck."

"It's more complicated than that. Tom, please, don't rush into anything. Sometimes it's better to just leave the past behind, for everyone's sake."

It was a week later, sorting through a box of his old clothes and belongings that had come from the Templeton Hall apartment and not been unpacked, that he found it. The key to the Hall. He recognized it immediately, with its large brass handle, like something from a fairy tale, a souvenir from his own childhood. Spencer had given it to him one afternoon, when they'd come back from the dam. "We've got loads of these. Mum and Dad will never miss it," he'd said to Tom. "You'll be able to get in whenever you want to now."

Finding it was a sign, Tom decided. The fact he still even had it meant something, surely? After the accident, when he learned that Nina had moved all they owned out of the Hall apartment in one afternoon, returning everything belonging to the Templetons to the Castlemaine solicitors, it had crossed his mind to tell her about it, to ask her to find it and return it then, too. But he hadn't.

He decided that day. He would get in touch with Hope, find out when Gracie was arriving, and go back to Templeton Hall. And if it would hurt his mother to know he was going, there was only one way around it. He wouldn't tell her. He would ask Hope not to tell her either.

His phone conversation with Hope lasted less than a minute. "You're coming?" she said briskly. "Good. Here are our flight details. We'll leave any further conversation until we're face to face."

As the date of Gracie's arrival grew closer, the parting lines from one of his recent girlfriends kept echoing in his mind. *You've got some ideal woman in your head, but you know what? She doesn't exist!*

But she did. Gracie had been that ideal woman, back when he was young, hopeful, full of vitality and optimism. He needed to see Gracie one more time, realize that he had built her up to be something she wasn't. He'd made her too sweet, too smart, too beautiful, too everything. If he saw her again, reminded himself that she had shown her true colors by deserting him when he needed her most, then he'd be able to move on. He just needed to be sure to protect himself first. Present himself in the best possible light. Do everything he could to avoid even a flash of pity in Gracie's eyes.

So why hadn't his plan worked? Why had seeing Gracie felt like a punch to the stomach?

"You two have unfinished business," Emily had said. *"I think you should cancel that plane ticket to Perth and drive straight back there."*

"Drink, sir?"

It was the flight attendant. He asked for an orange juice, then reached for his laptop. Enough thinking. It was time for work. Going over and over what had happened at Templeton Hall today was fruitless, no matter what Emily or Simon said. He was on his way to Perth, about to start filing stories, interviewing players, analyzing the day's play. This was his real life now. He'd done what he'd planned—seen her again, confronted his ghosts—and he could at last move on. All of that was behind him now. The Templetons, Templeton Hall, Gracie.

He didn't fool himself for a minute.

Chapter Thirty

IN MELBOURNE, Nina was sitting under an umbrella at her local swimming pool, watching Lucy splash around. She shaded her face as Hilary came back from the kiosk carrying cool drinks and ice-creams.

"Deep in thought?"

Nina nodded.

"Please don't tell me you're thinking about the Templetons."

"Just a little."

"Just constantly. You think I haven't noticed you glancing at the calendar every day? After I went to all this trouble to visit you again, to try and distract you?"

"If I could just be a fly on the wall—"

"That charming Hope would probably swat you, by the sounds of things. Nina, stop thinking about them. You made your decision, Tom made his."

"We think he made his."

"He texted you from the airport, didn't he? On his way to Perth?"

Nina nodded. "You're right."

"But if you don't mind me saying, would it have really mattered if he did go? You had your reasons, and fair enough, but the more I think about it, perhaps it would have been good for Tom to see Gracie again, to find out once and for all why she abandoned him like that."

Nina busied herself opening her drink.

Hilary continued. "I still find it so weird that she never even tried to get in contact with him again. Eleanor I can understand, especially after you let slip about what happened with you and Henry. But from what you used to tell me about Gracie, she seemed so much kinder than that."

After a pause, Nina answered. "Yes." She stood up then and went over to her niece with a towel. When she came back, she was careful to talk about anything but the Templetons.

TWENTY-FOUR HOURS LATER, the three of them were in Nina's car on their way to the airport, in plenty of time for Hilary and Lucy's flight home to Cairns. Usually Nina dropped her sister and niece in front of the airport, leaving them to check in and make their own way to the gate, none of them liking the farewell moment. This time was different.

"I have to talk to you about something, Hilary," Nina said as they drove into the airport grounds.

Hilary noticed her sister's serious expression. "I'm all ears," she said.

They found a café opposite a gift shop in the domestic terminal, took a table in the corner, and settled Lucy with a book and her iPod. Once she was occupied, Nina spoke.

"I need to tell you why I didn't want Tom to go back to Templeton Hall."

"That's what this is about? Look, I understand, Nina. It's fine."

"You can't understand because I haven't told you everything."

Hilary waited.

Nina took a breath. "If he'd gone there, he would have seen Gracie again. Talked to her again. And if he'd done that, he would have . . ." She stopped.

"He would have what?"

There was a pause before Nina spoke again. "He would have found out about her letters."

"What letters?"

"The letters she sent him, after the accident."

Hilary frowned. "But you told me that he never heard from her again. That she told you in Rome that she didn't want anything to do with him again."

"I didn't speak to Gracie after the accident. I only spoke to Eleanor."

"I don't understand."

Hilary listened in silence as Nina told her everything. How Gracie had written to Tom many, many times. How the letters had been sent to dozens of different addresses, each of them eventually finding their way to Nina.

"But you didn't pass them on to him?" Hilary stared at her sister. "Nina, you had no right. The letters were to him."

"I had every right. I'm his mother. Hilary, you saw him, saw how badly he was injured, how fragile he was."

"But she was his girlfriend."

"He was in a mess, Hilary. Physically, emotionally. I didn't want him upset any more."

"How would a letter from his girlfriend upset him? Wouldn't he have longed for that?"

"I couldn't be sure. I couldn't ask him, either."

"Why not?"

"Hilary, it was a terrible time. When I read Gracie's letters—"

"You *read* her letters? Her letters to Tom? You had no right to do that, either."

"It had nothing to do with right or wrong. Wouldn't you do anything you could, *anything,* to stop Lucy being hurt? If you felt there might be danger, wouldn't you stop her doing something? I didn't know what Gracie might be saying to him, if she would hurt him even more. I didn't know if she knew about me, about me and Henry. I was angry. I was shocked."

"But this was Tom's life, not your life. His relationship with Gracie, not yours. Nina, I can't believe this. You have to tell him she wrote to him. Now. As soon as you can."

"It's too late."

"But he must have always wondered. He must have wanted to write to her."

"He did." A long pause. "I didn't post his letters." She spoke quickly, before Hilary had a chance to react. "I thought it was for the best. I had to cut off all contact between our families, for all our sakes."

"So you let Tom think you'd posted them, let him wait to hear back from Gracie, knowing all the time that Gracie hadn't even re-ceived his letters? You didn't pass on the letters she had sent him, be-cause you thought that was protecting him?"

A nod. Nina waited for her sister's understanding. Instead, she got her fury.

"How *dare* you, Nina! How dare you do that to Tom, to Gracie." In the background, their flight was called. Hilary didn't move, just continued to speak in a low, cold voice. "I thought I knew you, un-derstood you, but I was wrong. I don't know you at all. Was this about Tom or was this about you? You and Henry? Anger at Henry because you never heard from him again?"

Nina could only stare at her sister.

"I thought you'd learned your lesson when Tom was little, with the lies you told him about his father's death."

"That's not fair. You know why I did that, how much I agonized over it."

"And yet you did it again? Lied to him again? Can't you see how wrong it was?"

"It wasn't. It was what he wanted, too. I asked him once, about a year after the accident, if he wanted to get in touch with Gracie. He said no."

"Of course he said no. How must he have felt? So hurt, so let down by her. You'd already done your damage by then. Can't you see that?"

Nina didn't answer.

Hilary abruptly stood up. "I have to go. I can't talk about this with you now." She took Lucy's headphones off and gathered up her be-longings. "Come on, honey. Time we went home."

Nina kissed Lucy good-bye. Hilary didn't lean forward for a kiss or a hug. She walked away, hand in hand with Lucy. She didn't look back.

IN PERTH at the end of the second day's play, Tom switched on his BlackBerry to check his messages. There was one from Simon, invit-ing him to a barbecue the Saturday after he got back. A pause, then he heard Emily's voice in the background, mentioning Gracie, Simon shushing her. Tom wasn't surprised. Emily was very persistent.

It was the other message that did surprise him. It was from his aunt in Cairns.

"Tom, it's Hilary. I want you to ignore all I said about going to Templeton Hall again. I think you should, as soon as you can. If you want to know why, ask your mother."

IN LONDON, Hope was on the phone to Gracie in Australia. Hope was reclining on the sofa in her sitting room. Gracie was calling from the front steps of Templeton Hall. She'd explained to Hope that the mobile phone coverage wasn't great inside the Hall.

"Never mind," Hope said. "I'll lobby a local politician to get it improved."

"In time for your visit this week? You're hopeful."

"By name and by nature," Hope said. "Tell me everything. How does the Hall look?"

Gracie gave her a full report. It was still standing, the basic furniture was still there, there were no signs of break-ins or floods or rats or mice. The garden was very neglected.

"I'll take care of the garden. What about the bedrooms? All still habitable?"

"Yes, but I've only made up your old room and mine. Did you want to try the others?"

Hope cursed her own big mouth. She was getting ahead of herself. Now her departure was this close, she was dying to see the Hall again and decide if her idea truly had legs. Her main worry had been that the building would need extensive repairs, and quite frankly, she'd had enough of that the first time around at Templeton Hall. But from what Gracie was saying, it was in good enough shape to start putting her plans into action immediately. Of course, there was the minor matter of tracking Henry down and getting him to agree to lease it to her—for a very cheap rent, of course—but why wouldn't he? The Hall had been lying empty for years. And hadn't Eleanor, Charlotte, Audrey, and Spencer already made it abundantly clear they had no interest in it anymore?

Hope realized Gracie was still waiting on an answer. "No, of course not. My old room is fine. I was just wondering what condition the rest of the place was in." Time to change the subject before she gave everything away. "So, you'll be okay there on your own until I get there on Wednesday? You haven't had any nosy locals sniffing around yet, I hope?"

"I haven't seen anyone," Gracie said.

"Really? No one at all?"

"No."

Hope couldn't tell if Gracie was telling the truth or not. When Tom Donovan had rung after getting her letter, she'd been very clear about Gracie's arrival date and time, and while he hadn't said anything specifically, she had the impression that he intended to meet Gracie on arrival, or definitely before Hope herself arrived. And he'd also been very insistent she keep their conversation to herself. He'd been very impressive, in fact. She did like that kind of strength of will in a man, young or old.

"Well, that's good," she said. "I'll leave you to it, then, Gracie. Thank you again. Do buy anything you need to make the place comfortable, and be sure to keep the receipts."

"Receipts?" Gracie laughed. "But it's your money I'm spending. Don't you trust me?"

Hope kicked herself again. Gracie wasn't to know Hope planned to write off this entire trip as a business one for tax purposes. It *was* a business trip, after all. An investigating-possible-business trip. "Don't mind me," she said with a casual laugh. "Victor was a stickler for paperwork. See you in two days, Gracie."

After she hung up, Hope checked the time. Not even midnight. She was too awake to sleep yet. Once upon a time she might have enjoyed a glass of wine, or perhaps even taken a small pill to help bring on sleep, but these days all of that was out of bounds. God, the *boredom* of it. The most she managed now and again was an occasional joint, the guilty feelings associated giving her as much a high as the drug itself. Her AA mentors would be horrified if they knew, as would her clients. It was a good thing they didn't.

She went into the spare room of the three-story townhouse that Victor had so kindly left her. The marijuana and the papers were hidden in the bottom of the antique bureau drawer in an old makeup bag. It took her only a minute to roll a perfect joint. Her next stop was her office on the first floor. The folder of paperwork she wanted to read again was on her desk. The hundred-page research document had cost her nearly ten thousand Australian dollars, but she considered it money well spent. If the Australian high-end residential drug-treatment market was anywhere near as lucrative as the English one, she'd make that ten thousand back from her first client in a fortnight.

Honestly, what had taken her so long to have this brainwave? It was almost criminal that Templeton Hall had been lying unused for so long. She should have thought of it when she heard about the failed attempt to use it as a meditation clinic. That had ended in disaster, from what Hope had gathered from Eleanor. Her own clinic wouldn't. She'd make as big a success of it as she had the three clinics here in London. Not only that, it appeared she might even be able to get Australian government assistance to establish it. What a wonderful country! It was all there in the folder. The research firm had certainly done their job. It was compelling reading, filled with data about existing rehabilitation clinics and programs, statistics on drug and alcohol addiction, even facts about referral procedures and treatment costs.

The one thing she hadn't asked the firm to do was find a location for any possible future clinic. She'd decided that for herself already. And once she'd visited the Hall again, with Gracie there beside her to record all the measurements and possibly stay on to do all the dogsbody preparation work for her regarding permits and builders' quotes and the like, she estimated it would take her less than six months to employ all the counselors and administration staff she'd need to get it up and running. A year at the very most. What to call it, though? The Templeton Hall Clinic? No, she'd have to change its name, or there would be endless streams of those ridiculous tourists turning up, convinced it was operating as a stupid living museum again. Something more discreet. She smiled. Why not? It was a vanity project, after all. Yes, she'd call it the Hope Clinic.

An hour later, she'd read all the research data she wanted to read and smoked another joint as well. She'd taken her shoes off, enjoying the sensual feel of the wool carpet under her bare feet. Her eyelids were fluttering, she was yawning and feeling pleasantly buzzy and languorous at the same time. Time for bed.

She was halfway between the first and second landings on the way to her third-floor bedroom when it happened. She'd been meaning to get the stairway carpet repaired since she'd noticed a snag in the expensive wool pile. Afterward she had no recollection of the moment she tripped, but she must have snagged a toe, twisted, overbalanced, and while trying to right herself, fallen back down a flight of stairs onto the first landing.

It took her several moments to catch her breath, sit up, check her head, then her body. There was no blood. She could move her neck. Nothing too serious, thank God. The dope must have relaxed her muscles. It was when she tried to stand up, putting her weight on her left leg and shrieking with sudden agony, that she realized what she'd done.

The pain was excruciating as she inched down the stairs to the phone. The first number she tried was Eleanor's. No answer. She tried again. Still no answer. Who else could she ring? She had no other friends in London. There was only one option. She dialed 999.

TWENTY KILOMETERS AWAY, in a fine French restaurant in the middle of Mayfair, Henry Templeton was entertaining a table of four men and one woman from Hong Kong.

He'd arrived in London only that afternoon and would be flying back to San Francisco before lunch the next day. The expense—and the jetlag—would be worth it. When he'd heard from a London contact that this Chinese investment team were in England on a brief business trip, he hadn't hesitated to make any arrangements necessary to meet them.

For the past two hours, he'd been sharing his best anecdotes of life in the antiques trade with them. There was nothing people liked to hear more than stories of dusty brooches found at the bottom of jumble-sale boxes being worth tens of thousands of pounds; of envelopes hidden inside the linings of cupboards turning out to be filled with rare and very valuable stamps. His guests had hung on his every word, even gasped collectively when he explained how a simple-looking red vase found in a charity shop had turned out to be an eighteenth-century Chinese masterpiece, made in 1740 for the Emperor Qianlong, worth not just tens but *hundreds* of thousands of pounds. So what if the stories he told weren't all from his own experience? This was a business dinner, and what he was telling them was best for his business.

Yes, it had been a very satisfying night, he decided an hour later as he shook hands with the last of his guests and returned to give the maître d' a handsome tip. Unfortunately the tip took the last of his cash, and his taxi fare, but a walk to his hotel in Belgravia would do him good. He was quite sure that by Monday morning, two, and possibly three, of the potential investors at his table would be in touch to say they were prepared to back his latest venture.

Why had it taken him this long to realize that the real money and real success lay not in the small items of life—antiques, jewelry, even cars—but in the solid concrete of property investment? And everyone knew that China was where the action was these days.

There would be obstacles, of course. The upfront construction expenses would be the biggest. But it was always about risks, wasn't it? That's what made it all so exciting. Who would ever have thought, for example, that he would make such a success of that vintage car business in the States? In the past decade, that had been by far his most successful enterprise. Even now, it still made an annual profit that quite frankly astonished him.

Reaching the hotel, he nodded good evening to the receptionist and took the stairs rather than the lift to his second-floor suite. Every bit of exercise helped. Letting himself into his room, he was pleased to see his personal mobile phone lying on a side table. He'd realized in the taxi to the restaurant that he'd left it behind, but knowing punctuality was all-important to Chinese businesspeople in particular, he hadn't gone back for it.

Four missed calls. He smiled as he listened to the first two messages, both from Adele, his girlfriend of almost two years now. A Harvard graduate, fluent French, Spanish, and Japanese speaker, and CEO of her own corporate translation company, Henry was growing very fond of her indeed. He'd been concerned that at thirty-nine she was too young for him—it hadn't been much fun explaining who Procol Harum were—but the positives about her certainly outweighed the negatives.

Her messages were warm, flirtatious, slightly bossy, a reflection of all he liked about her. He didn't need to call her back, she said. She was just reminding him of the dinner engagement they had the following night with possible new clients for her company. She'd collect him at the airport and they'd go straight on to the restaurant.

The next two messages were surprising. They were from Eleanor. It was years since she'd called him directly, even though his lawyers always ensured she had his contact numbers. Her voice was cool, her message brief. "Henry, can you call me, please?" No mention of the children. A good sign or not?

He rang the number she'd left immediately. No answer. Just her recorded voice calmly asking him to leave a message.

"It's Henry. Are the children all right? I'm in London on business. Please ring me as soon as you get this."

He waited for her to call back. Nothing. It wasn't until well after midnight and after two large whiskies that he managed to sleep.

Chapter Thirty-one

At home in Brunswick, it took Nina twenty minutes before she found it. The tin biscuit box was at the back of the hall cupboard under an old suitcase, behind the ironing board. She had moved it many times over the years but this was the first time she'd considered looking inside.

The lid opened more easily than she expected. The box was packed with paperwork: letters, faxes, postcards—twenty, perhaps even thirty, items, all addressed to Nina. Most of them were in Gracie's handwriting.

They weren't the letters Gracie had written to Tom. Nina had thrown them out immediately after reading them. Day after day they'd come, redirected to her from all over Victoria, from the cricket academy in Adelaide; even the police sergeant in Castlemaine. Nina had felt like she was under attack from Gracie, under attack from the whole family, Eleanor's words still ringing in her head, mingling with the shock and anger she felt every time she looked at her poor broken Tom. All her humiliation about Henry had come flooding back as well: his promises, his sweet-talk, how easily she had fallen for it, fallen into bed, fallen for him. Each time she'd thrown away one of Gracie's letters she hoped it would suppress some of that self-hatred. It hadn't. All it had made her feel was even more protective of Tom, determined to do whatever she needed to keep him from any more pain.

She still felt the sting of Hilary's fury at her in the airport the previous day. Her sister had phoned her that morning from Cairns, too.

"Have you rung Tom yet? Has he rung you? I won't lie to you, Nina. I left him a message last night. You have to sort this out while Gracie is still in the country."

"Hilary, you have to understand. It's nothing like the time I told him about his father—"

"No, it's not, because I understood your reasons that time. But to do it to him twice, Nina? To lie to your son twice, to try and wreck his life again? You had no right."

"It was so complicated. The accident, all that happened with Henry, with Eleanor—"

"What happened to you had nothing to do with Gracie and Tom. And yet you interfered. Overstepped. Lied to him, to Gracie, too."

"You didn't see him that day, in that hospital in Italy—"

"No, but I saw him when he got home. And I saw him as recently as this week. He's still not right, Nina, and you have to fix it, fix this whole situation, while you can."

"He'll hate me."

"*That's* what's stopping you? That makes it even worse. It's still all about you, not him."

"I have to think about it. I have to work out the right way to do it."

"You've got until tonight or I'm ringing him and telling him the whole story myself. I'm not giving you any more excuses, Nina. He might be your son but he's also my nephew."

"You can't."

"I can and I will."

It was only in the past hour that Nina's anger toward her sister had subsided enough for her to be able to think clearly. Now she just felt—what? Guilt? Or something else? Could it be relief? A strange relief that this was being forced out into the open at last?

In her heart, she'd always known it would come to this one day. That Gracie would turn up or Tom would go looking for her. But how to tell him? Where to start? How could she face his reaction? His anger? She already knew the first question he would ask her. Why? She could guess his second question, too. What had she done with Gracie's letters?

It was so long since she'd opened this box, but perhaps, just perhaps, she hadn't got rid of every single one of them. If she could even give him one, eight years too late, but one at least, perhaps it would be a starting point. She took the box out into the living room, sat on the sofa, and started to sort through it.

An hour later tears were streaming down her face. She'd stopped trying to wipe them away. There hadn't been any of Gracie's letters to Tom in the box. But there had been all of the younger Gracie's letters to her, from the first postcard she'd sent when the Templetons arrived back in London from the Hall, to the note Gracie had sent just before Tom arrived on his big solo backpacking trip. So many others in between, too. Eight years of Gracie's life, hopes, dreams, and worries, written on page after page and sent to her friend Nina in Australia. There hadn't just been letters from Gracie in the box either. There were letters, faxes, and emails from Eleanor. A thank-you letter from Charlotte in Chicago. Even several faxes from Henry. Proof in writing of the relationships she'd had with all of them. There was even a print-out of an email the then nineteen-year-old Tom had sent her during his first trip to London.

But it was Gracie's letters that affected Nina the most. How could she have forgotten what Gracie was like? She had turned Gracie into some kind of monster, a stalker, hounding her son. The real Gracie was there on each page, her spirit, her personality, her intelligence, her big heart obvious in every line, as her handwriting changed from that of a young girl to a teenager to a young woman. Her affection for Nina and for Tom obvious in every single line. That was the real Gracie. The Gracie who had fallen in love with Tom. The Gracie who Tom must have loved in return.

The Gracie who Nina had hurt so very badly.

Nina was still on the sofa, surrounded by the letters, when her phone rang. She looked at the caller ID. It was Tom. She couldn't talk to him yet. She wasn't ready. She had to take this slowly, make only the right decisions this time. She let it go to voicemail, waited, then replayed his message.

"Nina, it's me. I've had a message from Hilary, telling me she thinks I should go back to the Hall and that I should ask you why." He paused. "So this is me asking why." Another pause. "Okay, I'll call back later. Or you can try me. Bye for now."

Nina knew then what she had to do.

AT TEMPLETON HALL, Gracie had decided to go for a walk. Automatically, she found herself going through the garden and down the long driveway toward the main road. She made slow progress, having to stop every few meters or so to push a broken branch out of the way. She tried to mend a piece of the fence, twisting the wire until she realized it needed more than her strength to do it.

She stopped and looked back at the Hall now, ignoring the unkempt garden beds and the unpruned trees around it, focusing just on the building, on its graceful lines and the shifting colors of the stone. She had been so happy during the years they lived here, counting down the hours until the front door opened to their weekend visitors, showing groups around, asking her father all the family history, imagining and reveling in her own place in that long, unbroken story. It had never seemed like work to her, not like it had to Charlotte, Audrey, and Spencer. And every career guidance book she'd ever read had mentioned that it was a lucky person who managed to find work doing a job they loved, not just to make money.

Was it just a coincidence that the many jobs she'd tried doing after the accident involved working closely with people: the charities; the volunteering? Or that her study had focused on history, the stories behind the dates and the buildings? Had they all been attempts to relive the happiness she'd felt here as a child, in her job as a tour guide?

Perhaps. But since she'd been back here, since she'd seen Tom again, something had shifted in her thinking. Reality had replaced the layers and layers of stories she'd built up in her imagination. Not just about the Hall, but about Tom, too. She now knew one thing for sure. She still loved him. She'd known that the moment she saw him again. But she now knew something else, too. He was happy without her. He had recovered. Moved on. He was successful, in his work, with Emily. She couldn't think beyond that anymore, even if she still wished in her heart that their reunion had been so different. She now had something to move on from herself, facts about him rather than the unknown. Wasn't that exactly what she'd longed for all these years?

So why did she still feel so bad? As if it was all still unfinished?

She walked on, pretending to herself she was just meandering, knowing in her heart where she was going. To Nina's house. She came close enough to see that it was occupied. By a family with several children, by the looks of the swings in the garden, the array of small colorful T-shirts and dresses on the clothesline. She heard voices, and as she watched, a mother and two little kids came out onto the verandah, collected what looked like a handful of dolls, and then went back inside. Gracie had hoped it would be empty, that she could go right up to it again and say a kind of farewell to that house as well.

She had no choice but to keep walking. Before she knew it, she was at the yabby dam. The drought had been bad in Victoria in recent years, and there had been terrible bushfires, too, but there must have been rains in the area recently. There was more water in the dam than she ever remembered as a child. Standing on the edge, looking across to the other side, she saw a pile of wood and tin. She couldn't believe it. The remains of Spencer and Tom's half-built raft were still there, now covered in dirt, coarse grass growing through the rusting sheets of corrugated iron. The sight made her laugh out loud and then it made her want to cry.

She knew in that moment that she couldn't stay at the Hall any longer. It would have been hard enough even if she hadn't seen Tom. But this was more proof. Everywhere she went, everywhere she looked, she would be reminded of him.

She'd be letting Hope down, but of all people, she hoped her aunt would understand. She would still meet Hope at Melbourne Airport as arranged, still drive her up to the Hall, organize any supplies she needed, but she couldn't stay here for the week, when everywhere she looked reminded her of everything she needed to forget.

She'd walked a short distance from the dam back toward the Hall when she realized she was carrying something more than memories. It was in her jacket pocket. The whistle Tom had given her. She was near the actual spot where he'd first given it to her, the day she'd played hide-and-seek, the day he came looking for her. He'd told her all she ever needed to do was blow it and he'd come and rescue her.

She was crying as she lifted it to her lips. The noise she made was a feeble, strange one, more a squawk than a whistle. It made her laugh a little, even through her tears. That would teach her to be so melodramatic. What did she expect—one loud whistle and he would appear over the horizon, arms outstretched, telling her all was forgiven?

Now was the time to finally do it. Get rid of it. It was her last link with him. And what better place to leave it than the dam, where she'd first decided all those years ago, when she was eleven and he was twelve, that she just might have a little crush on Tom Donovan.

She returned to the dam, stood at the edge of the water, held the whistle in her palm, and squeezed it one more time, running her thumb along the inscription. Then she threw it away with as much force as she could.

She looked down. Her hand was still clenched. The whistle was still there. She couldn't get rid of it, no matter what memories it brought back, good or bad. She knew that even more surely now.

She held it safely in her hand the whole walk back to the Hall.

IN BRUNSWICK, Nina had never felt so alone, or so wretched. Once, she could have rung Hilary, confident of the comfort and sympathy of her support and advice. Or she could have rung Tom, always reveling in even a brief exchange with her son, her brave, strong, clever son. Not this time. The two people she loved and cared for most in the world were the two people who were now the angriest with her.

Telling Hilary what she had done with Gracie's and Tom's letters had been hard. Telling Tom had been a hundred times worse. It had taken three attempts before she was able to find the right time and conditions to talk to him. This wasn't a conversation for him to have in the cricket ground press box, or when he was at his computer, on a deadline. She knew how hard he worked when he was away, how important it was to him. She'd waited until he was back in his hotel room. She didn't waste time on general conversation. She got straight to the point as soon as he answered.

"Tom, I need to tell you something."

"I don't like the sound of that." His voice was relaxed, easy.

Ten minutes later, once she had finished telling him everything, his tone was like ice. There was no anger, no shouting. Just questions.

Where were the letters? How many had there been? Where had Gracie sent them?

Then the hardest questions of all.

"Why, Nina? Why did you do this to me? To Gracie?"

"I was trying to protect you."

"Protect me from *Gracie*? She would have helped me, not hurt me."

"I know that now, too. But at the time, Tom, I was so worried about you, so . . ."

She couldn't tell him the rest of it. She couldn't tell him about what had happened with Henry, when Henry was still married to Eleanor. He was thinking badly enough of her as it was. That would destroy their relationship forever. He didn't give her the chance to say any more, in any case.

His voice was hard and cold. "I have to go."

"But what will you do—"

He didn't answer. He'd hung up on her.

At first she just cried. Not just about Tom hanging up, not just about the hurt, the anger she'd heard in his voice. She cried for herself, for Nick, for her ruined, pointless life, for the wrecked relationship with Hilary, for the mistakes she'd made and kept making all her life. For the one thing, the one person, who'd given her a sense of accomplishment. Tom. He'd given her life meaning, and look what she'd done to him in return.

Her tears subsided eventually. The house was almost silent, just the humming of the refrigerator, the ticking of the kitchen clock. She stayed where she was, lying on the sofa. More thoughts were coming into her mind now. Uncomfortable thoughts and feelings she'd managed to ignore for eight years.

Had everything she'd done with the letters been for Tom's sake? To protect him? Or had Hilary been right? Had she done it all to protect herself just as much?

She made herself remember the confrontation with Eleanor in the Rome hospital. Both of them in shock, their children hurt. Nina had been jetlagged, reeling, unable to believe that all that was happening was real, enduring that long plane journey fearing the worst news would be waiting her arrival. Seeing Tom in bed, his face bruised and cut, his body motionless, trying to understand what she was being told in broken English, the terrible, shocking news that her strong, athletic son would never walk again.

And then seeing Eleanor again, afterward. The other woman was so calm. Controlled. The winner of that mothers' game of chance—her two children also in the car, yet Nina's only son was the one injured. Injured because of Gracie's driving. Injured because he'd become involved with the Templetons. Terrible, angry, distressing thoughts filled her head as she sought out Eleanor. She'd forgotten about Henry in that moment, her focus solely on Tom, on the hopelessness of his situation, the hardships ahead, getting him home, having to tell him he would never walk again, that his life of promise and health had ended.

At first there had been sympathy, understanding between the two women. But then the anger had spilled out of Nina, an urge to hurt, to strike back. She'd heard herself talking about Henry, telling Eleanor that she had slept with him, wanting a reaction, wanting her to feel even the smallest amount of pain in return. It worked. Eleanor's expression changed in an instant. All sympathy disappeared. Nina recalled raised voices, anger, accusations, denials, a moment of shared tragedy suddenly twisting into other, darker areas, her own shock and fear crystallizing into fury against not just the accident, but against Henry, Eleanor, Gracie, all of the Templetons.

It was that same fury that helped her keep going in the difficult times that followed. Her love for Tom was the bedrock, her reason to stay strong, but her anger toward the Templetons gave her extra adrenaline, extra purpose. She punished herself with the memory of Eleanor's face, anytime a part of her mind turned to thoughts of Henry. Deep inside, she'd still been waiting—hoping—for him to get in touch with her. Wanting—needing—him to express his sorrow over Tom. Wanting more of the feelings he'd given her, physically and emotionally. But there'd only ever been silence.

When the letters from Gracie started arriving, she had no compunction about reading them. There were letters from Gracie to her, too, begging forgiveness. Nina threw those away as well. All to protect Tom, she told herself at the time. It was the easiest thing in the world not to tell Tom about the letters. There was no longer room in their lives for any of the Templetons. Henry had chosen to step back from her, and she—and subsequently Tom—could do the same. She invented a conversation at the hospital in Rome with Gracie and reported it back to Tom without guilt or hesitation, telling him that Gracie didn't want anything to do with him. If Henry could hurt her with his silence, she, too, could hurt Gracie.

There it was, the truth. She'd finally admitted it to herself. She had kept Gracie's letters from Tom as a payback for the pain she was feeling herself—her hurt at Henry's silence, her anger toward Eleanor, that her charmed children and their charmed lives had emerged unscathed from the accident. She'd taken Tom's letters to Gracie, too, there in his hospital room, knowing that she wouldn't post them. It was for the best, she'd told herself. Not just for her, but for Tom as well.

Yet Gracie's letters had kept coming, week after week. Nina finally sent a two-line note to Gracie herself. She'd written it at the end of a terrible day at the clinic. Tom had been in distress all day, new pain meaning more tests, meaning constant movement. By the end of the day he'd been crying with frustration, Nina fighting back her own tears, wishing there was something she could do to stop him hurting. Arriving home to find yet another letter in Gracie's familiar handwriting waiting, she had lost her temper. She'd vented all her anger and helplessness on that letter, tearing it into the smallest of pieces, then doing what she had vowed not to do. She'd written back to Gracie. Her pen had nearly gouged a hole in the page as she wrote the words. She posted it that night. The next day she could barely remember what she'd written, but it worked. Gracie hadn't written again.

Nina had one period of soul-searching about her decision, as the months had passed, as she'd realized the reality of what lay ahead. At the end of another difficult day for Tom, a day of more pain and disappointment, she'd searched for something that might make him feel better. Gracie had come to mind, suddenly. She'd made herself ask him the question. Did he want to get in touch with Gracie again?

He'd said no, immediately. He'd been so definite. She'd taken that as proof that she'd made the right decision, that she'd done the right thing, for her and for Tom. She'd decided then that the only way forward was for her and Tom to become a unit again, the way they'd always been, the two of them against the world. She directed all her time and energy toward him. She allowed only people she was sure could help him into their lives. Stuart Phillips and his family. The doctors in the small rehabilitation clinic in Melbourne. All of them doing what they could to prepare Tom for his new, changed life.

Then came the day of the miracle, as she still thought of it. The latest in a series of tests showing something new, something positive. There would still be many months ahead of difficult rehabilitation, but there was now real hope.

Over the next year, Tom's determination to walk again had stunned his doctors, Nina knew that. He stunned her, too. She'd feared he had slipped into depression, his moods so changeable. The hope brought a new mindset. Tom became focused, driven, single-minded. He *would* walk again. Nothing would stop him. He poured his new energy and determination equally into his rehabilitation exercises and his journalism studies.

It took some adjusting on her part. She'd built her life around him again, as she had done when he was young. There were many fights, Tom snapping at her when she went to pick up after him, began to make his bed, tidy his flat. *I can do it, Nina.*

Hilary helped her through that stage. Hilary had always been there. "You have to let him be independent again, Nina. Imagine how he's feeling. He'd resigned himself to a life needing other people around him. Now he's back in charge of his own body again. You have to give him space."

That was more than six years ago now. It hardly seemed believable. Tom was now not only walking with barely a limp, but working full-time, traveling constantly, not playing cricket but doing the next best thing: watching it, reporting on it. And there she was, fulfilled in her own work—most of the time, at least. The school where she was now head of art was a small, alternative one, the children urged to express their creativity, art considered as important as math and science. They had both moved on, hadn't they? Left the Templetons far behind them?

Except they hadn't. Nina knew that now. Inside, had she always longed for something like Hope's letter to arrive? Something to happen to force her to confront everything she felt about the Templetons once and for all? Her own guilt about Gracie's letters. Her feelings about Henry. Her jealousy of Eleanor.

Her jealousy of Eleanor. There it was. Another uncomfortable truth. Because that had always been the case, she realized now. Even before she'd had the brief liaison with Henry. She'd always envied Eleanor's life, with her big happy family, her charming husband, her fulfilling and successful work life, even her elegance and poise.

That day in the Rome hospital, she'd seen a crack in Eleanor's perfect facade, but then it had sealed shut again, as she so coolly dismissed Nina, ridiculed anything Henry might have said to her, painted herself as a sophisticate with an open marriage, Nina as the gullible other woman. Even amid the shock about Tom, Nina had felt humiliated, embarrassed, ashamed of herself. Had that also been a factor in not telling Tom about Gracie's letters? Getting back at Eleanor through her daughter?

All of it was true. She could try to forgive herself, try her best to understand why she had done what she'd done, but she couldn't move past the facts. It was Gracie and Tom who'd been the innocent victims of all of these hurts and lies, both caught up in the fallout from their parents' messy, complicated lives. She could never make it all right again, give Gracie and Tom back those lost years. How could she ever explain? What could she ever do to make them forgive her? As for Hilary . . . could her sister ever forgive her?

Alone in her living room, more alone than she'd ever felt, Nina realized she had no way of knowing.

IN PERTH, Tom was pacing his hotel room as he spoke on the phone, hoping his editor back in Melbourne would agree. The next flight to Melbourne was in two hours' time. The flight took almost four hours. It would take him at least ninety minutes to drive there from the airport. If all the connections worked, if there were no delays, he could be back at Templeton Hall within eight hours.

"I can't explain, Jim, but it's important. Really important."

"So is this match, Tom. What can be so important that you suddenly need a day's leave?"

Just say yes, Tom urged under his breath. "I've spoken to Neil already. He said he can cover for me."

"It's hard enough getting copy out of Neil as it is. Seriously, what's so important?"

Tom could have lied, could have said there'd been a death in his family, but there'd been too many lies already. He told the truth. "The woman I love is in Melbourne for just another few days. If I don't go and see her now, I might blow it forever."

There was silence and then his editor started to laugh. "You're joking me."

"I've never been more serious."

"Tom, impressive and all as love's young dream is—"

"I'm begging you."

There was a sigh. "You've got one day. If you're not back in the press box at start of play on Thursday, you're sacked. Or you're not going to England for next year's Ashes. Whichever I decide first."

Chapter Thirty-two

IN LONDON, Henry was having a difficult conversation. It was his second difficult conversation of the day. Talking to Eleanor had been hard enough. While he'd soon established the children were fine, it was clear within seconds she was angry at him. Still. Even more so. Her voice wasn't so much icy as arctic. She didn't waste time on polite conversation. Once she confirmed that he was in London, she insisted he drop whatever he was there to do and "present himself" at her house at noon. She'd come home between lessons to see him. They had something extremely important to discuss.

"But my flight back to San Francisco leaves at two."

"Change it. This is more important."

"We can't discuss it over the phone?"

"No, Henry, we can't."

"I do have other plans—"

"Be there, Henry."

Now Adele was being as frosty. She'd started to ice up the moment he told her he needed to change his flight to attend an unexpected meeting.

"But that means you won't be back in time for the dinner tonight. You know how important it is to me. What's this meeting about? Who's it with?"

"An old business associate of mine."

"Male or female?"

"Female."

"An old girlfriend, is that what you mean?"

He was starting to wish he'd been more honest with her from the start. "Adele, darling, please. How busy do you think I've been in my romantic life? She's a business associate. We were partners in a property project some years ago and a few issues have come up that we need to discuss."

"What property project?"

Base a lie on the truth, Henry. "An apartment complex called Templeton Hall, in north London."

"Residential or commercial?"

"Residential but possibly commercial. That's what she and I need to discuss. Adele, my love, I'm sorry about tonight. Why don't you take one of your girlfriends instead?"

"I have an MBA and I'm a Harvard graduate, Henry. Don't patronize me. Are you having an affair with this 'business associate'?"

"No, I assure you."

"Do you intend to?"

"No. I assure you of that as well."

"Are you planning to finish things between us?"

"Adele—"

"Henry, do you think I'm a fool? You were with someone else when you and I met. I know you're capable of it. Would you please just be straight with me and save us both a lot of trouble?"

"I promise that breaking up with you is the last thing on my mind."

"Good." Her voice changed and became girlish. "Hurry home, then. I miss you."

In the taxi on the way to Eleanor's house later that morning, both conversations echoing in his mind, Henry took the opportunity to close his eyes. He was getting too old for all of this. But what was the alternative? Slow down? Give up all that gave him pleasure in life—the thrill of business dealings, chasing new dreams, and yes, wooing beautiful women? No, perhaps not just yet. He was only in his early sixties, after all. It was just a matter of keeping his mind sharp. His eye on the ball, as the saying had it.

He'd known from an early age that succeeding not just in business but in life meant being decisive. At school, the only scholarship student among classes filled with children of privilege, he'd learned to make the best use of what he did have—wit, charm, a sharp mind. It wasn't a matter of being calculating or self-serving. It was planning ahead, like playing chess. Weighing up options and making the best available moves. Recognizing opportunities when they presented themselves and maneuvering into position to gain the most advantages wherever possible.

And that had been the story of his life, hadn't it? Seizing the day, the opportunity, whenever it appeared, in work or in life. Sometimes it was luck, sometimes by design, sometimes it was a genuine emotional response. Meeting Eleanor, for example. That truly had been love at first sight for him. Of course he and Eleanor had had their ups and downs over the years. What married couple didn't? And all right, he had to admit his own role in some of those difficulties, but surely he'd behaved no worse than many other men of their acquaintance. And no matter what had happened between them in the end, they'd produced and raised four beautiful children together. In hindsight, their real problems had begun when tensions in his work life began to spill into his home life. He'd started to overstretch himself, take on too many clients, choose the wrong clients, make bad decisions, one or two bad judgment calls. Ruffle a few feathers. Was it any wonder he'd seized the opportunity of a fresh start, not just for him but the whole family, when it presented itself? Hadn't Englishmen been doing that for years, after all? Heading to Australia to reinvent themselves?

Even after the difficult years that followed, when Eleanor read him the riot act, when he was forced to work harder than he had ever worked until he had paid off every bill—every bill that she knew about, and more besides, unfortunately—he had only fond memories of the years in Australia, the fun it had been for the whole family. Even Eleanor had loved it there, at the start, at least, even if by the end she—

"Thirteen pounds, thanks, sir."

The taxi driver had to ask him twice. Henry hadn't realized they'd arrived. He'd never visited Eleanor at this house and didn't recognize the area. He passed over a twenty-pound note, told the driver to keep the change, and got out.

TEN MINUTES LATER, Henry was still waiting for Eleanor to explain the reason for this meeting. Her behavior was unsettling him, not that he allowed her to see it. He'd expected her to be angry at him from the moment he walked up the cobbled garden path and she opened her blue-painted front door. What he hadn't expected was this strange self-possession.

She'd casually exchanged greetings, as if it had been yesterday they'd last seen each other, not eight years previously. She barely acknowledged the compliment when he told her—truthfully—that she looked very well. She'd offered him tea, even poured it for him. As they took their seats opposite each other in her small but elegant living room, she filled him in briefly on the children. He felt a twinge of guilt that he didn't see them more often, but she didn't even censure him about that. He was surprised—shocked, even—when she mentioned that Gracie was currently in Australia, at Templeton Hall, in fact. Surely he should have been told about that? He hid it well, though, as he also hid his reaction to Eleanor's news that Hope had been going, too, until she had fallen down her stairs the night before and broken her leg.

"Fortunately her bank account is in such good shape these days she's been able to afford a very luxurious private hospital," Eleanor informed him, pouring more tea into their cups.

"That's good," he said, still wary, wondering why Eleanor felt the need to tell him all this.

"It's a terrible shame, really. She'd been so looking forward to going back to Templeton Hall. For her own recovery but also for another reason, it turns out. When I spoke to her this morning, when I told her that as a matter of fact you and I were meeting today, she got rather excited. It turns out she has a business proposition for us, Henry. To do with Templeton Hall."

"That's why you contacted me?"

"Not exactly, no. But isn't it perfect timing?" Eleanor took a sip of her tea. "She wants to know whether you and I would consider leasing Templeton Hall to her on a long-term basis, so she can establish a drug and alcohol rehabilitation center there. It's ideal, she told me. Beautiful, in an isolated setting, the right size. There's a fortune to be made in that industry, apparently. What a shame we didn't know that. All these years it's been lying empty over there."

Henry was even more wary now. He didn't know Eleanor in this mood.

"Perhaps we could ask her to prepare some paperwork for us," he said, trying to buy himself some thinking time.

"Perhaps we could." Eleanor put down her cup. "Henry, the reason I've asked you here today is to discuss what we'll do with the Hall when we die."

"Die? Are you ill? Have you had bad news?"

"No, Henry, I'm perfectly well. But I am getting older and I do want to update my will. And as Templeton Hall is the main shared asset between us, it's been on my mind a great deal. Especially since recent events have made it clear that none of the children appear to be interested in it very much, despite its place in their family history."

"They don't? Not even Gracie?"

"Even Gracie. In fact, she rang last night to tell me she's left the Hall. She said she'd realized it had been a special place but she didn't need to spend any more time there."

"That surprises me."

"Does it, Henry? I suppose it would. It's not as if you've shown much interest in your children recently, is it? How long since you've seen Audrey, for example? Charlotte?"

"We talk occasionally. But really, Eleanor, New Zealand? Chicago? Ireland? The children have hardly stayed still themselves."

"It's always someone else's fault, Henry, isn't it?" Eleanor stood up. "But let's leave any discussion about the children for another time, shall we? You and I have more pressing matters today." She picked up a folder from the small table beside her and put it in front of him. "This, for example."

He hesitated to pick it up. "What is it?"

"Perhaps you can tell me."

He opened it. A muscle twitched in his jaw. He didn't say anything.

"What is it, Henry?"

"It's a lease."

"Yes, Henry. It's a lease."

"I thought I had the only copy of it."

"Then you thought wrong. Your appalling filing was always going to be your downfall, wasn't it? You obviously took a copy and hid it, not very well, in a folder in your filing cabinet at Templeton Hall. Did you ever wonder what I would think, or what one of your children might think, if we found it?"

He didn't answer.

"Tell me out loud what it is, Henry, would you? Even after all these years, I think I need to hear it from you to truly believe it."

He paused. "It's the lease for Templeton Hall. A twenty-year lease." He didn't lift his eyes from the paperwork in front of him.

"Except it's not Templeton Hall, Henry, is it? Because we had no right to call it that. Because it had nothing to do with your family at all, did it?"

He looked up then. "Eleanor—"

"You didn't inherit it, Henry, did you? Your ancestors never went anywhere near Australia. You leased it, as some kind of hurried escape route, from one of your clients. That old man in Yorkshire, I'm presuming. You leased it, then you came home to me and you lied and you lied and you've kept lying. Why, Henry? Why?"

"Please, Eleanor, don't shout. Calm down. There's a perfectly rational explanation."

She gave a short laugh. "Calm down? A rational explanation? How can there be? You not only uprooted us all, not only made us go to the other side of the world to run a family business that had absolutely no basis in fact, not only wasted the last of my inheritance on extravagant and pointless renovations—"

"Eleanor—"

"But all of it, *all* of it, was based on a lie. You *must* have known I'd never have agreed to any of it, if I'd known you were only leasing the Hall."

"Of course I knew that. That's why I had to lie about it."

"'Had to lie'? So once again, it wasn't your fault? I *made* you lie, or otherwise we couldn't have done it?" She wasn't shouting now. Her voice was cold. "Did you even think for a minute what the repercussions might be? Think how the children might feel when they learned the truth? And of course that's why we couldn't sell it when we were in such debt, wasn't it? It wasn't ours to sell." She laughed then, a short, bitter laugh. "Tell me, Henry, have you still been paying for that lease? All this time it's been empty?"

The briefest of shrugs from Henry. "It was a watertight contract. I couldn't break it."

"So even more money down the drain? What has it been, Henry? Tens of thousands each year, to keep the Hall empty? Had you gone completely mad? Lost all sense? Did you never even think of telling me the truth?"

"And worry you more? Eleanor, of course not. But now I see that perhaps I should have." He smiled. "You see how much I needed you? You always did curb my worst excesses."

She swept the folder onto the floor, her fury obvious. "Don't even *try* to flatter me, Henry Templeton. Keep your false compliments and your lies to yourself. No, in fact, don't. Take them to my sister. I hope you do sublet the Hall to her, Henry. You deserve each other, with your lies and deceit. I hope you make a fortune out of her. I hope she opens her latest money-grabbing clinic and I hope the entire building collapses on her. On you both."

"Eleanor, you don't mean that. We had some very happy times there. Surely you remember? Please don't rewrite history."

"What history? Our entire time there was built on a foundation of lies. Your lies. And how did it end, Henry? Can you remember? Will I remind you? It ended badly. *Badly.*"

"At first, yes, but all our debts are paid now, aren't they? And I planned to tell you all one day, Eleanor. Of course I did. But what was the point until the lease was due for renewal? And I suppose I always hoped deep down that we might even renew the lease again, go back, start up the tours again, if not all the family, even one or two of us. Gracie, especially. It was such a special time for us as a family, Eleanor, wasn't it? Such fun at times. Please don't be too angry."

"Don't be too angry? You want me to laugh this off? You think it was all right to lie not just to me, but to all of us? Your own children?"

"It wasn't so much a lie as an elaborate story. There's a difference, surely. Eleanor, please, let's not be like this."

Eleanor tightly crossed her arms. "You're right, Henry. Let's keep it as nice as can be."

Henry stood up, too, smiling, ignoring the fact she had taken a step away from him. "Eleanor, how did it get so bitter between us?"

"Let me think," Eleanor said, tilting her head to one side. "Was it the first time you were unfaithful to me? Or the tenth time? Was it when I first realized you'd lied to me about the money we owed, the deals you'd done, the real trouble we were in? Was it when I found the lease for the Hall, when I realized you'd lied not just to me but to our children? Or was the final straw really eight years ago, when I discovered you'd slept with Nina?"

Henry's smile disappeared. "You know about that?"

"Yes, Henry. I found out about that the same day Nina told me her son would never walk again because of an accident caused by our children. The perfect circumstances for such a conversation." Eleanor's tone was still mild, her face composed. "How long had it been going on between the two of you? Will you tell me that? The entire time we lived there?"

"Of course not."

She gave a soft laugh. "'Of course not?' Because you would never do such a thing? Henry, what does it matter anymore? Can't you tell me the truth now, at least?"

"Eleanor—"

"Do you know what shames me the most, Henry? Not about you, but about myself? That up until the day in Rome that Nina told me about the two of you, if you'd asked if you could come back to me, I'd have said yes. When Spencer rang to tell me he and Gracie and Tom had been in an accident, all I wanted to do was ring you. I wanted to go through it all with you. I wanted you there with me and I knew for sure then that I'd never stopped loving you, as hard as it was so many times. It's been like a weakness in me, Henry, that I've loved you no matter how badly you treated me. I'd even decided that same day I wanted to try and make it work with you again. I hoped that you weren't with anyone else. But then I discovered you had been. That you possibly still were. And not just anyone else. You'd been with Nina. My friend Nina."

"It wasn't like that."

"Oh, really? You just happened to be in Australia? Just happened to bump into each other at Templeton Hall one afternoon? Happened to fall into bed together?"

"That's exactly what happened."

"No, Henry! No more lies." Her voice was suddenly loud. "Don't you ever get sick of it yourself, twisting yourself up further and further into these layers of deceit?"

"Eleanor, it was just a brief thing with Nina."

"You never saw her again afterward? But you promised her you'd be back, didn't you?"

Henry's silence was his answer.

Eleanor was very still now. "Then it wasn't just me you hurt, Henry. Because of you, because of whatever promises you made to Nina and never honored, I think Nina chose to punish not you, not me, but our daughter, Henry. She cut off all contact between Gracie and Tom, and now I think I know another reason why. It wasn't just about the accident, about Tom's injuries. It was because of what you had done to her."

"Eleanor—"

"Do you remember Gracie after that accident, Henry? Do you remember her pleading with both of us to contact Nina, to help her get in touch with Tom? To my shame, I didn't. I could have, but I didn't. And Gracie's heart has been broken ever since."

"I don't accept that. It was an accident. She and Tom were just children."

"Henry, I was nineteen when I met you. The same age Gracie was when she fell in love with Tom. I know that love like that can be real and lasting. I loved you then and stupidly, I kept loving you, no matter what you did. And what good did it do me?" Eleanor began to cry then, sobs from somewhere deep inside her. Henry hesitated only a moment, then moved toward her. Like two jigsaw pieces, their two bodies long-familiar with each other, he opened his arms and she stepped into them, her body molding into his.

"You ruined everything, Henry." She was speaking through her tears. "You ruined everything."

They were still standing like that, in each other's arms, when the door opened. It was Spencer, carrying a backpack, looking as if he hadn't slept for days.

"Mum, Ciara's kicked me out. Is it okay if—" He stopped and looked from his mother to his father. "Mum *and* Dad? Wow. Are you two back together again?"

Chapter Thirty-three

WHERE COULD Gracie be? Tom thought, as he knocked on the front door of Templeton Hall for what felt like the hundredth time. He'd knocked on the back door, each of the lower windows, the stables apartment, then returned to the front door, but there was no answer. He'd started to worry when he first realized there was no sign of a car, but he'd convinced himself that perhaps Hope had taken it somewhere. Or they'd both driven into Castlemaine for something. An hour later, he was still there, still waiting, still knocking.

Only then did he remember. He still had Hope's number. He reached for his phone and dialed. It rang eight times before a haughty, slurred voice answered.

"Who is this? Have you any idea of the time?"

"Hope, it's Tom Donovan."

"I don't care who it is. How dare you ring me in the middle of the night."

"Hope, this is Tom Donovan calling from Templeton Hall. In Australia. Aren't you here, too?"

A long, dramatic sigh. "No, sadly I'm not, Tom Donovan. I am, however, in a private hospital in London with a broken leg and I don't mind telling you I'm extremely pissed off about it."

Was she drunk? Stoned? She was definitely slurring. He tried again. "Hope, I'm at Templeton Hall—"

"You are? I'm glad someone is. It'd be a ghost town otherwise. Or do I mean ghost hall?" She started to laugh.

"Hope, please!" He had to speak up to be heard. "I'm looking for Gracie. She's not here."

"Tell me something I don't know."

"Where is she?"

"How should I know? She could be in Timbuktu by now."

"Please, Hope. Where is she?"

"No need to shout, Tom Donovan. I don't know, I told you. She didn't specify"—it took her several tries to say the word properly—"where she was going next."

"When did she leave here?"

"God knows. I'm all mixed up with the time difference. At least Gracie rang at a respectable hour."

"What did she say to you, Hope? When Gracie rang you, what did she say?"

Another sigh. "She rang me to tell me she'd decided she couldn't stay at the Hall on her own, too many memories or some such thing, at which point I told her that alas, I wouldn't be arriving there myself now either, at least not until this stupid leg of mine had healed. Still, what's a few months' wait in an international expansion plan? It will all work out, I'm sure of it."

"Hope, please. Where did Gracie go?"

"I. Don't. Know. She. Didn't. Say. Aren't you listening to me? All she said was that she was going to drive back to Melbourne, find a hotel—"

"There are hundreds of hotels in Melbourne. I'll never find her." Tom was thinking aloud.

"You could always ring her, I suppose. Ask her which one she's staying in."

"You have Gracie's number? She has a phone?"

"Of course she has a phone. Of course I have her number."

Tom's hands were shaking as he wrote down Gracie's number. After a hurried good-bye, he took a moment to compose himself. With hands still shaking, he dialed her number.

GRACIE WAS WALKING in the Botanic Gardens in the center of Melbourne. She'd found a small hotel around the corner and booked in for four nights. She'd at first considered changing her flight and returning to London immediately. What was the point of staying here now that Hope wasn't coming? But Hope hadn't seemed to care whether she stayed on or not. In fact, Hope, despite her broken leg, had sounded suspiciously carefree, as if she'd either hit the bottle again or taken far too many painkillers.

"Live it up, Gracie," she'd slurred. "Go and see Audrey and Bippie in Auckland if you want to. On me. Within limits. Keep receipts. See you when you get back. Sorry about the wasted trip. We'll do it again someday. Don't know when, don't know where—"

She was still singing when Gracie hung up.

The phone in her handbag rang again now. Gracie took it out, hoping it wasn't her aunt changing her mind. It wasn't Hope. Gracie didn't recognize the number.

"Gracie speaking."

"Gracie, it's Tom."

"Tom?"

"Where are you?"

"What?"

"Gracie, where are you? Where exactly are you?"

"I'm in Melbourne. In the Botanic Gardens."

"What can you see?"

She looked around her. "A pond. A café. The main gate."

"Gracie, stay there, would you? Don't move. Please, Gracie. Stay right where you are."

"Why?"

"I have to talk to you. I'm on my way. I'll be there as quickly as I can. Ninety minutes. Two hours at the most."

"But aren't you in Perth?"

"I was. Now I'm at Templeton Hall."

"Templeton Hall?"

"Gracie, please, don't go anywhere. I'll be there as soon as I can."

He hung up before she had a chance to ask anything more.

AN HOUR LATER, Gracie hadn't done what Tom asked.

Please, Gracie. Stay right where you are, he'd said. She hadn't stopped moving since he called. So far she'd changed tables in the small café four times. She'd been across to the gate of the gardens three times, checking the road in both directions. Which way would he come from? How long would he be? How could she just stay still and wait?

She had to check the call log on her phone to confirm she hadn't imagined it. Forty minutes after his call, a beep on her phone alerted her to a text message:

I'm not far away now. Please, Gracie, wait for me. Tom

Her head was filled with questions. What did he want to tell her? How had he got her number? Would Emily be with him again?

Exactly ninety minutes after he'd phoned, some sixth sense made her look toward the gate. It was him. She didn't move from her table. She waited, watching. His limp was more obvious now. He didn't have the stick with him. He was wearing a blue T-shirt, dark jeans. His hair was tousled.

He looked beautiful.

She stood up as he came closer. Neither of them was smiling.

The moment he reached her he leaned down and kissed her on the lips.

"Tom!" She stepped back, shocked. "What are you doing?"

"What I wanted to do at the Hall the other day. What I've wanted to do for eight years."

"But Emily . . ."

"She's not here."

She stepped back farther. "If you think I'll let you cheat on her—"

"She won't mind, I promise you. She's busy enough with her husband and baby son."

"You're having an affair with a married woman?"

"No, Gracie." He laughed then. "Emily and I are just friends. That's all we've ever been. I'm friends with her husband, too."

Gracie wanted to start this all over again. Nothing was making sense. "But I don't understand. How can you be engaged to her one day and not the next?"

"It's a long story. A short story." His smile vanished. "Gracie, I didn't even think to ask you or Hope. Are you married? Engaged? Seeing anyone?"

"No, of course I'm not." He looked as if he was about to kiss her again. She had to slow this down. "Tom, what's going on?"

"What should have gone on eight years ago." He took her hand, led her back to the table, sat opposite her. He didn't let go of her hand. His expression was serious. "Gracie, I spoke to Nina last night. I know everything now. About the letters you wrote to me after the accident. The letters she never passed on to me."

Gracie went still. "You didn't get my letters? Any of them?"

He shook his head. "She threw them away, Gracie. All of them. And that wasn't all." He told her about Nina's other lie. The fabricated conversation, that Gracie had told her at the hospital in Italy that she'd decided she could never see Tom again.

Gracie went pale, then red, then pale again. Shocked, she took her hand from his, sat back in her chair. "But I didn't even see Nina at the hospital. And I would never have said that. I'd have done *anything* to see you, anything to help you."

"I know that now. Eight years too late, but I know it now."

There was suddenly so much to say but no way to begin. A long moment passed as they just looked at each other.

Gracie spoke first. She knew her voice was strangely polite, her expression wary, cautious. It was as if this was now their first meeting, that the reunion at the Hall with Emily by his side hadn't happened. Above them, the sky was threatening rain. There were other people at tables a short distance away. Yet it felt as though they were alone, as though the next few minutes could change the rest of their lives. She searched for something to say, even as a hundred questions crowded into her mind. She wanted—needed—to know every detail of the last eight years of his life.

She had to start somewhere. "How are you, Tom?"

He gave the briefest of smiles, as if he understood all that lay behind those four words. "I'm fine, Gracie. I'm good."

There was too much distance between them. She wanted to reach across to him, to take his hand again, to touch him, but it wasn't right, not yet. "What happened, Tom? After the accident? With your back? With your life? With you?" Once she'd started, she suddenly couldn't seem to stop. "Have you been a journalist long? What paper are you with? Do you travel a lot? Do you live here in Melbourne?"

He smiled, laughed even, and shook his head. "No, Gracie, please. You first. What happened to you? What have you been doing? Are you still living in London? Did you go back to university? How is your family?"

She shook her head, unable to even begin to answer. All she had been doing for eight years was missing him. Her eyes suddenly filled with tears. She hurriedly brushed them away. "Why, Tom? Why did Nina do it to us?"

His smile disappeared. "I don't know. I don't care."

"You don't *care*?"

"All I know now is I don't want to see her again. I can never trust her again. How could I? How can she have done that to you, to me? Lied to us. Not just once, but again and again, telling me you didn't want to see me, telling me she had posted my letters to you, that—"

"Your letters to *me*? You wrote to me, too?"

He stared at her. "Of course I did. Of course."

There was silence again, as they could only look at each other. When Tom spoke again, his voice was quiet. "Gracie, the letters you wrote to me. What did they say?"

Her eyes filled with tears again. "That I loved you. That I missed you so much. That I was so sorry about the accident. That I knew it was my fault but I would have done anything, anything, I could to change it or help you. I must have written dozens of times. Hundreds. I don't know for sure. I wrote for six months, until I got Nina's, the one—"

"Nina wrote to you? From Australia?"

Gracie nodded.

"What did she say, Gracie? Please, I have to know."

"She asked me . . . she told me to stop writing. That you could never forgive me."

A flash of anger again. "*I*? I could never forgive you? But there was nothing to forgive. It was an accident, Gracie. It wasn't your fault. I always knew that."

"Nina meant you *and* her. The two of you. And it *was* my fault, Tom. It was."

"It *wasn't* your fault and it had *nothing* to do with her. It was you and me, Gracie. Us. Between us. She had no right." He stood up then, his hands clenched on the table in front of them.

This time Gracie didn't hesitate. She reached for his hands, held them tight for a moment. Again, that feeling that her next words were so important, that they could change all that lay ahead of them both. "She did, Tom. She did have a right. She's your mother."

He shook his head. "No, Gracie, you're wrong. How can you even try to understand what she did to us?"

She had to try, even if she was still reeling from seeing him, from what he had told her. She told him the truth. "I have to, Tom. I have to try and understand it. I have to believe she did it because she thought it was the best thing for you. Otherwise it hurts even more. Makes even less sense."

"Of course it doesn't make sense. How can it? Gracie, she kept us apart for eight years. It would have been longer, it could have been forever if Hope—" He broke off then, running his fingers through his hair. As she watched, as she stared up at him, his eyes suddenly filled with tears. "It's too much, Gracie. Seeing you again. Nina's lies . . ."

She moved then, closing the gap between them, straight to him, putting her arms around him. The feel, the warmth, even the smell of him was so instantly, gloriously familiar. "It's okay, Tom. It's okay."

He spoke into her hair, his arms tight around her, too. "How can it be? She took eight years from us. Nothing can ever excuse that, or change that. Nothing."

She held him closer, told him again that it didn't matter, it would be all right, everything would be all right. They were both crying now. If anyone was watching, they were oblivious. The rain was falling. They didn't feel it.

"It's all right, Tom. It's all right now. It is." She said it again and again, holding him, feeling his arms holding her so tightly in return. A minute passed, two, three.

He moved back from her, just slightly, enough to be able to look down at her. "Gracie, how can you be so sure? So calm? Aren't you angry with her, too? You must be. You have to be."

She shook her head, gazing up at him, her eyes still bright with her tears. "Tomorrow I might be. Tonight I might be. But how can I be angry now?" She reached up and touched his face. "I can't tell you how many times I wished that I would be here like this with you, close to you, touching you. Holding you." Her arms tightened around his back, and she felt the strength of his body through his T-shirt. "And now I am. You're here. We're here together." She smiled then. A big beautiful smile. "It's all right now, Tom. It wasn't, but now it is. Now it will be. Can't you see that?"

He laughed then, actually laughed, shaking his head as he gazed down at her, his face filled with love and something else—a kind of wonder. He tightened his arms around her. "Gracie, I'm sorry. That deserves an answer, a proper answer, but I have to kiss you again first. Just for a second."

He leaned down and kissed her for more than a second.

She felt it immediately, that slow molten feeling in every part of her body, stronger than ever. It was a shock to step back from him, to realize they were in public, that people were watching, that the light rain had become heavier, that it was now coming down in torrents around them.

His house was only a ten-minute drive away. Her hotel room was closer. They went there. There was more talking to be done, eight years' worth of talking to be done, but the moment they came into her room, to see the rain falling through the trees outside, to see the glow of her bedside lamps, the bed warm and inviting with its red covers, they moved back into each other's arms. The talking could wait.

LESS THAN twenty-four hours later, they were both at Melbourne Airport. Tom was catching the early flight back to Perth. Neither of them had slept much. They had made love, talked, laughed, cried, held each other, and made love again.

He had offered to stay longer, to resign, to never write a word about cricket again if that was what she wanted, but she insisted he go back to Perth. She knew where he was now, he knew where she was. She wasn't going anywhere. She would stay in Australia for as long as she could. And while he was in Perth there was something she'd decided to do. Something she had to do.

As she stood in Tom's arms at his departure gate, he told her again, as he'd told her since she made the suggestion, that she didn't have to do it, on her own or at all. Nina was his mother.

"I need to see her, Tom. I have to. And I think it might be better this way." Gracie felt strangely sure of it.

In the night, their bodies entwined, words and kisses being exchanged in turn, they'd spoken again and again about what Nina had done. Each time, they'd asked the same question: Why?

"She said she did it to protect me," Tom said, his voice soft in the darkness. "She was worried I'd be hurt even more. She thought it was for the best."

Gracie was still more confused than angry. Perhaps the anger was still to come. "But she knew me. She must have known I would never hurt you. That I loved you."

Wrapped in each other's arms, it felt miraculous to talk of their love again, to know that the eight years' separation hadn't changed how they felt.

"Are you sure you want to see her?" Tom asked once more, as they stood at the gate. "You don't have to, Gracie. I mean it. I'd understand it if you never wanted to speak to her again."

"I need to, Tom. I need her to tell me why she did it."

"Wait until I get back. Wait until we can go together."

She shook her head. "If I don't go and see her as soon as I can, then I think I never will."

He touched the side of her face, kissed her again. The softest of whispers in her ear, "I love you, Gracie Templeton."

She didn't need to tell him how she felt. She'd told him over and over during the night. But she told him again now, too.

She stayed at the gate until Tom had gone from sight. He'd be back in three days' time and she'd be there waiting for him. Now, though, she needed to make a phone call. It was early but she had to do it now. She took out her mobile and dialed the number Tom had given her. Her heart was thumping. It rang once, twice, a third time before it was answered.

"Nina Donovan speaking."

"Nina, it's Gracie. Gracie Templeton."

An intake of breath. Almost a sob. "*Gracie?* Where are you? Gracie, I'm so—"

Gracie couldn't talk to her here, like this. "I need to come and see you."

They arranged the time and place. In five hours' time, at Nina's house in Brunswick. Gracie hung up before either of them said anything else.

Within an hour, she was back at her hotel. In the taxi from the airport, she'd realized she needed help. In her room, despite the time, knowing it was late, she phoned her mother in London.

She wasn't sure how much she would tell her. As soon as she heard her mother's voice, though, as soon as Gracie assured her she was fine, she told Eleanor everything. Her mother's joy for her, for her and Tom, was immediate. Her anger, her confusion at what Nina had done, followed as quickly. Gracie interrupted her, with question after question.

"Why would she have done it, Mum? Hurt not just me but Tom as well? I need to try and understand before I see her."

"You're going to see her? On your own?"

"Today."

"Gracie, is that wise?" There was worry in Eleanor's voice.

"I have to, Mum. But I need your help first. You're my mother. Would you have done the same thing, if the positions had been reversed? If I'd been the one badly hurt?"

There was silence for a few moments before Eleanor spoke. "Gracie, it was a difficult time. Decisions made in the heat of it all, things said, words spoken that can never be unsaid. We were all in shock, remember. It was bad enough for me, but Nina had to fly across the world, not knowing what awaited her—"

"But it was afterward that she lied about my letters, that she told Tom I never wanted to see him again. She told Tom that she was worried I would hurt him somehow."

"Every mother feels that way for her children, Gracie. Even if we're mistaken sometimes. No one wants the people they love to feel any pain."

"But Nina was my friend. She must have known I'd never deliberately hurt Tom, or her. That's what I can't understand. At first, yes, but not to tell him about my letters for eight years?"

Eleanor's voice was soft. "Tom was the center of Nina's life for so many years, Gracie. Perhaps she did regret her lies, I don't know. But sometimes it's impossible to see a way to fix your mistakes, to admit you've made an error of judgment, especially when love like that is involved. Especially if you think you've done it for the right reasons."

"But what could be right about it? What reason could she have? You'd never have done something like that, would you? Lied to me for so long, even if you felt you needed to protect me from something?"

"It's not that black and white, Gracie. Nothing ever is." She paused. "But yes, I'd always do anything I could to protect you, too. To keep you safe. I can't begin to describe the feeling, but it's like an urge, an instinct, to give you the best life, the happiest life I can."

"That's why you didn't tell me about you and Dad for so many years? The truth about all the money? The reason you split up? To protect me?"

Another long silence from Eleanor. "That was part of it, Gracie, yes. I couldn't tell you everything. You were too young. You would have worried too much. And I still think that was the right decision."

Gracie suddenly needed to keep talking, to know everything. "But how did you know when it wasn't going to work out with Dad? When it was time to stop trying?"

"It wasn't one moment, Gracie. In the same way it wasn't one thing that made me fall in love with him. Many things happened to bring it to an end."

"The money problems?"

"They didn't help."

"Then what? If all you loved about him at first didn't change, and your personalities didn't change, couldn't you have stayed together, enjoyed what you could about each other?"

"It's not always that simple, Gracie. I had to decide how much I could forgive and I finally realized I'd reached my quota."

"I don't understand."

Across the world, in her London living room, Eleanor realized the conversation was taking a dangerous turn. She needed to think quickly before she spoke again. "Gracie, you know, I think, that your father and I had difficulties in our marriage even before we went to Templeton Hall."

"I guessed. And I'd hear you fighting. Charlotte used to hint at things, too. But you still stayed together for so long. Was it just for us? Or because you still loved him?"

"I loved your father very much, Gracie. Too much, probably. But the problem with Henry is he always wanted everything. Lots of money, big houses, a big career." Eleanor hesitated, then decided it was time to be as honest as she could be. "And not just me, I discovered, but other women as well."

"Women? He had affairs?"

"I think so, yes."

"Oh, Mum, I'm so sorry."

Eleanor smiled. "Gracie, it's all right. It is. It's all in the past now."

"Did you know any of the other women?"

"Most of them, no." She hesitated. "One, yes."

There was an intake of breath from Gracie. "It was Hope, wasn't it? Dad had an affair with Hope."

"No, Gracie, it wasn't Hope. She liked to tell people that they had, but it wasn't true."

"But one of the women was a friend of yours? Is that what you mean?"

"I thought she was, yes." Eleanor stopped there. "It doesn't matter now, anyway. It's all a long time ago now. And if it did matter once, it doesn't now, for so many reasons."

Gracie's voice changed. "It was Nina, wasn't it? Mum, is that what you're saying? Did something happen between Dad and Nina when we were all living in the Hall? Wouldn't that explain so many things? Why she might have done—"

This time, Eleanor didn't hesitate to lie. "No, Gracie, it wasn't Nina. And I'm not going to tell you who it was." She paused, before making another decision. "But there is something your father did that I need to tell you about. Something that will affect you more than the others. I've only just learned about it myself, but if this isn't the right time, Gracie, I want you to say."

"No, tell me, please."

Eleanor didn't hold anything back. She told Gracie everything, about finding the lease, about contacting Henry, about all she now knew about Templeton Hall.

Gracie was quiet for a long moment when Eleanor finished talking. "I can't believe it," she finally said. "None of it was true? We don't own Templeton Hall? We've never owned it?"

Eleanor already regretted telling her. "I'm afraid not, Gracie. Your father invented the whole inheritance story, from start to finish."

There was another long silence and then Gracie started to laugh. Really laugh.

"Gracie? Are you okay? Are you all right?"

"I am. I *am*. And I don't think I'm surprised about it. I really don't." She laughed again. "It actually makes sense. Being there this week, seeing it all again, it all felt like some sort of a dream, make-believe. And that's why, isn't it? It felt make-believe because it *was* make-believe."

"You really don't mind? I was worried that of all of you, you'd be the most upset. Gracie, I mustn't know you at all."

"I'm too happy today to be upset." Another laugh. "But now everything makes sense, all those heirlooms and paintings of our ancestors appearing out of nowhere, all the changing stories. . . . None of it was true?"

"Not as far as I can tell. If it's any consolation, Gracie, your father fooled me completely, too. He told me he didn't think I'd agree to moving the whole family to Australia if there wasn't a family link, if it wasn't an inherited property."

"Was he right? Would you have agreed to go if you'd known he was just leasing it?"

"Of course not."

They both laughed then.

"Are you furious with him?" Gracie asked.

"On one hand, completely and utterly. On the other hand, no. What's the point? I think I'm running out of fury, Gracie. The older I get, the more I realize I'm not in charge of the world or the people in it. I can't control them any more than I want them to try and control me."

"Try and tell Charlotte that. In fact, wait until Charlotte hears about this."

"I've told Henry he has to tell her. And Audrey, too. As for Spencer, he happened to walk in on us today so he already knows. Not that he seemed to mind—"

"Spencer's back in London?"

"And back living with me for a little while, yes. His Irish girlfriend has apparently had enough of him. Though I did hear him ringing Hope and offering his services as a highly paid nurse, so I suspect he won't be with me for long." Before Gracie had a chance to comment, Eleanor continued, "That's enough talking, my Gracie, for you and for me. I love you and I'm so very happy for you and Tom and please give him my warmest wishes." She paused. "And I'll be thinking of you with Nina today."

"Thanks, Mum. For everything."

"I don't think I was much help."

"You were. I promise." A pause. "Is there anything you want me to say to her from you?"

Eleanor didn't need to think about that. "No, Gracie, there's not. Nothing at all."

Just over three hours later, Gracie was in a taxi on her way to Nina's house in Brunswick. She'd spoken to Tom before she left her hotel. He'd just landed in Perth. When he asked her how she was feeling, she told him the truth. She was so happy and sad and confused, all at once, all the different feelings swirling inside her. There was anger now, too. The more she'd thought about it, the more she'd realized what Nina had done to her, to Tom.

"She's left message after message on my phone," Tom told her. "I haven't called her back. I can't talk to her yet."

Gracie didn't ask what Nina had said, or how she'd sounded. She didn't want to know. She needed to see her for herself. "I'll ring you afterward, as soon as I can," Gracie promised.

She stared out at the passing Melbourne streets now, at unfamiliar street names, rows of shops, neat houses, each on their own block of land, all so different from London. The sky was gray, a soft rain falling. She asked the driver how far away they were. Fifteen minutes at the most, he said. She glanced at her watch. She was on time. She'd be early, in fact.

After talking to her mother, she'd tried to rest, even for a little while. She and Tom had barely slept the previous night. Sleep proved impossible. Caught midway between happiness and anxiety, her thoughts were tumbled and tormented as she tried to prepare herself for this meeting. She wasn't even sure if she could picture Nina anymore. It was sixteen years since they'd seen each other. Sixteen years and a lifetime. She thought of the years at Templeton Hall, her friendship with Nina, how much it had meant, how sad she'd been to leave. Then her thoughts leaped forward, to Tom, to the moment they'd met at Paddington Station, her waiting for him, wearing the red coat he'd always loved. Their days in London together, traveling together: Scotland, Ireland, France, Italy. Image after image flashed into her mind, good times dissolving into the worst of times, the months after the crash, the crash itself. . . .

She glanced at her watch, asked the driver again. Ten minutes away. She tried to imagine how Nina might be feeling now. Angry with her still? Defiant about what she had done? She hadn't sounded angry on the phone. She had sounded upset. She hadn't sounded like the Nina that Gracie remembered.

More memories flashed into her mind, this time from childhood. Visiting Nina with her father and Spencer that day, asking to borrow Tom. Having cups of tea with her. Painting with her. Talking to her, so much, about everything, calling to see her every day, sometimes more than once a day. She remembered the day of Tom's cricket match, the party they'd held for him. . . . They'd held the party for Tom that day? Not Nina? Why? That thought sparked other images, of Tom spending so much time at the Hall. He and Spencer running riot, up to mischief all the time, at the dam, on the roof, in their tree house. . . . Tom had practically moved in with the Templetons. He'd loved it at the Hall. He'd told her as much, as they'd traveled around Europe together. They'd talked a lot about those times, their shared memories another bond between them.

Now, though, Gracie tried to imagine how Nina might have felt back then. It must have been hard for her. If she'd had a husband to talk to, other children, perhaps it would have been different. Perhaps it would have been easier to share Tom. But Tom was all Nina had. The center of her world. The person she loved most in the world. Even as a child, Gracie had somehow seen that. Now, as an adult, after her conversation with her mother, it seemed even clearer.

And if Nina had felt that way about Tom as a child, it must have been magnified a hundred-fold after the accident, when he was so badly injured. All she must have wanted to do was bring him home, keep him safe, protect him from anyone, anything, that could ever hurt him again. Protect him, especially, from the people who had caused the accident.

Protect him from the Templetons.

"Here you are, love."

They were in front of Nina's house. She'd arrived.

She paid, got out, a mass of nerves now. It was a small cottage. A neat front garden. She barely noticed it as she walked up the path. It felt like the longest walk of her life.

Before she had a chance to knock, the front door opened. Nina was standing there. She was wearing a blue dress, boots, even a necklace, as if she'd dressed up especially. She looked older, but with the same dark hair, the same blue eyes.

"Gracie . . ."

Gracie stopped short of the door. "Hello, Nina."

There were no smiles between them. No warmth. Only wariness, Gracie realized. On both their sides. And something else coming from Nina. It was fear. She saw it in her eyes. Nina was scared of her.

Nina seemed unable to move or to speak. Gracie glanced down. The other woman's hands were clenched.

"May I come in?"

"Of course. Gracie, of course." She stepped back and Gracie followed her, into her living room. She glanced around. It was as colorful as Nina's farmhouse had been, as beautifully decorated as the apartment in the Hall—bright paintings, warm-hued rugs, cheerful curtains. Young Gracie would have exclaimed over them. Now, Gracie said nothing.

She turned, seeing that expression on Nina's face again. Fear and something else. Nina looked sad. Desperately sad, and somehow defeated. As if she was waiting for one final blow. A blow from Gracie? Is that what she was expecting? A furious tirade?

This time Nina broke the silence. "Can I get you anything? Tea? A drink?"

Gracie shook her head. She couldn't pretend this was a normal visit. She couldn't even make any more polite conversation.

"Why, Nina? Why did you do it? Not just to Tom but to me, too?"

There was a split-second when she saw something flicker across Nina's face, something raw, something almost angry, then just as quickly it disappeared. Nina seemed to crumple in front of her, down into an armchair. "I can't explain, Gracie. I can't."

Once, Gracie would have rushed to her side, tried to console her. Now, she made herself stay still, kept her voice even. "You have to, Nina. You have to. We need to know."

The "we" registered. Nina looked up, her face still anguished, her eyes filled with tears. "Have you seen Tom?" At Gracie's nod, another question. "Is it . . . will it be all right between you?"

It was too new with Tom, too precious, too fragile yet. She didn't answer. "Why did you do it, Nina? Why did you lie?"

"If you had seen him, Gracie—"

"I wanted to, Nina. I wanted to do everything I could for him."

Nina shook her head. "He was a different person. He was broken. He was so frightened, in so much pain. His whole life changed in that accident, Gracie."

"All our lives changed, Nina."

It was as if Nina hadn't heard her. "All his life, all I'd ever wanted to do was protect him, give him the best life I could, and yet I'd failed him—"

"It wasn't you, Nina. It was me. I was the driver. It was my fault." Gracie was surprised at the strength in her own voice. She was no longer a child talking to Nina. She was an adult. The eight years of sadness, of grief, of soul-searching, and of worry seemed to have crystallized inside her, giving her strength, keeping her steady. "I hadn't been drinking, but it was my fault. I lost concentration and I ran into the truck. It could have been me injured or Spencer hurt, but it was Tom and I will never be able to forgive myself for that. Ever. But I still need the truth from you. Why didn't you give him my letters? Why didn't you send his letters to me? Why did you lie to us both?"

"I had to. I had to."

"No, you didn't. I would have helped him. My whole family could have helped him."

"We didn't want your help." Nina's voice had sudden force. "Can't you see that? He was my son, Gracie. My responsibility, not yours." Tears were running down Nina's face but she didn't wipe them away.

"He was an adult, Nina." Gracie was on less firm ground now. She'd expected excuses from Nina. Not this raw feeling. "He wasn't a child anymore."

"He was still my son, Gracie. He always was my son, before your family came along and again after you all left." Nina stood up then, too, the tears gone, the words pouring from her: sharp, angry words. "You Templetons always had everything, didn't you? Whatever you wanted. All that money, all that charm, even the Hall just fell into your laps. It was always so easy for all of you, with your perfect lives, the perfect family—"

"No, Nina!" Gracie couldn't let her get away with this. "It was never easy for us, for any of us. There was nothing perfect about any of us. Not then, not now. Why do you think I spent so much time with you, at your house? I needed someone like you in my life, Nina. And you're wrong about the Hall falling into our laps, too. I only heard the whole story today. We never owned it. We didn't inherit it. My father leased it."

Nina's expression changed. "Leased it? It wasn't yours? It isn't yours?"

Gracie shook her head. "My father lied about it. To all of us."

Nina's reaction shocked her. She laughed. It wasn't a nice laugh. "What a surprise."

Gracie stared at her. The mood had changed in the room and she didn't like it or understand it. She needed to take back control of the conversation again. "I'm not here to talk about the Hall, Nina. I just need to understand why you did what you did to Tom and me. Then I'll go. You won't ever need to see me again."

Her words had an instant effect on Nina. "Gracie, I have to know. Is Tom all right? Will he ever speak to me again?"

She told the truth. "I don't know."

"He won't. I know he won't." Nina started to cry again, talking quickly, not even looking at Gracie now. "He won't answer my calls. Hilary won't talk to me either. And I deserve it. I deserve it." She looked at Gracie then. "But at least you came to see me, Gracie. Thank you. *Thank* you."

Gracie felt strangely unmoved by Nina's tears. "I don't want your thanks, Nina. I don't even want an apology. I just need you to explain why you did it."

"Gracie, please, sit down. Please."

She sat down. As Nina began to talk, Gracie didn't move, didn't interrupt, just watched and listened as the words poured from Nina, a tumble of words, punctuated by tears, of her fears, her loneliness, her anguish and grief after her husband died, her love for Tom, the need—the desperate, all-consuming need—to protect him from harm, to give him the best life she could. She spoke about her pride in his achievements at school, with his cricket, and the realization that he was growing independent of her, that he wouldn't always be the center of her life anymore, that he was growing away from her, just as happy away from her, staying with his friends, or at Templeton Hall. Especially at Templeton Hall . . .

She looked at Gracie directly then, meeting her eyes for the first time since she'd begun to talk. "I can't expect you to understand, Gracie, the love a mother can feel for her son, but he was everything to me. He always had been, and when I saw him in the hospital in Rome, when I thought I'd almost lost him forever, I had to do everything I could for him, I had to protect him, do whatever it took—"

"No, Nina!" The anger inside Gracie spilled into the room with sudden ferocity. "You *didn't* have to do it. You were wrong then and you're wrong now. You don't think I know how it feels to love someone and have them be taken away? To miss them so much, every single day, that it hurts?" She couldn't stop talking now, even as she saw Nina had more to say. "You think I can't understand how you might have felt? Be feeling now? I understand more than you will ever know. I loved Tom, Nina. And he loved me. We were young, we still are young, but we knew what we felt then. We feel it still now. Whatever you tried to do to us didn't work. Tom didn't need your permission to be with me back then, and nor did I. We still don't." She stood up then and reached for her bag.

"Gracie, please, no. Don't go." Nina's tone was urgent. "I'm sorry, Gracie. I'm so very sorry for hurting you. For hurting Tom. I had so many reasons, I promise you, but I can't . . . it's not . . . I don't know how to . . ." She started to cry again then, sobs from deep inside her. "What do I do, Gracie? What do I do if he never wants to talk to me again?"

"I'm sorry, Nina. I don't know."

Nina started to cry harder then, her face hidden in her hands. "I'm sorry, Gracie. I'm so, so sorry, for everything."

Gracie watched for a moment. For a second, she was a child again, there with Nina sixteen years ago. She did now what she would have done then. She walked across to the other woman and for a second, just a second, touched her shoulder. "I'm sorry, too, Nina."

Nina was still crying when Gracie let herself out.

THREE DAYS LATER, Gracie was at the airport waiting for Tom's flight from Perth to land. They'd spoken before his flight left. They'd spoken many times, every day, about her visit to Nina, about what she had said, what they had both said. Gracie had relived her meeting with Nina again and again. She'd felt rushes of anger, felt sadness, pity, so many different emotions toward her. She'd talked about it with Tom, the two of them still trying to make sense of Nina's actions. Was understanding even possible? Was forgiveness? And if not, what was the alternative? Never speaking to Nina again? Cutting off all contact? Putting her through all the pain they'd experienced? Back and forth their conversations had gone. They'd talked about so many things—their past, the missing eight years, their future. So much seemed possible now. There were so many plans to make together. A life to make together. But each conversation had come back to Nina. What happened next with her was entirely in their hands, they realized. They could choose to hurt her, to punish her as she had hurt them. Or they could somehow keep trying to understand why she had done what she'd done. Find some way to forgive her.

That morning, Tom had rung Gracie and told her he had just spoken to his mother. He'd decided he would go and see her. Not immediately, but when the time felt right. She hadn't asked him for more detail. Not yet. Whatever happened next had to be between him and Nina.

Now, waiting for his plane to arrive, she felt as nervous, as excited, as if this was their first reunion. She paced the terminal. She checked the monitors every five minutes, in case his plane arrived early. She sat for a few minutes at the arrivals gate before her nerves made her resume her pacing. She browsed in a bookstore, looked at souvenirs, walked past a small clothes shop.

It was there she saw it, hanging on the front rack. A red coat like the one she used to have in London. As they'd traveled together, as they'd shyly swapped stories of when they'd first fallen in love with each other, Tom had always mentioned the moment he saw her waiting for him at Paddington station wearing her red coat. It suddenly seemed urgent that she be wearing red again this time, too. She tried it on. It was a perfect fit.

She returned to the gate, this time wearing the coat. Back to the monitor. Ten minutes to go. Five minutes. Then the message the plane had landed. Would he be first out? Last?

Fifteen minutes and many travelers later, she saw him. She stepped forward, stopped, waited.

She saw him scan the groups of people waiting, saw him catch sight of her, his expression changing as he smiled, the most beautiful smile she had ever seen. He started walking toward her. She met him halfway.

Around them, other passengers smiled, too, at the sight of the young man and woman in each other's arms. He was talking, then she was talking as, hand in hand, they walked together to a row of seats, sat side by side, hands still entwined.

An hour later, they were still there, still talking, the words interrupted by laughs, kisses, smiles, both of them with so much to say, so much to hear, as if there wasn't enough time for them to say all they needed to each other.

Epilogue

One year later

IN THE PLUSH Bobbie Enterprises office in the center of Auckland, Audrey turned away from the computer and urgently called her husband's name. "Greg! Quickly!"

He was there in seconds. "Darling, what is it?"

"That brother of mine, that's what it is. That amoral, immoral brother of mine. Look!"

Greg looked at the screen. On it was a scan of a newspaper article, attached to an email that had just arrived from Spencer. The subject line was long: And so the family tradition continues. Read and weep, siblings!

The article was from the local Castlemaine newspaper. Most of the page was taken up by a full-color photograph of Hope and Spencer standing in front of Templeton Hall. TRADITION GIVES WAY TO TREATMENT, the headline read. The article announced the opening of a new drug and alcohol residential rehabilitation center in what had formerly been the family home of the center's managers, Hope Endersley, and her nephew, Spencer Templeton. Both trained counselors, they'd each also had personal experience with addiction issues, the journalist had written. *"Our own journeys through the darkness of addiction mean we not only have empathy with our clients, but we truly practice what we preach," Ms. Endersley explained. "Our approach is called ASH, Abstinence through Strength and Humor. When you are in the grips of addiction, it can sometimes feel like there is no way*

out. We're here to personally show our clients the path to a better life, a
new life, lived with grace and integrity."

"Integrity!" Audrey said. "They're liars, the pair of them!
Spencer's never been an addict of anything except his own monstrous
ego. And he told me himself the only training he's done is an online
course on how to give up smoking. Mum told me she's convinced
Hope is drinking again, and as for it being our family home, we now
know we've got as much history with that house as, I don't know,
Bobbie has. And people are falling for it, can you believe that? Mum
told me they're booked out for the first three programs. It's scandalous, isn't it?" She looked at her husband. "Greg? Don't you think
it's scandalous?"

He coughed. He only ever coughed like that when he was feeling
guilty about something. She didn't like that cough. "What? Tell me?
What is it?"

"Look, darling, I haven't decided anything. And I don't need to
yet. She said I can take all the time I need, that she and Spencer are
in this for the long haul."

Audrey could only stare at him. "All the time in the world to do
what?"

"To decide whether or not to accept her invitation. Hope's been in
touch with me, Audrey. With a proposition. A very interesting proposition, in fact."

"And you didn't tell me?" Audrey's voice was getting louder.
"What is it? What does she want? You said no, didn't you?"

"I don't know yet what I'll say. I've decided to think about it,
meditate on it, and then I thought you and I could discuss it."

"It's about Bobbie, isn't it? She wants to trade on Bobbie's name?
Attract children to her clinics as well? Greg, no, we can't let her! I always hated Templeton Hall. I've only got bad memories from that
time. Why on earth would I want to go back there?"

Another cough. "Actually, the invitation was to me, not us. Audrey,
you know I love Bobbie as much as you do. But he's your career, not
mine. And I do miss the counseling, the interaction with patients, the
sense of satisfaction when you bring healing to another human being.
As Hope reminded me, that is my gift. And it wouldn't even be full-
time. She'd fly me in for week-long residencies, she said. Their pro-

grams run for three months per group, with experts on all manner of treatments coming in and out. And the pay is very good. Very, very good. Audrey, darling, please don't cry. Audrey, please . . ."

IN HER CHICAGO OFFICE, working late, Charlotte laughed loudly and for a long time when she opened Spencer's email. If nothing else, she had to admire their front. After all, who could ever prove or disprove that Spencer had or had not been an addict, if that's what he was now saying he was? As for Hope, whatever her formal credentials, she certainly had the jargon down pat, from what Charlotte remembered during their last unpleasant phone conversation over a year ago. If large numbers of deluded and troubled people chose to spend thousands of dollars holed up in a crumbling old pile in the middle of nowhere in the goldfields of Australia trying to get off drugs or drink or whatever took their fancy, who was she to say what they were doing was right or wrong?

She laughed again as she looked more closely at the photograph of the pair of them, there on the steps of Templeton Hall. Sorry, she couldn't call it Templeton Hall any longer, could she? Not that she could call it by its new name either. She enlarged the photo, shaking her head. Spencer was clearly trying not to laugh, and if she wasn't mistaken, Hope seemed to be pinching him and trying to maintain a suitably empathetic and authoritative expression. She just looked constipated, in Charlotte's opinion.

There was an address for the Hope Clinic's website at the bottom of the article. Charlotte couldn't resist taking a look. She gave a low whistle as it appeared on screen. It was very impressive, well written, consoling, businesslike. . . . She clicked on the fees page and whistled again. It was also very expensive. It seemed an addicted fool and his or her money were easily parted. Every possible service was on offer, too—treatment for drug addiction, alcohol addiction, sex addiction, gambling addiction, bad relationship addiction. . . . As Charlotte read on, she realized she hadn't even heard of half of these possible addictions. What kind of sheltered life had she led?

Had Hope thought about offering treatment for food addiction? Charlotte wondered now, as she reached for yet another biscuit from the large tin beside her. She'd been quite shocked to realize during her last clothes shopping trip that she'd gone up yet another size. She wasn't so much a plus-size woman anymore as a plus-plus-size woman. She'd also recently realized something else. The business was now running so well under Dana's expert, skinny guidance that Charlotte could think seriously about taking an extended break. Even Mr. Giles said he thought some time away would do her good. He'd been saying that a lot since he'd taken early retirement himself. He was a changed man, making most of his phone calls from his yacht. "All work and no play will make Charlotte a dull girl," he'd said cheerily last time they spoke. She and his son, Ethan, had agreed that Mr. Giles was possibly having something of a midlife crisis at the end of his life. But perhaps there was something in what he said. Perhaps it was time to smell the roses a little. Or smell the gum trees, at least. During a break of, say, three months. A break on, say, the other side of the world . . .

Charlotte started to smile. It really could be quite good fun to test Hope and Spencer's methods firsthand. Good fun to go back to Templeton Hall, too—sorry, to the Hope Clinic—after all these years. She barely remembered it, if the truth be known, and truly hadn't been at all surprised when she heard from her father that the whole inheritance story had been a big lie. Had any of them actually believed it could be authentic? All those ridiculous stories about ancient ancestors and early days on the goldfields? If her Templeton male ancestors were anything like the current bunch—her father and Spencer, to be precise—then the idea of any of them doing anything that involved hard work was out of the question.

As for the idea of Spencer being a counselor—she could just picture him trying to keep a straight face, trying to pretend he was interested in any other human being than himself. And Hope? If what her mother had said was true and Hope was back on the bottle again, it wouldn't be long before Hope would need counseling herself. The place would turn into a circus. Charlotte could just imagine the look on their faces if she was to turn up in the middle of it all, having registered and paid for her treatment under a false name. . . .

She was laughing out loud again as she clicked on the link for Client Enquiries.

"WE'RE DELIGHTED you're keen to work with us on an updated edition of your seminal work, Mrs. Templeton. As I'm sure you know, there's been a resurgence in interest in the methodology of home education as a viable alternative to mainstream educational approaches, and—"

"Mr. Drayson—"

"Please, call me Timothy."

"Thank you, Timothy, and please call me Eleanor. And I'm actually Eleanor Endersley these days. Eleanor Templeton was my married name. I was divorced four months ago."

"Of course, Eleanor. And am I right in therefore assuming that you'd like us to change your name to Eleanor Endersley on the new jackets of your book? You do like our proposed cover treatment, I hope?"

"Thank you, Timothy. I would like that name change and yes, I do like the cover treatment very much. You flatter me, calling me a world-renowned expert in home education, but what woman doesn't like a bit of flattery sometimes?"

"Mrs. Tem—, I'm sorry, Eleanor, I'm sure you spend your days fighting off flattery."

She smiled, and picked up the business plan Timothy Drayson had couriered to her house a week before. It had come with a very impressive letter introducing himself as the new managing director of the small publishing house she'd signed with all those years before. He'd been looking closely through all the company's backlist titles, the letter said, and had been astonished to see that her handbook on home education had been out of print for the past ten years, when cases of parents choosing to homeschool had been steadily rising. Would she be able to spare the time in her busy schedule to come in, meet his new team, and discuss their exciting ideas for the future of not just her book, but the whole company? he'd asked. When she'd said yes, he offered to send a car to collect her.

She'd been here in his small but very neat Haymarket offices for the past hour. It had been a surprising morning in many ways. His plans for her book were indeed exciting. He had been surprising, too.

She'd expected him to be a go-getting thirty-year-old, a new broom sweeping clean. He was go-getting, that much was clear, but he was closer to her age than she'd imagined. Not at all handsome. Quite short, too. But his eyes were full of life and intelligence, he had a beautiful voice, and she really did like his ideas.

She picked up the proposed cover for the reprint of her book, to which she had just agreed to add a new section, updating it to include today's university admittance standards and address the arguments for and against homeschooling.

She smiled. "It does seem quite amusing that people need to buy a handbook to learn how to homeschool. We'll be holding classes in how-not-to-hold-classes next. . . ."

"Now, it's funny you should mention that. . . ."

He explained to her that during his long career in educational publishing he'd spent two years with the Open University. He now wondered whether a short series of lectures in home-education methods might prove very popular. As he spoke, Eleanor couldn't help notice that very nice smile of his again. In fact, he seemed to be a very nice man all round. Quite possibly the very nicest man she had met in many years.

Once upon a time she might have been more cautious. She might have thought it best to wait to actually be asked, before leaping in and possibly making a fool of herself. But she wasn't getting any younger. She had a lot of ground to make up. She told herself this new approach had nothing, *nothing* to do with the fact that she had heard the day before that Henry was getting married again. To his much, much, *much* younger girlfriend, Adele. Henry himself had phoned from San Francisco and told her. Not only that, he'd invited her to the ceremony. It was taking place in what he called "a special place to us both." For an awful moment Eleanor thought he meant he was having the wedding at Templeton Hall, that he actually thought she'd want to go back there, until she realized he meant a place special to himself and Adele. She hadn't asked where that might be. It could be the prison on Alcatraz Island, for all she cared. It had taken some self-restraint to keep her voice calm and say that much as she appreciated the kind thought, and his continuing—now year-long—attempts to forge a closer, more cordial relationship between them, she really didn't think she would accept.

"As long as you know you'd be welcome. You know I only ever want you to be happy, too, Eleanor, don't you?"

She'd thanked him nicely and finished the call as soon as she could. She hadn't told any of the children yet. She'd decided to leave it to Henry to break the news.

Eleanor realized now that Timothy Drayson was still talking about a possible range of courses. She interrupted. "Timothy, may I ask one question before we go any further?"

"Of course."

"Are you married?"

He blinked. "I was. We're divorced, amicably. Two children, both grown up."

Eleanor nodded. "Did you ever cheat on your wife?"

He blinked again, twice. "No, I didn't."

"Are you lying?"

"No, I assure you."

"Are you seeing anyone at the moment?"

"No, I'm not."

"Would you like to have dinner with me tomorrow evening?"

He smiled that smile again. She was oddly relieved to see his teeth weren't very good. Henry had beautiful teeth. "I'd love to have dinner with you, Eleanor. Thank you."

She smiled, too. "Good. Now, I'm sorry, you were talking about a lecture series?"

IN MELBOURNE, Nina was doing her best to quiet down a classroom full of overexcited eight-year-olds. "Right, everyone. Listen to me, please. Put your listening ears on. Our special guest is here, he's outside, so have you all got your questions ready?"

"Yes, Mrs. Donovan," all twenty-four children chorused.

"Is the welcome banner ready?"

"Yes, Mrs. Donovan," the trio charged with the honor of waving the banner shouted.

Nina gave the room a last-minute check. Not that there was time to fix anything, but it did look fantastic, if she said so herself. Every desk, every chair, and every window was decorated in shades of green and gold: balloons, streamers, even little handmade flags bearing maps of Australia, all of them in the national colors, too. The children's excitement had gone straight to fever pitch when she first told them that a famous sports star had grown up just three streets from this very primary school and in fact had sat in this same classroom for three years before his family moved away, though his grandparents still lived in the area. They'd all gotten even more excited when she told them that her son, Tom, who'd once been a fast bowler and was now a cricket writer who traveled all over the world, had actually played several matches with him when they were younger and that they were still good friends. She'd even shown pictures of them together in their cricket whites, as well as other photos of her son as a little boy, not much older than them, beside the rainwater tank where he'd learned to bowl. Their shrieks had reached hysteria levels when two weeks after that she told them that Tom had rung her the night before and confirmed that yes, that famous sports star would be very happy to drop in to the school and say hello next time he was in the area visiting his grandparents, as long as there was no media and not much of a fuss made.

Did this count as a fuss? Nina wondered, taking in the sight of the fourteen girls and ten boys all dressed as mini cricketers in white shirts and white trousers, zinc cream on their noses, all of them holding either toy bats or plastic cricket balls. She hoped not. She did one last check of the balloons, the bottles of drink, the biscuits, all ready for their morning tea. A sudden image flashed into her mind, a memory from a night many years earlier—the kitchen at Templeton Hall decorated with balloons, the table covered with party food, all of it in celebration of Tom's first great bowling success. It was a relief, an unexpected and beautiful relief, to realize the memory made her happy.

She turned toward the door, got the thumbs up from the school principal and a slightly nervous smile from the young man standing beside him. She quickly reached for her camera, ready to take all the shots she'd promised to email not just to Tom and Gracie, but to Hilary as well, before turning to the wriggling children.

"All right, everyone. Let's invite him in, shall we? All together now, a big Brunswick welcome to the captain of the Australian cricket team!"

THE STREETS OF EDINBURGH were filled with performers, promoters, musicians, and jugglers. If it wasn't for the strewn paper from fast-food restaurants everywhere, you could almost mistake it for medieval times, Gracie thought, as if they had time-traveled back to carnival days. The atmosphere was wonderful: people calling out about comedy shows, theater performances, poetry readings, experimental plays, urging the public to take a chance, see a star on the rise. She and Tom had somehow managed to get the last outside table at a café midway down the cobblestoned Royal Mile and had been watching the passing parade for the past hour. Even if they'd wanted to have a conversation, the noise around them made it too difficult. There was so much to watch and listen to.

They'd been here for five days now. It was their honeymoon. Not that they'd told their families yet that they were married. They hadn't quite got around to telling anyone about their six-week-long engagement either.

It had happened in Liverpool. They'd been there for a weekend, having a short break before Tom returned to London to cover a match at the Lord's Cricket Ground. Walking hand in hand down a busy shopping street in search of a restaurant for lunch, they passed a travel agent advertising city breaks to European capitals: Paris, Prague, Vienna, Rome. A big poster in the window featured a striking photograph of the Colosseum at sunset, its stonework a warm, radiant shade of gold against a vivid, red-streaked sky. They'd walked on a few steps before Tom stopped, then pulled Gracie backward until they were standing right in front of the poster. Before she had a chance to ask what was going on, Tom went down on one knee. At first she thought he was just doing up his shoe, until there, on the crowded footpath, he took her hands, told her how much he loved her, and asked her to marry him. "I'm serious this time, Gracie. I was every other time, too, but I'm really, really serious now." She was crying and laughing as she said yes.

They'd decided they'd tell their families soon. Just as soon as they found exactly the right words to also explain why they'd eloped to Gretna Green in Scotland. They'd talked about a family wedding at first, either in Australia or England, before slowly coming to the conclusion that it would be too difficult, for too many reasons. Gracie wasn't sure whether it would be possible or a good idea to get her mother and father under one roof again, not to mention Charlotte and Hope. . . . And while they both had carefully, gently, slowly rebuilt their separate relationships with Nina, they also felt the time wasn't right—if it ever would be—for Nina and the Templetons to all be together again.

As it turned out, their wedding ceremony couldn't have been more perfect. They'd both worn their favorite clothes—not the ones they liked best themselves, but the ones they liked to see each other in the most. Tom wore his dark jeans and reefer jacket. Gracie had always loved that jacket. She wore her red coat. Fortunately the weather was cool enough for coats. They'd asked the couple who ran their Gretna Green B&B to be the witnesses. They'd agreed immediately. They did it a lot, they said. They were even thinking about adding "Happy to Be Witnesses at Your Wedding" to their sign. The ceremony was quick, matter-of-fact, and all Tom and Gracie needed to make their feelings official. They drove north straight after the ceremony and spent their first night as a married couple on the Isle of Skye, in the same small hotel they'd stayed in years earlier. They didn't tell anyone it was their honeymoon. They didn't want any fuss. Perhaps they'd have a small party when they got back to London or when they were in Melbourne next. Perhaps they could hold it in what Gracie and Tom had dubbed The Building Formerly Known as Templeton Hall. They couldn't quite bring themselves to call it the Hope Clinic. Perhaps not. They'd both said their good-byes to the Hall, after all.

In the year since they'd been reunited, they'd lived as nomads, in Australia, in England, even in India briefly, wherever Tom had needed to be for his work. They were still undecided about where they'd base themselves eventually. Gracie had decided to return to university to do a history degree, but she didn't know yet which university. London had looked the most likely. The previous day, though, they'd taken a walk around the grounds of the University of Edinburgh. She'd picked up course information. They'd also looked at ads for flats to rent. It was a serious possibility. Tom could travel from here for his work as easily as he could travel from Melbourne, or London. So much of his work was done via the Internet these days in any case. She'd travel with him when it was possible, stay at home studying when it wasn't. They'd managed to survive eight years of separation; a month now and again would be nothing to them.

A lull in the noise of the crowd gave them an opportunity for a quick conversation. They'd been trying to decide which shows to go to that evening.

"Why don't I see if there are tickets left for the condensed Shakespeare?" Tom suggested. "That might make the decision for us."

She agreed, then watched as he walked down the Royal Mile, dodging two jugglers, a harpist, three mime artists, and a man dressed as an Egyptian mummy. She glanced down at the program again, noticing there were two performances for the Shakespeare, one at seven, the other at nine. If there were still tickets, maybe they could go to the early one, and see some comedy later. Maybe even go to a third show after the comedy.

"Tom!" she called. He didn't hear her. "Tom!"

He was almost out of sight. She reached into her bag, pulled out the silver whistle, and blew hard into it, producing a loud, sure, strong note. Somehow her timing was perfect, the sound finding a path through the conversations and crowds between them.

Tom stopped and turned around.

Gracie blew it again, not so surely and loudly this time. It was more of a squawk. He heard that as well, laughing and shaking his head as he walked back toward her.

As he came closer, she smiled. "I was just checking it still works."

He smiled, too, then leaned down and kissed her.

"It still works," he said.

ACKNOWLEDGMENTS

Many people helped me with this book in many different ways. My thanks to Max Fatchen; Domhnall Drislane; Clare Forster; Jolyon Blazey; Penny Blazey; Paul Toner; Nick McInerney; Paul McInerney; Grant Wyman of the South Australian Cricket Association; Josh K. Stevens, Chelsea Stevens, Dorothy Rawlins of Alexandria House B&B, and Arlene Lynes and all at Read Between the Lynes bookstore in Woodstock, Illinois; Dr. James Cashman; Ursula Brooks; Suzi Clarke; Noelene Turner; Paul Buchanan; Jeannie and Richard Vallence; Maria Dickenson; Stephanie Dickenson; Sarah Conroy; Brona, Ashley, and Ethan Miller; Melanie Scaife; Sinéad Moriarty; Noëlle Harrison; Catherine Foley; Kristan Higgins; Carol George; Kristin Gill; Felicity O'Connor; Sister Margaret Mary Murphy; Sister Mary Mercer; Karen O'Connor; Bart Meldau; Milly Meldau; Karen Wilson; Peter Ritchie; Susan Owens; Rachel Leamy; Jean Grimes; John Neville; Una Collins; and Triona Collins.

My special thanks to Austin O'Neill, Lee O'Neill, and their cousin Dylan Smith.

Big thanks to my publishers: everyone at Penguin Australia, especially Ali Watts, Saskia Adams, Gabrielle Coyne, Louise Ryan, Peter Blake, Daniel Ruffino, Sally Bateman, Felicity Vallence, Andre Sawenko, Rachel Tys, Deb Billson, and Tony Palmer; the Pan Macmillan team in the UK and Ireland: Trisha Jackson, Jeremy Trevathan, Helen Guthrie, Thalia Suzuma, David Adamson, Michelle Taylor, Ellen Wood, Alex Martin-Verdinos, and Rebecca Ikin; and all at Ballantine and Random House in the USA, with particular thanks to Jennifer Smith, Jane von Mehren, Lisa Barnes, and Kathleen McAuliffe.

Warmest thanks to my agents: Jonathan Lloyd and Kate Cooper at Curtis Brown in London; Fiona Inglis, Grace Heifetz, and all at Curtis Brown Australia; Christy Fletcher, Grainne Fox, and Mink Choi at Fletcher & Company in New York; and Anoukh Foerg in Germany.

Once again, huge thanks to my sister Maura for her speed reading, eagle eye, insights, and encouragement; to my two families: the Drislanes in Ireland and the McInerneys in Australia; and to my husband, John, for everything.

AT HOME
WITH THE
TEMPLETONS

Monica McInerney

A READER'S GUIDE

A CONVERSATION WITH
MONICA MCINERNEY

Random House Reader's Circle: How did you come up with the idea for this book? And how long did it take you to write it?

Monica McInerney: The starting point for the novel was the idea of life in a stately home tourist attraction—or more to the point, the idea of *after-hours* life there. I've always loved the idea of what goes on behind the scenes in places like restaurants and bed & breakfasts (as I wrote about in *Greetings from Somewhere Else*), or in hotels (*The Alphabet Sisters*), or even businesses like travel agencies (*Family Baggage*). What I love exploring is what happens when the public have gone home, when the polite facade is dropped, when reality takes over. And what could be more intriguing than a stately home run as a living museum by a family who appear to have arrived quite out of nowhere?

In the early stages of writing, I visited a stately home in the north of England. As I toured the huge rooms with the rest of the group, I was struck by how little anyone listened to the guide. People seemed to be whispering to one another about what they'd had for breakfast, what they wanted for lunch, where they'd be going next, while the poor guide kept valiantly reciting facts and figures about the history of the house and the family who had lived in it for centuries. I remember thinking, *That guide could be telling these people anything—making it up as he goes along, in fact—for all the attention they're paying him.* And so the idea for the rest of the novel was born. . . .

I thought about the novel for more than six months before I started writing it, imagining my ideal stately home, deciding where to locate it, casting my characters, plotting my story. The actual writing took twelve months. I watched the four seasons pass by through my Dublin office window, looking out at a rainy Irish summer, a crisp, windy autumn, the low dark skies of winter—Ireland's coldest in years—the streets outside covered in snow, me at my desk with a hot water bottle on my lap. Spring arrived as I was doing the final edits.

RHRC: By the end of *At Home with the Templetons*, the main characters are spread out around the world, living in places like Australia, England, Ireland, New Zealand, and the United States. What is it that draws you to these locales? Do you do a lot of traveling yourself? And is there much research involved?

MM: I've definitely drawn on my own travel experiences in *At Home with the Templetons*. I visited nearly all the places featured in the book—some specifically for research (Yorkshire, Scotland, Sligo, the goldfields of Australia), others I'd been to for different reasons and then decided to use as locations. For example, I was in Chicago and Woodstock on a book tour in 2008 and knew within minutes of arriving in both places that I wanted to feature them as locations for this book.

My research initially involves a lot of walking around, taking photos, talking to local people—general sightseeing on the surface, but there's always another sound track playing in my mind, imagining my characters walking those same streets, seeing what I'm seeing, eating in the same restaurants, talking to the same people. . . . I rely on memory rather than photographs once I'm back at my desk writing, but then I go back to the photos and guidebooks during the editing process to make sure I have my facts right.

RHRC: You tend to write about large families. Did you grow up in a big family? And were there any similarities to the Templetons?

MM: I'm the middle child in a family of seven, and grew up in what I'd call a cauldron of words—there was always lots of action, drama, conversations, and laughter in our house. I'm sure it's no coincidence that my novels are always full of characters—as I know well, the more people there are, the more drama unfolds, often in very unexpected ways.

Like the Templetons, I grew up in quite an unusual house—the railway stationmaster's house in Clare, South Australia. It was a long way from being a stately home in the Victorian goldfields, but it was a beautiful, big house (it needed to be, for the nine of us), located on the edge of the town, up on a height, across from the railway station, beside the hills, with a large, rambling terraced garden. Living in a distinctive house definitely left its mark on me. I loved that it was special, that people knew it as "the railway house," that it had so many quirks and architectural touches, with its high roof and carved veranda posts, ivy-covered walls, and tree-filled garden. A local person once confessed to my mother that she always used to hurry past our house on winter evenings, convinced it was a haunted house. "It is, but with kids, not ghosts," Mum sighed.

Apart from that, and the fact that there were lots of us, too, there are no real similarities between my family and the Templetons. I'm very careful to make my fictional families as different as possible from my real one!

RHRC: The novel shifts between several points of view. Which did you enjoy writing the most? And did you relate to any one character more than the others?

MM: I loved Gracie. I wrote the book exactly as it unfolds for the reader, meeting the Templetons as children and following them all through to their adult lives, and Gracie arrived fully formed to me. It was such fun to write her mixture of sweetness, precociousness, earnestness, and intelligence. I also really enjoyed creating Hope, Charlotte, and Spencer—the troublemakers, basically! All three of them speak their minds, misbehave, and have a kind of devil-may-care approach. In real life I'm far more anxious and polite than they are, so it was very liberating and great fun to write their dialogue and scenes. Of all the characters, though, I actually related to Eleanor and Nina the most. While the story follows Tom and Gracie, and the plot revolves around their relationship, I think it is Eleanor and Nina and their different experiences of motherhood and marriage that are at the heart of the novel. I haven't experienced any of the true sadnesses that both of them go through in the novel—their grief over their marriages, both for very different reasons; their deep love for their children and their need to protect them at any cost—but I completely understood why each of them would make the decisions they did. I've already had some very strong reactions to Nina's actions in the book, but I truly have only sympathy for her. Which of us hasn't made mistakes of judgment in our lives, reacted badly to being hurt or disappointed in love, made decisions based on emotion rather than reason sometimes? I know I have.

RHRC: Is Templeton Hall based on any place in real life?

MM: It's an amalgam of many different stately homes I've visited in my life, in Australia, Ireland, and the UK. The seed for it, though, was Martindale Hall, a stately home that loomed large over my childhood in the Clare Valley of South Australia. It's a nineteenth-century Georgian mansion, two stories high and surrounded by palm trees and green lawns—completely incongruous in the usually dry landscape of the Valley. My two older sisters knew the family of caretakers, and as a ten-year-old, I used to listen with envy as they'd talk about being in the Hall after hours, having the place to themselves—and other hijinks that in the interest of good sister relations I won't go into here! Around that time, the Hall was also used as a location for director Peter Weir's film *Picnic at Hanging Rock*, which made it even more glorious in my eyes. I didn't want to star in the film, or be a caretaker—I wanted to *own* Martindale Hall: glide down its staircases, dine in its sumptuous rooms, sleep in the four-poster beds, lie in the deep, deep baths. . . . I would have quite liked a servant or two, too.

While I was researching the book, I visited many other stately homes in Australia, England, and Ireland, going on tours, reading brochures, talking to guides, etc., but the closest place to Templeton Hall is definitely Martindale Hall.

RHRC: Your novels are usually quite intricate—lots of characters, lots of story lines, and lots of locations. Do you plot them out before you start writing, or do you just wait to see where the narrative takes you?

MM: I think about the plot for more than six months before I sit down and start writing, so a lot of the intricacies are worked out before I face the blank screen for the first time. But once the writing begins, it truly does take on a life of its own. Characters I expected to be minor go center stage. Hope, for example, was initially a minor character but I enjoyed writing her so much she took on a much bigger role. Similarly, my idea for the novel was to bring two very different families into each other's orbit—the seven unruly Templetons and the smaller unit of the Donovans—but once I began writing, it was quickly apparent to me that their relationship was going to be far more complicated and long-lasting than I had expected. That's the magic of writing fiction, I've found—I can have a plan in my head, a cast of characters, even my locations decided, but once I'm there at my desk, every day, for months on end, the story and characters really do take on a life of their own.

RHRC: What are some of your own favorite books?

MM: I have hundreds of favorite books. Our house is full of them—sometimes I feel like I'm living in a library. I love classics like *Jane Eyre, The Secret Garden, The Railway Children, Little Women,* and *Wuthering Heights.* I love Rosamunde Pilcher's novels. Jane Austen's. Ian Fleming's. Marina Endicott's *Good to a Fault.* I'm a big fan of American writers like Garrison Keillor, Kristan Higgins, Curtis Sittenfeld, and Janet Evanovich; English writers including John le Carré, Laurie Graham, Clare Chambers, Philip Pullman, Joanna Trollope, J. K. Rowling; Australian writers Tim Winton, Craig Silvey, Helen Garner, Miles Franklin; Irish writers Maeve Binchy, Tana French, Paul Murray. Before I became a writer myself, I worked as a book publicist in Ireland and Australia for ten years so I have a treasured collection of signed books by writers I met, including Carol Shields, Joseph Brodsky, Edna O'Brien, and Seamus Heaney. I have a beautiful edition of Russian folk tales given to me by my uncle Phin when I was seven years old, which has traveled the world with me and which I know by heart. I'm also a very keen cook, so I have dozens of favorite ingredient-splattered cookbooks. I still like using reference books rather than relying completely on the Internet, so I also have shelves of dictionaries, history books, travel guides, gardening books, DIY books . . .

RHRC: We'd love to know what you're working on next. Can you share any details of your next book?

MM: I'm in the six-months-thinking stage at the moment, walking around talking to myself, naming characters, shaping their personalities, plotting their lives. I'm also about to start researching locations. This one will feature different cities in Europe, America, and Australia. I've already visited five of them, and am planning to visit the others soon, on flying visits only, to mirror what my main character does plot-wise in the story.

I'll also be exploring a different sort of family dynamic in this novel from my previous books, one with a much more complicated family tree, involving divorced parents, re-marriages, half-siblings, step-siblings—a whole complex web of relations. It can be difficult enough getting on with brothers and sisters you've grown up with. What is it like dealing with relatives who are virtual strangers? I know I'm going to enjoy finding answers to that question.

QUESTIONS FOR DISCUSSION

1. There are so many themes running throughout this book—family, love, redemption, forgiveness. Which do you think is the most important? And what did you think was ultimately the lesson here?

2. What do you think Templeton Hall represents to each character in the book, and how does that change over time?

3. Why do you think Tom is initially so drawn to the Templetons? Do you think Nina's instincts about them turned out to be fair or unfounded?

4. What is Hope's role in the family? Do you think she ultimately did more harm than good, or the other way around?

5. What role does money play in the book? How does it affect the actions of each character?

6. There are so many secrets floating around this family. How would things have been different if Henry hadn't lied about Templeton Hall for all those years?

7. One of the big themes of the book is second chances. Do you think Henry Templeton deserves one after what he did? What about Nina? And Gracie?

8. How do you think the characters were affected by the various places they ended up living? Do you think each one found the perfect home?

9. What do you make of the state of things between Nina and Gracie at the end of the book? Do you think they're on the road to reconciliation? How do you think their relationship will change going forward?

10. What do you think the four Templeton children will be doing in ten years? Will they still be in close touch with one another? What about their parents? And where do you think they'll be living?